Beyond a Reasonable Doubt
by C. W. Grafton

"Mr. Grafton has done a masterly job of construction ... the sheer ingenuity of it is constantly fascinating."
—*New York Herald Tribune Book Review*

OXFORD TOO
Bargain books & records and all categories
Trade your used books
For anything in the store

2345 Peachtree Rd. N.E.
Atlanta, Georgia 30305 (404)262-3411

Open 365 days a year

BEYOND A REASONABLE DOUBT

C.W. Grafton

PERENNIAL LIBRARY
Harper & Row, Publishers
New York, Cambridge, Hagerstown, Philadelphia, San Francisco
London, Mexico City, São Paulo, Sydney

The characters and events depicted in this book are purely fictional.
Any resemblance to persons living or dead or events which have
actually happened is purely coincidental.

A hardcover edition of this book was originally published by Holt, Rinehart
& Winston. It is here reprinted by arrangement.

BEYOND A REASONABLE DOUBT. Copyright © 1950, 1978 by C. W. Grafton.
All rights reserved. Printed in the United States of America. No part of this
book may be used or reproduced in any manner whatsoever without written
permission except in the case of brief quotations embodied in critical articles
and reviews. For information address Harper & Row, Publishers, Inc.,
10 East 53rd Street, New York, N.Y. 10022. Published simultaneously in
Canada by Fitzhenry & Whiteside Limited, Toronto.

First PERENNIAL LIBRARY edition published 1980.

ISBN: 0-06-080519-6

80 81 82 83 84 10 9 8 7 6 5 4 3 2 1

This book is dedicated to my severest critic whose intelligent and forthright comments have kept it from being any worse than it is.

The author wishes to acknowledge invaluable assistance from Elliot Maddox, Evelyn Bliss, W. S. Heidenberg, Jean Crawford, Bernice Baumgarten and Lillian Walker.

"The court charges you that the law presumes the defendant innocent until proven guilty beyond a reasonable doubt; that if you can reconcile the evidence before you upon any reasonable hypothesis consistent with the defendant's innocence, you should do so, and in that case find him not guilty. You are further instructed that you cannot find the defendant guilty, unless from all the evidence you believe him guilty beyond a reasonable doubt.

"The court further charges you that a reasonable doubt is a doubt based on reason, and which is reasonable in view of all the evidence. And if, after an impartial comparison and consideration of all the evidence, you can candidly say that you are not satisfied of the defendant's guilt, you have a reasonable doubt; but if, after such impartial comparison and consideration of all the evidence, you can truthfully say that you have an abiding conviction of the defendant's guilt, such as you would be willing to act upon in the more weighty and important matters relating to your own affairs, you have no reasonable doubt."

Instruction approved by the Supreme Court of the United States in *Hopt v. People of Utah*, 120 U.S. 430, 7 S.Ct. 614, 30 L.Ed. 708.

A Hair perhaps divides the False and True—
And upon what, prithee, may life depend?

—FitzGerald's Translation,
The Rubáiyát of Omar Khayyám

1.

IT WAS ABOUT two o'clock on that Friday in April 1940—a warm day with spring sweet in the air. A sign painter was working on the door of the law office. When I walked around his bucket of brushes and opened the door, there was a draft through the open windows and the steam heat was off and the papers on the stenographers' desks had to be weighted down with ash trays and books or they'd blow off on the floor.

Clementine was at the reception desk, young and black-haired and fat, so that the skin was stretched tight over her arms. She liked chocolates with cream centers and ate them greedily from boxes she kept in the lower left-hand drawer of her desk. There was a spike beside her typewriter where telephone messages were speared when you were out. I went over to see whether there were any calls for me and nodded agreeably, motioning toward the door. I said, "Looks as if it's actually happening, doesn't it?"

She said, "It seems definite all right. He's in there shuffling files with the Judge. I think he's got reservations on the early morning train. I thought he was kidding, didn't you?"

I don't remember whether I answered or not. I took my messages off the spike and went into my office and there on the desk was a funny-shaped package done in white tissue paper. I said, "What's this?"

Clementine came hurrying in with a manner some people think is officious and others consider merely an abnormal desire to be in everybody's business, which after all amounts to the same thing. She said, "That's a souvenir from the J. T. Pharis Steel Company on account of winning the patent case last week. It's really quite nice. Mr. Sothern got one and Judge Abercrombie got one and you and George Stern. Aren't you gonna open it?"

I said, "What's in it?"

She said, "Whyn't you open it, silly? Look, I'll show you."

The white tissue paper slid off smoothly and she held up a glistening steel ball. It looked heavy.

I said, "What is it?"

She said, "I guess it's one of the things they make out at the plant, but what could anyone possibly use it for? Mr. Pharis had them cut this hole in the top, and this gadget sticking out is a cigaret lighter with the works set right down in the steel. The thing's so heavy no one could possibly walk off with it, which ought to be a blessing. As a matter of fact it's so heavy I can't imagine anyone ever using it. Pharis says it's some kind of fancy-pants steel that won't rust and he thinks it's good advertising."

I hefted the thing in my hand and it was plenty heavy— not the kind of thing you would absent-mindedly whisk off the desk in the middle of dictating a brief, or slip in your pocket to take on a picnic. It must have been four inches in diameter and after you played with it awhile you definitely wanted to put it down. To satisfy Clementine and get her out of my hair I stuck a cigaret in my mouth and used the new lighter. It worked. She moved back to her desk in a glow of satisfaction.

Almost immediately I heard the buzzer and pretty soon Clementine called, "Mr. London."

I was reading a little note that said I was to call Mrs. A. P. Worthington at City 4872-J and I said absent-mindedly, "What?"

She said, "B. I. L. wants you in his office. I guess he's going to unload a file on you."

B. I. L. to Clementine meant "brother-in-law." This was her coy way of telling me that Mitchell Sothern had asked for me. I crossed the reception room, knocked once lightly on Mitch's door and went in without waiting for an answer. My brother-in-law was seated behind a disordered desk—a big man, solid, with a mass of wavy black hair and heavy features inclined to a brooding expression in repose. He was the middle partner of the law firm of Abercrombie, Sothern and Fant and the sign painter was busy taking his name off the door so that tomorrow the firm would be simply "Abercrombie and Fant."

In a deep leather chair beside the desk old Judge Abercrombie sat with a heavy gold watch chain looped across his fat belly. He was old and white-haired and tired—nobody knew how old, only that his face had a curious waxen quality, almost bloodless, and his lower lip sagged and bent out, and you could see the red linings of his lower eyelids.

Mitch said shortly, "Come in, Jess, I've got a job for you."

I said, "Yes, sir." Mitch Sothern was a man whose success I reluctantly admired, while at the same time distrusting and even fearing the qualities which he had parlayed into that success. He was domineering, unscrupulous, ruthless. I wondered if perhaps with even one scruple or one ruth he might not have been a fine man instead of merely a fine lawyer. He was energetic to the point of restlessness and when he was in a room there seemed to be a faint charge of electricity in the air. Whether you actually looked at him or not you couldn't help being conscious that he was there, just as you would probably be aware of a Bengal tiger. I had always wondered how my sweet and charming and unselfish sister Marcella had ever attracted his attention; or having done so, how she managed to hold it. In a way I had wondered why she had *wanted* to attract or hold him, for I was certain that they were of entirely different types. Or perhaps that explained it.

Mitch said, "How much do you know about redeeming property?"

I said, "How do you mean, redeeming property?"

He said, "God damn it, you've heard of an equity of redemption, haven't you?"

I said, "I've never done it but I've read about it."

Mitch squirmed around in his seat, not angrily, but impatiently. He half turned to Judge Abercrombie and said, "I guess I'd better take time to explain it."

He looked at his watch in quick irritation and then added, "There's a lot at stake and it's got to be done today. I was going to do it myself but the time keeps slipping through my fingers." The way he said it, you got a picture of time as a lot of obscene little creatures peeping out between his strong thick fingers, looking for a chance to wiggle through and run across the desk the moment he took his eyes off them.

Judge Abercrombie nodded, took a shapeless cigar butt out of his mouth and spat messily at a brass spittoon. A dribble fell on his untidy shirt front, and he wiped at it gloomily.

Mitch pulled a chair over next to him and it caught on the edge of the rug which didn't improve his frame of mind. Nevertheless when he spoke to me his tone was more of a resignation than anything else. He said, "Look, Jess. I'm going to take the time to tell you about this because otherwise you may think it's routine and unimportant, and it isn't. It's now eighteen minutes after two, and at five o'clock our time runs out. All you have to do is take this certified check that's in the file and the statement of redemption that I've already prepared, and go over to the County Clerk's office, tender the check, and get the statement stamped in the proper way. The thing I want you to know and feel is what you're *doing,* so you'll take nothing for granted and get it absolutely right. Understand?"

I said, "Yes, sir."

"We represent a man by the name of Alva M. Drysdale. He used to be a big shot and he isn't any more but that's none of our business. During the depression when he had more money than the rest of us and was playing things close to his chest, he bought an old farm-machinery factory out on the edge of town at a bankruptcy sale. He thought like Herbert Hoover that good times were just around the corner. It looked like a bargain. Then he went around four or five corners and prosperity wasn't there, so he got hard up and managed to get some damn fool to take a big mortgage on the place. Things went from bad to worse and he piddled around and staved off foreclosure until 1937 when the mortgagee got fed up and filed suit. I stalled in every way the law allows, filed every pleading in the book, got sick or went out of town whenever necessary and generally made hell's own nuisance of myself, but persistence finally beat me. The property was sold last April. No one was interested and the Tremont Realty Company, the plaintiff in the case, bought the property on a purely nominal sort of bid and simply took credit on its judgment. Even so, it had to pay out a lot of money for delinquent taxes and court costs, and by that time they were mad and made up their minds they'd collect the balance of the judgment out of Drysdale's hide if it took them fifty years. Between one thing and another they were either smug or careless and didn't bid as much as two-thirds of the appraised value of the property. Under the law, as you know, if they don't bid two-thirds of the appraised value you have one year in which to redeem the property by paying the amount of the bid plus interest and a ten-percent penalty. Get the picture?"

It wasn't a very difficult picture to get and I said I had got it.

"Okay," said Mitch. "That was in April 1939. In July,

as you recall, Senator Borah told the Senate there positively wouldn't be any war in Europe and on September first Hitler jumped on Poland. The war that wasn't going to happen *has* happened and a whole lot of things that were worth nothing in peace times are worth a lot now. I'm not supposed to know this, but for the last six months the Tremont Realty Company has been negotiating on the quiet with General Motors. But for stubbing their toe on our pathetic little equity of redemption they'd have sold this building and its grease-packed machinery and equipment at a profit that would knock your eyes out. Mr. Drysdale is toasting his arthritic joints at the expense of some harassed relatives in Florida and doesn't even know that we are about to hand him a gold mine on a silver platter— enough profit to pay off the Tremont judgment with plenty to spare. Judge Abercrombie and I are putting up this money ourselves for his account. I've deliberately let this go on to the last possible day so the negotiations with General Motors will get to the point where our deal is made for us out of the other man's sweat. I'll bet the Tremont people are watching the clock right now—figuring that in another two and a half hours we'll have missed the boat. Now, here's the statement and here's the certified check. It's something we can't miss on. Got it?"

I said, "Yes, sir."

He said, "I want you to go over between four and four-thirty. Not before and not after. It wouldn't surprise me if the papers are all laid out on somebody's desk waiting to be signed as soon as the clerk's office is closed and the opportunity lost." He slapped my knee and although the lines of his face said, "Aren't we having fun?" there was a fire burning behind his eyes. I thought as I had often thought before, that Mitch Sothern was someone I'd hate to have on the other side of a case I cared a lot about.

I looked at my watch and said, "Yes, sir. Between four and four-thirty, without fail." I picked up the file and nodded respectfully to Judge Abercrombie before leaving the room. On Mitch Sothern's desk was another of the shiny steel balls made into a cigaret lighter.

2.

I WENT BACK to my office and called Mrs. A. P. Worthington. While I was dialing the number I remembered who she was—an elusive witness to an automobile accident whom I needed in court next Monday if her testimony should prove to be worth anything. For three weeks, without luck, I'd been trying to locate her and make an appointment for an interview.

Her voice on the phone was one of those tired, resigned voices with a subdued sigh between each sentence, as if the world was perpetually taking advantage of her and she was kicking bravely against the traces. I talked her into letting me drop by on my way to work in the morning.

When I broke the connection I heard crisp steps crossing the reception room and Mitch Sothern strode into my office. "Strode" is really the only word for the way Mitch went into places, whether the place happened to be the court room, a directors' meeting, or the men's toilet. His voice usually had a resonant quality that would penetrate approximately eighteen inches of granite, but on this occasion he leaned over my desk and lowered his voice as he did when he was feeling particularly friendly.

He said, "By the way, Jess. In talking about that file, I forgot. Marty and I are having a few close friends around this evening. Informal. Just a little farewell party we scratched together at the last minute. Of course, we want you to drop over and join us in a couple of good-bye drinks. Think you can make it?"

I was pleased and said of course I could make it. Mitch and Marty had a reputation for good parties. Besides, when Mitch asked you to a party you went unless you had a broken leg.

Mitch started out of the room, glanced automatically at his watch, and then came back. He said, "Hell, after I turned that file over to you and the Judge and I looked at the piles of stuff on my desk and decided they would have to ride. There's nothing urgent that I haven't already disposed of. The rest of the files can work themselves out after you boys divide 'em around and study 'em. I'm tired and through for the day. Tell you what I'll do. Give me that Drysdale check and I'll run over and deliver it myself. I've nursed that baby so long I'll sleep better tonight on the train if I know it's done. Where's the file? This it?"

I said it was and he mussed my hair in the occasional fatherly way he had. He said, "See you any time after eight, with your drinking clothes on," and strode out again with currents of air swirling and clashing behind him.

As he crossed the room, he was stuffing the check and the redemption statement carelessly into the inside pocket of his coat.

3.

Now THAT Mitch had taken the check with him, the Alva M. Drysdale file was a dead pigeon and my plans for the rest of the afternoon had to be re-examined. I didn't take this little crisis too seriously. As a matter of fact I remember thinking that this was the sort of crisis I could do with more of. The big green blotter which Marcella had given me to celebrate the historic occasion of my admission to the bar was smooth and pure on my desk and the color was soothing almost to the point of fascination.

I took my desk pen and drew a circle on it, pretty good for a free hand job. The ink soaked fuzzily into the paper. I turned the pen over and used the back of the point to make a finer line, and put a square around the circle and then drew a triangle on each side of the square and then lines connecting the points of the triangle and finally a slightly shapeless circle to enclose the whole masterpiece. From this I derived considerable satisfaction.

I was dismayed to discover that at the moment I could not recall any legal responsibilities of Jesse London, attorney-at-law (which was me), and that I had better think of something to do or my days with Abercrombie, Sothern and Fant (about to be Abercrombie and Fant) would be numbered—and in very low numbers at that. I considered the diagram on my blotter and after absent-mindedly adding a few radiating lines to give a very pretty sunburst effect, I put away the pen, pushed the Drysdale file to the corner of the desk and dug out the only other file entrusted to my care.

The label on it was "International Chemical and Waterproofing Company vs. The J. T. Pharis Steel Company, Inc." To look at the outside you would never suspect that two trucks had rubbed fenders at an intersection and the judicial system of the Commonwealth of Kentucky was called upon to determine whether the International Chemical and Waterproofing Company, which occupied a disreputable one-story former garage near the city dump, should recover $42.32 plus $5.00 alleged to represent the fair rental value of the truck during the period of repairs; or whether the J. T. Pharis Steel Company should recover $59.84 plus $10.00 rental value on the same basis. There was a police report of the accident which disclosed that the police were not there and no skid marks were visible on the street. There was the name of one witness—namely, Mrs. A. P. Worthington. Each driver said the other was at fault so apparently the outcome rested in the browbeaten hands of Mrs. Worthington.

I buzzed for Clementine and asked if Mrs. Pennybaker could come in and bring her book. Clementine said she'd see, and I had more than a suspicion that she was sucking on a chocolate at the time. After a moment Mrs. Pennybaker made her appearance, very sprightly with her white hair and beautiful false teeth and a tiny knot of handkerchief into which her palms perspired lavishly. I put on what I thought was an air of complete absorption in my work and dictated with formality what I called a "Trial Memorandum."

Looking back, it must have seemed more than a little humorous to Mrs. Pennybaker, who had been Judge Abercrombie's secretary since only slightly after the pyramids were built; but if it seemed infantile to her, she gave no sign of it and gravely asked whether there were to be five or six copies. There was no use doing things halfway so I told her six would be enough and let her take the file in order that, as she explained, she could get the proper style of the case.

Having accomplished this much I felt that the day had been well spent and that I had earned a Coco-Cola in the drugstore downstairs. Since one form of dissipation leads to another I drifted from the soda fountain to a gaudy pinball machine which had long been a thorn in my ego. My touch was masterful and in what seemed no time at all I had mulcted the machine of thirty-five cents clear profit over and above my not unsubstantial investment. I then found that in some unaccountable way the time, as Mitch Sothern would say, had slipped through my fingers and it was eight minutes after five. I rushed up to the office, muttered some comments under my breath about the disorderly way in which the county tax records were kept, glanced around in the hope that someone had noticed my industrious application to the affairs of the firm, and clumped out with my hat on the back of my head. I had a general feeling that the world, after all, was not too bad a place to live in once you got the damn thing well under control.

4.

THE FIRST BUS that passed me at the corner was labeled "Riverside" so I let it go by, shifting my weight to the other foot and trying to read the headlines over the shoulder of a little man with an umbrella under his arm who apparently had the palsy and couldn't hold still long enough for me to see anything. The next bus said "Spring Lake Park" which was for me.

I climbed aboard and got a friendly nod from the driver whom I knew vaguely but satisfactorily as Joe. I sat down on the seat behind him, noticed once more the prohibition against talking to the operator and ventured that it was a pretty evening. Joe said the evening was pretty enough but his baby was sick and he had been up all night with her, and no evening looked more than ordinarily pretty under the circumstances. He said he had just come on duty and at the end of each run he was going to call the house. If the baby got worse he was going to ask for a substitute and go home and the hell with it.

This brought me to my corner so I patted him on the shoulder, said something appropriate about good luck, got off, and walked the two blocks to my apartment house. The lobby was practically deserted except for the potted palms, looking more secondhand than ever. Toothy Charley Pitts was reading the paper behind the counter and picking his nose. I waved my hand in passing and he waved back without comment. Cornelius Vanderbilt, the Negro elevator boy, took me up to the third floor.

I said, "How's it going, Wall Street?" and without cracking a smile he said, "How was the supreme court today, Mr. Hughes?" With this daily routine out of the way I let myself into Apartment 332, shed my clothes in various random ways and gave the evening paper a leisurely and meticulous going over. Then I took a musical shower, passing over the Lifebuoy soap in favor of Camay in honor of the party.

It was only five blocks to the party and I decided to walk it. Wall Street took me down in the elevator; Charley Pitts waved again as I went through the lobby, and the night air seemed cool and fragrant. I walked with spring in my heart, half tempted to skip occasionally, as I did at the age of sixteen when I was going for my movie dates. Three blocks to Cedar Avenue, then to the right with the big houses set well back from the sidewalk and the lawn sprinklers already working. Virginia Drive and beyond that Cedar Avenue again, lined with cars, bumper to bumper, in testimony of the fact that Mitch and Marty Sothern were about to go away.

The house was on the far side of the street almost at the end of the block. In the light from over the front door the grass showed wet and glistening and freshly cut, as the grass of Mitch Sothern would necessarily be. Irreverently I cut across the lawn, presenting myself at the entrance with damp shoes and stray blades of grass clinging on the toes. The house was overflowing with people and the chatter of voices was hospitable. The door was cordially open in testimony of spring, but the screen door was shut. I suppose I could have walked right in, but instead I put my finger on the bell. There was no response—no pealing of the bell, which I knew was in the kitchen and which I knew I would be able to hear if it went into action.

I tried again, feeling very much like the stableboy peeping in at big doings in the big house. People with glasses in hand were visible in the hall and through every doorway, but no one paid me any attention and I wondered if late entries were supposed to creep in via the alley and the servants' entrance.

Inez Wiggens came down the stairs, chubby-cheeked and black-haired and curiously exciting. Every time I saw her I felt the same little twinge of pleasure mixed with something bordering on jealousy as I wondered who she might be with. She noticed me and smiled and said, "Hello, Jess. What're you doing out there all by yourself? You look like a Western Union messenger."

I said, "Silly, isn't it? I tried the bell and it doesn't work and I was just making up my mind to come on in. After all, it's my sister's home, isn't it? But somehow I don't go walking into places. I like to be welcomed. And now that the honors are being done by my favorite business executive, my timidity is handsomely rewarded. You're lovely and beautiful, as always. Did you know that?"

She wrinkled her nose at me and said, "When you start kidding me, I wonder if my lipstick's on straight. As a matter of fact I don't feel lovely and beautiful. I feel depressed. Do feel depressed, too, will you? Then you may join me and we'll drink ourselves happy. I came early and I'm already at the point where another highball might produce a grisly sort of giggle."

I said, "My dear, leave us not be depressed. Tell Mr. London but everything. Is there a run in your best nylons? Anything else, I can cure."

The screen door shut itself quietly behind me. People in the hall were always pushing into the living room and those in the living room were always pushing out into the hall so that the big double doors resembled the subway station at Times Square during the rush hour. A servant took my hat and disappeared upstairs with it.

I took two highballs from a passing waiter who wore white gloves, gave one of them to Wiggie, touched my glass to hers in salute, and took a sip.

Wiggie said, "If you must know, the Assistant Buyer is being transferred to Memphis and I think I'm entitled to the job, but rumor has it that a snotty little creature will be sent here from St. Louis. Now I've told you, and I don't feel like discussing it. Be a help and say something funny. Oh oh, there's my date and he seems to be looking for me. You know George Stern, don't you, working daily as you do, with your shoulders practically rubbing together. Say hello to the nice man, George."

George said, "Hello, Jess. Your sister's been asking about you. Said for me to tell you to look for her as soon as you came in." He turned to Wiggie. "If I'm not mistaken, that makes four highballs. I suppose you know what you're doing, but don't you think you're laying it on a bit thick?"

She said, "I'll stop when forgetfulness rears its merciful head. Leaving now, Jess?"

I said, "I thought I caught a glimpse of Marty near those towering, naked shoulders over there. What a mass of flesh! So round, so firm . . . Yes, I do see Marty. I'll join you creatures later."

My sister Marty was talking to Stoakes Fant and his wife, but she saw me out of the corner of her eye and extended a hand out and back to bring me into the group. She said to Fant, "May I have permission to leave my kid brother in your care? I can't get over what a big boy he is, but at the same time I can't get over—you know, a sense of responsibility."

I said, "It seems only yesterday you were changing my diapers and blowing my nose for me, doesn't it?" I turned to Mrs. Fant and said, "Confidentially, I have recently learned to do these things for myself."

Marty said, "Excuse us, will you? While I have the chance

I'm going to whisk Jess into the study for a last heart-to-heart talk."

I said over my shoulder, "It's about the birds and the bees. Yesterday a big bad man gave me some fascinating hints . . ." Then I said to Marty, "Darling, I can't quite get it into my head that you're going away. It gives me a sinking feeling . . ."

"Yes, I know, Jess. I have it, too. Maybe when we get settled, Mitch can find a place for you in the new firm."

We closed the door of the study behind us. I said, "I'm a big boy now. Having to shift for myself might be a good thing. You didn't do a bad job of bringing me up, honey. Once I voluntarily washed behind my ears, and the other day when an ugly gorilla snarled at me for bumping into him in a crowd I snarled right back—and out of the side of my mouth, too. He was terrified, believe me. Slunk away and said, 'Curses, foiled again.' It was a big moment."

Marty held my shoulders and leaned back and looked at me a long moment, and then blinked and put her forehead on my chest. She said, "Jess, I'm very proud of you. In a way, I wish we weren't leaving, but then you have to take life as you find it, don't you? Dealer's choice is fair enough, even when you aren't the dealer. Will you come to see us when you have vacations?"

I said, "Sure thing. You know I will. And don't you worry. Promise?"

She leaned back and took another long look at me. Then she said, "I promise if you'll make a promise, too. If you get sick or get into trouble or need money . . ."

I laughed and said, "In any of those events, I'll know where I can turn. But no promises along that line. As of now I'm standing straight and solid on my own feet. Want to see if you can push me over?"

She laughed at me, and what might have been a small emotional crisis went by on the other side. She said, "No, you big handsome oaf, I'm not going to try to push you over, and I hope no one else tries, either."

I said, "I need another highball. Shall we join the ladies? Is it true what they say in the locker rooms—that they're made different from us men?"

We went out arm in arm and approached a group which somehow swallowed her up in one direction and me in another. I ate some absurd little things that were on a plate and then found another highball. Presently I was in an earnest group around an empty fire place discussing the possibility of an invasion by Hitler by way of Dakar, Brazil and the West Indies. The social currents eventually took me from this martial atmosphere into the sun porch where two young matrons were discussing their infants' formulas, and from this trap I was delivered into a passionate discourse on the desirability of Mr. Wilkie over Mr. Roosevelt in the fall presidential elections. During the course of this odyssey I spoke up an acquaintance with the white gloves on more than one occasion and eventually found myself in the kitchen, mixing drinks in a forest of glasses. It was nearly eleven when Mitch found me there and rested a cordial hand on my shoulder. He said, "Everything going along okay?"

I said, "All except pretty soon people had better go home and polish off on their own whiskey, on account of."

"Whiskey running out?"

I said, "This is the last bottle."

Mitch said, "We always ask a million but half of them usually don't show up." He stepped out to the back porch and motioned to me to follow. He said, "Look, Jess. I can't very well leave this mob. Some of 'em are starting home already and are just tight enough to insist on shaking hands with the host and hostess whether they give a damn or not. Be a good scout, will you? There's a liquor store three blocks away. You go down Cedar to Virginia, turn left on Virginia and it's at 18th Street, the second corner on the near side. Here's a twenty.

18 –

Three or four bottles ought to patch out the evening. Okay?"

I said, "Sure. Right away."

I started down the back steps but he followed me and held out something in his hand. He said, "Take my keys. The car's in the driveway. You don't want to lug a lot of whiskey around in your arms."

I said, "Okay, thanks." I left him and followed the drive around the corner of the house. I had thought there would be one car in the drive and that would be the end of it but I found four cars in a row, jammed in with their bumpers touching. I studied this situation in slight confusion, then shrugged and set out on foot.

5.

THE SIDEWALK on Cedar Avenue was flanked with trees which kept me walking as if in a dark tunnel. Beyond Virginia the trees were not spaced as closely together and in the occasional stripes of light I could see a man approaching the intersection. In the first band of light I caught no more than the impression that he was familiar. The second time I almost placed him. When he came into the light again, I recognized Joe the bus driver. I was sober enough to reflect that his baby must be pretty sick and he must be on his way home.

He reached the intersection before I did, turned to his left on Virginia, (opposite to the direction I would be going), appeared once or twice in the gaps between the trees, and was gone.

As I reached the corner and made my turn I reacted to the picture of his trousers as they had appeared for a moment under the street light—blue uniform trousers with a triangular snag at knee height, so that the snag part hung down and out, revealing a glimpse of hairy leg. Funny how in the kaleidoscope of an evening a chance picture here and there is developed and printed in the photographic laboratory of the mind, for obscure and illogical reasons.

6.

THE FOUR BOTTLES were in a paper bag and they made a pretty heavy package. I scrunched the top of the bag together to make something I could get hold of, but I began to feel that pretty soon the bag would come apart. By the time I was halfway back to the house the load seemed intolerable so I stopped and sat on someone's terrace steps and worried the cork out of one bottle and did what I could to lighten the load.

I was feeling pretty good when I went up the four steps to the back porch and didn't trip until I reached the top step. I went lurching off at an angle to one knee, clutching the package desperately.

Inez Wiggens was standing in front of the kitchen table with an empty whiskey bottle held straight upside down over a jigger, shaking it impatiently.

I got up and brushed the knee of my trousers and watched Wiggie thoughtfully. I said, "Forgetfulness must surely have reared its merciful head by now."

She turned and gave me a blurred look. Then she brightened and said, "Why, hello, Jess. What did you say?"

I went over and took the glass out of her hand and drank the whiskey myself. I said, "You were drinking to forget something. Now what was it you wanted to forget?"

She puzzled over that, frowning. Then she laughed and said, "Was I trying to forget something? I can't remember. Are you suggesting I shouldn't have another drink?"

"You're going to have an awful head tomorrow."

"Yes, I know. I ought to have better sense. I think I'll find a place and sit down. I think I'll be all right if I don't remember what I was forgetting."

Mitch came barging through the swinging door and his animal electricity charged the room as it always did. Wiggie walked uncertainly out through the butler's pantry. I looked down and saw there was still some dust on my knee, and brushed at it halfheartedly.

Mitch said, "What's the matter? Have an accident?"

I said, "Stumbled, but no casualties."

Mitch said, "It's probably just as well we ran out. It's a gummy enough brawl as it is. People have already started straggling home, thank heavens, and you should hear the way they go on when they hook bumpers out front. I've unhooked two sets already. By the time I got through you'd think I had hooked them myself."

In the absence of a convenient jigger, he poured a stiff drink for me in the bottom of a tall highball glass, poured one for himself, handed me my glass, and said, "Well Jess, here's how!"

I said, "How," and we downed our drinks at a gulp, made the customary face and put our glasses down.

I said, "What puzzles me, not that it's any of my business—"

"Not that what isn't any of your business?"

"Well, I mean . . . after all, a party like this and you and Marty leaving on the two-thirty train. What I mean is, well how do you do it? I mean, for example, glasses and stuff like that . . ."

Mitch said, "Not only that but the furniture and everything. In a way that's the fun of it. For once, you pitch a party

— 21

and make a hell of a mess and don't do a damn thing about it. You get on the train and go away."

I said, "You mean you just make a mess and lock the door and go away?"

Mitch waved his hand in an airy gesture and said, "Servants," and then added, "Anyway we'll have to come back to crate up all the stuff. What we're taking with us is packed and ready."

Marty put her head through the swinging door and said, "I've been looking everywhere for you, Mitch. The Craigs and the Andersons and the Terhunes are ready to go home and want to go through the motions."

I followed Mitch out through the babble of voices. There was a steady stream of people going upstairs for their hats and coming down with or without them; and people going into the powder room and coming out; and people clustering around the door, just about to go home but not quite doing it. Women who had already doctored their faces upstairs with the utmost care could not resist a passing glance in the hall mirror, and better than two out of three felt called upon to obstruct traffic and institute improvements. One couple was leaving when the girl thought of something she should say to another girl disappearing into the powder room, whereupon her escort sighed and threw his hat in the corner and went out to the kitchen for another drink. There was a cluster of die-hards nibbling the scraps left on a table which had once held trays of olives, anchovies, caviar, cheese and stuff like that. A few accepted highballs and showed every evidence of intending to spend the night.

Across the hall in the front parlor, a woman who had her hat on was playing very loudly on the piano, with her hat slipping down over one eye. Other people, who should have been on their way home, were singing such things as "Bicycle Built for Two," "Down by the Old Mill Stream," and "The Man on the Flying Trapeze."

In her best hostess fashion, Marty made the sprightly suggestion that the evening was young (Heaven help her!) and maybe they should all have another drink and stay awhile, but she was poor competition for barbershop harmony and the dutiful suggestion went unheeded.

I was standing as inconspicuously as possible near a corner in the big living room beside an end table with a lamp on it. I was conscious, but only in a passing way, of Wiggie coming unsteadily from the kitchen, brushing a strand of hair out of her eyes with the back of her hand and fumbling with a cigaret box in her puckered, nearsighted way.

George Stern was coming down the stairs with his hat in his hand. I made a gesture of recognition and he yelled something back. I didn't catch it and said, "What?"

He stopped, leaned slightly over the banisters and yelled, "A light! Behind you! Why don't you give the poor girl a light?"

Marty was in the big double doors between us. She turned and said mildly, "It's Inez, Jess. She hasn't a light for her cigaret. There's Mitch's new cigaret lighter on the table right behind you."

I put my hand in my pocket and found my own lighter which was small and easy to handle. As I turned, with my back to the room, I saw on the end table in front of me the round steel ball with the cigaret lighter built into it, given to Mitch by the J. T. Pharis Steel Company, the mate to the one on my desk down at the office.

Wiggie was standing by the divan with her left knee doubled up against one of the cushions, the strand of hair falling over her eyes again. There was a drowsy look in her eyes and she was reaching for the big cigaret lighter when I produced my own. The flame broke on the first try and she got her light with two deep drags while her free hand once more brushed the hair from her eyes. I put my lighter back in my pocket.

She said, "Thanks, it works, doesn't it?"

I said, "They always surprise me when they do."

George Stern came up to us and when he saw her condition he frowned slightly. Then he winked at me and came over to Wiggie, linking an arm firmly with hers. He said, "Look, honey, I'm absolutely all in. Matter of fact, I think I've had too much to drink. Think you could see me home?"

I was standing close to Inez Wiggens and a little behind her. She found my hand and gave it a squeeze. She said, "Every party it's the same way. George gets too much to drink and I've got to leave the fun and see he gets to his little door without falling flat on his puss."

She looked over her shoulder at me and said, "Good night, Jess. It was fun," and went away with him. She tripped over a wrinkle in the rug, only no wrinkle was there.

7.

THE EVENING had reached that stage where glasses stand around everywhere, some of them with lipstick smudges plainly visible; and there are bits of cracker on the rug; and a couple of cigarets are burned out on the edges of tables; and wads of cocktail napkins are on the floor like daisies on the lawn in the spring; and the table tops show ghastly white circles; and what's left of the crowd is a puddle around the front door like soap suds that stand around the drain after the water has run out of the washbowl.

That's the time when people wave back to the host and hostess before they get into their cars, and someone comes back to look for his pipe or his wife's purse, and the last few people are about to be persuaded to come back into the kitchen for just one last one for the road, whether they've been asked or not.

It's the time when the host and hostess have a great ache in their legs from standing up forever, and keep reminding themselves that if they can last a few minutes longer God will be merciful and let them go to bed and may He strike them blind if they ever give another party like this one.

I didn't want to get embroiled in the endless kitchen ceremonies so I sidled through the group at the door, shook hands with Mitch, kissed Marty lightly on her cheek, said good-bye, wished them good luck, nodded to whoever else was there, and went off down the steps to the side walk.

In the shadows toward the corner of Virginia, there was a lot of laughter and confusion over who should sit where in a car. They had all four doors open, and people kept getting in one side and out the other, and walking around and getting in again. It seemed very funny to the people involved, but not too funny to me. I had to walk that way but I was careful to step out into the grass of somebody's lawn to avoid getting confused in this whirlpool.

As I was passing, Inez Wiggens caught sight of me, smiled with pleasure, took my arm, and suggested that I would be a perfect solution to the problem if I would sit in the middle of the back seat. In the end, too many of us were in the car and there was much talk of who should sit forward and who should sit back, and it all seemed to be quite hilarious except to me, practically suffocated as I was with a boy on each side of me and two girls overlapping in front of me. As if this were not enough, they had to sing "The Man on the Flying Trapeze" and after that "Genevieve" and "Girl of My Dreams," and then I don't remember what.

It was a relief when we finally got down to my second-rate apartment house and stopped in front of it and took turns getting out like olives being dug out of one of those narrow-necked bottles. My legs were numb when I stood on the sidewalk. Being the soberest of the bunch, I had the acute feeling, which will be familiar to many, that the police department had operatives on the point of popping from every corner, shadow and lamp post, ready to herd the lot of us into a black wagon and trundle us into the rotogravure section.

There seemed to be a great tendency to resume the business of getting in the car on one side and out of it on the other, so at length I turned and went through the revolving door into the lobby with the singing and laughter very audible behind me. The lobby was empty and the light system above the elevator door showed that the car was on its way up. I glanced at my watch and it was a few minutes after twelve, which would mean that Wall Street had gone home long ago, and Charley Pitts would be operating the elevator.

I was at the stage when standing in one spot for any length of time is unprofitable. After a moment I walked up to the third floor, found my key without too much difficulty and let myself into Apartment 332. My first thought was to set the alarm while I was able to do so, and then, not trusting my will power, I called the lobby and got hold of Charley Pitts and asked him would he please call me three times at five minute intervals beginning at seven o'clock in the morning.

I had to get up at seven o'clock, naturally, because on my way to the office I had to stop and interview Mrs. A. P. Worthington so that, if all went well, the J. T. Pharis Steel Company, come Monday, perhaps could win $69.84 plus court costs from the International Chemical and Waterproofing Company, so help me.

I had my tie off and my shirt unbuttoned before I began to wonder where I had put the memorandum containing the address of Mrs. Worthington. Try as I would, the memory got away from me. I went over and fetched the telephone book and after discovering that there was no listing of a Mrs. A. P. Worthington, I remembered that she lived in an apartment house and had no phone of her own. I sat dismally on the side of the bed and wondered what in hell's name I had done with the memorandum. I distinctly remembered writing it out carefully at the office and doing something with it so clever that I couldn't possibly forget where it was. But where I had put it in the spate of cleverness, I couldn't recall.

Then I remembered dressing to go to the party, and all at once it was very clear that the memorandum had come to my mind and I had been concerned that in changing to my best suit for the party, and back again to another suit for work, I would lose this wretched bit of paper.

Finally I remembered that I had reasoned that suits may come and suits may go but my one hat would be on my head forever. I remembered then with what care I had folded this piece of paper and put it inside the sweat band of my hat, thinking with a chuckle that it would be on my head whether I knew it or not, when I would think of it in despair in the morning.

It was then I also remembered that in my hurry to get away from the dregs of Mitch's party, I had walked off without my hat. At the same time I remembered that I still had Mitch's keys in my coat pocket. Obviously, Mitch would need his keys. Obviously, I needed my hat and the information as to where Mrs. Worthington lived.

I buttoned my shirt, knotted my tie again, put on my coat and went out into the hall. The indicator was at the fifth floor, going up, so I turned to the stairway, walked down, passed through the deserted lobby and out into the sweet night air.

8.

As I approached the house I first had an uneasy feeling that I was too late, for the light over the front door was out and the house seemed dark and quiet. I walked by and looked in the driveway and when I saw two cars still standing there, I checked my watch. It was twenty-five minutes past one, so very likely the cars were Mitch's Packard and Marty's Buick coupe. I retraced my steps, turned in at the walk and went up and pressed the bell.

With the house so dark and quiet, I expected to hear the strident ringing of the bell in the kitchen, but I heard nothing. I pressed the bell again and once again before I remembered that I had done the same thing at the party a few hours earlier, and no one had seemed to realize there was anyone at the door.

I moved over to the glass panel next to the door and peered in to see if anyone was up and about. There was a faint night light in the hall. At the back of the house and to my left there was a knife-edge streak of light at the door of Mitch's study.

As I looked, a shadow moved and cut off the streak of light momentarily. I stood thoughtfully for a moment, scarcely knowing what to do. Then I remembered that Mitch and Marty would be leaving to catch the train within an hour and Mitch certainly ought to have his keys. Furthermore, I ought to have my hat so I could show up at Mrs. Worthington's in the morning. Anyway, why *shouldn't* I go in? No one would be going to bed an hour before train time. After all, Marty was my sister.

I opened the screen and tried the door, and although the latch was on so that the knob wouldn't turn, the door had not been pushed shut far enough to catch. It gave before my hand with a faint click and I went in and pushed it to behind me.

It was then that I first heard the voices in the study. When

I heard them I stood very still in paralyzed astonishment, for the voices were tense and furious and there had never been the slightest intimation that Mitch and Marty could ever speak this way.

Marty was saying, "—never heard of such a thing. You must be joking, darling."

Mitch said, cold and tense, "I never joke, not about things like this. You're not going and that's final. I'd rather you didn't make a scene about it."

There was a silence, full of vibrations which I could feel even out in the hall.

Marty said, "Have you planned this all along?"

"Of course. Don't be childish."

Marty said, with her voice rising, "Childish? Do you mean to say you planned all along to leave me here—to join this woman, whoever she is—and never said a word to me about it—even encouraged me to give this elaborate party to celebrate our leaving—and all the time you had it planned that you'd leave me here?"

Mitch said, "What difference does it make whether it was planned or not? I'm going and you're not going with me. That's the end of it. That's plain enough, isn't it?"

There was another stinging silence. Then Marty said, with faltering sarcasm, "Forgive me if I seem a little upset. How long has this been going on? Of course, I'm used to husband's walking out on me on Tuesdays and Thursdays, but well—you see, I guess it just never happened to me on Friday before."

Her voice broke a little and she said with a nervous laugh, "I guess in time one gets used to Fridays just like any other day of the week."

Mitch said, icily, "Nuts."

There was a silence. Then Marty said, slowly, "I suppose I'm a very mild sort of person, Mitch—too mild, now that I think about it. Is that what you're counting on? Well, I wouldn't be too sure. There are some things no one has to take lying down. What have you thought I'd be doing while you're designing a brave new life in a new world? Am I supposed to cry my eyes out and let it go at that?"

"No," said Mitch. "You'll feel that you must fight for hearth and home, the brave little moth flying straight into the flame. But you won't follow me and you won't say a word. You'll stay right here and swallow your pride and say nothing more than that we've separated. In due time there will be a divorce, and you will not make a scene about it. The script has been prepared, and you will say your little lines and jump through your little hoops when I snap my fingers."

Marty said, "You seem very confident. Are you sure you haven't misread the tea leaves somewhere?"

"No, I haven't misread the tea leaves. You have a vulnerable spot, and I know exactly how to reach it. Perhaps it would be better to tell you now, before you do anything hasty, and regret it."

"Well, all right. What is this vulnerable spot of mine that you're so sure about?"

I could visualize Mitch raising his eyebrows in assured insolence. He said, "Jess."

My stomach tightened in surprise and anger. My hands trembled and broke into a sweat. Marty said quickly, "*Mitch, you wouldn't?*"

"Yes," said Mitch. "I would. I have. I don't think there's any necessity for going into details. All you need to know is Jess is in trouble. He doesn't know it yet, but I'm quite sure he'll be fired in the morning, under circumstances which could indicate either carelessness or plain crookedness. Carelessness, he can probably live down. I might even help him. I probably will, if you act sensibly. If the other interpretation is applied, I'm quite sure he will be disbarred."

There was a long silence. Marty said quietly, "I see. The next question is useless, but I suppose I must ask it. You control this situation?"

"Yes," said Mitch, "I control it."

There was a new and softer note in Marty's voice. A shadow crossed the thread of light again and I gathered that she moved closer to him. She said, "What's happened, Mitch? Have I done something to let you down? I mean—well it may seem silly, but whether you believe it or not this is all a surprise to me. It never crossed my mind before. There's been so much between us— I shouldn't have to remind you of it. What's happened to all that?"

I could almost see the shrug that was reflected in Mitch's voice. He said, "What's happened to it? Nothing. Nothing happened to it. It was never there except in your imagination." A note of exasperation crept into his voice as he added, "For God's sake, Marty, where is this woman's intuition I hear so much about? You aren't wanted any more, can't you understand that?"

"But, Mitch—"

With irritation, "But what?"

The tenderness was there again. She said, "But, Mitch. Didn't you know? Maybe I shouldn't bring it up at this time, but I thought you knew. Don't you understand? *I'm going to have a baby!*"

This time the silence was longer than before and the intensity of emotions fairly crackled in the air.

I suppose I expected some exclamation from Mitch, but after an intolerable period of suspense, what I heard was the sound of a heavy blow and then the unmistakable sound of someone falling over a chair and striking the floor. There was a gasp of surprise and then of pain and before I could move there was a scramble; the door was snatched open and Marty ran across the dimly lit hall and up the spiral staircase with a crimson welt standing out against her white, strained face and one arm hugged tightly to her waist.

9.

I HEARD a door slam upstairs and then, with fury swelling in my throat, I walked lightly across to the study door, pushed it open, and stood glaring at Mitch. He was leaning back against a heavy oak desk, with his long legs stretched out in front of him and his ankles crossed. Someone had brought the new cigaret lighter in from the living room where I had last seen it. He was using it to light a cigaret.

He looked up at me through the smoke with only mild surprise—as completely at ease as if I had arrived by appointment. He said, "Why, hello, Jess. I didn't know you were still around. Thought you had gone home a long time ago. What's the matter? Forget something?"

The very lightness of his tone, remembered against the background of what I had just heard, made me so angry that for an instant he and everything in the room seemed fuzzy and blurred. A variety of blunt and insulting remarks were on the tip of my tongue, but what I said was, "I came back for my hat."

It sounded awfully silly. He gave me a crooked grin and said easily, "Okay, go ahead and get it. Getting a hat's a simple matter. You look like a typhoon about to phoo."

Again I opened my mouth to say one thing and said another. I said, "I also came back to give you your keys."

That sounded even sillier. A sense of frustration made an artery in my neck throb until I could feel every heartbeat against my collar. With a stupid feeling that I must look like a first grader bringing an apple to teacher, I dug the keys out of my pocket and held them out to him awkwardly. They were buttoned up in a little imitation-leather folder, and as I handed them to him the folder popped open and the keys jingled together.

He held out his hand for them, gave them a flip so that they lay together snugly, punched the snap with his thumb until it caught with a click, and slipped them into his pocket.

There was so much emotion piling up inside of me that when I spoke, the words came thickly and hurriedly, in little blurted groups. I said, "I was out in the hall and I heard it. Not all, but enough. You're a perfect son-of-a-bitch."

Mitch raised his eyebrows and said, "Oh, come now. Perhaps it isn't as bad as all that. It isn't as if husbands and wives don't have an occasional little squabble, you know."

I said, "Is that your idea of an occasional little squabble?"

He said, innocently, "I'm not sure I know what you mean. Don't be theatrical. How old are you, anyway?"

"How old should I be?"

"Old enough to be realistic, my dear Jess. For example, I suppose you're under the impression that because of your sterling merit and the fact that you made creditable grades in law school, the firm of Abercrombie, Sothern and Fant was in a perfect dither for fear it couldn't procure your services at a figure two or three times what they're actually worth."

His tone had the effect on me which might be achieved by pouring Worcestershire sauce into an open wound. I could feel the throbbing in my neck again, but I said with a quietness I was far from feeling, "Okay, you got me a job. I suppose on that account you're entitled to be whatever kind of a son-of-a-bitch may strike your fancy. If you didn't want me, just why *did* you hire me?"

He gave me a smug and superior look, but I do not know what he was about to answer for at that moment there was a clatter on the stairway and both of us instinctively looked toward the door. His eyes narrowed. He gave me a bristling glance, said out of the corner of his mouth, "Wait here and keep your mouth shut," went quickly out into the hall and pulled the door shut behind him.

The voices were indistinct through the heavy door, but

I was sure I could hear Beulah Mae, the Negro maid, saying something in shrill, urgent tones. Whatever Mitch said came to me only as a low resonant mutter, and then I heard heavy steps shuffling up the servants' stairway and a voice which I assumed was that of old Zack, Beulah Mae's husband, who lived with her over the garage and alternated as butler, chauffeur and general handy man.

I could gather nothing of the conversation except from the overtones—in Beulah Mae's case, one of alarm bordering on hysteria; in Zack's case, one of querulous incredulity; in Mitch's case, one of imperiousness to the point of contempt. Anger was beating heavily against my ribs and these few moments by myself increased rather than modified it. I heard Beulah Mae go back upstairs, taking the steps two at a time, which was unheard of. Then Mitch calmly opened the door, came back in and shut it behind him. He dug a cigaret from his pocket and picked up the heavy cigaret lighter.

He said, "Going back to the subject of your employment by the firm."

"Yes? What about it?"

"I don't know why I should tell you, but then again, why not? It isn't as if you could do anything about it, or indeed that it matters."

He said, "Everything goes according to plan. If you're smart, nothing just happens. It's all figured out in advance. Tonight it's your dear sister, Marcella, who is, let's say, a trifle upset. Tomorrow, it happens to be your turn. Judge Abercrombie doesn't know it yet but he'll fire you in considerable disgrace, I would say before noon tomorrow."

Here was a repetition of the same bewildering news he had given my sister. Before I could think of anything to say, there was another commotion upstairs and again both of us looked at the closed door with expectancy. A silence fell between us. We could hear footsteps on the stairway moving slowly and rather heavily as if they were carrying an unwieldy object. I assumed it was Beulah Mae and Zack carrying Mitch's baggage. As I listened, the sense of bewilderment over what Mitch had said about me gave way and was replaced by fury over what he was doing to Marty.

Neither of us said anything while the sounds continued. The baggage, or whatever it was, was carried out the front door, and the door was shut firmly. A few moments passed and then I heard the slam of a couple of car doors, the whine of a starter, and the roar of a motor as a car was backed out of the drive.

Mitch looked at his watch and said, "Well, that's that. Now if you'll excuse me, my *dear* Jess, I have just time to get my bags and catch the train."

He started for the door but I grabbed him roughly by the arm and jerked him around until he was facing me. A possibility was growing in my mind—something I had not considered before. I said, "What were Zack and Beulah Mae doing just now?"

Mitch threw off my grip roughly. He said, "Not that it's any of your business but since you asked, they are taking your sister Marcella to the hospital. Now, *if you don't mind*, I'll catch my train."

He started for the door again, but once more I grabbed his arm and this time I whirled him around so that he almost lost his balance. I said, "*Hospital!* For what?"

Mitch didn't shake off my hand this time. Instead he reached out and took my wrist in a grip that almost paralyzed me. He twisted my arm out and back until I thought a bone would give way. He said into my face, "It seems she's injured. Beulah Mae thinks she'll have a miscarriage. That's *her* business. My business happens to be catching a train and I'll thank you to keep your nose out of it."

We stared at each other at a range of six inches for a long, tense moment. Then he turned my wrist loose, shrugged his coat comfortably in place, and said, "Maybe you've got time to waste, but I haven't. Now take my advice and beat it."

My first thought was of Marty and I started for the door. He thrust out an arm, roughly, and rocked me back on my heels. He said, "On second thought, you'll wait until I give you permission to leave."

I saw the telephone on the desk. I said, "This is why we pay taxes and hire policemen." I picked up the phone and started to dial. Mitch hit me sharply across the face with the back of his hand and the room seemed vaguely pink. He twisted the phone out of my hand and slammed it back in its cradle.

For an instant we glared at each other.

His hat was on the table. He put it on, studied the effect in the mirror in the most infuriating manner, and started for the door.

I said, "No, you don't."

I grabbed his arm and pulled him around violently. The heavy cigaret lighter was on the desk a few inches from my hand. I picked it up and lunged at him with all my strength. At the last instant he saw and instinctively turned. My blow struck him in the back of the head with a deadly, sickening impact. He took a step forward. Then his head drooped on his neck, his body relaxed, and he struck the floor with a crash. His hat bounced on the floor in front of him and then wobbled over by the fireplace and came to a stop.

I stood there for a few seconds staring in horror at what I had done. The house was suddenly very still. Sweat broke out all over me. There was no mistaking the way the back of his head was crushed.

It seems to me, remembering those moments as best I can, that I must have spent a long time looking at the heavy steel cigaret lighter. I carried it doubtfully in my hand as I went out into the hall. Then I put it on a table, walked straight out through the front door, and pulled the door shut behind me until I heard the sound of the catch going home.

I went down the front walk without haste, turned to the

right automatically, and walked away. The street lights, shining between the trees in a lonely sort of way, made alternate bands of light and shadow through which I remember walking with my mind in a turmoil and the sweat drying on me in the cool April air.

10.

AT FIRST my thoughts were full of what had happened in Mitch's study, and I could think of nothing else. But presently, as I walked along, the preceding events came back to me and I realized that Marty was in a hospital somewhere. I stopped where the street light cast the shadow of a tree. I remembered that the City Hospital was on 18th Street, three blocks beyond the liquor store I had visited earlier in the evening. I debated a moment, standing first on one foot and then on the other, and then walked on up to Virginia and turned left.

It was when I was making the turn that I heard footsteps. Joe the bus driver came into the light on the other side of Virginia Drive, walking toward me and then turning to his left as he had done several hours before. He made a gesture of recognition with his hand and I nodded and made the same gesture in return. But as I walked away from the intersection the mental picture was different—there was something wrong about it. Then I figured out what it was. There was no longer a snag in his trousers.

The liquor store was dark now, and the streets were deserted. The globe over the door of City Hospital shone like cloudy milk, and black bugs were buzzing around it. I went through the revolving door and the lobby echoed gauntly to my footsteps. The lights were dim, the floor was marble, and there was a great deal of lonesome space without enough places to sit.

On my left there was a counter, and beyond it a woman sat at a desk under a shaded lamp that cast a cone of light downward. My heels clacked on the cold marble and I leaned over the counter. She scarcely looked up. I asked if a Mrs. Mitchell Sothern had been admitted that night. She examined her records, said there was a Mrs. Sothern in Room 412, and then added that no visitors were permitted—positively none. She was firm to the point of severity.

Behind me the revolving door swished. An old man and an old lady and a young girl clacked across the marble and asked a question. I felt ignored and walked disconsolately out and down the long flight of granite steps.

It was only a few blocks to my apartment house and since I could see no taxis on the streets I had to walk it. A block from the Albemarle I heard unmelodious voices trying to harmonize. For a moment I had that curious feeling that all this had happened before . . . that I had walked down this street, or another very like it . . . that the same song . . .

. . . Certainly, the same song . . . "Girl of My Dreams". . .

A car was parked at the curb, a yellow Hudson sedan. In it a flock of young people were passing a bottle around. As I approached they started "Dinah."

Beyond the next intersection a policeman turned his flashlight into the entrance of a building, wiggled it around. An unreasoning fear gripped me. A moment before I had been numb, as if I had been walking in a trance, but now all at once I knew I did not want to be seen by a policeman. The uniform was a threat. If a flashlight had been turned on me I would have covered my face, instinctively.

A thick voice said, "Hiya, Don, ole kid ole kid ole kid." A hand reached from the rear window and grabbed at my sleeve, pulling me up short. The voice said, "Good thing you come along—*came* along, that is. Car fulla girls and tenors." To the car he said, "If I hadn't of stuck out my hand he would never of known it was us, I guess."

He said to me, opening the door, "We been waitin' but we couldn't wait. Get in and have a gargle."

I was trembling—grateful for a place to become inconspicuous.

There was a great shifting of feet and knees and bodies as I crowded in. I did not want a drink but I took a swallow when the bottle was passed to me. It was dark in the car. I put my hand on a seductive knee and said, "Who's this?"

There was a giggle, halfway between indignation and pleasure and a girl said, "Hey! Don thinks this is feel day."

I said, "Well, who *is* it?"

She said, giggling again, "June."

I ran my hand through a head of curly hair in the front seat and said, "And who's this?"

A girl said, "Alice."

I said, "You must have a blue gown."

A voice from under the wheel said, "It's corny, but it's Don. Who else'd make a crack like that, for cryin' out loud."

From under me someone said, "Singing's all right, but let's go ahead and do it. And for a starter, let's get Don the hell off my knees."

I got the hell off his knees. Somebody said, "Give him the bottle again, he's behind."

The bottle came my way and I took another quick swallow. Evidently this was what Don would have done.

Somebody said, "The only thing he likes is 'Girl of My Dreams.' Somebody start it and let him earn his drinks."

I did very well with "Girl of My Dreams." From that we went into "Sweetheart of Sigma Chi" and then "Carolina Moon." The policeman was nowhere in sight.

I said, "Well, it was swell while it lasted. You understand, of course, that I've got to get going."

Somebody said, "Nice knowing you."

Somebody said, "Be seein' you around."

Somebody said, "See you in the funny papers."

I said, "Not if I see you first."

I walked away. There was no more singing. I was conscious of the people getting out of the car behind me, untangling and tripping and laughing. I was conscious of the uncomfortable feeling of a wrong hat on my head, but it didn't seem important.

A fellow tenant whom I recognized but didn't know came out of the Albemarle as I appeared under the marquee. I couldn't very well avoid him. He nodded and I nodded back. He walked north and I saw him turn into the Prince Garage, an all-night storage garage just above the Albemarle. The look he had given me was such a queer one that I took off the strange-feeling hat before I entered the apartment house.

Charley Pitts was sitting drowsily behind the counter reading a beat-up copy of the *Saturday Evening Post*.

With scarcely a glance he waved a hand vacantly and said, "Ever'thing under control?"

I debated saying nothing but realized it would seem peculiar.

I said, "Hiya, Pittsie, howza boy?"

It didn't occur to either of us that Charley should run me up in the elevator. I walked past his desk and climbed my two flights of stairs and let myself into Apartment 332. In the back of my mind there were plenty of reasons for anxiety. I sat on the edge of the bed and let them pass in review. They were ghastly. I went into the kitchen and found a bottle with an inch or two in the bottom of it. Presently there seemed to be no reasons for anxiety. . . .

With only very little difficulty I untangled myself from my clothes and made a limp diagonal of myself on the bed.

11.

I WOKE UP—staring wide awake with a first consciousness that the night had been tormented and without rest. I knew also that I had a bad hangover—just a jump before being nauseated. I had a headache too, one that pierced and throbbed. My mouth had a bad taste and my tongue was thick and without feeling.

It was early but I knew that there was no more sleep. I didn't consciously recall the successive events of the evening before, but neither had I forgotten them. They were simply there—all-pervading, and ominous, and creative of an impulse to be moving—to knock over things if necessary—to take something off or put something on—to turn on the water or light the gas—anything, so long as it didn't consist of sitting there on the edge of the bed.

Despite these urges I sat there awhile longer with my hands rigid on the bed beside me and my head slumped forward.

My thoughts ran in off-center circles, and after they passed a given point, I found it impossible to flag them down and make them sit in orderly rows so that I could call the roll and determine who was present and who was absent.

I got up and fumbled into the bathroom and pulled the chain that hung from the light bulb over the basin. I didn't pull hard enough and the light didn't come on but I was in such a stupid state that I didn't react to the continued darkness. With practised hands I opened the cabinet, found my toothbrush and tooth paste and actually brushed my teeth and put everything away before it occurred to me that when I looked in the mirror I didn't see anything. Maybe you'll think I'm crazy, until the day when in a moment of abstraction you go through automatic motions with great precision and afterwards fail to remember anything at all. Like when you're daydreaming and a truck comes suddenly out of a side street and your reflexes swerve and put on the brakes before your wandering mind has focused on the crisis.

After that, the problem of focusing was solved, suddenly and with a sense of shock. The state of near-somnambulism ended with a jerk, and I was the jerk it ended with. All at once I was Jess London again, very much aware of the happenings of the night before, but for the moment not frightened. Excited, yes, and tense to the point of quivering; but the quivering didn't have its origin in fear.

I know I did these things, and probably in this order: I reached beyond the shower curtain and turned on the cold water, sound evidence of the desperate measures I was prepared to take. I got out of my pajamas, found the aspirin bottle, poured two tablets into my palm, considered briefly, and poured two more. I put them in my mouth and felt disagreeable. Then with the shower running, and as unclothed as April Morn, I went into the kitchenette and started the percolator. I measured out the coffee mathematically, according to the directions, and then added a generous overdose and went back and stepped under the icy water. I stayed there, gasping and heaving, while successive waves of soberness came and went. At length I decided that I could step out of the shower without crawling straight into bed and going back to sleep.

I then rubbed myself briskly like Stover at Yale. I hooked a towel around my waist and went into the kitchenette and drank all of the coffee, standing up, and as fast as I could gulp it.

The phone rang. I stood in the living-room doorway and looked at it with alarm.

The police?

Not the police.

The police would scarcely ring and say, "I say, old chap, are you there?"

They would come and beat on the door with guns and

handcuffs, and there would be someone watching the fire escape at the same time.

The phone was still ringing. I went over and picked up the receiver.

"Mistuh Jess?"

It was Zack. His voice was anxious, trembling, desperate. I said, "Yes, Zack. What is it?"

"Oh, good God, Mistuh Jess, is I evah glad to hear yo' voice!"

"What's the matter?"

"It's Miss Marty, Mistuh Jess. She's down heah at the City Hospital and me and Beulah Mae is here, down in the furnace room, and we feel *responsible*, Mistuh Jess, but we don't know what to do. Miss Marty got took sick last night, Mistuh Jess, and Mistuh Mitch tole us to bring her down here and we done it, but now we don't know *what* to do. I called Mistuh Mitch foh instructions, and I called him and I called him, but the house don't answer, so I give up long time ago. I guess he must of gone on and went away on the train last night, Mistuh Jess, but it don't seem to figger, him going away with Miss Marty down here to the hospital. Den just now I figgered I ought to call you, Mistuh Jess, and I sho am glad you ain't gone, too."

I said, "You did right in calling me, Zack, only you should have called before, instead of waiting. You stay right there. When I'm dressed, I'll come down and then you can go home."

"Yessuh. Thank you, Mistuh Jess. We wait right here, like you say."

I heard a shuffling in the hall and the splat in front of my door that meant the morning paper had been delivered. I went out and got it and turned on the floor lamp in the living room and sat naked in the big chair.

I quickly found what I was expecting—a two-column head about a prominent attorney being found murdered in his home. It was the secondary headline that brought me up in a spasm of shock and anxiety. I don't remember the wording, but what it said was that the police were seeking my sister Marty who seemed to have disappeared under suspicious circumstances.

12.

I STOOD UP and I had the phone in my hand. The operator said, "What number, please?" and I put it down again with a clash. How could Marty have disappeared? Mysteriously or at all? What the hell were they talking about?

I picked up the phone again and when the operator asked me this time, I put the receiver down once more and looked up the number of the hospital. By the time I was on the wire again, the operator was in the middle of repeating her routine and she was getting very unhappy about it. I gave her the number and I could almost see her hips switch with annoyance. She plugged me in abruptly and buzzed the hospital with a vehemence which must have represented her nervous outlet after a hard night.

The woman on the desk at the hospital had evidently experienced a trying night of her own for she was laconical if not actually drowsy, and I am sure she was swallowing a yawn in the middle of her confession that Mrs. Mitchell Sothern was there and doing as well as might be expected, although she didn't say who the expecting was being done by. I asked if I could speak with her and was told I couldn't. Then I asked if I could speak with the doctor and I couldn't do that either. Then I asked if I could speak with the head nurse on the fourth floor and she told me frankly that I could if I wanted to but it wouldn't do any good.

I hung up and thought wildly of calling police head-quarters, but when I thought of someone answering the phone and asking me what I wanted and me not knowing the answer, I abandoned that idea.

I dressed and sat precariously on the very edge of the divan until I was almost slipping off to the floor. I held my head in my hands and meditatively shined the toe of my right shoe against my left trouser leg. This simple little action clarified my thoughts. Presently I went looking for my hat, put it on my head, and then, realizing that it didn't fit, held it stupidly under the light until I remembered that it *wasn't* my hat. My hat was on the bed in the guest room in Mitch's house. My hat was not the same color as this one. My hat fit my head, at least after a haircut, and this one didn't. This was the hat of a strange and rather hoarse tenor who didn't know how to harmonize "Tie Me to Your Apron Strings Again" but who had pressed into my hand a not too bad bottle of whiskey and hadn't counted the swallows on me.

The hat was green, of all things. Not the shade of green I would ever have owned, if indeed I could correlate my personality with a green hat of any shade whatsoever, Michael Arlen notwithstanding.

The sequence of association took me to the window and I opened it and peered down at the street. There, as if it might have been the place where the "Man on the Flying Trapeze" took off his trunks before going to bed, was a canary yellow Hudson sedan, with two doors hanging open over the curb and the general appearance of an empty beer bottle lying on its side.

There are times when life is a series of non sequiturs. It didn't seem odd that in the middle of murder and headlines and sisters in the hospital, the most important thing at the moment seemed to be the objectionable green hat. I went out and closed the door behind me and walked down the two flights of steps. Charley Pitts had been relieved by the day desk clerk, who had a carnation in his buttonhole. A big-bottomed cleaning woman, who wore grey cotton hose, was mopping around the potted palms with her behind looking like the silhouette of a disconsolate hippopotamus.

I walked out and went past the canary yellow Hudson, noted with interest a bedraggled pair of peach silk panties on the floor, (interesting at that), crumpled the hat and tossed it into a corner of the back seat.

I went on down to the middle of the block, turned in at a restaurant where the window was clouded with steam and ate scrambled eggs, fried ham, hot biscuits and coffee.

Then with my chin in the air and being careful not to step on the seams in the sidewalk, I stumped my way down to Cedar Avenue, turned to the right with an ear for the spring chatter of birds in the trees, walked down in the dewy morning past Virginia Drive and up to the door of Mitch Sothern's house where the door was open and a man in blue uniform was standing.

13.

THE POLICEMAN stepped out, half as if to meet me and half to bar the way. I said brightly, "Good morning!" It didn't sound too impressive.

He said, "Sorry, no one can go in. Little trouble inside. However, we'd like to have your name and address."

I said, "Who's in charge here?"

He had out a notebook and pencil. He said, "Lieutenant Richmond. Name and address, please."

"I want to see him. I have some information for him. He'll want to see me."

"I'm sure he will. What was the name?"

"Jess London."

"Address?"

"Albemarle Apartments."

"Apartment number?"

"Three thirty-two."

"Telephone?"

"Yes."

He looked up with a trace of impatience. "What's the number?"

I was getting impatient myself. I said, "Main eight two four three."

He made the entry, put the notebook in his pocket and said in a conciliatory tone, "I'm supposed to do it with everybody. Even if you're the F.B.I. I'm supposed to do it."

He shifted one foot sidewise and added, "That is, you've got to have some sense about it. The F.B.I. is just for example. A guy's got to have some sense, regardless."

I said, "I really do want to see Lieutenant Richmond. It's pretty important—really it is."

There was a stir inside the house and a man in plain clothes came and stood in the doorway. He said, "Who wants to see Richmond? You're seeing him now."

I said, "Well, if Lieutenant Richmond's the man in charge I want to see him and if that's you I guess I want to see you."

"What do you want to see me about?"

"Well, I saw in the morning paper what happened last night and Mitch Sothern's my brother-in-law—"

He broke in with, "Brother-in-law? Then you're Mrs. Sothern's brother? Or is it his sister's husband or what?"

I said, "No, I'm Mrs. Sothern's brother. I thought—"

"Then maybe you know where she is. They were supposed to go away on the train but she wasn't on it."

"That's what I came to tell you. She wasn't even *supposed* to go on the train. She's—"

"Then what did she have a ticket for?"

"She didn't have a ticket. She thought she did. It was a mistake."

"Mr. Sothern had two of them, didn't he? One for him and one for her. I don't get it."

I said, "Well anyway, what I mean is that Marty's in the hospital and didn't go away on anybody's train no matter how the tickets figure out. What I'm trying to tell you is she didn't go on the train because she was in the hospital."

"Marty? Is that Mrs. Sothern?"

"Marty's my sister. She's in the hospital. That's what I've been trying to tell you."

"What hospital?"

"The City Hospital. It's down on Eighteenth Street. She's been there since before the train left and that's why—"

"Look, never mind why or how long. If she's in City Hospital, that's all I want to know. Tell you what. We'll get Harry to drive us right down there now and you can come along and do all the talking you want to. How's that?"

He took me by the elbow while he was talking and we walked briskly down the steps and out to the curb where a police car sat with two red lamps and two search lights in addition to the normal equipment, and a radio aerial rod tapering in a graceful curve over the top.

Lieutenant Richmond opened the door and elbowed me in ahead of him. He closed the door behind us and said, "Okay, Harry. City Hospital."

When we were under way he turned to me, offered me a cigaret, held a light and then lit his own. He said, "All right. Now what's on your mind?"

48 –

I said, "You can go to the hospital if you want to but it's all a waste of time. She didn't do it. She couldn't have done it."

"Why couldn't she?"

"Because I did it myself."

He gave me a startled look. After a moment he said, "Just like that?"

I said, "I don't know what you mean. If you mean did I kill him, that's what I said. I suppose—well, just like that."

"Big party last night, wasn't there?"

"Pretty big, yes."

"You stay after everybody left?"

"No, I went home. There were still some people when I left."

"If you killed him, then you must have come back."

"Yes, that's what I did. I came back later."

"How did you get in?"

"Just pushed the door open."

"But we've already found the last guests to leave. Man by the name of Forman. Wife with him. They joked about whether the door should be locked and she fixed the catch herself and tried it. One of those button businesses."

I said, "Well anyway, it wasn't locked. The catch didn't catch. I just pushed it open."

"Didn't you expect it to be locked?"

"I don't know. I guess I didn't think about it."

"Well how did you expect to get in?"

I said doggedly, "Keys. I had a key."

"What key? Show me."

"I don't mean a key of my own. His key."

"Well, where's that?"

"I haven't got it. I—"

"We found his keys in his pocket and the front door locked. What about that?"

"I had 'em and I gave 'em back to him."

"What did you go back to the party for? Didn't you know it was over?"

"I went back for my hat. There was a memorandum in the sweat band and I had to have it for first thing this morning. I couldn't wait so I went back."

He took an envelope from his pocket, extracted a slip of paper and held it out for me to see. "Is that what you're talking about?"

I reached for it but he snatched it away. I said, "Sure, that's it. It was in my hat band and it says how I can get in touch with Mrs. Worthington. I had to have it on account of an appointment with her this morning."

"Then if you had to have it, why didn't you get it? This was in a hat on a bed in a room upstairs."

I said, "I went back after it but I forgot."

He said, "If you killed him, what did you do it with?"

I wasn't prepared for this sudden change of subject. I stared at him a moment and then said, "I hit him with the first thing that was handy. A gadget. A heavy thing—a—a—sort of ball made into a cigaret lighter."

"There wasn't anything like that in the room."

I stared at him again, tried to recall what I had done with the thing. Then I remembered. I said, "It's on the table in the hall."

"How did it get there?"

"It got there because I put it there."

"Just killed him with a cigaret lighter and walked out into the hall?"

"That's right. That's the way it happened."

"What for? Why take it out there?"

I said, "Jeest, I'm telling you, that's all. If you want to know, here I am telling you, and what the hell? You don't have to see Marty or anyone else. What I'm telling you, I killed him. You aren't even interested."

The car came to a stop and Harry said over his shoulder, "City Hospital, Lieutenant. Want I should wait or go in with you?"

Richmond said, "Did you hear all this, Harry?"

"Yes, sir."

"How does it sound to you?"

"I'm only a dumb cop, Lieutenant, but you asked me and I'll tell you. I buy these here two-bit mystery stories and I read the same thing three times a week. If it isn't a sister, it's a wife or a sweetheart or a mother. Young feller has got to run in and confess, irrespective and irregardless."

Richmond didn't comment but turned to me. He said, "So you picked up the cigaret lighter, or whatever the hell it was, and hit him. What'd you do that for?"

I said, "He was a son-of-a-bitch. He struck Marty—"

He interrupted quickly with, "Now we're getting somewhere. They had a quarrel, didn't they? That's what I thought."

I hadn't meant to tell him but now that it had popped out I didn't care. I said, "Sure they had a quarrel, but she didn't kill him. I've spent all this time telling you I did it myself."

He leaned back in the corner of the car and looked at me thoughtfully. He said, "All right, so you killed him. Was he dead when you left him?"

I said, "He was dead all right."

"How do you know?"

"Well, I mean, how can you be mistaken about a thing like that?"

"Feel his pulse?"

I hesitated a minute and then figured in exasperation that I might as well tie it up tight. I said, "Yes, I felt his pulse. There wasn't any pulse. I know where to feel and I kept at it to make sure. I tell you he was dead."

Richmond sighed, leaned forward and opened the door beside him. He said, "That does it. Don't try to make up such a good story next time. We got there at three-thirty and the Medical Examiner didn't get there until nearly four. He was alive then, but unconscious. He passed out while the Examiner was listening to his heart."

A thought occurred to me. I said, "How did you happen to go to the house anyway? I don't get it."

Richmond said, "Sooner or later somebody always finds the body. This time it was neighbors. Saw the lights and couldn't figure it out. For curiosity, give me a woman in the middle of the night. Me, I just say to myself the dopes left the lights on, but women aren't made that way. . . ."

14.

HE GOT OUT of the car and I got out behind him and slammed the door.

Richmond didn't seem terribly interested in me. He set off briskly up the long flight of granite steps that led to the entrance of the hospital. I had to yell, "Hey!" and run after him, feeling like a little boy whose mother has left him during a shopping tour. I remember the feeling of irritation. According to the scenario I should have been the center of interest, seated in an uncomfortable chair with the white light beating down into my face and perspiration pouring clammily all over me. And here I was, pulling at teacher's coattails, trying to get some small degree of attention.

I was only confessing to a murder—that's all.

Richmond went up the steps two at a time, a jump ahead of me. I was right behind him in the revolving door and caught up with him in the lobby. He seemed abstracted, as if he had forgotten me, but he remembered when I bumped his elbow.

He said over his shoulder, "Tell you what. Take that chair right over there and wait for me."

I said, "I will like hell. That's my sister upstairs."

He stopped suddenly and I ran into him. He said, "Look, sonny. It was a nice story and it was entertaining during a dull ride. I don't hold it against you. But for Chrissake's we aren't playing patty-cake and it would be nice if you'd just sit here and count up to ten a couple of times while I earn my living."

"But I've been trying to tell you—"

"Yes, I know. And don't think I don't appreciate it. But now if you don't mind . . ."

I said, "You don't have to be silly about it. It's hard enough to confess . . . I mean that's one thing you'd think there wouldn't be any sales resistance about. Stop me if I'm wrong."

He stopped and faced me with his hands on his hips. He said, "Confessions are swell. I love 'em. Given by the proper guy at the proper time they save the taxpayers a lot of money and that's right down my alley on account of the budget. You didn't know we had a budget, did you? Well we do, see? No matter how many murders or rapes or what the hell, they've got to fit in the budget. Now I appreciate your confession more than I can tell you but the budget says first I should go upstairs and talk to Mrs. Sothern. You follow that, don't you?"

I stared at him a moment in disgust and then shrugged and said, "Sure, if you've got a budget, that's different. I should have thought of the budget when I killed the son-of-a-bitch. Jeest, the budget!"

I sat dismally among the silent statuettes and held my head in my hands. He walked over and stood in front of the elevator, snapping his fingers nervously down by the seams of his trousers. When the door opened he stepped in with his head bent forward and everything about him indicative of attention to the problem ahead. If there was any sign that he was thinking about me, I failed to see it.

15.

I DON'T KNOW how long I sat there but I was very low, and it could have been a long time. Presently somebody touched me on the shoulder and it was one of those nondescript men who work in hospitals in uniforms that must have once been white. Presumably they empty cuspidors and carry out bedpans and throw away what they cut out of you when you have an operation. He was by no means neat and he was no Clark Gable either. He said, "Are you Mr. London?"

I admitted that I was.

"Feller wants to see you. Colored man, so he can't come in. He says please if you'd come outside, he's waiting for you at the foot of the ramp."

I got up mechanically and thanked him and went the way he pointed and walked out the door and down the ramp to where old Zack was waiting anxiously. He said, "Mr. Jess, I shore is glad you're here. It ain't right for the responsibility to be on Beulah Mae and me. I shore is glad you're here."

"It's all right, Zack," I said. "You did fine getting Mrs. Sothern here and it was wonderful of you to wait all night and let me know. I'd have been here sooner but I just didn't know. Now you and Beulah Mae had better go home and get some rest. Everything's going to be all right, and don't you worry about it for a minute."

Zack pressed my hand and shook his head and said, "I shore is glad you're here, Mr. Jess. I never had such a load on my mind in all my born days. I mean to say it shore is nice you're here. Beulah Mae and me, we done the best we could and now I don't know what we'd do if you weren't here."

I said, "Where's Beulah Mae?"

"Down in the furnace room. She sho' is worried about

54 -

Miss Marty. She sho' will be glad when I tell her you done come."

I said, "It's all right now, Zack. Everything's going to be all right. You and Beulah Mae take this ten dollar bill and go home and get some sleep and don't you worry about anything at all. I'm glad you called me. That was just exactly what you should have done."

I gave him the bill and a pat on the shoulder and he looked relieved and happy.

Someone would have to tell him sooner or later. I said, "I don't suppose you've seen the morning paper, have you, Zack?"

He gave me a foolish grin and shifted his weight from one foot to the other and said, "You know I don't see no mawnin' paper, Mistuh Jess. Whut it say?"

"It says Mister Mitch is dead, Zack. It says somebody killed him last night."

Zack stared at me gravely. At first there was no reaction, and then he frowned in distress. He said, "Mistuh Mitch, Mistuh Jess? You foolin'?"

"No, I'm not fooling. Did you see him last night? I mean, after the party and after the people all went home?"

"You mean daid? You got it wrong, Mistuh Jess. Ask Beulah Mae, she'll tell you same as me. Miss Marty come runnin' upstairs hurt—look lak she hurt real bad. Beulah Mae run right down and talk to Mistuh Mitch an' I come paddlin' right on down too. Mistuh Mitch jus' as live as you is. 'Fo God, Mistuh Jess, is you *sure* what it says in de paper?"

I said, "Yes, Zack, there doesn't seem to be any doubt about it. I know it'll be a shock to you and Beulah Mae, but it's something we've simply got to face. Don't worry now, see? You did right taking care of Miss Marty, and I'm not going to forget it. Now you and Beulah Mae get along home and have something to eat and get some sleep. Understand?"

Zack said, "I unnerstan' if you say so, Mistuh Jess. I shore is glad you come and took over. You got no idea whut a relief it is, takin' the load off us people . . ."

I went back into what I assume is called a lobby in a hospital, in time to see Lieutenant Richmond stepping out of the elevator. I crossed to him and took him by the elbow and said, "How is she?"

He was thinking of something else but when I brought him up short he looked at me and registered. He said, "Oh! Hello, you're still here. She's doing fine but you absolutely can't see her. Now take my word for it. She's doing fine and you can't do anything to help her. I talked to the doctor and the nurse, and everything's absolutely fine."

I said, "That's swell. Then I can go up and see her."

I started past him but he didn't let go of my arm and I had to swing around facing him. His face was grave. He said, "You can't see her. In the first place, the doctor said I upset her considerably. In the second place, there's a guard on the door and he has his orders."

"You mean I can't see my own sister?"

"You're pretty smart and you're doing fine. For now—no. You can't see her, no matter what. Now let's go back to the house, if you like, and have a big long talk."

I stood rebelliously for a long moment and then when I felt his pressure on my arm I realized the futility of resisting and went out and got into the car with him.

16.

THERE WAS a very long silence as we drove back to the house. We were almost there when Richmond said, "Getting back to how you killed him."

I thought dully that it was high time but I didn't say anything. He waited a decent interval and when I didn't answer he said, "What did you say you did it with?"

I said, "Figure it out for yourself."

"Something about some kind of cigaret lighter, wasn't it?"

I said, "You're so smart, figure it out for yourself."

"That's what I've been doing. I've been thinking you said a gadget that was sitting on the table in the hall. Am I wrong, or was the door open when you were talking to me this morning?"

Grumpily, "So it was open or it was shut. Where do we go from here?"

"Nothing. Only I was just thinking. Best I remember the door was open and you could see into the hall. If that's right, you could see the hall table, and if the thing was there, you could see that, too."

I didn't say anything because I was following his train of thought. I didn't have much trouble following it. I kept my mouth shut. Presently he said, "Funny thing. According to your sister, they had a quarrel. But to hear her story, he was alive when she left him. She even says the servants talked to him after they separated, and he was alive when she was taken to the hospital. When did you talk to her?"

"Me? I haven't seen her since . . . I don't know when it was. Anyway Mitch was very much alive at the time."

"That's what I thought. At least that's what I thought you'd say."

I said, "Have you talked to the servants?"

"No, but I will. But what am I supposed to get out of a couple of Negroes who have been with Mrs. Sothern and her family since they were born? Anyway, they had left the hospital when I asked."

"What difference does it make? You aren't going to believe whatever they say, are you?"

He gave me a funny look and said, "I'm not going to swallow it, if that's what you mean. I wasn't born yesterday."

"No, I didn't think you were. But don't let that make you forget that sometimes people tell the truth."

We pulled up in front of the house on Cedar Avenue. Richmond reached across me and opened the door nearest the curb and got out ahead of me. I followed him and tagged along behind as we went up the walk and into the house.

At the door he hesitated an instant to say something to the guard and I pushed past him. I said, "There's the cigaret lighter I was talking about. Look, I'll show you . . ."

I didn't know the Lieutenant was behind me but as I reached for the cigaret lighter his hand clamped on my wrist like a vise. He said, "Never mind showing me. If there are any fingerprints, we'll find them ourselves if you don't mind."

I stood back helplessly. He drew a clean linen handkerchief from his pocket, draped it carefully over the cigaret lighter, gathered it underneath with great caution, and beckoned to the guard at the door. He said, "Find a box or something and don't touch it. Tell the Sergeant to get this down to headquarters and give it a good going over for fingerprints."

I stood by the table and watched. All at once my knees felt a little shaky and I put out my hand to steady myself. The tiniest trickle of sweat tickled the calf of my leg.

Richmond said, "What about these servants? Do they live on the place?"

I said, "Out in back over the garage."

He said, "Show me," but he set off ahead of me with assurance and it was all I could do to keep up with him. He went briskly through the screen door at the end of the hall and I had to put up my hand abruptly to keep it from swinging back into my face. I followed him almost in a trot as he struck out across the little patch of back lawn and went straight up the outside wooden stairway that led to the living quarters above the garage.

As he went up he said over his shoulder, "Is this the place?" But he didn't wait for an answer and I didn't bother to give him one. He didn't hesitate in front of the door at the top of the steps but opened it and walked in—not with the air of one who tests a door to see whether it is locked but with the unchecked motion of one who knows what to expect. Obviously he had been over this ground before.

I waited without comment in the tiny living room while he disappeared briskly into the adjoining bedroom. I could hear him opening drawers, looking into closets, the bathroom, the kitchen and finally even stepping out to have a look down the kitchen steps at the far end, out of sight of the house.

He came back with a look of impatience on his face and when I offered him a cigaret he took it and let me hold a light for him without paying much attention. He said, "What do you know about them? If they left the hospital and didn't come here, where did they go? Relatives? Friends? Servants next door? The burial society?"

"How should I know? After all, so what?"

"Yes, I know. You killed him with the cigaret lighter. Well, maybe you did. I'm not saying you didn't. But at the moment what I want to do is talk with these servants. Know their names? Your sister said there were two of them. Man named Zack and woman named Beulah Mae. That right?"

"That's right."

"Zack what? The doctor hustled me out before I was half started. Doctors are a nuisance, aren't they? I haven't seen one yet who didn't hover and beat his wings like an old hen. Hell, a man's got to attend to his business—I don't mind that. It's the hovering that gets me."

I said, "I don't know that I ever heard their last name. Zack and Beulah Mae don't need last names to get around. What for?"

He said, "Big help you are," and I had to catch another screen door to avoid a broken nose. On the way down the steps behind him I said, "I gave Zack a ten dollar bill at the hospital. They'd been up all night. Maybe they stopped somewhere for a bite to eat."

He was at the bottom of the steps and stopped and turned so sharply that I ran into him. He said, "Oh! You did?"

"Why not? What would you have done?"

"You didn't tell me you had talked to them."

"You didn't ask me."

He just stood and looked at me and I had the impression his mind was on something else. I said, "Go on. What would you have done?"

He went on looking at me and then almost grinned as he turned away. He said, "Considering the budget I'd probably have given them a buck a piece. Ten bucks. My God!"

In the front hall he stopped again, but by this time I was getting used to him and pulled up short of a collision. He said, "Let's have that story of yours again."

"And let you make fun of me?"

He shrugged and said, "No use getting sore. You confessed, you know. I could take you down to headquarters as easily as not."

"Yes, I suppose you could. But all you're doing is trying to kill time while you figure out how to go about locating Zack and Beulah Mae. All I'm doing is taking up space. I'm about to walk out of here and go down to the office and ask Judge Abercrombie to get his feet wet and look after my sister. If you don't like it, you can arrest me. How about that?"

He said mildly, "Well, how about it?" And then he said, "Oh hell! Run along. Mind if I arrest you some other time?"

I said, "No, not at all. Give me a ring. And now would it be okay if I picked up my hat?"

He looked at me without any particular expression. "You mean the one you especially came back for last night? When you just pushed open the door?"

I didn't dignify these remarks with an answer. I tried to look as if I wanted my hat.

He said, "Sorry, no hat. It's already got a tag on it. You get it back after somebody's been electrocuted. By then you won't want it."

I was beginning to get angry in a frustrated sort of way. I walked out the door feeling like a fool, and then halfway down the front walk, I turned and came back. I said, "After all, the law must go on. If you must keep the piece of paper out of my hat, keep it and be damned as far as I'm concerned, but be a sport and give me the address, will you? I'm supposed to see the lady about an accident."

He thought that over a minute and then fished out my memorandum and let me write down the address.

17.

I WENT DOWN the walk and turned right on Cedar Avenue under the trees. By now I had done it so many times that it seemed natural, and the difference between daytime and night-time lost its significance. Pervading everything was that wonderful sense of life and growth and greenness that doesn't happen in tropical countries where there's no real spring. The dew on the grass was drying in the morning sun but it had not entirely disappeared and certain blades of grass here and there had a proud shine that just missed being a sparkle. The stripes of light and shadow that were so marked at night, and that shook in the spasms of the arc lights, were not now so notice-able nor so bright, but they were there nevertheless—perhaps more in the background of memory than in the foreground of actuality.

What I want you to feel is what I felt at the time, with thoughts of past and present challenging each other in my mind so that as I walked along the now familiar sidewalk, day and night were scarcely removed from each other in my thoughts.

It seemed not only natural but inevitable that when I approached Virginia Avenue I should once again encounter the almost monotonous repetition of events in the person of Joe, the bus driver, coming toward me. Absorbed as I was, my unconscious thought was that all this had happened before at exactly the same time and in exactly the same way and I caught myself wondering if perhaps it would not happen again, and perhaps again, as a cracked record plays a fragment over and over because it cannot help itself.

We both started our turns—mine to my left and his to his left, and then I caught his eye and stopped and said, "Hello, how's your baby?"

He gave me a gesture that expressed despair better than words and said, "Not much good. She's pretty low. Like I told you I called at the end of each run last night and when it didn't sound good I asked for a substitute and went home. Well, by the time I got there she was asleep—all flushed in the face so it would tear your heart out, but she was asleep and the doctor was there and said she was doing all right. So it didn't look like I could do any good and God knows I couldn't sleep so I thought the best thing I could do was go on back and finish out my tour and that's what I did . . . now, I don't know . . . I just don't know. . . . She ain't rational and what the doctor says I don't understand at all. I don't know what's wrong with her or anything. The doctor says she ought to have a transfusion but it's some kind of blood type they don't have down at the hospital . . . Jesus, I'm only a dumb bus driver. I don't know what to do."

He looked completely dejected and then added automatically, "Look at all the blood I got and don't even want.

But what good does it do? I hate to say it but I swear sometimes I wonder if God knows what He's doing."

During the course of this conversation we had somehow met in the middle of Virginia Avenue, perhaps because a soul unloading its burden wants to be near the unloading platform. I know that urgent thoughts were clamoring to be heard but somehow even at such a time I couldn't quite turn and walk away from his bewilderment. I patted his shoulder and I guess I said that everything would turn out all right because that's what people usually say. All at once I felt that a mist of warmth and gratitude—almost love—came from him and gathered like a cloud around me. He was tired and worried, and a hand on his shoulder was almost more than he could stand.

To break the awkwardness of the situation and without stopping to think of the consequences I glanced down and said, "Your wife must be a honey. Even with all your troubles I see she fixed the snag in your pants."

He looked down and grinned with one side of his face and said, "Yeah. Wanda's okay. In the middle of the battle of the Marne she would be mending and sewing on buttons, and I don't suppose it would really matter to her which side she was mending for."

A car honked and he sighed and went his way.

18.

THE SIGN on the door now said "Abercrombie & Fant" and I remember thinking that the sign painter had unconsciously recorded history in advance. I even wondered if perhaps, in the curious way that life operates, it might have been Mitch himself who gave the order to take his name off the door. I had a silly thought like this: "Take my name off the door. But keep it handy and remember how to spell it because tomorrow you can cut it in a piece of stone and put it out in the cemetery."

Mrs. Pennybaker was playing her typewriter as if it were the *Nutcracker Suite*, and Clementine had her mouth shaped as if in the hope of concealing a succulent bit of chocolate, and Miss Tarbo was pushing up and down on one of those things that makes holes in paper for filing purposes. They all stopped what they were doing when I came in, except I'm sure Clementine kept on caressing a great big chocolate cream with her tongue.

I was clearly a problem to the secretarial force. None of them knew what they should say to me, and as a matter of fact I didn't know what I should say to them either. I supposed I should be properly overcome with grief and I tried to look at least a little grave and funereal, but I was sure I wasn't doing too well with it and was glad to get into my little office with no more than a nod.

Once there, I sat down and didn't know what to do. Perhaps it would have been better if I had gone straight to Mrs. A. P. Worthington after all. Strange—the typewriter in the next room had not resumed its noisy syntax and I didn't hear the pleasant crunch of Miss Tarbo making holes in paper.

It was Mrs. Pennybaker who came and stood in the door, perspiring frantically into her little wadded handkerchief and giving every evidence of white-haired confusion.

I looked up and she mistreated her damp handkerchief and said nervously, "The Judge wants to see you right away."

I said, "Thank you," and she went away. I got up with a feeling of weariness, thinking, "All right. Let's go see the old man of the sea and find out what he wants." I had never got over my original feeling of awe, almost fear, of bleak old Judge Abercrombie. Now I remembered my first reaction to him— the general idea that he must have been around racking up the balls in the corner poolroom about the time Noah was born.

I knocked faintly on his door and then remembered that he was a little deaf (and no wonder). I sensed that all eyes were on me—the way you feel when you discover that one of your trouser buttons has been unbuttoned probably since 9:30 A.M. I looked over my shoulder and Mrs. Pennybaker, who did everything for the old Judge except blow his nose, made a slight gesture with her head to show I should go on in. I took a deep breath and went in and shut the door behind me.

Judge Abercrombie was sitting by the window in a black leather chair which his mother had given him when he was a Judge of the Court of Appeals back in the 1890's. Tufts of ancient horse hair, so old that no modern mouse would be interested, showed in a number of places where the leather was cracked. I stood there with a touch of dread and remember thinking in an impersonal way that this was probably how people had to look before they became "Greenleaf on Evidence" or "Cooley on Torts" or any of the other saintly patriarchs of bad print in legal libraries.

He was sitting well down in the chair with his short legs crossed but not quite touching the floor and his chin reinforced against his chest so that the loose jowls, not very well shaven, bagged out on each side of his chin like a goat's wattles. His black alpaca suit was shiny and there were spots of tobacco stain on it. He looked abstracted and gloomy, and the red linings of his lower eyelids showed with more than usual sadness.

I coughed and he glanced at me through his bushy white eyebrows. A degree of animation manifested itself, but not a very great degree. By resting his elbows on the arms of his chair and wiggling his bottom from side to side he maneuvered himself to an erect sitting posture and his little feet in the high button shoes groped for and found the foot stool which was all he could hope to reach.

He indicated a chair and said, "Come in, Mr. London," and his jaws wobbled a little so that he grimaced to get his loose lips out of the way and then clamped his false teeth together aggressively. I wouldn't have dreamed of sitting down but I pulled up a chair and stood beside it wondering what next.

He nodded to himself, indicating that his thoughts had been examined and more or less met with approval. He said, "I'm not as young as I used to be." It was one of the most complete and comprehensive understatements I have ever heard. It was obvious he couldn't have summoned me purely for the purpose of confiding such a thought so I tried to look sympathetic and understanding, and cautiously wet my dry lips with the tip of my tongue.

He said, "You have read the paper?"

"Yes, sir."

"Well, what have you got to say for yourself?"

I don't know what I had been expecting but this wasn't it. When I didn't answer at once, he looked up at me viciously and worked his lower jaw from side to side. From observation in the past I judged that this movement was either an effort to adjust his badly fitting plates or an effort to get an extra bit of juice from a tidbit of Climax plug.

I said, "I'm afraid I don't know what you mean, sir."

He looked around for his big brass spittoon, missed it, and wiped angrily at the new spots he had made on his vest. He said, "Hey?"

I said, "I don't know what you mean, sir. Mitch—Mr. Sothern, I mean—was my brother-in-law and I owed a lot to him. We were very fond of each other. His death is a shock to me too, sir."

He shifted in his chair. "Of course it is. Death's a nuisance, but when you get to be my age it doesn't shock you any more. It's regrettable, but everybody's born and everybody dies. Tomorrow it may be me or you. More likely you. I ought to have died thirty years ago."

That was a poser. I couldn't agree, and if I disagreed he might want to argue about it and where would that get us? I thought of all the noncommittal remarks I could make and finally ventured, "I'm sorry, sir."

He looked puzzled for a moment and said, "What were we talking about?"

"I don't know, sir. I believe you asked if I had read the paper. And then I think you said what did I have to say for myself and I'm afraid I don't follow you, sir. I mean, I just don't understand."

He said, "Oh!" and seemed to be groping around for his train of thought. Finally he said, pointing, "Paper, give me the paper there on the desk." I gave him the morning paper and he held it in hands that shook violently so that all the while he was holding it, the paper crackled. He was conscious of his infirmities and to cover his embarrassment he would shake the paper every few seconds.

He paid no attention to the article on the front page about Mitch's death but scanned the rest of the page with growing impatience and then licked his thumb and made futile attempts to turn over to page two. Finally in an access of rage he roared, "Mrs. Pennybaker!" with astonishing volume. I don't suppose the windows actually rattled but they seemed to. Almost instantly the door burst open and Mrs. Pennybaker appeared in fluttering alarm.

He roared, "Get my glasses," and when she found them on the desk and handed them to him he said, "Here, take this goddam paper and find that—that *thing* for me. I don't know why I have a secretary. It's customary, but I always have to do everything myself. Seventy years of law practice and no one ever finds anything for me."

Mrs. Pennybaker found what he wanted, creased the paper carefully, took his glasses from him, opened out the earpieces and practically put them on for him. She said, "Here it is, Judge, right here. Look, I'll put your finger on it."

He shook off her hand and roared, "Goddamit, I'll put my *own* finger on it!" In a milder but still complaining tone he said to me, "These flighty young bitches are always messing around."

He became conscious again of the fact that he had lost the connection, and peered blankly at the page. At length he centered on the article Mrs. Pennybaker had indicated and studied it in frowning concentration until he recovered his original idea. He tapped the paper explosively and handed it to me.

As I read it I had that strange feeling of constriction around my heart that hits everyone occasionally. The story said that the Tremont Realty Company had announced the sale of the old so-and-so plant at the intersection of so-and-so and so-and-so to General Motors for $1,250,000. I read it twice to make sure, scarcely breathing.

I looked up, and now there could be no doubt that Judge Abercrombie knew why he had wanted to see me. He was trembling all over. He said, sticking a shaking finger out at me, "I sent Mr.—Mr.—what's his name? That young feller out there—Stern. Stern. I sent Mr. Stern over to check up. You didn't tender that check, did you?"

When I didn't answer at once, he thundered, "*Did you?*"

I started out, "Well, Judge . . ."

He was almost beside himself and tried ferociously to heave himself out of the chair. He kept slipping back and at length the foot stool flew out from under his feet and he gave up with his feet dangling helplessly.

He said, "Just answer yes or no."

I was getting calmer now, because I knew all I had to do was explain something he didn't know about. I said, "No, Judge, I didn't. I wasn't supposed to. Mitch—Mr. Sothern—came in and got the check from me and said he would do it himself."

"Young man, I *heard* him explain it all to you and delegate this job to you."

"I know, Judge. You're exactly right. But what I'm telling you is that after that—after I had left you—he came to my office and said he would do it himself. He put the check in his pocket and went off with it. That's the last I saw of the check. Something must have happened, Judge. Mitch explained how important it was—you know that."

He looked at me uncertainly with his head trembling more violently than ever. Suddenly he roared again, "*Mrs. Pennybaker!*"

She came paddling in almost on the instant. He roared, "That file. Bring me that file!"

I expected her to ask what file, but she didn't. She gave me an agonized glance and then padded out and presently back in again. I recognized the Alva M. Drysdale file which I had left on the corner of my desk. Judge Abercrombie seized it with hawkish eagerness and licked both thumbs before contriving to fumble it open. Then he held it out to me in speechless triumph.

I was speechless too, but my feeling was one of dead, bottomless panic. There on top of everything, secured with a paper clip, was the redemption statement and the pale green check which should have redeemed the Drysdale property and prevented the sale by the Tremont Realty Company.

I looked frantically at the Judge and then at Mrs. Pennybaker and said, "But how did it get here? I tell you, Judge, honestly—Mitch—Mr. Sothern that is—yesterday he came in and got the check himself. I tell you I saw him putting it into his pocket . . ."

The silence was so frigid that I realized the uselessness of saying anything more. I stopped in the middle of my sentence.

Judge Abercrombie was looking at me with a sad glower. His lower jaw was clamped bulldoggishly against the upper, and the ill-fitting teeth made his lower lip protrude.

We stared at each other. Finally he made his usual messy spitting job, wiped his flabby lips, and turned to Mrs. Pennybaker who seemed to be on the verge of tears. With a wave of his hand that carried dismissal and complete finality he said, "It's bad enough to be negligent. Young people will always be careless." He whacked his fist resoundingly on the arm of his chair and then shook his finger at me, "But when it comes to dodging your responsibilities—not having the guts to take your own blame—trying to shove something off on a dead man who can't talk back . . ." He shook his head to indicate that he was incapable of finishing a statement of such perfidy. He said to Mrs. Pennybaker, "Go out and figure up what this—this—what *he* has coming to him. Add full pay for a month. Hell, don't be niggardly. Pay him for three months extra. It'll be cheap at the price."

I tried to say, "Judge, you aren't being fair. I tell you—"

He broke in and said to Mrs. Pennybaker, "*What is this person doing in my office?*"

I said, with my lips trembling, "Under the circumstances, of course I won't accept a dime. I'd cut my throat first."

There were angry tears in my eyes. I considered a multitude of things that wanted to be said, but in the end I turned and walked blindly out of Judge Abercrombie's office and went into my own room and sat down and put my head in my hands.

19.

I DO NOT KNOW how long I sat there but it was long enough. I was conscious that life was following its usual and customary course which seemed callous and somehow not quite fair. Mrs. Pennybaker beat on her typewriter firmly—you might say resolutely; and Miss Tarbo punched her monotonous holes in pieces of paper and clicked and unclicked the Acco fasteners which took isolated documents and made them part of integrated history. Perhaps it was my imagination, but I'm sure a drawer opened with that air of guilty caution which indicated Clementine was searching for a chocolate rather than grubbing forthrightly for carbon paper.

George Stern's door opened and he walked across the reception room into Judge Abercrombie's office. He had the appearance of one who has not been fired and who doesn't anticipate being fired. After awhile he came out again and walked into my office and sat down with something that was not quite embarrassment but wanted to be.

George was a nice guy but he was self-centered and impatient. He seemed to think it was apparent that the firm was wasting valuable time each day it delayed admitting him to full partnership.

There was a long moment of awkwardness. I could see George did not want to mention Mitch, but knew it would be odd if he didn't. He said, "The news in the paper this morning was a terrific shock. I can't take it in. I know how you must feel."

I said, "I'm afraid I don't feel anything much. It takes time to realize such things. I mean, to understand that it's really true."

"How's Mrs. Sothern taking it? Awful thing, for her, especially."

"Awful thing is right. She's in the hospital." I didn't mention her injury because it didn't seem to be any of George's business.

He said, "Hospital? Poor girl! I hope she's getting along fine."

I nodded and there was a strained silence.

At length he said, "The Judge seems upset. I don't know what happened and it's none of my business but it seems I'm to take over your files. Sorry, but I guess you understand how it is."

I said quickly, "Oh, sure. I understand. But it's a laugh to talk about files."

I went out and got my one case from Mrs. Pennybaker and brought it back and handed it to George with what I hoped was an appropriately wry but not bitter smile.

"There," I said, "are my legal responsibilities. Outside of working on the Pharis patent case and a little leg work and odd jobs here and there, you have in your hands all I happen to be chargeable with at the moment. Not counting, of course, the absurdly simple little thing, that, according to Lord God Abercrombie in all his wisdom, I managed not to do. But let's not go into that."

George showed very plainly he had no desire to go into it. Since I was leaving the firm with a blot on my escutcheon, he had no intention of being any part of a piece of blotting paper to absorb any of it in passing. He glanced through the file, nodded once or twice to show how quickly he was absorbing the substance of it, and put it on the corner of the desk as constituting a mere incident in a busy life. I handed him the scrap of paper on which I had jotted the information Lieutenant Richmond had reluctantly furnished me from the memorandum which had been in my hat band. George accepted it stoically.

With the future stretching rather vacantly before me, I said, "Doing anything tonight? All this rather leaves me at loose ends, and I thought if you weren't busy maybe we could have dinner together and chew the rag or something."

He looked at me uneasily and said, "Sorry, wish I could. The fact is I have a sort of date or something. Wish I could get out of it, but you know how it is."

I said, "Sure, I understand."

I understood, all right.

He picked up the file, nodded absent-mindedly, and walked over to his own little cubbyhole which was no bigger than mine.

I sat there a moment and then opened and shut the drawers of my desk to verify what I knew to be a fact—that there was nothing personal in them. I shut the top drawer on the left side and then hesitated, puzzled. In the drawer was something I didn't remember seeing before. Something I had not put there.

With my hand on the knob of the second drawer I stopped, trying to remember. Then I opened the top drawer again and stared at an envelope that had typed on the front of it, "Deliver to Mrs. Mitchell Sothern—Personal and confidential."

I lifted out the envelope gingerly and turned it over in my hands. It was unsealed, and papers were inside. I took the papers out and unfolded them. There were three stock certificates, made out in three strange names, and endorsed to me, each representing five shares, of the par value of one hundred dollars each, of the common stock of Tremont Realty Company. A note said, "I have photostatic copies."

I simply sat there and looked, wondering what this was all about. I had never in my life possessed enough money or property to buy fifteen hundred dollars worth of stock. I had never in my life had enough credit to borrow that much, or half that much. Until yesterday, I had never heard of Tremont Realty Company.

Then, suddenly, I understood.

This, then, was what Mitch had been talking about last night. This was Mitch's hold over Marty. This was supposed to be the motive for my failure to redeem the property yesterday afternoon, as I had carefully been instructed to do, in Judge Abercrombie's presence. Without this stock, endorsed to me, I might get off lightly on the ground of mere negligence. Which, at that, would be hard enough to live down.

But with stock of Tremont Realty Company, in my name, that explanation would never stick. Now it would appear that I failed to redeem the property because I knew how much that failure would enhance the value of my stock, and who would believe, or even listen to, my desperate explanations?

You could be disbarred for a great deal less.

Was it also a crime? Not larceny, certainly. Not really

embezzlement, although its equivalent. I couldn't think. . . .

I remembered that there were people right outside my door, and that they might come in at any moment. I put my hands below the level of the desk—out of sight. I wanted to slink, to look over my shoulder.

The papers folded easily in their old creases. I put them back into the envelope, licked the flap, and sealed it. Then I put the envelope in my inside pocket. I went out self-consciously, said good-bye briefly to Clementine, Mrs. Penny-baker and Miss Tarbo, and walked out of the offices of Aber-crombie & Fant.

20.

As I MADE my way through the revolving door I caught a glimpse of Inez Wiggens passing swiftly by in the crowd on the sidewalk. Suddenly I wanted company. I fell in behind her and caught up at the intersection where she was waiting for the traffic light to change. I came alongside with our shoulders touching and said, "Miss Wiggens, I believe?"

She gave me a startled look and then a bright smile. The light became green and we struck out ahead of the surge of pedestrians. I took her elbow lightly to prevent separation in the crowd. We were several shops beyond the intersection before there was an eddy in the sidewalk traffic and I could swing her into an open space in front of a drugstore.

To make conversation, I said, "How do you feel this morning?"

Her expression indicated that she was wondering what, if anything, she should say about the newspapers and Mitch

Sothern, but her struggle was brief and the decision was plainly written that since it was my brother-in-law I would be left to set the pace. She said, "I feel all right. Specifically, I'd rather like a Coke. Since it's my idea, may I buy you one?"

"No, you may not. But we'll have a Coke nevertheless. You wouldn't want to embarrass me, would you? Not for a dime anyway."

She hooked her arm in mine and said, "For a dime it would scarcely be worth it. All right, my defenses are properly weakened. You may buy me a Coke and thanks very much."

We beat our way into the drugstore very much like C. S. Forrester beating his way up the channel against a head wind, and found a booth where we sat with dirty glasses, used ice cream dishes, cigaret stubs and crumpled paper napkins between us. Presently, an untidy waitress rushed up with a tray, threw everything on it, reorganized the glass table top with a few frenetic sweeps of a revolting greasy rag and careened away. Since any other behavior would have been a surprise to both of us, we paid little attention to this performance except for the tacit observation that the table was no place to put one's elbows.

I dragged a paper napkin from the tenacious metal container and wiped the table top. By that time the waitress appeared again in a gust of wind with her hair straggling over her face and made a few more passes with her objectionable cloth. She said positively there were no more oranges, lemons or limes and that the chocolate ice cream was all out. I said in that case perhaps Wiggie would like a Coke and she said on second thought she believed she would. The waitress left us suddenly, managing to convey the impression that if she had known we only wanted Cokes she would scarcely have bothered. The menu said the special for the day was a banana split with a whole banana, three scoops of ice cream, sauce, nuts, cherries, whipped cream, and two kinds of jam.

I said, "I suppose you've seen the paper?"

She nodded.

The next move was up to me so I put my elbows on the table and looked away and said, "I suppose things like this happen, but it's hard to realize, isn't it? After all, how long ago was it—a few hours? He seemed so—so—alive."

She nodded again but said nothing.

I said, "I suppose it's queer the way people react to the unexpected. It all seems unreal, and if that's trite I suppose it's because most of life itself is pretty trite. I've already been down and confessed."

There were wrinkles of a frown between her eyes. She said, "You did?"

I said, "Yeah, but they didn't believe me. Seems stupid, doesn't it?"

"What seems stupid?"

I looked at her evenly, "Now what do you mean by that?"

"I don't know. What do you think I mean?"

I said, "Well, I don't know, really. You could mean it sounds stupid to confess or you could mean it's stupid of them not to believe me."

She put her hand quickly on mine and said, "Don't be touchy. You were the one who said something was stupid, and I didn't follow you. So I asked, that's all."

I said, "I'm sorry. Didn't mean to be rude. The fact is, I'm pretty much upset, and for a number of reasons. I don't suppose you knew, but it happens Marty's in the hospital. Some sort of injury, last night, and I can't even get in to see her. Nobody'll tell me anything. I don't know how bad it is or what it's all about."

Wiggie said, aghast, "What did you say?"

"Marty's in the hospital. Don't ask me, because I don't know. Either the doctors or the police or both have put out orders no one may see her—not even her own brother. I'm frantic, but what can I do?"

76 –

"Maybe they'd let me see her. No, I guess not. So that's why the paper this morning said they couldn't find her. Does that mean anything—I mean in connection with—with the other?"

I said, "You know as much about it as I do, which is nothing. I'm going to send flowers to Marty when we're through here, but I don't know what else I can do. Except keep trying to see her, and of course I'll do that."

We each took a couple of sips through our straws and then I said, "You'd think Mitch and Marty would be enough, wouldn't you? But you haven't heard all of it."

I turned my Coco-Cola glass around two or three times in the puddle of water in which it was sitting. I said, "As if that wasn't enough. When trouble comes, it really comes, doesn't it?"

"Yes, that's what they say."

She didn't know what I was talking about and she waited. So presently I said, "What I mean, on top of everything else it seems this morning I'm fired. Things are a little rough."

She was silent but there was a feeling of warmth and sympathy between us, and oddly enough it was that feeling which I was unprepared for and which I seemed unable to combat.

I said, "But I don't know why I should burden you with all this. Shall we go?"

I was getting up as I said it. She found her purse and got up with me. I looked around and caught the eye of the waitress and signaled to her and put a fifty-cent piece on the table because I didn't want to be bothered. In passing between the little round tables out in the middle of the floor we had to squeeze against each other and it seemed natural enough that our arms should be linked together when we emerged on the sidewalk.

She seemed to be in no hurry. I said, "Thanks very much. I enjoyed the Coke and enjoyed being with you. I didn't mean to pop off about my problems."

She gave my arm a little impatient shake and said, "Don't be silly."

I took my arm out from under hers and said lamely, "Well, thanks anyway. It did me a lot of good, just saying it. Even though that doesn't accomplish anything." I gave a little nervous laugh and added, "I guess that's just the way people are. Well, so long and thanks again."

As I started to move away she was against me—possibly following and possibly pushed by the crowd, I couldn't tell which. She said, "You shouldn't be alone in this frame of mind, you know."

I said, "I shouldn't?"

"No, really. It isn't good for you. Look, what are you doing this evening?"

I said, "Oh, I don't know. Nothing special."

"That's what I thought. Maybe it would be better if you came by and took me out to dinner. As a friend, I'm entitled to volunteer in a time of trouble without seeming to be forward, don't you think? I mean, afterward we could see a show or something like that. That is, if you'd like to."

Her seriousness gave way to a smile and she said, "Or would you rather do nothing special?"

I was surprised at my own eagerness and realized, all at once, that this was what I had been wanting. Perversely I said, "Oh, I'd just be a bother. You know—being low in your mind is contagious."

She gave me that little impatient shake again and said, "Oh, nonsense. Don't start pitying yourself. I'll be expecting you at eight, and don't keep me waiting. Do you think you can remember the address or must you write it down?"

I said, "I'll remember."

She said, "Six twenty-two Magnolia Drive. Apartment three-C. Eight o'clock?"

I said, "Eight o'clock. I'll be there."

Two doors away my eye caught a grey snap-brim hat that

was almost a dead ringer for the one I had left in Mitch's guest room. Conscious of my bare head and the demands of civilization, I stopped in. At my demand, the clerk took that very hat out of the window. It fit and I bought it on the spot.

A block beyond, I turned into a florist's. I debated between roses, which wouldn't last very long, and a potted geranium, which I didn't think would brighten up a room much. I finally settled on some pink gladioli and bought as many as the money in my pocket would pay for. I pondered a long time over the card, then decided there was no use trying to send a message—the police would see it didn't get through, anyway. So I finally wrote nothing but "All my love—Jess" and asked them to send the flowers right away.

21.

I WALKED DOWN to the hospital and met Richmond getting out of the elevator on the ground floor. He said, "Hello, there," and took me by the arm and maneuvered me into a corner of the lobby.

I said, "How is she?"

"The doctor says she's doing very well. Still no visitors, but being her brother I don't suppose it would hurt anything if you looked in for a moment. I left word with the guard at the door."

I said, "I suppose I can exchange three words with my sister as long as one of your men is under the bed."

He smiled in a way that seemed to say "not very funny" and shrugged his shoulders. He said, "Look at it from my side. Even the nicest people are always fixing up silly things to tell the police. They think it's a game like button, button, who's got the button."

"Then I was right, wasn't I?"

Richmond said, "Not exactly," and then he grinned in spite of himself and said, "Not under the bed. Just in the room."

"Even that's a concession. This morning I couldn't get in at all. What happened? You've talked to the servants and she's in the clear. Is that it?"

He looked away uneasily and then suddenly glanced at his watch and seemed to be in an awful hurry. He said, "Sorry, I've got to be running along."

"I'll bet I'm right, at that. This morning you thought Marty killed her husband and you had it down cold. Now the servants have blocked off that road and you're looking for another one."

He said, "We always look at all of them. As a matter of fact, there may be a couple of things I'll want to talk to you about before long. You'll be around?"

I said, "If I had other ideas, how far would I get?"

He smiled and was a little embarrassed. He said, "Not far, I hope."

I was glad when he went away. I was conscious of the envelope in my pocket. It felt as big as a victrola record.

22.

THE MAN in the hall said his name was Phelps. From seeing a lot of movies you think of a policeman as a shapeless middle-aged Irishman with a thick red neck and heavy black shoes with knobby toes. Phelps was young and lean and clean-cut. He was in a civilian suit and it fit him. I said he was in the hall but that's not strictly true, for when I came out of the elevator and headed for Room 412 he was in a sort of sun porch, sitting in a chair reading a book. By the time I reached Marty's door he was there, casually and without hurry.

I said, "Hello. It's all right. I'm her brother. I saw Richmond downstairs and he told me I could see her." Then I added, "I mean, *we* could see her."

He said, "Sure. Then you must be Jess London."

I nodded and he said, "Not over three minutes. Don't blame us, it's the doctor."

He bumped his knuckles softly against the door and when there was an indistinguishable sound from inside we went in and Phelps had manners enough to make himself more or less inconspicuous.

I took Marty's hand and sat in the chair beside her bed. There was a redness and puffiness around her eyes which indicated the emotional crisis she had been through. She was on the solemn and serious side but I knew at once that she was in complete control of herself.

I said, "You look fine. Feeling okay?"

Marty said, "I'm all right. They tell me you've been here two or three times already and they wouldn't let you see me. That's silly, isn't it? Hospitals always seem to exaggerate."

"Never mind. It doesn't make any difference. I'm only glad to see you looking so well."

The real subject was thick in the air between us but neither Marty nor I knew how to touch it. Finally, I said, "There must be something I can do. I mean, with you here in the hospital and everything . . ."

She said, "I wanted to ask you, Jess, but that man—Lieutenant Richmond, is it?—seemed so vague and difficult that finally I sent a message to Stoakes Fat. You know, he was always very fond of Mitch and I didn't think he'd mind."

"Sure. Anything I can do?"

Marty squeezed my hand and said, "No more than you've already done, Jess, and that's a lot."

I said, "What do you mean by that? I haven't done anything yet."

She was silent for an unnaturally long time and then said, "That man—Richmond—told me about the way you came in this morning and confessed. I don't think he meant to, but he was asking me a lot of questions and the doctor wouldn't let him stay, so he was in a hurry and let it out in order to get to his next question. It really was awfully sweet of you, Jess, and I appreciate it. But it's all right. Honestly, I don't know a thing about what happened and I know they'll find out I'm telling the truth. From what Mr. Richmond said a few minutes ago, I'm sure he realizes it. But it was loyal and sweet of you. And just like you, too."

I said, "Oh, hell, forget it."

Phelps managed to catch my eye. He nodded, opened the door and stepped outside. I kissed Marty on the forehead, patted her arm and went out into the hall, waving airily to her just before Phelps closed the door behind us. The last glimpse I had I was sure her lips were trembling.

23.

THERE WAS a delay at the elevator because a patient was coming up. It was a little girl looking pathetically small in a tiny little lump of covers in the middle of the long stretcher-bed. She was lying on her back with her eyes half closed, and one hand was on top of the covers with the doll fingers curled gracefully and naturally in the way that a child's fingers seem always to lie in moments of relaxation. The breathing was quick and alarming.

I stood aside until they got her out of the elevator and then I saw Joe getting out behind her. He needed a shave and his eyes were tired and worried. I fell in beside him as he walked down the hall behind the nurses. He noticed me and nodded abstractedly. There was a woman on the other side of him who was obviously Mrs. Joe, but there were no introductions and I didn't expect any. He seemed to be glad there was someone to talk to. He said, "They're going to put her under an oxygen tent. That's not good, is it?"

I said, "You can't tell. Sometimes it's only a precaution. Sometimes a few hours under an oxygen tent does wonders. Especially when they're little. I don't have to tell you. One minute they're sick and one minute they're well. That's the way it goes."

Joe seemed unconvinced but he appreciated my effort to be of comfort. He said, "It's a pity about the transfusion. It isn't anything peculiar about the blood, from what they say. Only that not very many people have it. They've got two of the what-you-call-'em—donors, on the list, but one of 'em's sick and one's out of town. I told 'em to wire Chicago or any damn place and they're doing the best they can. I guess that's all anybody can do." Then he said, "Jesus, she's only two."

There was a doctor in the room and they were bringing contraptions down the hall. When a nurse came out I walked with her and said, "Is it a very funny kind of blood? Couldn't almost anyone have it?"

She said, "Of course. You could be the right sort of person and have it and not even know."

"You mean type A or type O, as simple as that?"

"That's just the beginning. Now we have to test for something called the Rh factor. It's the combination that's so unusual. It's a funny combination."

I walked a few steps more and then said, "Any trouble giving me a test?"

She stopped and looked at me, wondering how serious I was. I grinned and said, "I'm a very funny guy. My blood ought to be funny, too."

There's a lot of luck in the way things turn out. She hustled me down to the laboratory and someone took a sample of my blood. I sat and read the advertisements in yesterday's newspapers for thirty minutes and then learned that I was the kind of Joe Doakes they were looking for. One nurse seemed excited and rushed off to tell the doctor. Another nurse took me in and stretched me out on a table, and rubbed alcohol on the inside of my elbow. She told me to turn my head away, and I did.

She said, "You're supposed to skip eating anything for several hours before giving blood, but this is an emergency and we haven't time to argue about it."

I said, "I ate some breakfast, but that seems long ago. I didn't eat much, anyway."

She said, "That's fine."

I lay a long while in silence. At least it seemed long to me. Because I knew I shouldn't move my right arm, I thought I would go crazy if I didn't move it.

The door opened brusquely. The doctor came in, frowning. He said, "How much have you got?"

The nurse said, "Hardly more than 200 cc."

The doctor said, "That's enough for a child of this age. I can't risk waiting any longer. The donor will come back another day if we need more. Perhaps tomorrow."

He looked at me for confirmation, but not as if he had any doubt about my answer. I said, "Of course."

There was a painless tug as the needle came out. The nurse swabbed the spot with alcohol again, then put a piece of alcohol-soaked cotton in the joint of my elbow and bent my arm to hold it in place. She said, "Wait here. Don't leave until I come back."

The doctor said, "I suppose we know how to reach you?"

I nodded.

The doctor and the nurse went away. Lying there was pleasant enough. I'm not sure I didn't go to sleep.

After a long while the nurse came back. She said, "Hello."

I said, "Hello."

She said, "The little girl was very low. A little later might have been too late. The improvement was immediate and remarkable. You're very lucky, you know. Most people never have a chance to save a life."

I said, "Two things about me, I'm funny and I'm lucky. Shall I come back tomorrow?"

She said, "It may not be necessary, but if it is, we'll let you know. Ordinarily you wouldn't be allowed to give blood again for several weeks. But we took very little today, and after all, this is an emergency. Our regular donors—"

I interrupted and said, "You didn't take as much as I lost snagging my finger on the last beer-bottle cap. I sometimes bleed that much through my eyeballs after a party."

Joe and his wife were waiting in the hall as I went by on the way to the elevators. I stopped. They looked at me with great solemn eyes but they didn't know what to say. She silently pressed my hand between two moist palms and bent her head and dripped a tear on me. I was embarrassed. I waited until she turned me loose, then patted her gently on the shoulder and went away.

24.

ALL THIS didn't seem to have taken much time but when I left the hospital it was after two o'clock and I was feeling very, very hungry. There was a hamburger stand or a juke joint on almost every corner, but what I needed was something a good deal more serious. I walked to the business district, getting hungrier at every step, until there were dancing specks in front of my eyes every time I blinked in the bright sunlight.

I went into Minterno's on account of the sea food and ordered a dozen blue points as a starter because they didn't have to be cooked. On the same theory I ordered a double crab cocktail as a follow up, still in the appetizer class, and then called for red snapper with shoe string potatoes, spring salad and coffee.

When the blue points came I tested the sauce and added a big spoonful of horse radish and rather too much pepper sauce so that after the first mouthful I was going strictly by feel rather than taste.

George Stern came in and saw me and wondered if he could sit at my table, which he could.

I speared another oyster and swallowed it with such pleasure that he ordered blue points himself. I half expected him to request a couple of mine while he was waiting.

I said, "How was the honorable Mrs. A. P. Worthington?"

He said, "Okay. It's in the bag. There's only one witness and she's on our side so we collect for the J. T. Pharis Steel Company. It's a breeze."

I ate another oyster with his fascinated eyeballs following each movement. I said, "Swell," but only to make conversation. I didn't give a damn about his case, now that it wasn't mine any more.

His oysters came and I passed him the horse radish and pepper sauce which he administered timidly. He said, "About this evening. As it turns out, it's okay. How about getting a bite somewhere and maybe taking in a show?"

I said, "Sorry. As it happens I've been invited somewhere. You know how it is. One of those things. Give me a rain check?"

"Sure, anytime. Date?"

"In a way. I guess you could call it that. More of an invitation than a date. Just one of those things that turn up."

I finished my oysters, received the double crab cocktail and tackled it with my appetite unabated. George studied me with an almost glassy expression in his eyes and then summoned the waitress and duplicated the order. After awhile he said, "You were at the party last night. Police been bothering you?"

I said, "Police?"

George said, "A Lieutenant of detectives. Rich or Richmond or something like that. When I called the office just before one, they said he had been in and wanted to see me. What do they do? Talk to everybody?"

"Nervous?"

George said, "Why should I be nervous? Hector, I wonder if this dope thinks I did it." He laughed and then ate another bite and said, "What the hell am I laughing at? It ain't funny."

25.

THE RED SNAPPER was good and George ordered that too. The coffee was too hot and too weak, which is a bad combination, but the peach cobbler was delicious to the very end of the unnecessarily large portion and I was particularly pleased with the hard sauce. Considering one thing and another, including rather dull attempts at conversation between George and me in our satiated condition, it was after three-thirty and I was dopey with sleep when I left Minterno's and started back to the apartment.

A short distance this side of the entrance the Hudson sedan, much too bright in its yellowness, stood at the curb with the two doors still hanging open as if, having spent a very tough evening indeed, it shared the hangover of its occupants. To stop and peer in at the green hat and silk panties would have been evidence of indecent curiosity, but I checked these items out of the corner of my eye in passing and noted that they were still there, complete with all their sinister implications.

I heard a door close and a cheerful voice said, "Well, if it isn't Mr. London."

I stopped and looked around. It was Lieutenant Richmond, walking down the steps from the house opposite the Hudson sedan. I said, "Hello, Lieutenant. I see you at every turn. I would call you ubiquitous except that I can't pronounce it."

He said, "You just did. What does it mean? Never mind, I was only having fun."

I said, "Tending to your little chores, I suppose. Putting the cat out of the county jail, winding the city hall clock, and other little civic items."

"No, you might call this my homework, forgive the pun." He looked up at the house and shook his head, almost in admiration. "What a hangover! Sweetest and most vicious collection of hangovers I've ever seen."

"I thought you were working on this Sothern case. You mean you're switched over to parking tickets all of a sudden?"

"Parking tickets?" said Richmond. Then he remembered the sedan, grinned and said, "Oh, that. No, not parking tickets. I'm still on Homicide."

I said, "I see. Some other case. Didn't know you had 'em two and three at a time."

"Not me. If I'm working on a case and another one comes up, it goes to somebody else. I stay on one job until it's finished or dried up—you know—sometimes it's a dead-end street and we let it sit for awhile. Wait for tips and squeals and then go after it again."

"You mean these people with the hangovers have something to do with Mitch Sothern's death? How could that be? And how do you get to know a thing like that, if it's true? You fellows really get around, don't you?"

He said, "Breaks. Sometimes you get the breaks and sometimes you don't. I was following up a small idea and it gave me a lead and I followed up on that—see how it goes? A little luck does it. As a matter of fact, this is a subject you and I ought to have a conversation about."

"Don't tell me you're still hot on my trail?"

Richmond gave me a funny look. He said, "Still making jokes?"

I said, "I'm a card. I joke about everything. Tell you what. Maybe detectives haven't got a union but I'll bet all the veal in a chicken salad sandwich that you don't work from dusk to dusk like Philo Vance. If it's about time for the deductions to stop deducting why don't you come up to my place and have a snort? If it'll put your mind at rest I'll show you the revenue stamp on the bottle."

Richmond raised his eyebrows and said, "I couldn't dream of accepting, but on the other hand since you're a suspect, naturally I must go on suspecting you. Sometimes in line of duty we have to make the supreme sacrifice."

I said, "It's only a blend, you know."

He said, "Sometimes we have to make the semisupreme sacrifice. Or perhaps we should call it the supersupreme sacrifice."

I said, "After I'm convicted and electrocuted, let's you and me pitch a binge together."

He said, "I'll do it with you while you're in the death house. It stands to reason alcohol would make you a better conductor."

I said: "Conductor, hell. It'd make me a goddam motor man."

26.

I WAS AHEAD of Richmond as we went through the revolving door into the lobby of the apartment house. It wasn't time for Charley Pitts to be on duty for the night, but he was sitting with his chair tilted back against the counter in obvious discomfort, looking without absorption at the pages of *Redbook* magazine. When he saw me the front legs of his tilted chair hit the composition floor with a whack and he jumped to his feet. He started to make a gesture to catch my attention, and then stopped and converted the gesture into the business of running his fingers through his hair.

He shifted his glance pointlessly to an uninteresting spot in the street and then sat down in the most amateur fashion and looked at his magazine again.

I graduated from the second grade many years ago, though

I must admit it was without distinction. When Charley converted his wave into a poor adjustment of his hair-do, I automatically turned my head and caught the tail end of a surreptitious motion by Richmond.

As we crossed the lobby and entered the elevator there was an acute sense of awareness all over me like goose pimples. As I had been doing constantly throughout the day, I readjusted my estimate of the man behind me.

And as I had done on every previous occasion I raised his percentage.

27.

WHEN WE ENTERED my apartment I held my hand out for Richmond's hat and then unceremoniously threw it on the couch and started for the kitchenette. I said, "This way. You can get out the ice while I'm doing the rest of it."

He tagged along and I pointed and he got out a tray and held it under the tap while I found the bottle and a couple of glasses. We took our drinks back to the living room and made ourselves comfortable.

I said, "Excuse me a moment." I went into the bedroom and closed the door. Then I went on into the bathroom and closed that door. I turned on the cold water tap to make a noise, and then took the envelope from my coat pocket, carefully tore it and the stock certificates into little pieces, flushed them down the commode, and rejoined Richmond.

I said, "Your health, Lieutenant."

"And yours, Mr. London."

"With reservations, of course?"

"Naturally."

I said, "Just for fun, are you working or playing at the moment?"

"Oh, working, definitely. Do you mind?"

"No, not at all."

"Then I may as well ask some questions. Should I remind you that anything you say may be used against you?"

I said, "By all means do. Do detectives read detective stories along with other people?"

He said, "Oh, indubitably."

"Well, go ahead."

He put down his drink without touching it and said, "Maybe you're kidding, but I'm not. I really want to ask you some questions."

I nodded and didn't say anything but I took a long swallow of my drink and it was good.

Richmond said, "I keep getting back to this confession of yours. It all seemed very melodramatic and dashing at the time, in the tradition of *Beau Geste* and *Graustark* and Douglas Fairbanks. But as a matter of fact you really *were* back at the house, or at least in the neighborhood, around two o'clock. Upon re-examination I began to lose my sense of humor."

"What makes you think I was in that neighborhood at any such hour as that?"

He spread his hands to indicate impartiality and helplessness. "Nothing but evidence. I have some imagination, but not much."

I began to feel a certain rigidity in the muscles of my legs. They were crossed, with my right leg over my left one, and I wanted to cross them the other way but it didn't seem the right thing to do at the time so I let the muscles ache.

I said, "What kind of evidence?"

He said, "Oh, the usual sort. Only people who saw you, that's all."

I put on the best puzzled frown I could manufacture and

then raised my eye brows and frowned again. I hadn't watched Lionel Barrymore over a period of years for nothing. I said, "Hell's fire. You mean somebody is telling you he saw me somewhere around that house when I was home and in bed?"

"I don't know whether you were home and in bed or not. But somebody saw you, yes. Or to give you the benefit of the doubt, we can say he was somebody who *thought* he saw you. Not one person. More than one."

I pinched a knuckle between my teeth and tried to look thoughtful. It was no problem because my mind was making a frantic effort to run through the entire evening; to preview this film he was about to show me.

I said, slowly, "If these people you're talking about are honest, they rather put me on the spot, don't they?"

He said, "It looks that way to me."

I stayed silent as long as I could and then I said, "But how could they have seen me if I wasn't there?"

Richmond said, "That's the question I'm asking myself. You can answer it two ways. You were there and they saw you, or you weren't there and they're mistaken."

I said, "What do *you* think?"

"I don't know. I wasn't there myself. I'm asking you just as I asked them."

I got up and put my hands in my pockets and walked up and down the room a couple of times. I said, "When I popped off this morning I was full of the "Star Spangled Banner" and stuff like that. I was ready to be locked up and have my picture in the paper and the *Trial of Mary Dugan* or what the hell. Maybe that's what getting up at a foolish hour does for you. Now everything seems sane and normal. Marty seems to be in the clear and I find myself cherishing the great out-of-doors. Handcuffs don't seem dramatic any more and I don't want anything around my wrists except a watch band. If you're going to start being silly, perhaps our beautiful friendship is in shoal water and rapidly approaching the rocks."

He shrugged and said, "There's no reason to take it personally. I've got a job and I'm trying to do it."

I said, "That's okay by me. Only it seems you're always smelling *my* footprints. Try some other trail some time, and I hope you follow somebody who's got athlete's foot."

"You must admit—"

"Let's skip the grammar and say from now on out I don't admit nothing. Whatever you think, I think something else."

He stood up and shook out the creases of his trousers. He said, "That's the taxpayer's privilege, but you needn't think you're going to make me mad. What I do is try to earn my pay check and keep my nose clean on account of the pension when I'm an old broken-down man. I ask questions until I find everybody who was at the party and I talk to all of them. I talk to everybody they talk about. I talk to who you're kin to and who you work for and then I start and ring doorbells. When it's all done they give me another job and I do it over again. Nights I listen to Fibber McGee or Bing and sometimes on Sunday I see a double header and boo the umpires."

I said, "I didn't mean to be personal. Let's get back to the subject. You said we ought to have a conversation about something."

He went over and looked out of the window a long time with his hands thrust into his hip pockets. "I thought so, and then I didn't know whether I should mention these things or not. I was about to skip it, but on reflection—well, this is no poker game and I'm not playing hide-and-seek and I don't know any tricks. All I'm trying to do is find out what's true, so I'll come out right now and see what you've got to say. Want to talk?"

I raised my eyebrows. "Sure. Any time."

"Fellow name of Block, lives here in the building. Know him?"

I said, "Block? Can't say I do. Probably one of the goons who steps back into the elevator to make room for me at the third floor, going down. What does he have to say?"

Richmond put his head on one side and thought that over and then said, "I can't think of any good reason why I shouldn't tell you. It's a free country and you can talk to him yourself if you want to. He says he saw you coming in around two-thirty. So does this boy Pitts who seems to be the night elevator man. That checks with your original story, doesn't it?"

I said, "How do you figure that?"

He said, "Let's see. Mrs. Sothern and the servants say he was alive when they last saw him. She was admitted to the hospital at two-twenty-five. That about figures, doesn't it?"

I said thoughtfully, "Oh, I see. Still barking up that tree, are you?"

He said, "Well, what about it? The hell with the file. Why don't you break down and save the taxpayers some money?"

"No thanks, Lieutenant. It seems that people are getting mixed up but I'm not sure I understand how or why. I came in about twelve. Miss Wiggens, as it happens, was in the car. I saw Charley all right, but it wasn't anywhere near two-thirty. Does he say he saw me twice?"

Richmond had his serious expression on his face, and his eyes were alert. He said, "No, as a matter of fact he didn't mention but one time. I'll have to check again with Mr. Pitts. He seemed certain enough about the hour, though. He remembered some people singing just before you came in. Then there's Block, who saw you at the same time."

I pinched my lower lip and considered this. I said, "Whoever he is, how well does he know me? How can he be so damn sure it was me if I wasn't there?"

Richmond said, "He seemed sure enough. Sees you around and about and knows you by sight. Doesn't seem to be any doubt in his mind. Full of details, as a matter of fact. Remembers you had a hat on. Green, that's what he said."

I said incredulously, "*Green* hat? Now where would I get a green hat? This is a new one I bought this afternoon. The only other one I've owned in the last year is the one you've got a tag on. Why would I wear a *green* hat? I don't even *like* green hats!"

Richmond was thinking again. He said, "I don't know. I'm only telling you what he said, but maybe you've got something there. Oh, well, back to the grind. I guess I'll have to have another conversation with Mr. Block, too."

He seemed about to leave and I had to hold him a minute because there was an idea I wanted to think about. I said, "Now what about these people with the hangovers? What have they got to do with it? I thought that was what you wanted to talk about."

"Oh, yes, the people with the hangovers. Well, we might as well go into that, too. It all ties in. Seems these youngsters, two boys and two girls, were parked right there in that yellow car. Same time, more or less, as Pitts and Block are talking about. Two, two-thirty, three—all pretty vague, but then you should see the shape they're in. Must have been—well, never mind. As I was saying, there they were, sitting in the car. Somebody comes along the sidewalk, heading up this way. From the description, about your height and shape. They're having fun, see? Singing and kiddin' around—harmonizing and all. The way they put it, the boys are tenors—if they're anything—and they needed a baritone or a bass to put some body—some oomph—into the singing. So as this character goes by, one of 'em sticks out a hand—you know how kids can be—and grabs his sleeve and invites him in. This passer-by takes it in a good-humored way, gets in, has a drink or two with them, puts in a right nifty baritone, and then comes on up and walks into this apartment house."

I said, "Well, is that supposed to tie in? Maybe I'm not on the ball today. I don't get it."

"I forgot something. Funny thing, but when this strange guy walks off, seems he's wearing a green hat. What do you think of that?"

I stuck out my lower lip dubiously and shook my head and frowned. I said, "Beats me, but I can see your point. Let's say all these people remember pretty well—the time and everything. Let's say they're telling the truth. All right, then maybe someone walked up this way from that yellow car about two-thirty this morning, wearing a green hat. Block comes out of the building at the same time and sees this man wearing the green hat. Whoever he is, he walks in and Pitts sees him. That could be, Lieutenant. There's only one thing puzzles me. It's screwy. All this time I've been in bed asleep for a couple of hours or more. Now how could all these people think that man was me? The kids in the car might have it wrong, but how about Pitts and Block, who say they know me? Block—well, he could be mistaken because I hardly know him and he hardly knows me. But Pitts"— I looked down and shook my head— "Pitts could hardly make a mistake like that."

Richmond said, "I'm afraid I've got to think maybe they weren't mistaken. Still, it's inconclusive at the moment. I want to talk to Pitts again about whether you came in once or twice, and I've got some more questions for the youngsters down the street, after they're a little more *compos mentis.*"

I said, "You've got your job to do, I can see that. What do you want to do, arrest me?"

He said, "No, that won't be necessary, at least not yet. The heat's not on as early as this, and I don't like to make mistakes. Hurts people and don't help the Department. Anyway, I'm not afraid of you disappearing if I need you."

"I'm curious. Why not?"

Richmond said, "People think disappearing's easy. Maybe so, for a few hours, few days. Once in a lifetime a Judge Cramer does a now-you-see-me-now-you-don't, but it's one case in ten thousand. The rest always turn up sooner or later—shacked up with a blonde in Seattle or trying to sell typewriter ribbons in Yuma or digging ditches in Opelika, Alabama.

My mind was working on the green hat. If Richmond

should walk past the Hudson sedan and see the green hat there would be hell to pay. Somehow I must see that he did not see it. If only I could maneuver him so he didn't see the hat, and then come back later and . . . and what? Burn it? Hide it?

My good sense came home in time. A green hat was just a green hat. Its significance lay only in its relationship to time and space . . . that is, a green hat lying in a certain car, parked at a certain place, at a certain time. If I were to take it away, a potential asset would immediately become a liability. If I were caught with it in my possession, no explanation on earth would ever explain myself out of trouble.

I was glad that my mind had worked fast enough. At the moment I felt as if I were about to scoop up a hot grounder and go into a fast infield double play. I said, "You aren't leaving your drink?"

He gave me an oddly serious look and surprised me by saying, "Perhaps it's better if I don't break bread with you. There's something about it that tends to bias the judgment."

I bumped his shoulder gently with my fist and said, "Oh, hell. Don't be a fool."

He laughed suddenly, picked up his glass and drank almost half of it without stopping. He said, "Okay, but the drink's at arm's length, just like you and me." Then he laughed again, infectiously, and said, "But who can drink at arm's length? It's all figurative. Well, good health, temporarily, and all the luck you'll need."

He drained the rest of the highball and put the glass on the table. I said, "Wait till I get my hat. I thought I'd go over to the hospital and see if they'll let me talk some with my sister. We can walk part of the way together, unless you're headed the other way."

To my relief, he said, "No, I'm headed that way, but I won't be going far. Car's parked a little ways behind the one we were talking about. I'll go that far with you.

I said, "That's fine," found my hat and his, and we went out together.

We walked along, not saying much. When we came abreast of the Hudson sedan he wasn't looking that way and I had to take over. I stopped suddenly—so suddenly that he was two strides beyond before he noticed and turned. I stared into the car and said, "One moment, Sherlock."

He said, "What?"

"Strange and devious thoughts are being suggested to my mind. Could be you're about to witness justice emerging triumphant over a mishandled imagination. Did your chum Mr. Block say he saw a green hat?"

Richmond came back and I pointed. "Look. No, tear your mind away from the lady's pants if you can, and observe yon crumpled object."

He put one foot on the running board and bent to look in, but didn't touch anything.

I said, "Okay, it's only a green hat and it doesn't mean a thing."

Richmond backed out and straightened up. He put his finger on his upper lip and pressed it so that he could do a better job of hooking his teeth over it. He said, "Pretty nice that it should turn up at this particular time and place, isn't it?"

I gave him a long incredulous look and then lifted my hands and let them drop helplessly at my sides. It was supposed to give the impression that I was speechless, so I didn't add any words.

He said, "Remarkable coincidence, don't you think? I'm only asking."

"I see. When you mentioned a green hat upstairs, I hurried down and planted this object and then popped back, through the water pipes, perhaps, and brought you here for the amazing discovery. Is that it?"

"There's no use trying to make it look foolish. After all, suppose you were in my shoes."

I said, "Well, you and your police suspicions can act as you damn well please. For my purpose we're going to fetch out this green hat and see what we can see."

He started to say, "Oh no you don't," but I was ahead of him and lunged into the back seat and brought out the green hat before he could stop me. I said, "Here, look for yourself. All I mean is, we aren't going to walk off and leave it while you get a couple of photographers and your fingerprint outfit. Ten minutes later we come back and it's gone and then what?"

At first Richmond looked as if he might be inclined to be quarrelsome. But the hat had been moved and there was nothing he could do about it, so at length he accepted the situation with poor grace and looked resentfully at the hat. He uncrumpled it and turned it over in his hands two or three times and then looked at the sweat band. He said, "Your initials aren't P. W. T. by any chance, are they?"

I said, "Odd, isn't it? With a name like Jess London it happens that those are exactly my initials. Incriminating, don't you think?"

Richmond was studying the hat and then my head as if mentally trying it on. I said, "I suppose the Constitution protects me against unwarranted searches and seizures, but I waive the Constitution in the presence of a witness." I bent down and said, "Go ahead. Try it on before you dislocate your eyeballs."

He made a wry face but he was nobody's fool. He put the hat on my head and did a lot of wiggling and adjusting with it before he was satisfied. It was ridiculously small for me. I said soberly, "Maybe it would fit me if I had a haircut. You know how fast hair grows with all these modern tonics."

Richmond said, "Very funny."

I said, "Justice is blind but I doubt if a hat salesman could be as blind as that."

He made with the hat as neatly as possible and followed me reluctantly, his face bearing an expression that indicated his mind was restless and dissatisfied. He didn't say a word as we started off. When we came to his car, a little way down the street, he paused with his hand on the door handle, jingling some change in his pocket with the other hand. He looked at me and then looked down at the sidewalk and finally shrugged his shoulders in a baffled sort of way.

I said, "You don't like it, Lieutenant?"

He said, "I don't like things I don't understand. I don't like things that're too pat. If this is the hat people saw on somebody's head, how did it get back in the car? And if it isn't, then what? Then it doesn't mean anything at all, which is probably right, because of the initials in it. But how many green hats do you see around? I don't like it. Something's screwy."

I said, "I agree something looks screwy, all right, but just the same I don't want you misplacing that hat, Lieutenant. You're thinking nasty thoughts about me and I've got a hunch all these little bastard details that don't add up will prove something before we get the answer. Whether you like it or not, you mark that hat and hang onto it, see? If I'm under suspicion I've got some rights, and this is one of 'em. You keep track of that hat or I'm going to raise pluperfect hell."

Richmond said, "I hang on to everything. You give me a burp and you'll find it marked for identification and sealed in an envelope."

28.

AT THE HOSPITAL they told me Marty was asleep and it wasn't visiting hours and the doctor said nobody could see her and the police wouldn't allow visitors—anybody. That appeared to cover all the possibilities about three deep, so I went back to my apartment.

I stood alone in the middle of the room and looked at the closed door and wanted to tingle but didn't quite. If you've ever had malaria, you've felt that way a few minutes before your bones start shaking with a chill. There are alternate feelings of hot and cold, or perhaps it's better described as being either hot or cold, you don't know which.

I went out to the kitchen and took a rather large straight drink of whiskey and let it give me what amounted to a temporary chill. The whiskey was hot and it made me as conscious of what happens to something you swallow as when you eat that bismuth combination and let them take a candid picture of your digestion.

I went back to the living room and there was a knock at the door. I admitted a very sheepish and embarrassed Charley Pitts, who didn't know whether to clasp his hands in front of him and crack his knuckles or put his hands in his pockets or scratch his neck. He tried some of each.

I induced him to come in and closed the door behind him. He blurted suddenly, "Heck, Mr. London, you know I'm sorry, heck, I didn't mean to make trouble for you or anything like that. Heck . . ."

I said, "What're you talking about?"

He seemed more embarrassed and self-conscious than ever. With an extra effort he managed to crack the one knuckle which had resisted him before. He said, "Hector. I mean hell. He was up here, wasn't he? All I did was answer his questions. I mean, I didn't have time to think. Any way, I'm sorry."

"There's nothing to be sorry about, Charley. What was there to tell him?"

"Nothing. Nothing, that is, except that you came in about two-thirty."

I said, "How's that again?"

"Two-thirty, Mr. London. That's how it was and that's what I told him."

I looked as puzzled as I could, which was probably puzzled enough for Charley Pitts. I said, "Listen, Charley, it's absolutely all right to tell Lieutenant Richmond, or anybody else, anything you know. But let's be sure we aren't mixed up about things."

He said, "Well . . . all I know is, that's how it was and he asked me and I told him. You came through the lobby and I was reading, remember?"

I put my thumb in my mouth and frowned and said, "Y-e-e-e-s, I remember seeing you. You were sitting there reading and I waved and you waved or something like that. But what the hell's all this about two-thirty? It was around twelve when I came in, wasn't it?"

A firm stubbornness began to appear in his jaws. He said earnestly, "No, sir, it was after two. I remember outside, a couple of doors away, some people were singing in a car. That's how I remember particularly."

Walking up and down the room had done very well with Lieutenant Richmond so I tried it again. Finally I shook my head and said, "Okay, Charley. However it looks to you, you go ahead and tell it that way. Somehow it'll all get straightened out. There's a mix-up down the line somewhere and I'm damned if I can understand it, but maybe the cleaners will find it when they look through the pockets."

Charley looked slightly relieved. Then he said, "Is there anything I could do, Mr. London? I mean, I'll go to him and say I was mistaken if you say so."

I put an arm around his shoulder and gave him a squeeze. I said, "No, don't do that. When you start trying to cover up for somebody all you do is get into trouble, and you'll have trouble enough of your own without borrowing from other people. Your old third grade reader was right, and don't let anyone tell you different. Honesty is the best policy, the early bird gets the worm and a stitch in time saves nine, or anyway eight and a half. Don't you worry about it. Things will all turn out all right."

"That Mr. Richmond seemed a little excited. Have I got you into serious trouble?"

"He's nosey, of course, but there's absolutely nothing to worry about." Then I said, "He said something about a Mr. Block. What about him?"

Charley said, "He was asking about who else was up late. You know, coming in or going out. I told him about Mr. Clegg, best I remember he came in about two-fifteen. And Mr. Block. He went out with a suitcase right about two-thirty. You must have seen him, or pretty close to it. Don't seem like he was hardly out of the building before you come in."

I was thinking back. I lit a cigaret and realized I shouldn't have done so when I saw the way my hand was trembling with the lighter. I covered it by cupping both hands and taking my time. I could only hope that Charley was unobservant.

I said, "Jeest, Charley. Things are really messed up somewhere. Like I told you, I came in right around twelve, maybe a few minutes one way or the other. Your Mr. Whatever-his-name-is I may have seen now and then in the elevator if he lives here, and I guess I'd know his face if I saw him. But hell, how could I have seen him at two-thirty last night? Oh, well, never mind. Whatever all this business is, it'll straighten itself out."

Charley said, "All I know is, that's the way I remember it. This detective asked Mr. Block's apartment number and I told him, and he went up. That's all I know."

I said, "Well, no harm's done. Like a little drink before you go?"

When he hesitated, I said, "Just a quickie. I'll give you some chewing gum."

He looked uncertain and then said, "Well . . ." and then

I took him to the kitchenette and gave him a drink and a stick of chewing gum and saw him to the door.

29.

SOMEBODY once said in Latin that time flies and he was a pretty smart apple because it still does. Where it flew I don't know but when I got over a case of the mild jitters it was after six o'clock. The late afternoon paper was on the table and I had to think hard to remember that I brought it in when I got back from the hospital—one of those natural and automatic actions that doesn't register.

I glanced through what it had to say on the front page about Mitch Sothern, which was the morning story with embellishments but no substantial additions. Then I looked down at the sports flashes to see what teams were winning and what teams were losing and whether Joe DiMaggio and Ted Williams and Hank Greenberg and Mel Ott had got themselves any home runs or contrived to be a colossal disappointment.

I like to undress when there's no occasion for hurry— one thing at a time and maybe stop and scratch your leg and read the funnies and notice those little column fillers that contribute such interesting but obscure facts as that the mean annual rainfall in upper Nigeria is so many and .54 inches.

It was twenty minutes to eight when I went out. The tie had been a very happy selection and my new hat was in a pleasant mood and I was almost jaunty as I waited for the elevator despite the depression in my gizzard. After awhile I gave up and walked down to the lobby, bouncing up and down to give my arches a workout.

Charley Pitts was there and he seemed relieved that I seemed cheerful and gave him a friendly wave. I felt a zing in my blood and the ugly implications of Lieutenant Richmond and his vulgar thoughts were not enough to give me concern at the moment.

I took a bus and at three minutes to eight got off two blocks from the address Wiggie had given me.

The illuminated glass sign said "Monticello Apartments."

I had not yet begun to recognize the coupe so I was surprised when Wiggie met me at the door and took me into the living room where Lieutenant Richmond was sitting. He tried out his experimental grin and said dryly, "Hello. Just checking everything."

"I know. You get lists and ask questions and ring doorbells. If I see you one more time you've got to buy me a drink."

He said, "You've never operated on a budget, have you?"

I said, "You buy me the drink and I'll pay for it."

Wiggie said, "Have I walked into a lodge meeting?"

Richmond said, "Don't tell anybody, but it's mostly a question of building up a file. Sometimes we don't catch the guy, but they don't skin your tail if you've got a lot of reports where you've been places and asked plenty of questions and looked under the bed and put some things in envelopes. By the way, any objection to fingerprints?"

Wiggie said, "I had a manicure this afternoon. Is it necessary? Can you do it without mussing my nails?"

I said, "Dear, dear Miss Wiggins. Asking for your fingerprints is a mere figure of speech. What the Lieutenant wants is strictly *my* fingerprints. Tell him he can have yours if he can get the price of a manicure out of the budget and that's the last you'll ever hear of the subject."

Richmond said, "*You* haven't had a manicure, have you?"

I said, "My manicurist is having her vacation in Bermuda.

I couldn't risk her displeasure by taking my nails to anyone else."

He said, "Then you're just the guy the budget can stand. A touch of alcohol on the fingers tips makes things tidy enough for a working man. Hold everything and I'll get the kit from the car."

I said, "Let's don't debate about it. If you must give my dainty fingers five o'clock shadow, let's have at it."

Richmond hustled down to the coupe and came back with his equipment.

He said, "The stuff doesn't taste bad, but then I assume you don't suck your thumbs anyway." He looked apologetically at Wiggie and added, "I don't like to delay the festivities, but I'd like to get done now, if you don't mind. The laboratory promised me pictures of what they find on that cigaret lighter Monday morning."

If I kept on hearing things like that I was not sure my appetite for dinner would be anything to brag about. I let Richmond busy himself with his kit, and when he was ready I let him take my fingers and thumbs and roll them in his sticky black ink and then roll them again on his cards to produce lovely fingerprints—rather too clear and distinct in an alarming sort of way.

30.

WIGGIE'S APARTMENT was on the third floor. We stood at the window together and watched until Richmond walked out to his car, tossed his fingerprint kit carelessly on the back seat, and drove away. Then I realized that I had scarcely paid any attention to Wiggie. I said, "Sorry. How would it be if I went out in the hall and knocked on the door and we started the evening all over again?"

She was even more attractive than on the other occasions when I had seen her. She was dressed very trimly and there was a sparkle in her eyes and a general air of suppressed devilishness which was altogether entrancing. She said, "I think that would be a very good idea. The place seems faintly official, doesn't it?"

I went to the door and opened it and closed it and put my back against it and took off my hat and said, "Good evening, Miss Wiggens."

She took my hat and held it behind her and I put an arm around her and bent as if to kiss her and then stopped. I smiled and said, "I don't want to carry this too far."

Her eyes sparkled even brighter and she said, "I'll stop you when you do."

I looked at her a long while, and stopped smiling, and so did she. Then I went ahead and kissed her and after a moment my hat dropped on the floor and it was a very sweet kiss.

Presently I took my arm away and looked at her and she said, "Maybe it would be better if you went out and came in another time. I think we're rehearsing the wrong script."

I put my hand behind me and opened the door an inch and closed it again and said, "Now what?"

She blushed a little and said, "Frankly, it's the same script, but we mustn't be monotonous. Wouldn't it be better if we ad libbed a few lines and had a change of scenery?"

I said, "We'll go anywhere you like. I have no ideas at all."

"We mentioned a picture. Is that what you'd like to do?"

The only thing I wanted was whatever she wanted so I looked at her, trying to get a line on what I should say. She read my thoughts and with a solemn look still on her face, shook her head almost imperceptibly. And then we couldn't help it and laughed and, impulsively, I put my arms around her again and laughed into her hair. I said, "Darling, you're wonderful."

She pushed me away and said, "Well, you wanted to know what I was thinking. It seemed silly not to let you know. Really, I don't feel like seeing a picture but that doesn't mean I won't sit through a double header and a flock of previews if that's what you want."

"I don't want to go to a show either. Now, what *do* you want to do?"

"Why don't we go some place that isn't too conspicuous and just have dinner and talk?"

"Such as, for example?"

"Well, I was thinking about a place out on the Nashville pike. In a way, I suppose it's something of a joint but the food isn't too bad and there's a five piece orchestra that you can dance to if you have some imagination." Then she added hastily, "I don't mean we have to dance, if you don't feel like it or if it isn't appropriate under the—well you know, the circumstances."

I said, "Maybe we ought to skip the dancing if that's all right with you. I'll be honest— I've been disillusioned about the great Mitch Sothern recently and I must say I don't feel the slightest twinge of grief over his death. Understand, I wouldn't have wished him anything like that but now that it's happened, under whatever unfortunate circumstances, I just can't squeeze out a regretful tear."

She said, "No, I didn't get the impression that you were heartbroken. How's Marty?"

I said, "I've been allowed to see her once, with the police very much in evidence. She's recuperating, best I can tell. Wouldn't let me in this afternoon."

"I'll fix my face."

31.

WHEN SHE CAME out of the bedroom, all prettied up, we went down to her car and drove to the place she was talking about. She felt very gay and there was a lot of incidental chatter I can't remember, and then we fell silent.

I thought of Marty, emotionally shocked over Mitch's infidelity, and his death, and the loss of her expected baby. Even with her balance and healthy outlook, the adjustment would be difficult. The suddenly smashed bits of a sunny, serene life would take a deal of picking up. Was Marty capable of meeting the challenge, or would she become moody and self-pitying? I'd have to watch that. For the moment I was helpless, but flowers again tomorrow might be a good idea. And a visit—a longer visit —as soon as permitted. It wouldn't do to tell Marty about being fired—or would it? Perhaps letting her worry about me might take her mind off herself? That problem would bear thinking about. . . .

What was I going to do about Charley Pitts and this man Block?

Wiggie said, "Why did Lieutenant Richmond want your fingerprints? And what did he mean by his reference to fingerprints on a cigaret lighter?"

I debated a moment, trying to decide whether to laugh it off or make some cautious explanations. It was the growing necessity of discussing things that made me say, "You may as well know it now as later. I'm in trouble, of a sort. Richmond thinks I killed Mitch, to put it baldly. I didn't, but even being suspected is trouble, naturally."

Wiggie pulled abruptly over to the curb, pushed the ignition switch, and turned an anxious face toward me. She said,

"But why? Is it simply a hunch, Jess, or does he think he has something to go on?"

I offered her a cigaret, took one myself, and felt for my lighter. When I touched it, an alarm signal flashed in my brain. I felt around in other pockets. I said, "Sorry, I must have forgotten matches."

Wiggie produced a package of paper matches from her purse and I held one for her and then lit my own cigaret. I said, "He thinks he has plenty to go on, but it's really absurd. This morning when I saw the paper—about what happened to Mitch, and that the police were looking for Marty—well, I did the first thing that popped into my mind. Being in the dark, all I could think of was taking the heat off—if only for a little while. Well, it was while I was wondering what to do, that old Zack called me from the hospital and told me Marty was there. Knowing her as well as I do, I was positive she had nothing to do with Mitch's death. But still, she was crazy about him, as you know, and when she learned of it she might have—you know, got hysterical or something. I knew it wouldn't be an hour before the police found her, with the story spread all over the front page, so I went straight to the house, asked who was in charge, and told Richmond that I killed Mitch. That's what I was talking about in the drugstore this morning."

"But didn't you say they wouldn't believe you?"

"Right then, they didn't. Richmond saw through me in a minute. I had to tell him where Marty was, because I didn't want them to get the idea she was hiding. I went with him down to the hospital and before that little drive was over he had pulled my story to pieces in half a dozen different ways. Made me look like a fool."

"That doesn't sound like much to go on."

"No, it doesn't. But when he satisfied himself Marty was out of the picture, I guess he turned on me as the next best bet. Now it seems he's dug up, or thinks he's dug up, some people who saw me outside my apartment around two-thirty, which he says would be about the right time, and which happens to have been some two hours or more after I went to bed and went to sleep. He says this evidence that I was in the neighborhood of Mitch's house pretty close to the time Mitch was killed ties in with my ridiculous confession."

"But you could have been out of the apartment without killing somebody, Jess. No, you were home in bed. Still, it's pretty thin."

"Well, that's not all. You see, I had to invent a weapon as a part of my story. The newspaper report said it was something heavy and roundish or flat, so I chose that heavy steel-ball cigaret lighter, not knowing anything better to choose. Now he's testing the lighter for fingerprints, and if he should chance to find my prints on it, even mixed up with other people's, you can see how excited he'll get."

Presently she said, "In spite of all that's happened, you don't seem to be worrying very much."

I said, "Well, I am, really. This fellow Richmond seems to be all right enough in his way but I've an idea he wouldn't mind casting me in the role of the goat. The power of suggestion is a wonderful thing. I don't know what he's said to these people to make them think they saw me at two-thirty, but the idea seems to be there. With an opening like that, all he needs is to find some fingerprints on that cigaret lighter and I'd be in bad shape."

She was quiet so long that I glanced at her. She was looking fixedly ahead, with her lower lip in her teeth and a speculative expression around her eyes. She said slowly, as if feeling her way along, "But of *course* they'd be there. It's a little confused but a definite memory is coming back. Didn't you light my cigaret with that fancy cigaret lighter, at the party?"

I said, "Maybe I did. When was that?"

She said, "I was pretty tight. I think I was actually bumping into the furniture and maybe putting out a hand occasionally to keep from falling. It's no wonder I don't remember everything with crystal clarity. But how it seems is that I had a cigaret and you were looking the other way, and somebody called to you, and then you turned around and the lighter was right there and you picked it up and gave me a light. I can remember swaying around but at the time it seemed that I was steady enough and *you* were weaving. Does that sound reasonable?"

I let a decent interval of time pass as if I were searching my memory in the same troubled way. I said, "That's so. It was late in the evening, wasn't it? Some of the guests were already leaving. I could see out through the living-room arch. George Stern was coming down the stairs, out in the hall. He saw you and I didn't, so he called and pointed and then I turned around like you said. Does that check pretty well?"

She said, "Of course. It was George, because when we were in the car someone was kidding him about his loud voice."

After a moment, she said, "I'd rather you'd drive."

I started the motor and pulled away from the curb. There wasn't much talk during the rest of the drive.

32.

She said, "There's where we turn off."

At the entrance to a lane overhung with trees there was a modest sign of the type that shines in your headlights although not itself lit up with electricity. All it said was "Oak Lawn." There wasn't a word about dining or dancing or a floor show or anybody's orchestra.

I said, "You mean here?"

She said, "That's what I like about it. They aren't after the crowd that simply drives by and sees the sign and wants to stop for a beer. They're after the people who hear about it from other people and will take the trouble to look for it. It's—well, it's maybe a little higher than some places but if you don't like it we can go some place else next time."

I liked the casual way she said "next time." There was an absence of coquettishness about it which appealed to me. More than that, a next time was beginning to appeal to me anyway. Very much.

The lane went straight away from the highway for perhaps two hundred yards and then turned twice to the left, still overhung with massive trees, and brought up in front of a white, low, one-story place with old English coach lamps on either side of the door.

This was a different sort of place with a small entrance hall from which you passed, on either side, into a fairly large dining room with fire places at both ends. It was done in maple and the decorations were confined to a couple of spinning wheels, a grandfather's clock and hand-painted china plates in racks around the walls. In one corner, music stands were set for an orchestra which appeared to be made up of a piano, violin, cello, guitar and drums. There were arches here and there leading to a number of smaller rooms, almost alcoves.

A hostess came to meet us, and since Wiggie knew her way around the place, I let her take the lead. She made a gesture and we were shown to one of the alcoves at the farthest corner of the room. Stoakes Fant and his family were at one of the tables we passed. When he caught my eye he nodded in recognition, obviously not knowing whether to smile or not, things being as they were. I nodded back, resisted the impulse to smile, tried to look grave, and took my eyes away from his.

When we were seated we were out of sight of all but a corner of the main room. Wiggie seemed pleased.

I looked at the menu and said, "Cocktail?"

She said, "Yes, let's. I'd like a martini."

I glanced at the hostess and held up two fingers and said, "We'll order when the waitress gets here with the drinks."

When she was gone I said, "It's a nice place."

"Do you really like it?"

"Yes, I do. It's decent and quiet. Something a little apart from the slot machines and juke joints and beer and pretzels. Hungry?"

"Starving. I feel more like a farm hand than a career woman."

I said, "What does an assistant buyer do?"

She smiled and said, "Oh, I don't know. One assistant buys and things like that."

Stoakes Fant appeared in the archway, looked around, and came over to our table. I pushed back my chair and stood and said, "Good evening, Mr. Fant."

He said, "Hello, Jess. Sit down. I won't be a minute."

I said, "I'd like you to meet Miss Wiggens. Miss Wiggens, this is Mr. Stoakes Fant. You must have met at the—party last night."

The reference to the party was awkward and I felt a hotness in my ears. Wiggie acknowledged the introduction and Fant reached out and took her hand in his rather courtly way. I've forgotten what they said but it was appropriate. I remained standing and Fant turned to me. He said, "I hope Miss Wiggens will pardon the intrusion, but I've been wondering how I'd get in touch with you over the weekend. Marty sent me a message and I dropped in at the hospital this afternoon. She wants me—that is, you and me together—to look after all the —you know, details. I couldn't locate you at the moment and things—well, certain things have to be done, of course. Hope you don't mind. I went ahead and made all the arrangements —the undertaker, cemetery lot and all that sort of thing. The funeral's at four tomorrow afternoon, from the house. Drop in Monday some time and I'll show you what I've done."

I suppose it will seem silly, but the idea of undertakers and cemetery lots and funeral services and flowers and hearses came to me as a shock. Looking back, I realized that twenty-four hours had not yet passed since Mitch and I were glaring at each other in the study of his home; and I had been living in a dreamlike state—aware with all my senses of surface hazards, and the puzzle of curious events following rather too rapidly one after the other. I am conscious now of the light-headed almost feverish way in which I had lived through the day, parrying instinctively, rolling with the punches as they came, but never quite conscious that I was in the first round of a real heavyweight fight with a championship at stake.

Stoakes Fant was saying, ". . . the lockbox at the Second National Bank. I've already arranged for the man from the State Revenue Department to be there. I could handle it by myself if necessary but after all, being Marty's brother, I'd rather have you there. Think you can make it?"

I said, "What time did you say?"

He said, "Monday morning, nine o'clock."

I said, "Second National. I'll be there." Then I said, "What about the funeral?"

He and Wiggie both gave me sharp looks. Fant said, "I just told you. Four o'clock tomorrow afternoon, from the house."

I ran my fingers through my hair, shook my head ruefully, and said, "Of course. Sorry. I must be going nuts."

Fant put his hand lightly on my shoulder, said to Wiggie that he was glad to have met her, added a good evening to both of us, and went back to his table.

I sat down and my face was burning. I was conscious of the fact that one shoe was tied too tightly, so that it hurt. I didn't want to look at Wiggie until I had had a chance to pull things into reasonable order again. The thought of a cemetery lot and an undertaker's parlor sat heavily in my chest and I couldn't think of much in the way of small talk. I was glad when the waitress brought our martinis and the menus.

33.

WE HAD FINISHED our pie and were in the middle of the second cup of coffee when there was that moment of stillness and expectancy which seems always to precede an orchestra's first number. During that moment Wiggie was looking at me and I was looking at her. Her hand was on the table between us holding a cigaret and almost unconsciously I put mine over it as we listened.

She said, "The door back in the corner opens on the out-door dance floor. They don't use it now because it rains so much, but later in the summer it's lighted, and you eat and dance outside if you want to. It's dark and no one will know."

I said, "Would you really like to?"

She said, "Oh, yes, let's. Do you mind?"

We were outside in time for the second chorus. The out-side dance floor hadn't been swept in a long time and there were leaves from the trees that overhung it—trees that were green now. Somewhere there was a lilac bush in bloom and its fragrance was heavy in the air. We danced with her hair against my cheek. When the piece was over she said, "It was a nice moment. Now let's go home."

We sat in our corner behind the table and I put my hand palm up on my knee and she put hers in it. I waited for the check, added a rather more than generous tip, and at her sug-gestion went out by the door that led to the dance floor. Neither of us wanted to encounter Stoakes Fant again, or anyone else we knew. Our feet shuffled through the leaves as we felt our way around the outside of the building. She was leading, holding my hand, and I hung back a little and she came and put her arms around me and I kissed her again.

We were silent on the drive home and silent as I took her up to her apartment. I didn't know whether to come in or not, but I did not want to be alone with my depressing thoughts and my eyes must have begged. She shut the door behind us and put her head on my shoulder and said, "Only for a minute. You can't stay long."

"When may I see you again?"

"When do you want to see me again?"

"Whenever you can be seen. You wouldn't have breakfast with me, would you?"

She leaned back and looked at me. She said, "I would."

"If you've got anything to drink let's have a highball and then I'll be a good boy and go home. Tomorrow I'll come by for you and we'll have breakfast together. Why don't we spend the whole day together?"

She said, "Sit down and make yourself comfortable and I'll fix the drinks."

"No, of course not. I'll come with you."

We went back to the kitchenette and I leaned against the refrigerator and watched her as she found a half-bottle of whiskey, got out ice cubes and fixed the highballs. She had a disturbing effect on me. She made me feel happy in spite of the gnawing sensation of danger and depression that was deep inside me.

Wiggie handed me my highball and said brightly, "You go first and I'll turn out the light."

I had been thinking during the day that I was pretty good at hiding my feelings, but almost immediately my confidence was shaken when she sensed the difference in my attitude and said, "What's the matter, Jess?"

I tried to look mildly surprised. I said, "Matter? Nothing's the matter. Why do you ask?"

"Nothing. I just wondered."

She said, "I have a car and you haven't. Tell you what. I'll come by for you about ten-thirty or eleven and we'll go somewhere and have breakfast together. How does that sound?"

I wanted her to come to me and she understood and came, and I kissed her a long time and then held her tightly in my arms with her head against my shoulder.

After a long while she said, "Jess?"

I said, "What?"

She pushed back from me and there was a troubled frown on her face. She said, "Jess, there's something I don't understand."

My heart turned over in a spasm. I said gently, "What don't you understand?"

"Something that Lieutenant Richmond said to you. It's been worrying me. Did he say someone had seen you in the neighborhood of Mitch's house around two o'clock this morning?"

Even so, it was a relief because I was thinking of the cigaret lighter.

I laughed, perhaps a little nervously, and said, "Oh, that," with an air of dismissal.

"No, don't laugh, Jess. I don't know what it's all about but things like this can be serious and you ought to face them. There's no telling what circumstantial evidence might do to you."

I forced a grin. "It's just a silly mistake somewhere. It'll all come out at the proper time and let's not worry about it. I told you what he claims—Charley Pitts and this fellow— whatever his name is—Block, or something. What they say is full of holes right on the surface and by the time he talks to them again it'll all be cleared up. Take the singing, for example. See? And the green hat. My God, it's all too ridiculous."

She was still serious. She said, "That's not what I'm talking about. Don't you see, Jess? There must be someone else. Charley Pitts and Mr. Block, even if they *aren't* mistaken, only show you might have been *outside the apartment house* at two-thirty. Why did Richmond say you were seen *near Mitch's house* if that's all the evidence he had?"

It went over me like electricity. My mind raced over the entire catalogue of last night's events, struggling with the vagueness that whiskey had given me. Suddenly I wanted to get away and think about this alone.

I said, "The way you talk, you're almost frightening me. Between you and Richmond, one of these days I'll begin to believe it myself."

Her eyes were wide with concern and apology. She said, "Oh, Jess. Don't say things like that. Now you're frightening me and I feel like a perfect heel. Always remember this, will you? I'm on your side."

I said, "Remind me to tell you you're sweet."

She came to me and I kissed her again and then put on my hat and went out and closed the door.

34.

I MET A BUS at the corner as if by appointment. There were no other passengers. I felt solitary and perverse so I walked straight to the back of the bus and sat in the corner and thought in frantic torment of Richmond and Pitts and Block and Wiggie and cigaret lighters and fingerprints and green hats. Maybe

120 —

I ought to drink a lot of whiskey, even though tomorrow the overhang would be like the eaves of St. Agnes.

Wiggie had suggested a shocking thought. Was there, indeed, more evidence against me than Charley Pitts and this man Block? Wiggie was right. Between the two of them, they only tended to prove that I was outside the apartment house after two o'clock and what they said was by no means hopeless, considering the way things were going.

But Richmond had said there was evidence I was in the neighborhood of Mitch's house.

Was he bluffing or was there another element of the unknown?

Perhaps an old maid who sat in the dark, peering beneath the cracks of her drawn blinds, hoping to spice her uninteresting existence with a dash of scandal.

Perhaps someone casually returning to his home at an odd hour . . .

Of course. Joe, the bus driver. Joe, who started work between five and six in the afternoon but who had a very sick little girl at home and therefore left his job early.

But that wouldn't do. Two o'clock, if anything, would be late rather than early. But then he *had* come home early, for I had seen him, even though he hadn't seen me.

How was that again?

I noticed with a start that we were passing my apartment house. I reached up and jerked the cord and when the bus stopped at the next corner I swung out, let it pass in front of me, and then crossed the street and walked back. The yellow Hudson was still in the same position at the curb and the doors still hung open as if the entire day hadn't happened. I was reminded of the pictures of bleached skulls on the desert, never moving but staring impassively at successive generations. As I went by I could no more help glancing in than you can help looking at a woman's legs when her skirt blows up. The peach panties were as eloquent as ever.

I walked briskly to the apartment house, nodded to Charley, and let him run me up to the third floor. When I was undressed I felt that sleep would never come. I turned off the light and sat on the edge of the bed and drank all the whiskey I could find. In the middle of the third cigaret I retained just enough presence of mind to feel for the ash tray, and went off into a dark and troubled sleep.

35.

I AWOKE with a cramped feeling that indicated I had probably not turned over once during the night. There was a disagreeable brightness about the room. The clock said it was six-thirty and I accepted this statement at face value. I would have been glad to admit it was six-thirty even if I had known positively that it was three o'clock in the afternoon. Feeling my way from one piece of furniture to the next, I went around and drew the shades—three of them. Then, as long as I was up, I went into the bathroom and found the aspirin bottle and poured two tablets into the palm of my hand. They looked so small and futile that I nudged the bottle and poured out more—I don't know how many. I ate them like a handful of peanuts and eased myself diagonally across the bed and hoped that I would die quickly.

I woke up again and the front door buzzer was making a nuisance of itself. I found a dressing gown, put one arm into a sleeve, fumbled for the other armhole until I gave up in baffled exasperation, and finally wrapped it around me like a Roman toga and reeled, barefooted and still half asleep, to the door.

Wiggie was dressed in yellow and looked as fresh and cheerful as a dew-covered jonquil in the morning sun. I opened the door and stood aside, speechless.

She studied me from head to foot and finally burst out laughing. I didn't feel like laughing but for the sake of friendliness I finally managed something creaky and grim which I hoped would do. I turned discourteously and made the rounds, raising the shades so that the odious sunlight could come in.

She said, "I'm glad you can't see yourself. You're unattractive, not to say revolting. The other sleeve of your dressing gown is inside out. Shall I fix it for you?"

I said, "No" rather shortly.

She said, "I see what you mean. I'm sorry, but personally I feel marvelous. I feel the impulse to be the little housewife and find something to revive you."

I said, "I don't care whether I'm revolting or not and a little housewife sounds like a very timely idea. While I stretch out, please go away and fix some hot coffee and don't make any more jokes."

She went into the kitchenette and I turned over with my nose pressed flat against the back of the couch and in this preposterous position I went sound asleep.

Wiggie shook me. She was sitting on the floor with a cup of coffee and when I turned over she held it up for me. With some clumsy blowing it became cool enough to endure and I swallowed it and mutely asked for more. After the second cup I went into the bathroom and closed the door and was sick. Then I stood under the shower, put on the dressing gown again, and went out blearily and presented myself in the living room. If I had been a six cylinder engine I would say I was hitting on about one and a half cylinders.

I said, "What time is it? Don't answer that. It doesn't matter."

She looked at her wrist watch and said, "Ten-forty-five."

I said, "As late as that? As early as that? Hand me the rat

poison. I feel incompetent, irrelevant and immaterial. I sustain an objection to myself. Let me be stricken from the record. Is there any more coffee?"

She steered me to the divan and I sat heavily and leaned forward and held my head in my hands. She knelt in front of me, sitting back on her heels, and touched her lips to my hair. She put her fingers gently on my temples. She said, "Head ache, about there?"

"There, yes. And everywhere else."

"Hangover? Or that and something else?"

I shook my head miserably, but gingerly, from side to side. I said, "What I used to think of as a hangover, beside this is little children. Little innocent children, you should hold a handkerchief for them to blow their noses into, Lord love their little carcasses."

"Oh, it can't be that bad. You didn't have much to drink when we were together last night. Did you find a lot more somewhere?"

I said, "Ordinarily, I can hold half again as much without anything like this. I don't understand."

She said, "Lie flat on your back and we'll try some more hot coffee. What you've got is a whiskey hangover and a nervous hangover at the same time. Didn't you sleep?"

"I guess you'd call it sleep. A corpse full of formaldehyde couldn't have been out colder. I guess I didn't move for hours. There was a wrinkle in my pajamas, and it made a regular crease in my side. Look. No, that wouldn't be modest. Point is, it was a *rigid* sort of unconsciousness—merciless. I think Dracula came to see me."

Wiggie disappeared into the kitchenette and after a minute returned with more coffee. I took a reckless sip, and was scalded, and endured an impossible, intolerable moment when I could neither spit it out nor swallow it nor hold it in my mouth. A spasm shook my hand and I spilled some of the coffee from the cup, but the white-hot effect in my mouth did much to bring my hazy eyes into focus. I took another sip, swallowed it in agony, and put on what must have been a fantastic sort of grin.

I said, "Hello."

She smiled and said, "Hello, Jess."

"I'm coming around. Was I—pretty messy?"

"No, Jess. You weren't a mess. I don't think you could ever be."

I said, "You're either naive or you have much to learn. Anybody can be a mess." I took another shocking swallow, grimaced, and shuddered. I found the four walls of the room, located the doors and windows, and began to wonder what I had said and done before this faint degree of sanity had returned. I said, "If you'll be patient, I think a cold shower—a long one—might fix me up. If you look around, you might find a magazine or a book or something."

Wiggie said, "Never mind. You go take a shower and come to life. I'll find some way to kill the time."

36.

THE COLD SHOWER was an ordeal but I stood under it in desperation, gasping and shaking and determined not to give up. The water was cold and my flesh rebelled but I stood my ground and took the punishment. I deliberately presented the vulnerable spot in my back and would not move until it began to get numb. I ducked my head and let the icy stuff cascade across my neck. I held my chin up in the air and let the stuff run across my chest until I felt like the Merchants Ice & Cold Storage Company, or anyway a majority stockholder.

Then one day I shut the water off and got out of the tub and dried myself. I put on clean underwear and clean socks and a clean shirt and a suit fresh from the cleaners. I felt wan and washed out and my knees were uncertain, but I was alive. I no longer felt like a charge account at the undertaker's establishment.

I went into the living room.

Wiggie came over and knelt in front of me again, sitting back on her heels. She said, gravely, "Jess, you *are* in trouble, aren't you?"

I said, "Isn't everyone? Always? It's only a matter of degree."

She said, presently, "If I ask you a straight question will you give me a straight answer?"

I said, carefully, "Of course."

"And you won't take offense?"

"Offense? Why? Of course not."

She looked away and bit her lip.

I said, "Come on. Shoot."

She wouldn't look at me. I took her face in my two hands and made her look at me. Her eyes were deep and troubled.

At length she said, "Jess, is it all right if I ask you this question—honestly? You won't be mad with me?"

I said, "No, I won't be mad with you."

She said, "I have a feeling this is a question I shouldn't ask."

I said, "Go ahead. Ask it anyway."

There was a long pause. She said, "We've known each other a fairly long time, haven't we? I mean, we aren't exactly strangers."

"No."

"As a friend, I'm entitled to certain privileges, I think. Or is it all right to think we're a little more than friends?"

I said, "Last night I thought we were more than just

friends, and I hope it's still that way. But if you doubt your right to ask me something, I don't know."

She turned and studied my face, as if trying to be sure of something. Then she put her head under my chin for a moment, and then leaned back and looked hard at me again.

I said, "Well?"

She said, "You're hiding something from me, Jess. I can feel it. I know you didn't have anything to do with Mitch's death, it isn't that. Just tell me this—when you went into your apartment house about midnight, after you got out of the car, did you really go straight to bed and stay there?"

I tried not to show any reaction, but evidently I didn't succeed. I wasn't able to say anything, right away.

Wiggie said, "No, look at me, before you answer."

With a conscious effort, I looked at her—straight and with as little dissembling as I could manage.

I said, "You took me a little by surprise. I don't know what I expected, but that wasn't it. There's no trouble giving you a straight answer to that question, Wiggie. When I left you and the others who were in the car, coming from the party, I went straight up and went to bed and never left the apartment house again that night."

Wiggie looked hard at me, and it was only with the greatest difficulty that I avoided turning my head away. She said flatly, "I don't believe you."

I thought it was a good time to create a diversion. I said, "Why don't we see if we can get a bottle sent up from the desk? I don't know how you feel, but a few mouthfuls of the hair of the dog . . ."

There wasn't any response, so I went over and called the desk, trying to be chattily noisy about it, to cover the embarrassing silence. At this hour it wasn't Charley, of course, who was on duty; but all of them are Charleys, when you analyze it. I put down the receiver with forced gaiety and said, "You see, even on Sunday, all you have to do is know how it's done. The greenback is more powerful than the flat-foot."

Wiggie didn't move. I went into the bedroom and fetched a five dollar bill from the dresser and went in and threw it carelessly on the table.

The real trouble with buzzers is that they have no sense of timing.

I said, "Oh, hell. It couldn't be the whiskey, as quickly as this."

She gave me a push toward the door and said, "Go ahead. I'll fix my face."

She got her compact from the handbag and went to the window. I crossed to the door, wondering how long it would take me to get rid of whoever might be there.

I said, "Hello, Joe."

He was more haggard than ever. His whole aspect was one of utter weariness and discouragement. His clothes were wrinkled and his tie was crooked and his face sagged and there was a dead look in his eyes. His expression of entreaty made me think of when I was a kid and my dog used to say with his eyes that he wanted to do whatever I wanted him to do, if only he could understand.

I said gently, "Come in, Joe."

He made no motion to come in but when I took his arm he came with me and I shut the door. I said, "I guess you know Miss Wiggens." You could see he guessed he didn't but he made an effort and said, "How do you do?"

Wiggie, with rare good sense, nodded and said nothing.

Joe drew in a long deep breath and looked at the floor. He said, "I feel like a heel but even a heel can have a little girl." He looked at me defiantly. "I got no call to ask you for your blood but I'm not asking for myself. For Joanna it's different. If we had plenty of time I'm sure we could find somebody else but the doctor's in a hurry and there ain't no time to look."

It was not a good idea to leave Wiggie, with questions un-settled between us, but there was only one thing to say. I said, "Of course."

I looked desperately at Wiggie, and bless her heart, she came and stood by me and linked her arm in mine. "Of course, he'll go," and then she turned to me and said, "I'll wait here for you. Don't hurry. And afterwards maybe you'd take me to lunch?"

I said, "They want me to lie down afterwards. If it seems long will you wait?"

She nodded and I found my hat. At the door we met the desk clerk with my order, poorly disguised in a brown paper bag. I said to Joe, "Don't you think you'd feel better if you had a drink of whiskey?"

His eyes located the bottle and then looked away and back again and finally at the floor. "Me? I feel all right."

I said, "Nonsense, you're out on your feet. Take a drink and pull yourself together. Remember, your wife's depending on you."

I poured him a stiff straight drink in the bottom of a tumbler. He made an automatic gesture of greeting to each of us and took it at a gulp. Then we went out together.

37.

JOE HAD his car. I got in under the wheel without discussing who was going to drive. After looking blank for a moment, Joe walked around without protest and got in beside me. Approaching the hospital, I said, "There's nothing to be apologetic about. It's my good luck I have the right kind of blood. Joanna can have all she needs of it, Joe. So could you. If I needed your kind of blood, I'd get it, wouldn't I?"

He didn't answer, and when I gave him a sidelong look his eyes were moist and blinking. To keep the conversation going I said, "Wouldn't I?"

He tried once and a curious noise came up out of his throat. He coughed and tried again, and said, "You can have it to fill your gas tank if you say so."

I said, "Sure. Anybody'd be the same way. You don't have to call yourself a heel."

He said stonily, "That's what I am, just the same." Then he said, "You can go on beyond and turn in at that driveway. There's a place to park, behind."

I turned in and we found a place to park. As soon as the car came to a stop he was out and on his way to the rear entrance of the hospital, looking back over his shoulder at me impatiently.

When we stepped out of the elevator the nurse sighed with relief and took charge of me briskly. This time I knew the routine. I stretched out on the table and turned my head away and let her go about her business.

She said, "Feel okay?"

I said, "In the pink."

"That's good. Counting yesterday and today, we're going to hit you a little on the heavy side. Lie here and take it easy. Don't try to sit up until I come back and say so."

I said, "I've got a wrestling match in thirty minutes. I won't leave until then."

Much later they let me look in at Joanna. She was white, but a tinge of color was coming back to her as my blood became a part of hers.

The nurse looked at my face and then rather absurdly took a firm grip on my arm and walked me to the sun porch where Mr. and Mrs. Joe were waiting. By the time I was there

I felt foolish and was glad to have the muscular little body beside me.

Mrs. Joe looked at the nurse and received a nod. She stood up and took one of my hands in both of hers and pressed it moistly and then went off down the hall to Joanna's room.

Joe took out a pipe and filled it with hands that shook and spilled bits of tobacco on the floor.

He said, "I want to tell you."

I said, "All right."

He said, "That detective asked me. Well . . . I told him what I saw, that's all. It seemed right to tell him the truth—that is, it did then. Now I'm all mixed up and I don't know what's right and what's wrong. God help me, I've thought about it and thought about it and now right and wrong don't seem the way they used to seem."

I didn't think he was finished so I went on and listened. He lit his pipe and when it suited him he said, "Used to be, right was white and wrong was black and one was one and the other was the other. If you did black, you knew it was black and did it anyway. Afterwards you asked God to please forgive you. Now there's a place I never saw before where you might say it's gray—sort of. Your blood being in my baby just damn well changes the color of things. That's all I know."

I said, "Joe, there isn't any reason to be all upset. Truth's white and telling it doesn't change the color. If what you told is the truth it can't hurt me, so quit worrying about it. Let's get it off your chest. Just what is this truth that's making you so confused?"

"Well, he asked me if I didn't pass near this house on my way home at night and I said yes I did. Then he asked did I see anybody that night. What night I don't rightly know now. What day is this?"

"Sunday."

"Sunday already? Then I guess it wasn't last night. No,

because I was here all last night. Friday night, that's when it was. He asked if I seen anybody on my way home and I said yes I had. I forgot your name but he tried several names out on me and then I said it was you, because that's who it was. Like I said, it seemed all right, then. I just couldn't help it. Anyway, he said when was that, and I said around two o'clock because that's the way it was. Now, thinking about it, I guess I got you into trouble and I wish I'd said I didn't see anybody."

I put my head down in my hands and thought for a long time. I wanted to tremble and I suppose I would have, except for the fact that my hands and elbows and knees and head were all braced against each other.

With something of an effort I went back to the train of thought of the night before. I couldn't wait long enough to test it logically. I had to say something before the moment got cold.

I raised my head and put a wrinkle of concentration between my eyes. I said, "Joe, I think I understand something. What time did you say it was?"

He said, "Right around two. Maybe a little before or a little after. I wouldn't know down to the minute."

I said, "Was that the only time you went home Friday night?"

He looked out of the window and took a puff from his pipe and said, "No, I went home once earlier than that on account of being worried about Joanna. Then the doctor said she was asleep and it looked like maybe the trouble was over so I went on back and finished out my time. That's how it was."

I said, "Think about this now. Are you sure you didn't see me on the first trip instead of on the second?"

He looked hard at me and then his eyes shifted uneasily and the blood came up into his neck so that I could see it. He said, "No, I'm not sure. I could be mistaken."

I said, "Look at me, Joe."

He brought his eyes around reluctantly and then looked at me squarely, but not for any length of time. His eyes kept meeting mine and looking away and coming back and the color grew higher in his face and he shifted his feet restlessly.

I said, "You don't have to be dishonest for me, Joe. You *are* sure, aren't you?"

Then he met my eyes and looked miserable. He said, "Yes, I'm sure. There ain't any doubt at all. But I swear that don't cut any figure any more. I could just as well be confused as not."

I said, "All I know is that I wasn't there at two o'clock or anywhere near that time. If your eyes and memory say I was, don't you ever budge from that and say anything different. But there's something wrong somewhere—what, I don't know. If we believe in right and wrong then we've got to believe right will come out in the end, don't we? Well, that's what I believe, Joe, and instead of helping it, telling a lie will only hurt."

He said, "It'd be awful easy to be confused. Whether it's maybe ten or ten-thirty or whether it's two, it's still dark. I came from the same direction and went the same way. How could I be so sure it was one time instead of another?"

I shook my head and said, "No, you know better than that."

He looked up wistfully. "You ain't sore?"

I said, "No, Joe, I'm not sore."

His eyes met mine again and this time they were steady. He said, "I'm not much civic minded. With me, first comes Joanna, and Wanda—that's the Missus. Next comes Joe himself. Me, I mean. After that comes people I like. People who do good by us. Only after that comes other people. To tell you the honest truth I don't give a damn whether you kill somebody or not, but I know what you done for me and I ain't the kind that should forget it. I could be confused easy as anything only I don't want to be confused on my own hook, on account of I'm too dumb to think through how things come out in the end."

I said, "I'd rather you just let it lie. Nobody needs to lie for me. At two o'clock on Friday night you saw somebody you thought was me. You're sure, so that's what you ought to say and nothing else. I happen to know I was home in bed at that time and I know I'm not guilty. So in the end, what you say will have its explanation and everything will be all right. That's what justice means, Joe—that everybody tells the truth and yet what's right becomes apparent simply because the truth is being told. Justice doesn't grow out of lies. It can't."

Joe said, "It's all right, if you say so. The way it looks to me, sometimes maybe justice needs a little help. A little lie nobody can catch you up on wouldn't hurt anything, just in case."

I shook my head. The nurse was coming down the hall. She said, "The reaction has been amazing. The little girl spoke to her mother and asked about her daddy. It's all right for you to come now."

Joe took his pipe out of his mouth and his lower lip was trembling. Tears piled up in his eyes and when he blinked they ran down on each side of his nose and followed the deep wrinkles around the corners of his mouth.

I said, "That's swell. If you need me again I'll be around."

I walked with them as far as the door of Joanna's room, and when they turned in I walked over to the stairs and went up to Room 412. The young cop was there, but I was not as respectful as before. I said, "Enough is enough. This is my sister in here, and I'm going to see her or raise seven kinds of hell. Come along, if you like, but keep your damn mouth shut."

I wasn't fooling anybody, and I knew it and he knew it. He put a twisted smile on his face and said drily, "Yes, sir." That meant he had instructions I could see Marty. There wasn't any kind of misunderstanding between us. I felt superior, nevertheless.

Marty was sitting up against banked pillows. Her face was grave and there were indications of new lines in it—perhaps the beginning of realization that life was not all the beer and skittles she might have imagined it to be.

I sat in the chair by her bed and took her hands in mine and kissed them. I said, "Honey, darling."

She said, "Jess, it's so good to see you. I've been feeling so lonely."

I said, "You have me. You mustn't feel lonely any more. We're standing together, aren't we?"

Marty put a hand on my head and said, "Are we? You've no idea how much that means to me. I feel as if there's been a great commotion and all the world has gone rushing by, leaving me here, all by myself."

I pressed her hand against my cheek. I said, "I know. But you and I were together before the storm ever came up, and now that it's come and gone, we're still together. If you want to hang on to something, hang on to me. I'm pretty stout, and I like to be hung on to."

She said, with her eyes misty, "The flowers were lovely. I read the card and almost felt that you were here in the room."

I said, "I would have been here, but they wouldn't let me. You know that. I sent some pretty things and a nice smell to represent me."

Marty said, "I'm not going to be pathetic, God forbid. But the plain truth is, Jess, that now I am looking to you for the pride and joy and fulfillment of my life. Is that all right with you? I mean, I don't want to be a nuisance or a source of embarrassment."

I said, "If you turn to me, it only makes me proud. If you need to lean on somebody, don't lean on anybody else—that is, unless and until I prove to be a failure."

38.

NATURALLY at such a time I wouldn't suggest that Joe take me back to the apartment. There were no taxis in sight and it was a pretty day, so I walked. There was the slightest trace of shakiness in my knees and the sun on the pavements seemed abnormally bright, but my heart was happy and the few blocks didn't seem long.

As I turned the next corner I saw Richmond parking his coupe near the entrance. I had no desire whatever to see him but I knew if I didn't head him off he would call my apartment before I reached the lobby, and then Wiggie would have a problem she wasn't counting on. That is, assuming she was still there. The possibility that she might have gone away was one I hadn't thought of and it gave me a twinge.

Acting on impulse I put two fingers between my teeth and gave one of those shocking whistles you either learn when you're a kid or never learn at all. Even a block away it almost unbalanced Richmond. I could see his relaxed body jump. But for a quick instinctive grab, his hat would have fallen from his head. He flashed a startled, angry look in my direction, and then when he saw me he relaxed again and waited, grinning a little foolishly.

When I came up to him I said, "You ought to look at a calendar. It's Sunday. Or didn't you know? Budgets being what they are, how the hell can the city pay time and a half for overtime? Or does it?"

He said, "Nuts. The city doesn't pay time and a half for anything. But then in the long run it isn't so bad. When the heat's on you don't pay any attention to time. Afterwards, just so long as the file's okay and you haven't been stupid about it, you sleep late or take a day off and nobody says a word."

I said, "Then I gather the heat's on now."

"Oh, indubitably. Aren't you beginning to feel a hot breath on your neck?"

I said, "Funny thing. I was thinking about it only the other day. Before they put you in the electric chair they shave your head, don't they?"

"Sure. You know—good connection."

I said, "What I was wondering, suppose the barber nicks your scalp a little. Does he put iodine on it or use one of those styptic pencils to stop the bleeding?"

Richmond looked thoughtful a moment and then raised his eyebrows. He said, "I never thought about it. I suppose that's something a barber does naturally, wouldn't you think so? You know, professional standards and all that sort of thing. Still, it does seem silly now that you mention it. Doesn't seem a germ would bother infecting a corpse, does it?"

I said, "Waste of time, that's the way I look at it. I was just wondering."

He said, "Well, it's a good point. You can't tell what people will do. There was a suicide once—a doctor—happened right down here on Fulton Street. Remind me some time and I'll show you the place. Committed suicide by cutting his wrists and bleeding to death. Know what he did? Got out a bottle of alcohol and carefully swabbed the place first. Habit. Can you beat it?"

I said, "Why are we discussing this anyway?"

Richmond looked at me in exasperation and then recovered his sense of humor and a twinkle came into his eyes. He said, "You started it, remember? Wondering whether they'd put iodine on your scalp."

I said, "It's a natural thing to wonder about. The iodine I use has to be weaker than usual or it sometimes gives me blisters. Hell of a note, being electrocuted with blisters. Makes your flesh crawl to think about it. Why don't you drop whatever you're doing and come up for a drink?"

– 137

He said, "Being as it's Sunday and I don't really have to be on duty anyway, the idea isn't half bad. Especially since I can do it without dropping what I was doing."

"That's what I thought. It's only a question, whether I ask you or whether you insist. The way I feel about it, I pay the taxes anyway. And if I don't ask you up and give you a drink, you'll come anyway, which isn't courteous. And then later on you'll have the drink and find some way to get it on the expense account so that I pay the bill after all."

He was silent. We walked through the lobby together without saying a word. We had to wait for Cornelius Vanderbilt and the silence was so long that it became uncomfortable. I said, "Something on your mind?"

He said, "I was thinking. Why do we spar around with a lot of monkey business like this? It doesn't prove anything and it isn't amusing to either to us. When you're a copper— that's a phrase my kids get out of the radio and the movies— people either want to ball you out or be witty. Same way in all the detective stories. It doesn't really make any difference but what the hell?"

I had my key in my hand and was about to put it in the lock when I thought better of it and turned to Richmond. I said, "This isn't a casual visit—not on Sunday. There's something special on your mind so we might as well talk it out."

He said, "Here? Why not inside?"

"Company."

He raised his eyebrows. "Anyone I shouldn't see?"

"Of course not."

We stood there eyeing each other. Finally I put my finger on the bell. I said, "It's only Miss Wiggens—I hope. She dropped in this morning and then when Joe came by and asked me to go down to the hospital with him she said she'd wait."

"Joe who?"

"I don't know his last name. All I know is, he's a guy

named Joe with a sick little girl in the hospital who needed a transfusion."

"Joe Herdt?"

"Who's he?"

"He's a fellow who lives down on Cynthiana Street. That's about three blocks from Virginia, down in the valley where the surroundings are a little less rarefied. He happens to have a little girl in the hospital is what made me ask."

I looked at him.

He looked back. He said, "This fellow Joe Herdt happens to be a bus driver."

I said, "Then it must be the same man. This one's a bus driver too."

Wiggie opened the door, seemed radiant when she saw me and then less radiant when she saw Richmond. She said, "Hello. What time is it? I think I've been asleep."

We went inside and closed the door. I said, "Lieutenant Richmond is beginning to be unhappy about how much I see of his witnesses. He's beginning to remember I saw Marty's servants before he did. Now I've just come from Joe and here you are waiting for me. The Lieutenant doesn't like it."

Richmond said, "I didn't say anything. Have you got a guilty conscience?"

Wiggie said, "Am I a witness? That's nice."

Richmond made an impatient gesture. He said, "Everybody's always playing games. For my part I stick to business and do the best job I can. If a card turns up that isn't what I like it to be, I put it right on the table face up along with the rest of them."

I said, "What's the card you don't like?"

He said, "The choice of words was bad. It isn't a question of what I like or don't like. It's a question of what fits. When a whole lot of things look one way and then something looks different it upsets me. Not that I care. It's only that I try to understand what happened."

Wiggie said, "Well, what did happen?"

Richmond said, "It's about the green hat. Those people who were in the car have finally gotten over their hangovers. That is, it's a question of degree. They're less hung over than they were. What they say now is, this guy who got in the car and sang with them was somebody they know. Fellow by the name of Don Stith, so they say. I haven't been able to locate him yet. It seems they persuaded Don to join them in the car and they had a few more drinks and this fellow Stith, whoever in hell he is, walked off with this green hat on his head."

Wiggie said, "That ought to be easy to check. Get hold of this Don Stith and if he's anywhere near the same shape as Jess, there goes Mr. Block and his story about seeing Jess come in at two o'clock."

Richmond said, "According to his wife, he's out of town. Claims he left town Friday afternoon. Now where does that put us?"

I said, "It doesn't put me anywhere. That's one for you to figure out. Maybe when you find him you'll quit being so damn suspicious. How could I come in at two o'clock when I was already in bed?"

Richmond said, "Don Stith and his green hat doesn't affect Charley Pitts saying you came in right at the same time. It doesn't affect Joe Herdt either. And another thing. There's a woman on the desk at the hospital who says a man came in and asked for Mrs. Sothern a few minutes after she was admitted. From the description it might very well have been you."

I said, "What kind of description? Does she say it was me or just that it wasn't a giant or a midget or a humpback or a man with a harelip?"

This time Richmond shifted his eyes and looked uncomfortable. He said, "Of course the description isn't like a photograph. What do you expect from one glimpse at two-fifteen in the morning?"

Wiggie said, "How was the light? Good or bad?"

Richmond didn't answer that one. He said, "There's one way we can tell. Any objections to going down with me tonight and seeing if she recognizes you? If she says it wasn't you, definitely, then that's that."

I said, "No objection at all. One request, though, out of plain common sense. If I go down there and you ask was this the guy, she'll probably fasten my picture in her mind whether it was me or not. Let's take down four or five people about my size, and no tricks. If she looks over the batch of us and picks me out, that's different."

Richmond looked doubtful for a moment and then sighed and said, "It's the same as the old police line-up. That's fair enough. Okay, it's a deal. She sleeps all day and doesn't come on duty until after supper. Shall we meet at the hospital?"

I said, "All right. Let's make it about ten-thirty or eleven o'clock. I'll be taking Miss Wiggens out to dinner—that is, if we ever get lunch first. Only look. Don't drag in a flock of policemen in plain clothes. Let's get some ordinary citizens."

Richmond made a face. "You sure want to do it the hard way. How would I round up a flock of citizens in the middle of the night?"

"Well, I'll compromise with you. You bring along two of your stooges and I'll bring two or three of mine."

"It's a deal."

"And no tricks?"

"No tricks."

Wiggie said, "If that's settled, personally I want a drink. Is anyone going to join me?"

Richmond debated with himself and then said, "Well, maybe a small one since I'm not strictly on duty anyway. Then I've got to hoof it home."

We went into the kitchenette and while I was taking the cork out of the bottle Richmond said, "Better make mine straight. I haven't much time."

Wiggie said, "Make mine straight, too. It's getting late and I'm hungry."

I said, "Hungry! Now that you've mentioned it, I'm starving. What time is it?"

Wiggie said, "Nearly two o'clock."

When I had poured the drinks, Richmond looked at me with a wry sort of amusement and said, "I'll wish you long life, for whatever good it will do."

Wiggie said, "You joke about the weirdest things. However, it's a nice wish."

It was good whiskey and I made a mental note to have another slug before taking Wiggie to lunch. At the door Richmond turned and said, "I almost forgot. Coroner's inquest at ten-thirty in the morning. You're expected to be there, or do I have to get out subpoenas and haul you in?"

I said, "Aw, beat it."

39.

BY THE TIME we were looking for places to eat, the nice eating places were beginning to be disinterested. Through the plate glass windows you could see the mops going to work and the chairs being stacked around the tables. This was Sunday and midafternoon business was dull and the clean-up boys were beginning to hope they could make the second half of the double-header at the ball park.

We went into a miscellaneous place, and ate miscellaneously. I didn't expect the food to taste good, and it didn't. Life itself didn't taste very good. I felt a something between Wiggie and me.

Wiggie was very quiet as we ate. She looked down at her plate a great deal.

She did not look at me.

At length I said, "Something's on your mind, stuck in your craw. Why don't you say it?"

Still she wouldn't look at me. She said, "It doesn't make any difference."

I said, "In that case, all right, it doesn't make any difference."

So there was a silence.

Wiggie said, "I assumed some things, and now I know I shouldn't have assumed them."

"What shouldn't you have assumed?"

"Nothing. It doesn't make any difference."

I kept my mouth shut.

Presently she said, "I suppose I'm supposed to be supremely loyal and deaf and dumb and accept your statement that you did not leave your apartment after midnight last Friday night, despite a lot of evidence that appears to be to the contrary. I suppose I'm not entitled to any explanation of anything. I suppose I'm not to be trusted—that I can't know all the truth and help you face whatever there is to be faced. That's what I suppose."

I said coldly, "If you want to assume that everything you hear is true, and everything I say is a lie, then it shouldn't be surprising that I don't take you into my confidence. I'm not saying you *aren't* in my confidence. I'm just supposing."

She waited a moment and then said, "I see."

I said, "So you think I didn't really go to bed when I say I did? You think I subsequently left the apartment house, and am afraid, or ashamed, to say where I went and what I did?"

Wiggie shrugged and looked out at the street, but didn't deny it.

I said, "Richmond says some people claim to have seen me here and there under circumstances that sound thin to me.

I tell you categorically that I was in my apartment all the time. I feel it shouldn't be necessary to defend myself beyond that point—to my friends. I expect my friends to believe me—at least until they've heard the evidence at firsthand. Even then, I'd expect them to give me a hearing."

She looked at me gravely, almost sadly. She said, "I've heard some of the evidence at firsthand. That's the trouble."

Puzzled, I said, "What evidence? When? What do you mean?"

Wiggie said, "I thought about you a lot, last night. I didn't like the way things were going. I wondered if Richmond could be making up his stories about witnesses, hoping to trap you or scare some lame explanation out of you."

"So then what?"

"So then, this morning I found Joe Herdt at the hospital. He didn't want to talk, but I told him I was trying to help you, and that I couldn't help you without knowing what he might have told Richmond. I finally got it out of him. I even cross-examined him, trying to find a weakness or an explanation . . . I've seen Charley Pitts, too."

I sat back and stared at her. At length I said, "Then you constituted yourself both judge and jury, held court, and convicted me. Didn't you think I was entitled to be heard?"

Wiggie appeared to be on the verge of tears. She said, "No, Jess. That's not so. I don't believe for a minute you had anything to do with Mitch Sothern's death. That's not the point. I simply believe you're being very foolish not to admit you left the apartment house. Go ahead and tell Richmond whatever there is to tell. It can't get you into trouble worse than suspicion of murder, don't you see that? All I want to do is help you, and all I get for it is a pretense that I'm hurting your feelings."

I said, "It doesn't take any pretense. How can you help me, as you claim you want to do, if you start out marking me down as a liar, and believing every Tom, Dick and Harry who may have been roaming around at two o'clock in the morning?"

There were no longer any signs of tears. Anger was rising in her, and there was a set grimness about her lips. She gestured impatiently and said, "What's the use? Never mind. What difference does it make, anyway?"

I said, "No difference, I guess. Only it leaves me knowing how I stand and what you think of me. That's interesting, as a passing thought."

"Yes," said Wiggie, "I suppose it's interesting, but only as a passing thought."

There was no warmth in the atmosphere between us. The waiter came with the check and I paid it, and there was a dismalness of no words while he brought the change and received his tip. I held Wiggie's chair aside for her and went to the door and out to the car.

She fumbled in her purse and found the keys and held them out to me. She said, "We're only a few blocks from my place. You'll need the car to go to the funeral."

The gesture was calculated to hurt me, and it did. I said, "Of course not. I can rent a car, or I'll walk. Don't be silly."

She continued to hold the keys out at arms length, and there was hostility around her mouth.

I said, "If you insist, it's awfully nice, and thanks. I'll drop you at your apartment house and bring the car back as soon as the funeral's over."

She held the keys a moment longer, and then dropped them on the sidewalk and turned on her heel and walked briskly away. I let the keys stay where she had dropped them and hurried awkwardly after her.

I said, "Wiggie, *please!* I'm not holding out on you. I'm telling you the truth, really I am. Don't let me down this way. I . . ."

A man and his wife, fat, and fanning themselves on an adjacent porch, looked at us with gathering interest.

I stopped, and Wiggie went on without turning her head. I said in a despairing whisper, "*Wiggie . . . !*"

She went on, putting her heels down in the most determined way.

The fat couple stopped fanning themselves and showed every evidence of wanting to become a part of this drama.

I stood still and watched, listening to her receding heel-taps, with a very low and melancholy cloud hanging in my stomach. Then I walked slowly back and stood by the car, unable to resist a last hopeful glance. Wiggie was still walking away. She turned a corner and was out of sight.

Very conscious of the fat eyes boring into my back, I bent and retrieved the keys, unlocked the car, and drove violently away.

40.

Mitch Sothern had as many guests at his funeral as he did at his parties. I drove by the house twice, and finally found a place to park two blocks away and on a side street. I dug out a pocket comb and checked my hair, with difficulty, in the rear-vision mirror. I was glad I had on a dark suit and a dark blue tie. Black would have been better.

Phelps was at the door, still unaccountably looking like a plain civilian. His expression was suitably grave, and if I hadn't known better I would have mistaken him for one of the undertakers. I whispered, "Am I late?"

He whispered, "No. On time. The family just came downstairs."

"Family?"

"Mother and sister. From Hopkinsville."

"I guess being in the family, I'll have to speak to them. Where's the Lieutenant?"

He gestured toward the door.

I said, "Waiting for me?"

He gave me a funny look and raised his eyebrows.

I said, "Skip it," and went on in.

There was a formal smell of people all dressed up, and a buzz of hushed whispering. The undertaker had brought in a small organ and a grave woman was playing "Safe in the Arms of Jesus." Three steps inside the door I was stricken with the heavy-sweet, oppressive scent of too many flowers. The living room was banked with them.

An undertaker's assistant with white gloves indicated the register and I signed it. He half bent with delicacy and whispered into my ear, "Would you like to view the remains?"

I whispered, "If it isn't too late. I don't want to hold up the proceedings."

He shook his head and gestured smoothly with a white glove that turned palm-up to indicate I should go on in.

The living room was packed with little folding chairs that were too close together. The bottoms of people hung over the edges, and their knees pressed against the backs of the chairs in front. By turning sideways I could edge through the narrow space against the wall and up to the massive casket.

Lieutenant Richmond, in an oxford grey suit, was managing to look fairly inconspicuous. As I looked down at the man I had killed, I could feel Richmond's eyes on me as plainly as if they had been raw oysters sliding down the back of my neck. I wondered if my expression would be wrong.

Mitch Sothern made a very fine corpse. He was not old enough to be flabby around the jowls. The line of the jaw was firm, the set of the face was aggressive, as always, and the placidly closed lids gave the impression that they might roll back at any moment and reveal one of Mitch's fierce, elec-

- 147

trifying scowls. I reminded myself, with a twinge of revulsion, that he was full of embalming fluid.

So this was Mitch, the son-of-a-bitch. Well, you were hurt worse than Marty after all, weren't you? You got me fired, but who's got a hole in the back of his head? You or me?

I stood looking down at him until I thought I had looked as long as a brother-in-law was expected to look. I raised my eyes and met Richmond's, without flinching. The organ was playing "Asleep in Jesus, Blessed Sleep." Richmond gave me an imperceptible nod and I noticed a chair in the front row. I sat down gravely beside a heavily veiled old lady. She whispered, "You must be Jess London," and pressed my hand. I pressed back gently, and didn't say anything.

The organ tapered off into a succession of tremulous chords and then sighed and quit. The minister appeared from somewhere, gave us a calm, heavy look, and started to talk in low tones about the shape of a pigeon's egg. I looked at him gravely, noted the first few words, and then wandered off on my own train of thought.

Why did Mitch bother to get me fired?

If the equity of redemption was so important, why did he turn it over to me in the first place? Why did he take the file back? Why didn't he redeem the property? Why did he put the check back in the file? All this for no other purpose than to use me as a threat against my sister?

The minister was saying, ". . . stricken down in the fair flower of early manhood, in the very prime of life. But who are we to question the wisdom of the Almighty? Let not your heart be troubled, ye believe in God, believe also in Me . . ."

Now that Friday night's moment of sheet-lightning anger had passed, I could understand, in a way, about Mitch and Marty. Men sometimes stop loving their wives, just as wives sometimes stop loving their husbands. "Till death do us part" sometimes turns out to be a figure of speech, and "for better or for worse" sometimes means "as long as it's better, and the hell with you when it's worse." With divorces accounting for ninety per cent of the suits filed in Circuit Court, a guy would be a fool to pretend otherwise. The sun comes up, the sun goes down, hello, good-bye, so sorry, next case.

But why did Mitch bother to get me fired?

Was it a sort of extra twist he was giving to the knife he was sticking in my sister? A sadistic touch?

". . . In my Father's house are many mansions; if it were not so, I would have told you; for I go to prepare a place for you. And if I go to prepare a place for you, I come again, and will receive you unto myself; that where I am, there ye may be also . . ."

It was too hot. Much too hot. Steam came up inside my clothes and my face felt flushed. The smell of the flowers was sickening . . .

When I glanced up, Richmond was looking at me. I returned his gaze levelly, and fought down the sickness in me.

Would all this never end?

Take him out reverently and lower him, with mechanical devices, until he is below the surface of the ground. Cast flowers upon his casket. Let ashes be returned to ashes and let dust be returned to dust. Cover him over with sod and let the birds twitter in the branches overhead. This once was Mitch Sothern, so help me. These are his mortal remains. Why talk about it? If he wants peace, let him have it. Give it to him, and let's go about our business . . .

It did end, finally. The organ went into "Nearer My God to Thee" and they let us go out, sideways, bumping each other and bumping the little folding chairs which were too close together.

I managed to maneuver out of the living room, and backed up in an eddy in the hall while the main stream stumbled against one another on the way out the front door. Richmond was there. He would be. For a moment we were almost alone.

I said, "Want to feel my pulse?"

He said, "No. Should I?"

"Want a specimen of my saliva?"

He just gave me a look.

"Lie detector test?"

The look was sharper. He said, "Afraid?"

"No."

"It's an idea."

I said, "The patent office is full of ideas."

"Don't turn into a wise guy. You're in trouble enough without borrowing any."

"Thanks for warning me. Will anything I say be used against me?"

"Yes. It will."

"But not *for* me?"

He laughed and said, "Oh, go to hell."

41.

I NOSED my car into the funeral procession, and we went to the cemetery. I watched, with properly folded hands, while they put him down into the earth. The veiled ladies were supported in their grief by persons who seem always available for the purpose, and we went back to our cars and drove away. The traffic lights were working as if nothing had happened, and a garbage truck, careening at a corner, spilt a couple of soiled cabbage leaves on my fender. Somehow it had got to be ten minutes after six.

I parked and went up to my apartment, feeling very lonely and a little abused. There was a gloomy lump of misery in my chest over the way Wiggie and I had parted. I had hurt her feelings, but what else could I have done? I certainly couldn't tell her, or anyone, that I had left my apartment after midnight. If I did that, the next question would be, "Where did you go?"

The next questions after that would be, "What did you do? Who were you with? When did you come back? Who saw you? Who did you see?"

And all of them were questions I couldn't answer. People in stories are always going out and simply walking around, alone, in the middle of the night, not seeing anyone they know, not being seen by anyone they know. Making up a story like that couldn't help me, and it could make the hand of the executioner fiddle with the switch.

If I should ever admit I wasn't at home and in bed all the time, then Joe Herdt's testimony would crucify me. If I stuck by my guns, there might be a chance. While I had been going to night law school I had many times sneaked away from my daytime job, or used a late lunch hour, to sit in courtrooms and listen to trials. I had watched the lawyers and the judge and the jury and the witnesses, trying to memorize the mistakes and the successes, trying to figure out how they happened, and why. The main thing I had learned was that witnesses who depart from the truth, or try to garnish it, are asking for trouble. There seems always to be a catch, somewhere . . . a catch that can be proven in some unanticipated way, by some odd, unpredictable person.

No, it was painfully regrettable that Wiggie had to guess part of the truth and become offended because I wouldn't confide in her, but it was a painful regret that would have to stand. In time, perhaps she would forgive me. My only chance was to adopt a simple, basic, fundamental lie and then cling to that in spite of everything.

The feeling of loneliness increased. I did not want to be by myself. I wanted, desperately, to be with Wiggie. I felt sure I could hold her in my arms and talk the hurt away. If she would forgive me, take me on faith, then this gnawing emptiness might leave me; and if it left, then maybe I could get myself in hand and bluff this thing through to the end.

I went to the telephone and called Wiggie's apartment. There was no answer. I waited ten minutes and tried again. Still no answer.

The chief buyer at Harley & Farnsworth was Thelma Joyce. I found her number and called it.

Someone said, "Hello."

It was Wiggie. I felt happy. I said, "My luck is good. This is Jess. I thought maybe you'd have dinner with me."

Wiggie said in a remote voice, "No."

I said, "Don't keep on being angry, darling. I was telling you the truth. When you get right down to it, I'm the one who ought to be hurt, if it has to be one of us. Don't you think you could trust me, a little?"

She waited a very long time. Then she said, "I'm convinced that part of what you told me is true, and part is a compromise with the truth. Very likely for a reason which you think is sound. If you don't think enough of me—trust me—to let me know all of the truth, so I can share the trouble and the problems—"

"Look, Wiggie, let's don't talk about it on the phone this way. It's so—well, impersonal. Let me come by and take you out to dinner so we can talk. Then if you still feel the same way . . ."

"No, I don't think it'd do any good. . . ."

"Anyway, I have your car. I want to bring that back, of course."

"No, you can park it in front of the Monticello and leave the keys in the mailbox or mail them to me."

She hung up on me. I called back and let the bell ring a dozen times, but there was no answer.

42.

I wENT TO the window and looked out. The street lights were on. There was a pain in me—an ache.

The pain was still in me, only bigger now, and getting worse. I looked out the window some more. The pain was very bad.

All right, so I'm in love with her. What's wrong with that? Whose business is it? Mitch is dead, but I'm alive. That's my good luck and his tough luck. The world is full of prudes, but I'm not one of them. Take today, for whatever it's worth. Yesterday's gone and tomorrow isn't here yet, and when it gets here I may be somewhere else.

I went back to the phone and called Thelma Joyce's apartment again. There was no answer. I let it ring and ring and ring. No answer.

I waited five minutes, walking up and down the room in a sweat. I called again. No answer. Five minutes later I called again. Still no answer.

Was she there, pouting? Or had she gone?

My head began to ache and I went in and washed my face with cold water. My insides were all drawn up tight. A gulp of whiskey and a couple of aspirins were a help, but not much.

At seven-fifteen I got Wiggie's car and drove around to the pile of limestone where Thelma Joyce lived. The elevator took me up and I put my finger on the buzzer and let it stay there. To freeze me out, this was going to have to be a very deep freeze.

Suddenly the door was snatched open and I faced Thelma Joyce, a tall, greying blonde, slick and well-groomed and maybe in her fifties. The noise of the buzzer bounced out at me and I took away my finger. We had met once at a party but she didn't recognize me. She said, "Well?"

Very hostile.

I took off my hat. I said, "Could I see Miss Wiggens?"

"Who're you?"

"My name's Jess London. I'd like to see Wiggie—that is, Miss Wiggens. You're Miss Joyce, aren't you?"

She said, "I guess I am." She snapped it at me. She said, "Miss Wiggens doesn't want to see you—now or at any time. Besides, she isn't here."

She shut the door firmly in my face. I put my finger on the buzzer. The door came open again. Miss Joyce said, "If you do that again, I shall call the police."

I said, "Do that. I love 'em. I see the police every day. I want to see Miss Wiggens."

"She isn't here."

"She was here awhile ago. I want to see her."

"I tell you, she's gone. Now go away."

I put my hand against the door and gave a little push. I said, "Mind if I see for myself?"

Through clenched teeth she said, "Don't you dare!"

Down the hall a door opened and a large man came out and stood watching us with his hands on his hips.

I said, "Friend of yours?"

She wavered, bit her lip, looked down, and then stepped aside and let me in. Her face was crimson.

I said, "You don't like scenes. Shall I go ahead and look?"

She shrugged and sat down and lit a cigaret. It took me thirty seconds to satisfy myself that Wiggie wasn't there. I sat down and helped myself to one of her cigarets. I said, "I beg your pardon, will you forgive me? I'm in love with her and I'm not thinking very straight."

She said, "Don't tell me about it. I'm not interested. Please leave now."

"Did she tell you about me?"

Silence.

"Did she?"

She gave me a long, grim look. She said, "Wiggie is very deeply hurt. She wanted to help you, but she says you're holding the facts to yourself. That means you don't trust her, so she signed off."

I sat there for a long time. Then I said, "Miss Joyce, I'm a louse. I didn't lie to Wiggie or hold back the truth. But if I hurt her—gave her the impression of not trusting her—I'm sorry."

She crushed out her cigaret viciously, picked up another, and rolled it in her fingers. I held a match.

I said, "I'm in with her. I think you know it and believe it. Could I be this big a fool and not be in love?"

I thought there was a softening of the lines around her mouth. I said, "People have been calling love a funny thing for a long time, but I'm just now finding it out. It makes you listen to things you know aren't true, and makes you believe them just because they hurt. It makes you say things you don't mean, and then won't let you take them back. It takes away the power of forgiveness. It makes you hurt people only for the delicious sort of pain you get out of it yourself. Does she love me?"

She looked at the end of her cigaret.

I said, "We've known each other casually for some time. These last two days we've been pretty close. I know that's an awfully short time, but you've no idea all the things can happen in forty-eight hours. Maybe she told you. I haven't done a thing, but I'm in trouble with the police. Bad trouble." I put my hand under my chin and said, "About up to here."

She wouldn't look at me. There was no telling what she was thinking. I said, "How would you like to be in trouble and in love, all at the same time?"

I said, "Tell Wiggie something for me. Tell her I love her with all my heart. Tell her she doesn't have to love me, I'll love her anyway. Tell her I know I'm a louse, but I love her. Tell her if she never speaks to me again I'll still love her."

I found my hat and went out and shut the door behind me.

43.

THERE WAS a parking space under the trees in front of the Monticello Apartments. The car went into it mathematically, beautifully. A truck driver couldn't have done a better job. Too bad there was no one around to admire me. . . .

The buzzer in Wiggie's apartment had a peculiar sound. I put my ear against the door and tried again. Don't think I'm silly. It was not the sound of an apartment with no one in it. It was the sound of an apartment *unoccupied*. It was a very lonely sound. It said *Don't ring any more, it's no use. Nobody's here and nobody's going to be here for awhile. Come back later —much later—or not at all. Don't you see there's no use ringing anymore?*

I went downstairs and around the side and found the back stairs. Two floors up, I saw what I thought I'd see. The buzzer was right. A note in the milk bottle said, "No more milk until further notice. Apartment 3-C."

The top step was very hard, but there was no other place to sit. I leaned against the bannisters and smoked a cigaret. The pain was bad, and now it was mixed with a nameless, formless fear. It would be hard to banter with Richmond, next time he turned up.

Where would Wiggie go?

I didn't know.

Who was she?

'Did she have a family? Where?

And if I knew, what then? Very deeply hurt, Miss Joyce had said. How deeply?

Deeply enough.

Hell hath no fury. . . .

Remember also thy Creator in the days of thy youth, before the evil days come, and the years draw nigh, when thou shalt say, I have no pleasure in them; before the sun, and the light, and the moon, and the stars, are darkened, and the clouds return after the rain; in the day when the keepers of the house shall tremble, and the strong men shall bow themselves, and the grinders shall cease because they are few, and those that look out of the windows shall be darkened, and the doors shall be shut in the street; when the sound of the grinding is low, and one shall rise up at the voice of a bird, and all the daughters of music shall be brought low; yea, they shall be afraid of that which is high, and terrors shall be in the way; and the almond-tree shall blossom, and the grasshopper shall be a burden, and desire shall fail; because man goeth to his long home, and the mourners go about the streets. . . .

44.

I AM A MOURNER and I am about to go about the streets. Loose the silver cord, go ahead and loose it. Break the golden bowl. Break the pitcher at the fountain. Break the wheel at the cistern. Return the dust to the earth as it was. Return the spirit unto God who gave it.

The cigaret burned my fingers and I jumped and it fell into the cuff of my trousers. I turned the cuff out frantically, and beat out the sparks and stepped on the glowing butt.

No matter how you feel, you still want to live.

In a dark, remote corridor, under a bulb that must have been less than five watts, a sign on a door said, "Manager."

I knocked.

A voice said, "Yes, please?"

I said, "Please."

The door opened two and a half inches, on a chain. The voice said, "What was it?"

"I want to talk to the manager."

"That's her you're talking to."

"It's about Miss Wiggens. Has she moved out?"

There was a pause. She said, "Three-C, that is?"

I said yes it was three-C.

"Moving out, no. Leaving for awhile, yes."

"How long?"

"I should know?"

"Where's she gone? Can you tell me that?"

She said, plaintively, "Please. I should know?"

I said, "Thanks. Sorry to have bothered you."

She closed the door.

So that was that.

45.

ONE THING was for sure. I couldn't go on driving Wiggie's car. It was a point of honor. If you're mad at me, your car's mad at me, too. If I'm a louse, I'll not drive your car. I'll not sit where you usually sit. I'll not hold the wheel you usually hold.

This is your clutch, I shall not use it. This is your brake, I shall not step on it.

Your cylinders shall not be my cylinders. Your God shall not be my God.

I'm not mad at you, you're mad at me. Meanwhile, my air shall not come through your carburetor, my electricity shall not come from your generator.

I locked the car, forcefully and permanently, and walked home. It seemed extremely logical, inevitable. That's what being in love will do to you.

Find an envelope. Address it. Wrap the keys carefully, and seal it with finality. Go down to the desk and have it meticulously weighed. No postage-due on this one. Hell no. Paid in advance.

Now, are you satisfied? Take your car. See if I care.

46.

AT NINE-THIRTY I remembered my date with Richmond at the hospital. I sat up in my dark room with the sweat on me again. I should have made arrangements. Now I was in a hell of a fix.

I went to the telephone and picked it up and then put it down again. Who did I know, about my size?

George Stern. Who else?

Hayden Grove. No, he's a blonde. Too short, anyway.

Stoakes Fant. Too old.

Who the hell else did I know?

Think.

All right, George Stern. One's better than none.

I dialed his number and waited. He said, "Hello."

I said, "Hello, George?"

He said, "Okay."

"This is Jess."

"Okay."

"Busy?"

"No."

"How about doing me a favor?"

"You mean down at the hospital?"

I hesitated. "How did you know?"

"Wiggie called me."

I said, "Oh."

He said, "It's all fixed. Forget it. It's in the bag."

I waited, thinking. Then I said, "That's fine. Thanks a lot. See you there." I hung up.

What's fixed? What's in the bag?

47.

So IF SHE called George Stern, she must have called other people, too. Whatever was in the bag, was in the bag.

It was all arranged. My life or my death, spinach or baked ham, salmon croquettes or rhubarb pie.

I called the desk. Charley Pitts answered.

I said, "What're you doing on duty at this hour?"

He said, "Beg pardon?"

I said, "This is Jess."

"Oh. Hello, Jess."

I said, "What the hell are you doing on duty before ten?"

He said, "Aw, I'm kindhearted. The guy had a date, you know how it is. We trade around."

"I'm low on whiskey. You aren't out of it, are you?"

"Not so's you could notice."

"Okay if I come down for some?"

"I'm not hoarding it."

"I'll be right down."

I walked, because it was less trouble. Cornelius Vanderbilt was off duty at this hour and there was no use putting Charley to a lot of trouble. I was going to need Charley.

He was in a cane-bottom chair, tilted against the wall as usual. He was reading the inevitable magazine. When I appeared in the lobby he marked his place with a stubby thumb and said, "Pint or fifth?"

I said, "Fifth, I guess. Saves time."

He said, "Help yourself."

I went into the little room behind the counter, opened the cupboard, and selected a fifth of Yellowstone. Holding it by the neck I went out and put the right amount into Charley's shirt pocket, stuffing it down with my finger. He was embarrassed with me, and didn't raise his eyes.

I said, "I'm going out in a few minutes. Why don't I put in a call now, for in the morning?"

He said, "Go ahead, the book's right there."

The book was on the first shelf under the counter, a grey-backed account book with "Journal" printed on the cover in big black letters. I said, "Any trick to it?"

He said, "How many tricks could we play on each other? We write 'em on the left page in the order they come in. Then I put 'em on the right page in the order they go. That's as complicated as we can take it."

I flipped the pages until I found a place with the right date at the top. There were four calls on the left-hand page. The right-hand page was blank. I looked to see how the other entries were made, and then wrote "332—seven."

It was a simple matter to turn back two days. Friday night's page showed the call I placed when I came in at midnight. There were two or three calls entered after mine.

I said, "It's all fixed. In case I don't see you as I go out, good night."

Without looking up he gave me a gesture with his hand and said, "Good night."

48.

THE GLOBE over the door of the City Hospital was still like cloudy milk and black bugs were still buzzing it. One month or the next, one year or the next, I guess the bugs go on doing the same thing. I guess if I were a bug I'd do it, too. Maybe being a bug is no bed of roses, at that.

George Stern was a few steps ahead of me and I didn't speak to him. I followed him and stood outside the door, watching him through the fingerprinted glass. He went across the marble floor and leaned across the counter and spoke to the woman under the lamp that cast a cone of light downward. Whatever they said, I couldn't hear it. George nodded and went to a corner and sat in a cold chair among the cold statues.

I waited until some other people came up the steps, and went in behind them. When they walked to the left, I walked to the right and sat in another cold chair. After a moment I went over and spoke to George. Richmond came in, saw us, and came over. We walked down a hall until Richmond opened a door. George said, "Mr. Olney, Mr. Spencer, this is Jess London. This is Lieutenant Richmond, I guess you know him. The rest are his Joes. I guess you can introduce them, Lieutenant."

I said, "Hello" and "Hello" and "Hello" and "Hello."

Everybody said the same thing. We shook hands.

Lieutenant Richmond looked at his wrist watch and said, "Well, I guess everybody's here."

It looked as if someone ought to say something, so I said, "I guess so."

He said, "What do you call the head nurse, Mother Superior?"

My silly brain thought, "Mother Superior, Mother Huron, Mother Michigan, Mother Erie, Mother Ontario."

There was a telephone on the desk. Richmond picked up the receiver and said something into it. We waited.

After awhile a woman came in. She closed the door and stood with her back against it. She was nervous. So was I.

Richmond said, "I think you know why we're here. Someone came in Friday night and asked for Mrs. Mitchell Sothern. It was not necessarily one of us in this room. All we want to know is this, do you recognize one of us as being that person?"

She looked at each of us in turn, briefly. Then her eyes came back to me and lingered. My heart was beating very fast, but I looked back at her steadily and wouldn't let my eyes drop. She spent an extra long time on George Stern, too.

There was a handkerchief in her hand and she started twisting it. She looked at me again and then turned to Richmond. She said, "You put me in a very difficult position. So many people come in. How could I know it was important?"

Richmond said, "Of course. If none of us brings up a memory, no one will blame you. But it's something we have to try, just the same."

She said, "The light, you know. It isn't very good. It's shaded."

Richmond didn't say anything.

She said, "How can I be sure anything happened on Friday night. What if it was some other night? Should I say anything if I'm not sure?"

There was a glint of excitement in Richmond's eyes. He

said carefully, not looking at me, "We want whatever reactions you have and we'll make allowances for uncertainty. What you say may have a negative value, you know. If you point out someone who couldn't have been here, perhaps we wouldn't pursue the point any farther. On the other hand, to point out someone who stirs a memory isn't to be taken as an accusation. It would be considered with other evidence, for whatever it's worth."

She said, "It would be so awful to be mistaken."

Richmond didn't say anything.

She looked around almost desperately and then seemed to come to a decision and grew noticeably pale. She put her hand to her throat and said in a voice we could barely hear, "Two of these faces mean something, but I couldn't swear about Friday night. That's the best I can do. I'm sorry."

Richmond was disappointed and a little annoyed, but he kept it out of his voice. He said, "Who?"

She pointed to George Stern and then to me, and suddenly sat down on the edge of a straight-backed chair and put her face in her hands. She was trembling. She said, "I'm afraid I'm upset. Could you ask them to let me have some ammonia in a little water?"

Richmond moved his hand and one of the policemen went out swiftly. My hands were trying to shake so I put them in the pockets of my coat. My collar was too tight. Richmond, watching me narrowly, offered a cigaret. I shook my head and turned to the window. My mouth was dry.

Richmond said to Stern, "When were you here?"

George said coolly, "Is that a fair question, Lieutenant? I mean in the presence of a confused witness?"

Richmond flushed.

The woman said, "I feel a little better now. There's a rest room down the hall. May I go?"

Richmond offered his arm and she went out with him, a little unsteadily. In a moment he was back. George didn't wait for him to repeat his question. He said, "Sorry, Lieutenant. It just didn't seem sporting. She gave it an honest try but it was inconclusive, to say the least. A discussion in her presence might clarify things, or it might distort them. You wouldn't want that to happen, would you?"

Richmond said shortly, "Of course not. I shouldn't have asked the question under the circumstances, but I can ask it now. When were you here?"

Stern took his time. He got out a package of cigarets, struck a match, and inhaled deeply. He said, "Really, Lieutenant, I'm sure I never saw her before this evening."

"You mean before she came into this room?"

Stern hesitated. "No, I didn't say that. I said before this evening. I got here a little early. She was at the desk, taking over the switchboard, I believe. You weren't around, so I asked for Mrs. Sothern. Thought I'd pay my respects. Wasn't that all right?"

Richmond was furious. He said, "Who put you up to that? Of all the goddam things!"

Stern frowned and took his cigaret out of his mouth. He said, "What do you mean by that?"

Richmond set his lips in a firm line and then shrugged his shoulders in disgust. He said, sarcastically, "You didn't know, I suppose, that we were going to test her memory. You merely introduced yourself casually, to the right person, and just happened to ask the only perfect question. You had no idea it might cause uncertainty and confusion."

It was George's turn to shrug. He said, standing his ground, "Miss Wiggens called and asked if I'd come down. She said you and Jess and some other people would be here, and you'd explain. If you don't want people to ask questions at the information desk, why don't you put up a sign?"

Richmond stared at him and then wiped his face with his handkerchief and sighed and said wearily, "All right, I apologize. She got here a little early and I guess I was a little late. I guess it was just a damnable coincidence. I ought to turn in my badge."

I was fairly calm, by then. I said, "Too bad, Lieutenant."

He said, "Don't forget, she picked you."

I said, "That's right. Do you think a jury will convict me of murder on her testimony?"

"Maybe not. It's cumulative, one more thing to explain. Do you think you can explain them all?"

I said, "Can you?"

He raised his eyebrows. "I'm sleeping good at night. My digestion's fine. If I were you, I'd be worried."

"I'm not worried, Lieutenant."

"Maybe you should be."

George said, "It's Sunday, or I'd offer to buy a drink. By the way, Jess, I guess you know Steve Spencer."

I shook hands and said, "Sure. Long time no see. Thanks for coming down. How would a beer sit at a time like this?"

Steve said, "No trouble, glad to do it. A beer sounds swell."

I said, "Lieutenant?"

Richmond said, "No, thanks."

George said, "I'll match you."

I said, "Nonsense. Let's get going."

49.

BEER IS SOMETIMES good for the jitters; beer and people to talk to. I don't know how many we had. The place was full and the juke-box always had nickels in it and there was a crowd around each of the pinball machines.

Steve Spencer was a lot nicer guy than I remembered. The third beer got under his tongue and from then on he gave us an endless prattle, without conceit and without guile, relaxed and amusing, and with most of the laughs at his own expense. George Stern is strictly from no imagination, but even George found an occasional thing to say. Toward one o'clock he began to show a tendency to put his hands on the waitresses, and I thought that was enough.

I said, "Sorry, boys. All you have to do is work. For me, I'm a man of leisure and I can't afford these hours of dissipation. My idleness starts at an early hour tomorrow, and I have to be in shape."

"Work," said Steve, "is an expensive luxury. In order to afford it, I often have to sacrifice the bare necessities of life. If there's any money in my coat pocket, take it, will you? I gotta go to the johnny."

His coat was on the back of his chair. When he had gone I said, "Keep your hand in your pocket. The check's mine."

George said, "Split it three ways. Anyway, two. Don't be an ass."

I said, "This is my party."

George removed his glasses and polished them. He said, "Don't be a fool. Pretty soon, what're you going to use for money?"

I said, "Coupons. I got a million of 'em."

George said, "In that case, of course . . ."

So I paid the check.

50.

THE PHONE was ringing when I entered the apartment. I needed
to go to the bathroom but I took a grip on myself, a half nelson,
and answered it.

Stoakes Fant said, "I bet I got you out of bed."

"No, I was coming in the door."

"Sorry to call at this hour."

"It's okay. No trouble."

"About tomorrow morning. You won't forget?"

Forget what? Oh, yes.

I said, "Nine o'clock. No. I won't forget."

Where? Oh, hell, where?

He said, "That's right. Second National."

I said, "On the dot. I'll be there."

I put down the phone and went over and wrote on the
back of an envelope. "Nine o'clock—First National." I looked
at it hazily and then crossed out "First" and wrote "Second."
Jeest, it was a good thing he called.

I went to the bathroom and then took the cork out of the
bottle of Yellowstone. I turned out all the lights and went
to the window and raised it. There was a stir of air and it felt
good. The beer had made me warm and my face was dis-
agreeably sticky. I went back into the bathroom and washed
my face with cold water. When I came back I turned up the
bottle and took three gurgles out of it. Some of the whiskey
ran down my chin and I wiped it off with the back of my
hand. I had a succession of shudders. My mouth tasted bad.

I fumbled with the cork, dropped it, felt for it, found
it, put it firmly in the bottle. I put the bottle on the floor.
I backed up, felt the bed against my knees, and sat down
heavily. I lay back with my arms stretched out over my head.

I'd go in and brush my teeth, and then I'd undress and go to bed. . . .

The next thing I knew was when the phone rang at seven o'clock.

51.

I WAS AT THE Second National Bank at nine in the morning. I knew there were big, red veins in the whites of my eyes, but no one could say I wasn't there. The body was present, with two cups of scalding coffee doing their best for me.

Stoakes Fant did not stare at my eyeballs. He was a nice Joe. He introduced me to the representative of the State Revenue Department, who was Steve Spencer.

Steve and I shook hands and said hello. He had red veins in his eyeballs, too, but not as big as mine. Evidently there had been no bottle of Bourbon waiting for him when he got home. We went down the stairs to the vault in single file, Steve ahead of me and holding to the rail. Me too.

Fant produced a key to Mitch's safe-deposit box and we solemnly watched while the attendant produced a matching key and drew the steel drawer from the steel bowels of the bank. We fell into line again—first the attendant with the sacred commercial remains of Mitch Sothern, then Fant, then Steve Spencer, and then me. We went through the corridors and into a little room with a table.

Stoakes Fant was disgustingly normal. You could see he had been to a show with the family, slept soundly, and filled his belly with a solid breakfast. His face had a healthy glow and there were no swollen veins in his eyes. He said, "We shouldn't expect to find much, you know. He was leaving town."

He had a yellow pad in front of him. All right, let him write it all down. Damned if I would.

Steve was strictly business, as much as he could be. He took things out of the box, jotted down notes, and handed them to Fant. Fant was gusty and cheerful, wrote things down, and passed things on to me. I put them in a pile in front of me. I didn't jot anything down.

"Life insurance policy," said Steve, noting name and number and amount. He passed it to Fant.

"Check," said Fant. "Life insurance policy." He noted name and number and amount. He passed it to me.

I said, "Check." I didn't write anything down. I put it in front of me.

"Deed," said Steve. "Property known as 1918 Cedar Avenue. Joint, with survivorship."

"Check," said Fant.

I took it and said, "Check."

"Envelope," said Steve. "This seems to be the will. Mind making me a copy?"

Fant said, "I think there are copies at the office. Looks like the one I drew for him right after the marriage. He kept talking about changing it, but I guess he never did." He passed it on to me. I unfolded the will and glanced at it briefly. It was short and simple. Everything went to Marty. That was a relief.

I said, "Will. Check." I put the will on the pile in front of me.

The envelope had once contained papers that made it bulge, but now it was empty. A line showed where a rubber band had once been around it. It was empty, but it still bulged, and when you pinched it, the air went out and said sqoosh.

Steve put his finger nails noisily around the inside of the box to indicate there was nothing else. He held it upside down, to be sure. Nothing fell out. He handed the empty box to the attendant and said, "Okay, that's it."

"Well," said Fant, "I guess that's all."

I said, "I guess it is."

We stood up and I handed the policy and the deed to Fant. I didn't see a wastebasket, so I folded the empty envelope and put it in the side pocket of my coat.

We shook hands all around. Fant took out his watch, made an apology, and went away quickly. He didn't know what to say to me, and I didn't know what to say to him. The attendant disappeared. That left Steve and me.

He said, "Join me in an aspirin or two?"

I said, "Where have you been all my life?"

52.

WE WENT INTO the drugstore near where my office used to be—the same one I was in with Wiggie . . . Good Lord! only two days ago. Steve stopped at the cashier's desk and bought one of those little flat cans of twelve aspirin tablets and then joined me in a booth. I took two and he took two. He said, "When I own an aspirin mine, I'm going to jack up the price. Think of all the people you could blackmail on Monday morning."

I said, "You could sell 'em by the carat, like the crown jewels."

A waitress flounced up with two glasses of water. She had had a nice weekend with a little sunburn and she was feeling good. The muslin bow on the back of her apron hadn't wilted yet. When she smiled, there was a great shining of white teeth.

I said, "Coke, with lemon."

Steve said, "Coke, with about five drops of ammonia."

The waitress went away briskly. Steve watched her. He said, "Isn't youth amazing?"

I said, "Remember, it's early in the morning."

"Yeah, I know. Give her a few hours. Luncheon-sag sets in about two. *A lettuce sandwich on thin slices, and just the barest little bit of mayonnaise. Not too much. And weak tea. Hot, you understand, but not too strong.*"

Before I could say anything, he looked at his watch. He said, "George comes in about this time."

I shook my head. "Not this morning. He's got a case in quarterly court. Big automobile accident, thirty-five cents damage. That's the way lawyers waste their best years. Either that or studying up a storm on a case somebody else will handle."

He said, "His case was supposed to be at nine. It's nearly ten."

I said, "Silly boy. Everything's scheduled at nine. He'll be lucky to get to trial at three-thirty, and then his witnesses will be gone."

But surprisingly enough, George Stern came in before we were half through our Cokes. He caught Steve's wave, nodded, and came back and slid into our booth. He held his head in his hands.

I said, "How'd it go?"

He said, "What a life! If we could only do without witnesses."

The waitress came up, bouncing. Her white teeth came out of her head in a big smile. She took George's simple little order with an air of pleasure and triumph and hurried away.

Steve looked after her sadly and wagged his head. He said, "She thinks she'll wind up running the jernt, but she won't.

The older ones are smarter. They come to work all beat up and bitter to begin with. That way, you avoid the letdown."

I said to George, "You mean the J. T. Pharis Steel Company isn't going to get its fender paid for?"

George said, "You and your Mrs. Worthington McGillicuddy, or whatever her name is. She's a daisy."

"Bad witness?"

"Look," said George. "Saturday we go over the whole thing together. Everything's straight and everything's fine. We're going this way and they're going that way. Get it? We're hardly moving, they're speeding like nobody's business. We give a signal, they don't. We get to the intersection first, they come busting through. It's open and shut. We're a cinch."

I said, "And then what?"

George said, "Lucky it's a small case, or I'd beat my brains out. This watchamacallem witness of yours takes the stand. She's been to a lot of movies, see? All dressed up. It's her day in court, star witness and all that sort of thing. No lawyer is going to tie *her* up in knots. No sirree."

I said, "I get it. I'm away ahead of you."

George said, "You don't know the half of it. She tells it fine. Everything down to the inch. How many miles per hour, how many feet away, you never heard anything like it. Too good, but anyway, she got it out." He hit himself on the forehead with the flat of his hand. "If only she could have dropped dead, right then."

I said, "Go ahead."

"Okay," said George, "Okay. It's the other guy's turn. Frank Hathaway, know him? Must be sixty. So he starts in on her. She does all right until pretty soon he asks her which one was the red truck. Right away I can tell she doesn't remember, see? It's eight months ago, she doesn't remember. I can see what's coming and I sweat straight through my underwear, but what can you do? The judge says sit down, you got to sit down. Inside me I scream she should just say she doesn't know. But will she do that? Moses in the bullrushes! She's got to guess!"

He stopped and spread his hands helplessly. He said, "If you got to guess between two things, half the time you could be right. Even if you weren't there, averages will do it. What did she do?"

I said, "She guesses wrong."

George threw up his hands. "Judgment for the plaintiff. Without a witness, we would have won, hands down."

"Well," I said mildly, "maybe next time she'll guess right."

All I got for that was a dirty look.

53.

PRETTY SOON George had to go to the office. Even if you lost a case, if you had an office you could go there. If you didn't have anything to do you could talk to somebody, or read something in the library. Or even go down and shoot a pinball game, just as long as you had a base to operate out of.

Then Steve had to go. Somebody's safe-deposit box was going to be opened at eleven, and he had to be there.

For me, nobody's nothing was going to be opened nowhere, and I didn't have to be there anyway. You could sit in a drugstore, not waiting for anyone, maybe thirty seconds. Then you had to get moving. When you're a stranger in a town, you can't loaf on the street corner. You don't belong.

I walked to my apartment house. I walked the longest way you could walk. I still got there too soon. The air was stale so I opened all the windows. It was a bad place. I wasn't used to being home at eleven in the morning. The place seemed *uneasy*.

I found an old *Reader's Digest* and pulled a chair to the window and put my feet on the sill and tried to read. Pretty soon I put the magazine face down on my knees and just looked out of the window at the clouds. The backs of my knees began to ache, so I put my feet on the floor. Then I put them up on the sill again.

I went to the phone and called Harley & Farnsworth and asked for Miss Joyce. I said, "This is Jess London. Please don't hang up on me."

She said, "All right, but I'm busy. What is it?"

"Wiggie's gone away. I guess you knew."

"Yes, I knew."

"Would you tell me where? Please?"

"No. I'm sorry. I promised I wouldn't."

"Is the promise that important?"

"I'm afraid it is."

"More important than me? I mean—oh well."

"Sorry. I'm wanted on long distance now. Good-bye."

I said, glumly, "Good-bye."

I took off my coat and vest and lay back across the bed. Then I got up and found my bank book and looked at the balance. One hundred sixty dollars. The rent was paid for April. That was good. By the first of May I had better find another place. Maybe a boardinghouse.

No more reaching for beer checks. That was out.

I went through my pockets and found sixteen dollars and seventy-eight cents. I also found the empty envelope that came out of Mitch's box at the Second National Bank.

On the front of it someone had written "T.R.C." in pencil. The jerky, vicious motions reminded me of Mitch Sothern. I kept looking. No ideas came to me. I guess I dozed . . .

54.

THE BUZZER brought me up with a jerk at noon.

Richmond was at the door. I stepped aside and asked him in. He was nervous and irritable.

He said, "You weren't at the inquest."

I said, "I'm sorry, I forgot all about it."

"Miss Wiggens wasn't there, either."

"No. She's gone."

"Fine thing. You said you'd be there. Made me look like a fool. No subpoenas."

I said, "Sorry."

He said, "You'll be sorry, all right. Guess what happened."

I waited.

He said, "The Coroner's jury found it was intentional homicide at the hands of Jesse London."

I said, "What's next?"

"Well, you're under arrest, as a starter. The Grand Jury's in session now. The Commonwealth's Attorney will present the case this afternoon. If there's an indictment, you'll be arraigned tomorrow morning."

"I'll waive arraignment. I'll ask for trial immediately. The sooner the better."

"You'd better start out by getting a lawyer."

I said, "I'm a lawyer myself."

"Isn't there an old saying . . . ?"

"Yes, there's an old saying, that a lawyer who represents himself has a fool for a client. I guess I ought to hire Clarence Darrow. How much would I have left over out of a hundred and seventy-six bucks? That's after allowing myself sixty-eight cents for lunch. Wait a minute. If I'm under arrest, do I eat lunch on the Commonwealth?"

Richmond sat down in the most comfortable chair in the place. There was a frown on his face. Presently he said, "Listen, Jess. Take off a minute and forget I'm a policeman, will you? Somebody ought to talk to you straight, and if I don't, maybe no one will."

I said, "Yes, uncle."

That annoyed him. He said, "I think you're probably a nice boy, Jess. You could grow up to be a fine man. I mean it. If you live that long. But you'd better put your feet down on some solid ground, and pretty damn soon, too. You'd better take that smirk off your face and wipe the wisecracks out of your mouth. You're in trouble, and laughing won't get you out of it." He pointed at the whiskey bottle. "Neither will that."

I said, "The difference between us is you think I killed Mitch Sothern. I know I didn't. I don't think I'm going to be convicted for something I didn't do. Look, Lieutenant. Why would I want to do anything to him? What reason are you going to give the jury? He was good to me. He got me my job."

"Have you got it now?"

I said, "So you've dug that up, too? That's pretty thin, isn't it? Am I going to kill somebody Friday night for something that came as a complete surprise on Saturday morning? Or did you bother to get all the details?"

Richmond said grimly, "I dug up the details, all right. Maybe you ought to think about them. Sothern gave you a responsible job to do—very responsible, but very simple. All you had to do was walk over to the courthouse. But you got excited playing a pinball machine and forgot all about it. I gather Mr. Sothern was a tough customer when he was angry."

So even the people at the office were telling on me. Well, what should I have expected? Mitch had been the office dynamo, of many years' standing. I was a cub—practically a stranger. Why should they cover up for me?

I said, "That's their version of it. It doesn't happen to be true. Maybe people won't believe me, but I'm going to tell what actually did happen. Because it happens to be the absolute truth, I'm just childish enough to think a jury will believe it."

"That's the trouble. Suppose they believe it, have you thought about that? Call it the absolute truth, and see where it gets you. I know your version, too. Sothern gave you this check to redeem some property. He went out of his way to impress on you the importance of taking it to the clerk's office before five o'clock. According to your story, he changed his mind, took back the check, and said he'd do it himself. For some reason, the job isn't done. Nobody saw him take back the check. No one knew he had it. The check goes back into the file. Now, who's going to get the blame if Sothern calls you on the carpet? Are people going to believe you or him? How long is your job going to last under the circumstances? And how easy will it be to get another one?"

"But why would he do that?"

"Exactly. Why? It's your own story, and you're stuck with it, or else you're going to have to admit you lied, and won't that be a big help? Suppose they do believe you. Don't you see? Either he framed you, or he was merely careless, but in either case it was fixed for you to take the blame. That's going to sound like reason enough. It makes pretty good sense. Somehow you find out about it. You go back to the house after everyone else has left. You finally understand the spot he put you on. In a moment of anger—wham! How does that sound?"

It didn't sound very good. It sounded like hell. In a curiously exact way, it accounted for everything except the real reason I hit Mitch Sothern on the back of the head. And disclosing the real reason wouldn't improve things, either.

One thing kept bothering me. Why would Mitch go to all that trouble just to get me fired? I couldn't figure it.

I said, "Why're you telling me all this?"

Richmond came over and put a hand on my shoulder. He said, "You're so pathetically young and cocky. Nobody has ever slapped you down or kicked you in the shins. My job's finished when I fill up the file and hand it over to the Commonwealth's attorney. Nobody pays me to have opinions. I don't know whether you're guilty or innocent—all I know is what people say. It adds up to a lot. Maybe you were home in bed, like you say. A hell of a lot of difference that's going to make if some high-powered explaining isn't done."

He waited a long time and let that soak in. Then he said, "Get yourself the smartest lawyer in the business, even if you have to hock your future to do it. Ask the Court to appoint somebody if you can't raise the price. Then get into a room and shut the door and tell him everything. Maybe your best bet is to plead sudden anger and see if they'll call it voluntary manslaughter. You might even get off with a suspended sentence if it's put up to the Commonwealth's attorney in the right way—by someone who knows how. Maybe self-defense. Get some advice. Do something. Haven't you got some people somewhere? Get on the phone over there and call 'em. They've got a right to know you're in trouble and they've a right to be with you and help."

I said, "I'm not going to plead sudden anger and I'm not going to plead self-defense. I'm going to plead I was home in bed because it's the truth. Put on all your witnesses, Lieutenant. I don't believe they can take me out of bed and put me somewhere else. I know most of your witnesses, and I don't believe they're lying. Somehow everything is just screwed up, that's all. One way or another, it'll all come apart of its own accord. It's got to."

He raised his arms and let them fall to his sides. He sighed and shook his head. "The little knight, all in shining armor," he said in a tired voice. "Don himself, jousting with the windmills."

I said, "Thanks, just the same. When it's all over, we'll go to a ball game together. Will you?"

"Look," he said. "One more try. The batter hits a slow

roller to the shortstop. He beats the throw to first base. That makes him safe, doesn't it? Now what happens if the umpire says he's out? Which is he, Jess, safe or out?"

"Out."

"But he beat the throw. We just said so."

"He's still out. The umpire said so."

"How much satisfaction does he get out of knowing he was safe?"

I said, "Still no soap. Thanks for trying. I'll have to do it my way."

"Well, in that case, get your toothbrush. They're waiting to book you, down at headquarters. On the way, we'll stop and get a bite to eat. You wouldn't have much appetite for what we have to offer you inside."

I grinned with my face muscles and said, "Not only that, but it's easier on the budget."

Richmond said, "I hope you're still cracking wise when the trial's over."

55.

THE EARLY afternoon edition of the paper was out. A block away there was a stack of them in front of a spaghetti joint, weighted down with a brick. My face was there, under a black headline. Not the best picture that was ever taken of me, but enough of a likeness for everyone I knew to recognize. I put the nickel beside the brick, slipped a paper out of the stack, and folded it under my arm.

Richmond shouldered me into the door of the spaghetti joint and to a table near the narrow door that said "Men." I chose to sit with my back to the room. He sat opposite me. He ordered spaghetti and beer. I ordered ravioli and milk, not looking up while the waiter was at the table. The back of my neck was burning. I felt as if everyone in the world were looking at me.

Richmond said, "Ever eat here?"

I shook my head and then said, "Once. A long time ago."

"Lot of your friends eat here?"

I said I didn't know.

He said, "Then quit carrying the chip on your shoulder. Hold your chin up. When the waiter comes, look at him. He won't know you from Adam. Suppose Al Capone pulled up the chair right next to you and asked for the mustard. You'd just hand him the mustard."

I guess I must have winced.

He said, apologetically, "Al Capone was only for an illustration. I might just as well have said Lindbergh or Gracie Allen."

It didn't really make any difference. The starch wasn't in me anymore, nor the volts, or whatever you call it. I couldn't think of anything smart to say. The muscles wouldn't make a grin.

His spaghetti seemed to be good, considering the way he ate it. The beer, too. It didn't appeal to me, but you could tell he thought it was fine. I picked around at the ravioli, knowing I ought to eat, not understanding why I couldn't. The milk went down under the drive of will power alone. It kept catching in my throat.

We walked down to police headquarters, coming up through the alley and entering by the side door. The reporters and photographers were there. I was the story of the day.

My impulse was to hang back, to turn away, to hold my hands up over my face. Out of the side of his mouth, Richmond said, "Take it easy." Somehow it gave me back some of my balance. A few hours ago I would have met these people without self-consciousness, even cheerfully. One picture and one headline couldn't destroy me. But now there was definitely no eagerness to laugh.

I said, "Well, I'm here. I wasn't going anywhere. They didn't have to get out a three-state alarm."

Richmond's look had some respect in it. I felt better.

Thurston Galloway of the AP came over. "Any objection to pix?"

"No, if you'll give a break. Anything you want, within reason, but no gags. Is it a deal?"

He looked around at the rest and said, "Sure."

I said, "No cheesecake."

That got a nervous sort of laugh out of them. Nervous for me, not for themselves. The atmosphere was friendly; they were pulling for me. They were half afraid I'd do or say something idiotic. If I did, they'd take a picture of it and write it down, but they'd go out with an uneasy feeling of shame. Anyway, that's the impression they gave me and it kept my lips from quivering.

One of them asked if I wanted to make a statement. I said no, maybe later, unless just to say I didn't know what it was all about. They asked if I had known about the inquest and why I wasn't there. I told them about being down at the bank, and then that I plain forgot about the inquest. Richmond had told me to be there, but I didn't realize I was even a witness. I just forgot about it.

If I had been there, would I have had anything to contribute? I didn't know. I hadn't read the paper, so I didn't know what had gone on. I didn't have anything to contribute, as far as I knew. I guessed under the circumstances I'd be entitled to a transcript of the evidence. After I'd seen it, I'd know better. Was there anything else?

Yes, I had heard the Commonwealth's attorney would go before the Grand Jury this afternoon. I didn't know whether they'd indict or not. I didn't know what the evidence was. If there was an indictment, I'd waive arraignment and ask for a quick trial. As far as I was concerned, the quicker the better. I had nothing to be afraid of. No, I hadn't employed counsel. I didn't see any reason to need a lawyer. I didn't even have anyone in mind. I didn't know whether I'd represent myself. I might. There was no reason to decide anything. I'd wait and see. Yes, if I had a statement to make later, I'd let them know.

I was docile with the photographers, too. Richmond and I let them snap us walking up the steps together. We did that twice, an extra time for the guy whose flash bulb didn't go off. They took me getting fingerprinted. They took some close-ups. Someone suggested a shot through the bars but the suggestion wasn't repeated and another guy changed the subject. They were a pretty decent lot. I don't know how much more I could have taken. The strings were stretched pretty tight.

They couldn't make the home editions, but they had time to catch the five-star finals and they went off to file their stories, leaving only the men who ordinarily covered the City Hall beat. I knew them by sight and promised I'd see them again if the Grand Jury took action. When they had all gone, Richmond closed the door and said, "Guy wants to see you. It won't hurt them not to know."

I followed him down a hall and into a room where Stoakes Fant was sitting patiently in a stiff chair. Richmond stepped aside and let me in, and then went out again and closed the door behind him.

I said, "Hello, Mr. Fant."

He indicated a chair and I sat down. He tapped the folded newspaper in his hand and then tossed it on the desk beside him. He said, "As soon as I saw the story I got in touch with Matt Bolden. He'll be considerate—within proper limits, of course. At my insistence he turned his office upside down. We were in law school together. The witnesses go before the Grand Jury this afternoon. Suspense is the worst part of something like this. Don't let it get you down."

I said, "Thanks, Mr. Fant. I'm a little bewildered, I guess. I appreciate the thing being pushed along. It's more the suspense than anything, like you say. A few hours ago things were perfectly all right, like when we were down at the bank, and now . . . well, it's all happened so fast I don't even know what went on at the inquest. I was just sitting there, and bingo . . . and here I am with people taking pictures of me."

He said, "You can stay in here until we know what the Grand Jury does. If there's a true bill, Bolden won't be unreasonable about bail. It'll be stiff, in view of the charge, but not impossible. That will be arranged. I've agreed to take responsibility, personally, which means the ante will be lowered. You can come home with me. Matt won't stand in the way of a trial whenever you're ready. No reason for the thing to drag out indefinitely."

"No," I said, "no reason for that."

He got up and walked back and forth. "You'll want one of the specialists, of course. Schiarelli or Joost or Halloran."

I said, "No."

"Well, all right. Maybe you've got a point there. We can go to one of the deacons of the bar, Abercrombie himself or Hansford or old Judge Grace, maybe. You'll want somebody like Schiarelli at the table, though. Somebody who knows the ropes. There's a lot of difference between civil and criminal cases."

I said, "Wait."

He stopped and looked at me.

I said, "Would you mind sitting down a minute?"

He sat down.

I said, "I appreciate all this a lot, Mr. Fant. I really do. I mean, worrying about me. You and Judge Abercrombie have a sense of *noblesse oblige*, haven't you? You have to look after the chicks, even if they've bitten the hand that feeds them. Things like that."

I waited, and when he didn't answer, I said, "Thanks for

going through the motions. Honor of the regiment, dignity of the flag and everything."

He gave me a very queer look.

I said, "You're defending a criminal. I know you didn't mean to, but you started out by indicting me. Now all I'm getting is a fair trial and the smallest possible sentence. A deal, if it can be arranged. The smallest possible blot on the scutcheon. I'm sorry, no dice. You're doing it with misgivings anyway, aren't you?"

His answer was so long coming that it made me look up. His face was serious, but he had not taken offense. He said, "Did you say you haven't read the accounts of the inquest?"

"I haven't had a chance."

"There's plenty of time. Maybe you should read them now." He pushed the papers across the desk at me.

I spread the papers elaborately and read everything, including continued on page seven, column two. Joe Herdt, Charley Pitts, Block, fingerprints on the cigaret lighter, the reported confession I made on Saturday morning, the dubious lady at the hospital—everything.

I looked up and said, "Do they usually spread it all out at the coroner's inquest like this?"

Fant opened his hands eloquently.

I said, "They must think it's a weak case if they want to try it in the newspapers like this."

Fant said, "Does it sound weak to you?"

I looked at him a very long time. At first he wouldn't meet my eyes but finally he did.

I said, "Let's not pull any punches. I won't bail out. I'm going to see it through the hard way. I'll give you A for effort, and now let's call it a day."

There was no mistaking the expression of relief, but he wasn't quite through. When he walked around, it reminded me of Richmond. He said, "My wife and I are very fond of Marty. We always have been. May I tell her I did all I could?"

I said, "Yes, you can tell her that."

"May I tell her you know what you're up against and still won't take any help?"

"Yes, you can tell her that, too."

"Is there anything else you want me to tell her?"

I thought it over. I said, "Yes, I guess there is. Tell her I'm not worried and she shouldn't be worried, either."

I wasn't worried—much.

56.

FANT AND Richmond came in together about four o'clock. They didn't have to tell me— I could see it in Fant's expression. The reporters were congregating again in the room down the hall, which meant the same thing. I drew in my breath slowly, and stood up.

Fant said, "The Grand Jury's in the courtroom, just handed up the indictment. Bolden is willing to go along on the idea of a quick trial and the docket's pretty well cleared up at the moment. Feel like going over and talking about it now?"

I nodded. My mouth was so dry I was afraid to say anything for fear my voice would sound queer. I was empty without being hungry and I recognized the beginnings of a headache. My finger explored the inside of the cigaret package and I crumpled it and put it on the table. All the meat on my face wanted to hang down straight but I made it turn into a tasteless smile as I indicated the ash tray, piled high with half-smoked butts.

I wasn't worried—much.

Richmond went first, I followed, and Fant came along behind. There was a water cooler in the corridor and I stopped and washed out my mouth and then drank thirstily. For a moment there was an impulse to retch but I fought it down.

Richmond said, "How about it, boys? Shall we skip the pix? Plenty of time later. We're going over to see Bolden and the Judge."

Galloway said, "Is Mr. Fant your attorney?"

I said, "Mr. Fant's a lawyer, but he's here only as a friend. A very good friend whose services are timely and appreciated. That's all. We haven't discussed any other relationship."

"Do you mind?" said Richmond, pushing toward the door with his hand on my arm.

I said over my shoulder, "I'm asking for the earliest trial I can get. The Judge and the Commonwealth's attorney are waiting to discuss the matter. We don't want to keep them waiting."

The press was close on our heels as we walked briskly across the street. We made quite a procession. A loafer on the courthouse lawn took a toothpick out of his mouth and fell in behind to see what was going on. Eight or ten small boys were yelling shrilly and throwing a baseball around.

Matt Bolden, the Commonwealth's attorney, was in his early fifties, smooth-shaven, lean-faced, with rimless bifocals that slipped down his nose a little whenever he blinked. He had a habit of putting the middle finger of his right hand against the bridge of his spectacles and pushing them back up. I knew him by sight and he knew me the same way, relics of a sanity hearing in which I had handed papers to Mitch Sothern.

When we came into the shadowy courtroom there were nods all around—of recognition rather than of greeting—and we pushed up to the bench. Judge Thornton sat above us with a dignity that managed somehow to be friendly. In a horseshoe game at the last Fourth of July picnic, he had thrown a ringer on top of mine—a triumph he had never forgotten.

He said, "Hello, Jess."

I said, "Hello, Judge." I was suddenly overcome by his use of my first name and had to blink a couple of times and clear my throat. I was glad no one noticed.

Stoakes Fant said, "I'm here only as a friend, Judge. Jess wants to do his own talking. He wants the case pushed up on the docket as far as it will go, with the Court's permission. Mr. Bolden sees no reason to ask for delay."

We were talking in low tones, as people at the bench seem to have a tendency to do. Stragglers were hanging around the room for no good reason. The Grand Jury had been dismissed and no case was being tried. Galloway was leaning heavily between Bolden and Fant, trying to hear what was going on.

Judge Thornton said, "It isn't the kind of thing you rush into. You'll want counsel. Counsel, of course, will be allowed time to prepare the case. When will we have a jury again, Mr. Bolden?"

Bolden put up his finger and pushed his spectacles up his nose. He said, "If Your Honor please, this jury's summoned for the rest of this week but we've pretty well filtered through the list of cases ready for trial and there've been a lot of continuances. The Grand Jury has returned a lot of true bills and there'll have to be arraignments, you know, but other than that . . . well, the attorneys will want time, of course. My office will be grateful, too. We're understaffed. Always have been."

Judge Thornton said, "What did you have in mind?"

I said, "If the Court please, the witnesses have appeared before the Grand Jury, so they must be available. Mr. Bolden has just presented his case, so it's already prepared. I'm going to represent myself, and I'm ready any time."

Judge Thornton said. "Why don't we adjourn to chambers? I want to smoke." He said to the clerk, "Bring along the docket and we'll see what we can do."

We went back into a darkish room and the clerk turned on the lights. We sat around in the chairs and looked for ash trays and spittoons. The reporters stood against the walls. Judge Thornton sat in the swivel chair behind the desk, on the leather cushion that the years had impressed with the shape of his rear end.

He said abruptly, "Jess, you mustn't be pigheaded about this thing. The charge is murder. Have you read the indictment? Well, never mind, the clerk will give you a copy, of course. Being a lawyer, you ought to realize the gravity of the charge. It's my duty to bring it home to you. If you can't afford counsel, the Court will appoint someone. I'll let you take your pick. Members of the bar are officers of the Court. A little work for nothing won't hurt them." He said to the reporters, "This is off the record. I guess you understand that."

I said, "I think I understand my rights. It isn't a question of the money. I'd rather represent myself. That's one of my rights, too, isn't it?"

He leaned back and clasped his hands behind his head. "Yes, if you put it that way, I suppose that's one of your rights. In the case of a more mature member of the bar, I'd let the question rest. How many criminal cases have you tried?"

"Police Court. A few cases."

"Running a red light? Speeding? Making a book? Keeping a bawdy house?"

"Cases like that, yes."

"How about civil cases?"

"A few divorces. Forcible detainers. Collections."

"Judgment by default? Undefended divorces?"

"Some of them, yes. But I've watched an awful lot of trials. A lot of them."

"I see." He looked up at the ceiling. He pursed his lips and blew out his breath. "The Court is not impressed with the qualifications. If I were appointing counsel in a capital case, I should feel constrained to appoint someone else."

He sat up straight and took a cigar out of a hand-tooled leather box. "However, the accused has rights, and I suppose they must be respected, even in a backhanded sort of way. When the case comes to trial, we must make this a matter of record, of course."

I said, "Yes, sir."

He was impersonal now, as if I had hurt his feelings. He had an air that said, you wired your own electric chair, now sit in it. The whole atmosphere of the room was different. A large brown creature sat with folded arms on my pancreas.

Judge Thornton said, "How soon do you want the trial?"

I licked my lips and said, "Whenever the docket's got room for it. Tomorrow."

"Mr. Bolden?"

"I'm looking over the docket now, Your Honor. Flagerian, that's the embezzlement case, Judge. We're still looking for the woman—that will have to go over to another day. Addison —he's pleading guilty, that won't take long. That leaves Ruby Esther Long—you know, the charge of poisoning three husbands. I meant to take that matter up with the Court. The subpoenas have been served and the Commonwealth is ready but there was a message just before the afternoon Grand Jury session—it seems old Judge Grace had a stroke. He's the lawyer in the case. . . ."

"That's distressing," said Judge Thornton, breaking in. "I hadn't heard. Still, what is he? Eighty? Very well, let the case go over. When she's employed new counsel we'll find another date. There's the question of the jurors. Were they instructed to come back tomorrow morning?"

The clerk said, "Yes, sir. The Court instructed them to be back at nine-thirty."

"All right, Mr. Bolden, you will be heard on the subject. What have you to say?"

Matt Bolden looked at Fant. Fant deliberately looked away. Bolden rubbed his chin and said, "Only that it's rather precipitous—I mean, on a capital offense. We wouldn't want the record to give the wrong impression. However, if the accused will join in a stipulation . . ."

I said, "That's agreed, Your Honor. Mr. Bolden can prepare written stipulations and I'll sign them."

"Then," said Bolden, "there are no objections from the Commonwealth's attorney. There's the question of the availability of the witnesses, of course. I suppose subpoenas could be got out. How about your witnesses, Mr. London?"

I said, "Your witnesses will do, Mr. Bolden. I'll want to go over the list, of course. Isn't there some way we could let one subpoena do the job for both of us?" I turned to Richmond. "What about the people in the yellow car? Did I overlook them in the story on the Coroner's inquest?"

Richmond said, "They were there. I don't think we'll have any trouble producing them again."

I said, "Then I guess that's all. Wait a minute. No, I'm sorry. I'll want to call Miss Inez Wiggens. She wasn't there today, was she?"

"No," said Bolden, looking at a list in his hand. "There wasn't any Miss Wiggens."

Richmond said, "We can get out a subpoena."

I said, "I don't know where she is. Perhaps out of the jurisdiction of the Court."

Judge Thornton said drily, "Is there a suggestion the case shouldn't be tried tomorrow?" Between the lines, around the words, curling over the syllables, the hint of sarcasm was there —faint and thin, but enough to bring my jaws together, tight.

I counted to five, slowly. I said, "No, Your Honor. If Mr. Bolden will produce the witnesses who testified before the Coroner and the Grand Jury, the accused will be prepared for trial."

"All right," said Thornton. "Trial at nine-thirty. Now if you'll excuse me, gentlemen."

Fant cleared his throat. Judge Thornton looked at him. "Were you about to say something, Stoakes?"

"Only as a friend."

The judge smiled. "There's nothing wrong with friends. The Court recognizes them."

"I was thinking of bail. It would be particularly important to the accused, preparing his own case. It's a matter within the discretion of the Court."

"Mr. Bolden?"

"I suppose so. Mr. Fant mentioned the matter earlier and I've considered it. The Commonwealth's attorney has no reason to fear the accused will not appear for trial. Still, there's the question of policy. The charge is serious. Ten thousand?"

Fant said quickly, "The amount is a little surprising, under the circumstances. A reputable member of the bar. . . . I'm prepared for five, and will take personal responsibility . . ."

I said, "The accused has made no request for bail."

Thornton ignored me. He said, "Five will be enough. This is not to be taken as a precedent, you understand. The Court finds there are special circumstances."

57.

WE LEFT THE judge's office and went across the hall to the place where Bolden managed the affairs of the Commonwealth. The press would have to wait. We filed between the typewriters to Bolden's private office. It was dark and dingy. Bolden dug out an old pipe and started grubbing in a humidor, spilling tobacco on the top of his desk.

Bolden and Richmond put their heads together and scribbled on a yellow pad. Finally they straightened up. Bolden said, "It's irregular, giving out a list of witnesses before the Grand Jury but there it is. God knows it's fair. They heard everything—for and against."

I looked at the list. Mr. & Mrs. J. T. Forman.

I pointed and said, "Who're these people?"

Richmond craned his neck to look. "Forman? Last people at the party. Live next door. Got uneasy and gave the alarm. That's how we happened to show up."

I thought, okay.

Dr. Albert Maxwell. Medical examiner.

Lt. Alpheus T. Richmond. (Alpheus? Oh well . . .)

Cpl. Harry Lautzenheizer. (Harry)

Zack Woods. Beulah Mae Woods. (Never knew they had a last name.)

Elaine Grotznicht. I said, "Who's this?" Richmond came and looked over my shoulder. He had to consult his notes. He said, "Nurse at the hospital."

"You mean—that one?" Richmond nodded.

Joseph Herdt. Check.

Charles Pitts. Check.

Horatio Block. Check.

Philip Thomas. I said, "Who's this?" Richmond consulted his notes again. He said, "Him and the next three, the people in the car.

I said, "I get it." I read on down the list:

Frank Hicks, June Gravura, Alive Gravura. In the car, check.

Sgt. F. Lohrman. I pointed. Richmond looked and said, "Fingerprints."

I said, "Okay."

Richmond paused, enjoying himself. He said, "The F stands for Fauntleroy. He's sensitive about it."

I said, "It's a secret."

Milton T. Abercrombie. I looked hard at that one. Richmond caught my eye and looked away.

I pushed aside the list. I said, "The list is okay. I'll stand on it."

Bolden said, "Shall we initial it?"

I said, "Why not?"

He scribbled his initials and I scribbled mine. Now I'd play hell getting a continuance if Wiggie should fail to show up.

And I needed Wiggie.

I thought, *This is why you ought to have counsel.*

Bolden said, "Nine-thirty. If you want to check in early, we'll report on the subpoenas."

"Thanks," I said. "That's fine. Much obliged."

58.

FANT WAS WAITING, and so were the reporters. I didn't want to talk to them but I didn't want to be rude, either. I couldn't afford any nasty cracks in the newspapers.

I accepted a cigaret from Dobernik of the *News-Scimitar* and sat down as if I had all evening. I said, "I hope you fellows go easy on a guy. I'm tired and there's a hard day ahead. If you've got any questions, shoot, but don't make it too long, will you?"

"Are you going to be your own lawyer?"

"Yes, I am. If I don't get to trial tomorrow it might be a month—maybe in the fall. I can't have a charge like this hanging over my head indefinitely. I've watched them gather what they call the evidence against me and I think I know what it amounts to. Another lawyer would have to spend days or weeks learning the score. That's all there is to it."

"You mean they're rushing you into trial?"

I said, "No, certainly not. It's the exact opposite. I'm the one who insisted—ask Bolden and he'll tell you the straight of it. When we found the docket was unexpectedly clear tomorrow, Mr. Bolden was very nice about it. I'm grateful to Judge Thornton, too."

"Are you out on bail?"

"Yes, the Court was considerate. Mr. Fant, here, made the arrangements after the amount was fixed. He's been gracious enough to ask me home for the night. Incidentally, I'd appreciate it if you fellows would lay off the telephone."

"How're you going to plead? Or would you rather not answer that?"

"I have no objections whatever. The plea will be not guilty, of course. Now I'd like to be excused."

Fant had showed no signs of impatience. Now he stood up and when he saw I was ready, he put on his hat and pulled the door shut behind us. We went out the front entrance and down the stone steps. I knew the parking lot where he always kept his car and we turned that way.

He said, "You made out very well with the press boys."

I said, "Thanks."

"I spoke to Carl Amery. He's rushing his transcript of the Coroner's inquest. He might have a copy by eight or nine tonight—said he'd bring it around to the house."

I said, "That's swell. I don't know how to thank you. I meant to ask about it, but I forgot."

He said, "No trouble. Forget it."

We got into his car. He said, "You'll want to go by your place, I guess."

I hadn't thought about it. I said, "Pajamas, yes, and shaving things and a clean shirt and socks. Won't take but a minute.

Would it be better if we came back after supper? I don't want to upset your family schedule."

"No hurry, let's do it now."

We rode to the Albemarle Apartments in silence. I was glad Charley Pitts wasn't on duty. Cornelius Vanderbilt nodded but didn't know what to say to me. The five-star afternoon paper was on the stool in the elevator, with my picture, one of the shots at headquarters, prominent on the front page. He turned it over without looking at me.

When I came out of my apartment and locked the door, the elevator was waiting. Evidently he had been rehearsing. He said, "Wish you lots of luck, Mr. Hughes. I mean, Mr. Jess."

I said, "Thanks, Wall Street."

Then I said, "Know who lives in four-oh-eight?"

He stopped the car between floors and closed his eyes. "Yessuh. He's a gemmum fixes up prescriptions at the drugsto' down here next to the Bijou. He comes in late, after the show over. I don't see him much. Little bald spot in the back."

"Is he in town?"

"Far as I know, yessuh. He go out about four o'clock, I saw him then."

"How about six thirty-seven?"

"Take it slow," he said, thinking hard. He grinned even while his eyes were squinted up tight. "You ask me, Mr. Jess, I got to have a picture I'm up on the sixth flo' walking down the hall. Six thutty-seven on the left, at the end. Now I got it. Name Miss Eugenia Small. Don't know what she does. Hair beginning to turn gray."

"One more. Who's in six ten?"

"Mr. Block in six ten, Mr. Jess. You know Mr. Block."

I said, "That's right. I forgot. All right, let's go on down, and thanks a lot."

I found a fifty-cent piece in my pocket and gave it to him without explanation.

When the car was headed out toward Fant's place, I said, "How old are the children? I'm very bad at remembering."

He said, "Stoakes is sixteen, he's third year high. Griselda will be twelve in August. Georgia's the baby, she was six last week. They keep us humping."

I said, "I don't want to be a lot of trouble, but if you and Mrs. Fant don't mind I'd rather go in the back way and maybe have a sandwich and a glass of milk in the room I'm going to sleep in."

"You don't have to worry about the kids, if that's what you mean."

"Partly. The main thing is I don't want to eat and I'm afraid I couldn't talk to anyone."

"Well, all right. I'll bring up a highball for you. Then maybe later a sandwich will sit better."

When we got to the house I was polite, with all the effort I could muster. Griselda was practicing scales on the piano and paused only long enough to put out a hand and shake mine. Georgia was on her stomach on the living room floor, using crayons on a big coloring book. Young Stoakes was overdue —no one knew where. I was glad of that.

I followed Fant upstairs and into a neat little room at the back of the house. When he left me alone, I took things out of my coat pockets and put them on the dresser, then found a hanger and put the coat in the closet. I pulled a chair in front of the window and loosened my collar and put my head down on my folded arms, on the window sill. . . .

After awhile I looked for my cigarets on the dresser. The envelope was there, folded, but still with the bulged-out effect from things that had been in it.

I picked up the envelope and looked again at the writing, "T.R.C.," unmistakably in Mitch's energetic strokes.

T.R.C.

Then for the first time, I thought I had an idea.

Fant tapped on the door and came in with a highball. It

had a lot of tinkling ice in it. When he saw my smile his face smoothed out and he came in almost jauntily. My spirits were on the way up.

I said, "Where's yours?"

"Downstairs. Should I bring it up?"

I said, "Of course. And I hope you can spare a couple of minutes."

"You look as if you could stand that sandwich now. One of the kids can bring it up."

Half my drink was gone by the time Fant got back upstairs. I kept staring at the envelope, and the longer I looked the more certain I was. I turned the chair around and sat astride of it, with my chin over the high back. Fant sat on the bed.

I said, "Think along with me a minute. Mitch and Marty had their bags packed to leave Friday night, didn't they?"

He nodded.

"Marty's been in the hospital. All the things a woman would need must have been in those bags. Did she send for them?"

He thought a minute and said, "Yes, as soon as she could sit up. She asked for them Saturday evening. I routed out Zack and Beulah Mae, made them find the bags, and took hers to the hospital."

I took a turn around the room and then came back and straddled the chair again. "Now," I said, trying not to be excited. "What about the other bags—Mitch's. Did you see them?"

He frowned and said, "Yes, I guess so. The bags were in the upstairs hall. Beulah Mae knew which ones were Marty's and we took those. I believe there were two others. Zack must have put them in Mitch's room. Why?"

"Has Richmond been through them?"

"I don't think so. Why would he? I don't think it ever occurred to him. It didn't occur to me."

"Have you had your dinner?"

"Good Lord, yes. It's after eight. The children die of starvation before six-thirty. This house is practically in bed."

"And the keys? How about the keys? Is there any way we can get into Marty's house?"

"The keys are in my pocket downstairs."

"Then come on, let's go. Do you mind?"

"Here's your sandwich." Griselda was in her nightgown, one hand holding it up to keep from tripping her and the other hand holding a plate. It was a ham sandwich, cut fancy in four pieces, with an olive and some pickle and two stalks of celery to make it appetizing. Mrs. Fant peeped through the door behind her.

I suddenly realized I was trembling with hunger. I sat down and laughed. I took Griselda on my knees and admired the sandwich and gave Mrs. Fant a grin. Against my will, I ate it slowly. I could have eaten five of them.

Griselda gave me a kiss on the cheek and ran off to bed. I said to Mrs. Fant, "Your husband is a very wonderful guy. I'm going to take him off on a little expedition, but it won't take long. Could you possibly fix me about two more magnificent sandwiches like that to eat when we come back?"

She said, "Marty's worried sick about you."

I said, "You tell Marty not to worry, will you? I'll come to see her again when this is all over. And in case things are in a hurry in the morning, thanks for everything."

It wasn't a long ride to 1918 Cedar Avenue. We parked in the side drive, let ourselves in the front way, and went upstairs. Two bags were on the floor, inside the door of Mitch's room. I picked up the nearest, flopped it on the bed, and opened it.

My hand, groping under shirts and shorts and pajamas, found a package almost at once. It was flat, and not very thick —enough to bulge out an envelope, but no more than that. There was a rubber band around it.

I motioned to Fant. When he was beside me I took off the rubber band, unfolded the sheets and held them under the light so he could see clearly.

There were eight certificates for common stock of the Tremont Realty Company, issued in various names and endorsed in blank. They added up to nineteen hundred forty-one shares. The fine print on the certificates said the authorized capital stock of the corporation was 5,000 shares. These certificates, then, represented about forty per cent of what General Motors had paid for the building.

I said, "Here, you take 'em. They don't make me innocent and they don't make me guilty, but they answer the only question that has really worried me. Show them to Judge Abercrombie, will you? Then use your own judgment. Let's go home."

Fant didn't say a word all the way back to his house. In the kitchen there was a plate on the table, complete with two ham sandwiches all cut up fancy, olives, pickle and celery. I ate the whole works, methodically and with enthusiasm. A note said there was milk in the refrigerator. I found it and drank it. I felt fine. There was a load off my mind.

Fant was sitting there, looking at the stock certificates. He said, "I'll show them to Judge Abercrombie. I'll tell him where we found them. I'll have to tell Marty, too. It's a shame, but she'll have to know. I wouldn't believe it, but I have to. Now I feel different about the whole thing. I wouldn't believe it."

I said, "It's time to go to bed. Good night."

He stood up and came over to me. He said, "What I did today was for Marty. You're entitled to know I didn't do it for you. I would have told you sooner or later but today it didn't seem to matter. Now it's different. What can I do for you? I mean really, down the line."

My impulse was to cry, because I was braced against hard things and had no defense against soft ones. I said, "Nothing.

You've done enough. You can hold your breath if you want to, that's all."

He said, "I'm holding it now."

On the dresser in my room was a copy of the transcript of the Coroner's inquest. I put on my pajamas, read it once, and went to bed. I fell asleep almost at once.

59.

FANT DROVE ME down to the courthouse at nine and we went straight to Matt Bolden's office. He had been on the job since seven-thirty and was beginning to look tired already.

"There's a small snag," he said, pushing his spectacles up his nose. "Fortunately it's not serious. Forman is under the weather this morning—fever—doctor—looks as if it might be tonsillitis." He waved his hand vaguely as if to indicate all the other things it might be. "I've been over the testimony before the Coroner and I suppose you have, too. He and Mrs. Forman were together all evening and their testimony is the same. I'm not inclined to ask for a continuance."

I said, "No, as long as one of them is here. The other witnesses?"

"The Sheriff's office reports they've all been served. I suppose we must assume they'll answer when their names are called."

"How about the stipulation?"

He pawed around on his desk and handed me two type-written sheets. "I've prepared something. Rather too elaborate, perhaps, but we don't want grounds for reversal, do we?"

You can't ask for reversal in a criminal case except in the

event of conviction. Nagging thought. "No," I said, "we wouldn't want that."

Even the word "elaborate" was an understatement. This was a regular crucifixion. It was stipulated that the indictment (copy attached) was returned by the Grand Jury of Calhoun County on the 29th day of April, 1940. The accused was immediately notified and received a true copy of the indictment. At the request of the accused, and over the protests of the Commonwealth's Attorney(!), an immediate trial was sought. The Court urged delay and the employment of counsel which were expressly waived by the accused. The Court endeavored to appoint counsel, but the accused insisted vigorously upon his right to represent himself. It was stipulated that the accused was a graduate of the Jefferson School of Law in the Class of 1939, that he had taken and passed the Bar Examination prescribed by the Commonwealth of Kentucky, that he had been duly sworn and admitted to practice in the Circuit Court of Calhoun County, the Court of Appeals of Kentucky, and the District Court of the United States for the Western District of Kentucky. Since October, 1939, the accused had been, and until April 27th, 1940 he continuously was, associated with the law firm of Abercrombie, Sothern & Fant, and as such was engaged in the general practice of law during that period. Accused acknowledged the gravity of the charge contained in the indictment and acknowledged his realization of the possible statutory penalties in the event of conviction. Accused expressly waived any possible defects in the indictment or irregularities in the procurement thereof or in the obtention of evidence. At the request of the accused, trial was set for the 30th day of April, 1940 at the hour of nine-thirty in the forenoon, all of which was expressly agreed to. The accused had furnished a list of witnesses and the same had been duly subpoenaed. If said witnesses appeared and testified in due course, accused expressly waived the privilege of seeking a continuance because of the absence of any other witness, or witnesses.

An addendum had been added. The accused expressly waived the right to seek a continuance because of the absence of the witness J. T. Forman and expressly agreed that the trial might proceed without him.

This stipulation had been prepared at the suggestion of the accused in order to cure any possible charge of irregularities growing out of the foregoing facts, and was signed by the accused in the presence of witnesses and in open Court, without constraint or compulsion from any source whatsoever, and of his own free will.

Fant had been reading it over my shoulder. He said, "It seems complete enough, except for the Washington Monument. That seems to have been overlooked. You won't sign it, of course."

I said, "It looks all right to me. I'll sign it. Have you a pen handy, Mr. Bolden?"

Whether he went to law school with Stoakes Fant or not, Matt Bolden didn't like the remark about the Washington Monument. He said coldly, "It should be signed in the presence of the Court as provided in the final paragraph. Now, if you don't mind, I'd like to have a few moments alone. I'll join you in court in"—he looked at his watch—"twelve minutes."

I said, "In thirteen minutes you'll be late."

That got me a frigid look, too. I gave him one, right back. Mine was pretty cold.

60.

THE COURTROOM was crowded. George Stern was waiting for us inside the railing and gave Fant an envelope. Fant handed it to me. "Jury list," he whispered. "One of the court reporters gets them up every time a panel's drawn. Name, address, occupation, previous jury service, what the verdict was."

I had practiced law six months and didn't know. I guess a question must have showed in my face because Fant said, "It's all a matter of record. Bolden's got one, too. Go ahead, take it."

He sat with Stern and I made my way alone to the table allotted to the defense. Stern came over and brought me a yellow pad and a couple of pencils. The room was full of eyes—too many eyes. I looked down at the yellow pad and made doodles—a something that might have been a duck, rather lopsided. A sailboat with a very large sail. . . .

Bolden came in at nine-twenty-eight, an assistant following with a handful of papers. They whispered together and shifted the papers in various piles. If I looked straight at the crowd I saw no faces—only a lot of people who seemed eternally to be murmuring and moving about in their seats. If I looked at the window, a face would occasionally take shape in the corner of my eye. Charley Pitts, chewing gum very rapidly. Joe Herdt . . .

There was a commotion at nine-thirty-two and then quiet. Judge Thornton came in. We stood up and the deputy sheriff pounded and said his piece, and we sat down. It took about five minutes to dispose of the Addison case.

The clerk said, "Commonwealth against London."

Bolden said, "We'd like to have the witnesses called."

"Very well," said Judge Thornton, "Mr. Sheriff, you may call the witnesses."

They stood up, one by one, and Bolden carefully marked them off on his list. He said, "The Commonwealth is ready, Your Honor."

I said, "Defendant's ready."

Bolden signaled to me and we went up to the bench. He produced the stipulation and handed it up to the Judge. The clerk turned on the little shaded desk light and Thornton read it, frowning. He looked down at me and said, "You've read this, I presume?"

"Yes, Your Honor."

"This part about waiving any possible defects and irregularities in the indictment?"

"Yes, Your Honor."

"You're calling no witnesses for the defense?"

"No, sir."

He drummed on the bench with his blunt fingers and looked over our heads for a moment. The assistant handed Bolden a fountain pen and Bolden handed it to me. I tried to sign the paper but the bench was too high and I had to take it over to the clerk's desk. Bolden came and bent over it. The clerk handed it up to Judge Thornton and he signed it and handed it back.

"Is the jury here, Mr. Bolden?"

"Yes, sir."

"I shall make a brief explanation and the general interrogation, as usual. You understand, Mr. London, that you may defer making a statement to the jury until you open the case for the defendant?"

"Thank you. I'll make mine right after Mr. Bolden's."

"As you wish. That's your privilege. All right, Mr. Clerk, you may call the jury panel."

All very formal. We weren't pitching horseshoes now.

I went to my table and sat down. I studied my lopsided duck while Judge Thornton explained, somewhat laboriously, that the Grand Jury had indicted the defendant, Jesse London, for the wilful murder of one Mitchell Sothern at his residence on Cedar Avenue, this city, between the hours of twelve midnight and four A.M. on Saturday the 27th day of April, 1940. The defendant had entered a plea of not guilty. In order to assure a fair and impartial trial, the Court would first interrogate them on their qualifications as jurors and then counsel for the Commonwealth and for the defendant would be given an opportunity to interrogate them further. The jury should understand the sacred nature of the duty it was their privilege to render, both to the defendant and to the people of the Commonwealth as a whole. The jury should consider the questions carefully, and answer them thoughtfully.

When Thornton had asked them the general questions—whether any of them was related to the defendant by blood or marriage whether any of them knew me; whether they had any knowledge of the case or had been led to form an opinion; whether they knew of any reason why they could not render a fair and impartial verdict—Bolden stood up.

I said, "If the Court please, perhaps we can save a little time. I'll take the first twelve names on the list if Mr. Bolden will agree."

Bolden was nonplused. His spectacles slid down his nose and he pushed them back up with his characteristic gesture. After a moment he said, "Your Honor, we all want to save as much time as we can and I think I can say that I shall be the last to cause any unnecessary delays. However, I have certain duties—duties to the defendant as well as to the Commonwealth, I might add—"

"That's understood," said the Court. "You have the right to question the jurors and the Court will not require you to waive it. Do you wish to address the jurors one at a time, or will you ask the panel as a whole?"

Bolden bent to whisper with his assistant and they took another hurried look at the jury list. Mine was still in my pocket. In response to my offer, he would probably either select his jurors in a hurry, or lean too far the other way and wear everybody out. He decided to make it snappy.

He said, "If the Court please, this is the same panel we had last week and we've interrogated them before. The preliminary questions asked by the Court cover the essential points, except as to the matter of the death penalty. On that, I shall be content with a question addressed to the panel as a whole. After that, saving of course the right to challenge without cause, I think we will be ready to proceed."

Thornton nodded. Bolden's assistant, thumbing through some notes, was putting a big black "X" opposite certain names on the jury list. I could see that the second name was one of them. I got out my copy of the jury list and noticed that one Adam Springer, salesman, 1142 Pine, age 46, had sat on two juries last week and there had been an acquittal both times. I put the list back in my pocket.

On the death penalty question only one juror raised a hand—a gray-haired woman at the end of the line. Bolden cupped his hand behind his ear to catch her name and wrote it down carefully. In a sharp voice she announced that she didn't believe in the death penalty. People who committed crimes were mentally sick and should be given care in state institutions. Putting them to death was a confession of helplessness and weakness . . .

Bolden said, "Challenge for cause, Your Honor."

"That will be all. You may be excused."

There was another whispered conference between Bolden and his assistant and a slip went up to the clerk. The clerk crossed two names off his list and looked at me. I shook my head. Twelve jurors answered to their names and found seats in the jury box. This time I had out my list and put the number opposite each name.

I looked at Fant. It was twelve minutes after ten.

Fant looked serious.

61.

WHEN THE JURY had been sworn, Bolden made his opening speech. I knew, in general, what it would be. . . . The purpose at this time, ladies and gentlemen of the jury, is merely to furnish you with an outline of what the Commonwealth will show by the testimony of the witnesses, to enable you to follow what may sometimes appear to be a disconnected narrative . . . blah . . . blah . . . blah. . . . The Commonwealth will show you that so-and-so and so-and-so and so-and-so . . . After the evidence has been heard, the Court will instruct you with respect to the law of the case and then I will attempt to be of assistance to you in sorting out the facts established by the evidence, assigning to each fact its proper value, fitting it into its proper place. . . . A fair and impartial verdict upon the law and the facts . . . confident you will find the defendant guilty as charged. Thank you. He had taken twenty-five minutes.

I stood in front of the jury and put my hands on the railing between us and looked at each of them.

I said, "I'm the defendant Mr. Bolden has been talking about. I'm charged with murdering my brother-in-law. Put in simple terms, the charge means I thought about killing a man, laid some sort of a plan, and then killed him. My defense is that I didn't do it.

"My defense is that when the crime was committed— that's what Mr. Bolden says—I don't even know whether a crime was committed—I was somewhere else. From the books you've read and the pictures you've seen, I'm sure you know such a defense is called an alibi. But you'll find this is a curious sort of alibi because I haven't any witnesses to prove it. That is, unless Mr. Bolden's witnesses prove it for me.

"It happens that I know some of the witnesses Mr. Bolden will put on that stand over there. They aren't crooks or liars. They're good people. I'm sure they're going to tell you the exact truth—as they know it. As a matter of fact, if I had given them permission—well, I won't say that. I'm sure they didn't mean it anyway.

"There'll be a lot of testimony about last Friday night, as Mr. Bolden has told you. I understand some of the witnesses will say they saw me—or think they saw me—at various places outside of the Albemarle Apartments where I was asleep in bed. I'm sure they think so, or they wouldn't say it. All I can do is sit here and ask them questions and try to find out how they happen to be mistaken. You have a right to ask questions, too, and I want to urge you to do it.

"Under our constitution, no one can require me to take the witness stand and submit to questioning under oath. And if I should stand on my rights, Mr. Bolden cannot argue that any inferences are to be drawn from that fact. I waive that right. At the proper time I shall take the stand and be sworn and answer all the questions anyone cares to ask—yours as well as Mr. Bolden's.

"You are entitled to know what I'm trying to show from the questions I ask, just as Mr. Bolden has told you what the Commonwealth is trying to show. I don't think my questions will give you any trouble. I know that somehow—in some way—I wish I knew how, but I don't—there is a ghastly distortion of facts in the minds of perfectly honest people. My effort will be to find the causes of that distortion and reveal the truth."

I looked at each of them again, hard. I said, "I'll be trying hard. My life depends on it."

I went back to my chair and sat down. I looked at the yellow pad, and at the lopsided duck, and at the sailboat with the very large sail. I searched the crowd carefully, but couldn't find Wiggie.

Two reporters slid out from under the table reserved for them and pushed their way toward the door. With luck they could make the home editions.

Judge Thornton said, "The usual separation of witnesses, I suppose."

Bolden said, "I suppose so."

I stood up and both of them looked at me in curiosity, if not surprise. The reporters hesitated at the door, wondering if a moment's delay might produce something significant.

I said, "If the Court please, what's the matter with letting the witnesses stay in the courtroom? As a matter of fact, I'd like to tender a motion that they be *required* to stay."

Bolden pushed his spectacles up his nose. Here was something he hadn't been looking for, and he didn't like it. He said, "The witnesses are always separated."

I said, "They're your witnesses, because I haven't got any. If not hearing each other is supposed to be for my protection. I don't want to be protected that way."

The Judge said, "This is not the place to discuss the matter. Counsel will join me in chambers. There will be a ten-minute recess."

We formed a procession into Judge Thornton's chambers —the Judge, Bolden, the clerk, the official stenographer, the reporters for the morning papers, Fant, Stern, and me. A buzz of conversation was swelling in the courtroom before I closed the door behind me. We rustled around until everyone was settled.

"All right," said the Judge, lighting a cigaret. "Suppose we hear Mr. London first."

I said, "My point is a simple one. I suppose the idea is to keep witnesses from hearing each other on the theory that their testimony may be influenced. Well, where all the witnesses are called by one side of the case, it looks like it's the other fellow who is being protected. I'm the other fellow, Your

Honor, and if something's for my benefit, I don't see why I can't waive it."

Bolden said nervously, "We wouldn't want any reversible error, of course. It's customary to separate the witnesses."

I said, "I couldn't ask for reversal because of something I not only agreed to, but actually requested. Look, Your Honor, I really believe this is something I have a right to demand if I want to. I know these people couldn't have seen me anywhere but home in bed after about midnight last Friday night, because that's the only place I was. Somehow I've got to find out how this train got off the track. Maybe I'm foolish, but I've got a notion the witnesses themselves will figure this thing out if they hear the whole case. With the Court's permission, I'd like to dictate a motion at this time to the official reporter."

Thornton frowned and said, "You may, of course, tender any motion you like."

I took a deep breath and said, "My motion will go farther, if the Court please. I wish to request that all the witnesses be required to remain in the courtroom throughout the trial, and that the defendant be accorded the right and privilege to recall them from time to time for further questioning on anything that may develop."

Bolden's assistant plucked his sleeve and he bent his head. The assistant said in a whisper that everyone could hear, "This is screwy."

Thornton said, "Dictate your motion and the Court will then consider it."

I said, "For the benefit of Mr. Bolden, I'm inclined to believe the denial of such a motion would constitute reversible error in itself." I didn't know whether it would or not, but I got a rise out of the Commonwealth's attorney. He came out of his whispered consultation and stared at me in alarm. He pushed his spectacles up his nose. His assistant put down his notes and went into the library.

There was a profound silence in the room as I dictated the motion I had described. I got into the spirit of the thing and mentioned my rights, the ends of justice, and the Constitution. Thornton said, "Do you want to be heard, Mr. Bolden?"

The Commonwealth's attorney edged forward in his chair, pursed his lips, and then took the plunge. He said, "This is a new one on me, Judge, but I can't see how the Commonwealth could be prejudiced. As Mr. London says, the witnesses who have been subpoenaed are all mine. There might be a catch in it if he's got some undisclosed witnesses sitting around looking for ideas, but there's no law requiring him to tell us who he's going to produce. Unless the Court has some ideas that haven't occurred to me, I'm inclined to confess the motion. I wouldn't want to risk reversible error."

Thornton said, "Let the motion be filed and granted with a notation that it is agreed to by the Commonwealth. Court will reconvene."

62.

THE FIRST WITNESS was Mrs. J. T. Forman. She was nervous at first, but calmed down as the minutes ticked by. Before long it was apparent she was enjoying herself.

She was Mrs. J. T. Forman and she resided at 1920 Cedar Avenue, next door to 1918 Cedar Avenue, the residence of Mr. and Mrs. Mitchell Sothern. She knew Mitch and Marty —what? Oh, yes, of course, the witness meant Mr. and Mrs. Sothern. Such *dear* friends, you know. On Friday evening, April 26th, she and her husband attended a party at the home of the Sotherns—a farewell party. Yes, they were leaving the city. As a matter of fact, they were leaving on the two-thirty train Saturday morning. The witness had been with Mrs. Sothern when the reservations were made.

The witness testified that the party began to break up around midnight. Yes, it had been a good party—*very* good. Mrs. Forman and her husband stayed until everyone else had left. They had thought they might be of help—you know, neighbors. Their offer of assistance was declined. Marty—Mrs. Sothern, that is—had said the servants would clean up the —the mess, the next day. And then, of course, in a few weeks Mrs. Sothern would be returning to select what furniture would be stored and what furniture would be shipped.

The witness and her husband left around a quarter to one —well, maybe a few minutes one way or the other. No, they didn't look at their watches, but when they went to bed it was one-thirty, so that would be about right. The witness went straight to sleep. No, she didn't hear anything after that.

What was the next thing? Well, she woke up. It was around three-thirty, because she looked at the bedroom clock. Luminous dial, you know. Then it occurred to her something was wrong next door—you see, the light was shining into the window against her ceiling—and at that hour—I mean, after all. She knew the Sotherns were supposed to have left an hour before. . . .

No, she didn't arouse her husband right away. She got up and looked from the window. The lights were on next door— even in the servants' quarters. First she decided she'd call on the telephone, but there was no answer. She let it ring and ring, but there was no answer. Then all of a sudden she began to feel sort of—well, *queer*. She had never taken any stock in this talk about a woman's intuition, but (bridling a bit) in view of the undisputed facts she thought there just *might* be something in it, when all was said and done.

She awakened her husband and they talked it over—the

two of them. They agreed they should investigate. She "en-robed" (to use her own word for it) and went over and rang the front door bell. When there was no answer, her husband went back to the servants' quarters and found that Zack and Beulah Mae were not there.

What was one to think? Then her husband went around looking in at the windows. Wherever there was a light, of course. The shades were drawn in the den, but one of them wasn't all the way down. Through the little crack that was left, Mr. Forman saw Mitch—sorry, Mr. Sothern—lying there, apparently injured. Yes, she was the one who called the police . . .

Bolden whispered with his assistant and looked at me.

I didn't leave my chair or even look at the witness. I made a new doodle on my yellow pad and said in a conversational tone, "Was I at the party, Mrs. Forman?"

She smiled, pleased with herself. I caught the smile out of the corner of my eye.

She said, "Unless you were an optical illusion, Mr. London."

I thought, so that's the way it's going to be. A cutie. "I don't suppose you noticed when I left. You wouldn't have an idea of the time, would you? I mean, approximately."

"Well, yes, approximately. People were beginning to leave. I would say you were well toward the first. Twelve, or a little after."

"And did I understand you to say you and Mr. Forman were the last to leave?"

"One doesn't like to be categorical, of course, but I should say we were the last. It had been a—a successful party. Not in-toxicated, you understand—I wouldn't want to give the wrong impression. Such *nice* people. But—well, shall we say *gay*? All sorts of amusing things were said and done. I believe Marty and I—yes, of course, I'm referring to Mrs. Sothern—actually went around looking under the furniture to see if any of the guests, perhaps . . . Ridiculous, of course, but it *was* amusing. . . ."

I said drily, "You didn't find me hiding under the baby grand, did you?"

She said, bridling again, "We didn't find even a leprechaun. I'm sure all the other guests were quite gone. Quite."

"I gather you left around a quarter to one. Was the door locked or unlocked at that time, or do you know?"

"Locked. I'm quite positive. As it happens, I set the night-latch myself. I mean the little buttons. You press one, you know, and the knob on the outside won't turn. They're quite common. Everyone locks one's doors that way, I should think."

"You pushed the little button so the door wouldn't open from the outside? Did you try it to make sure?"

"I couldn't be mistaken. There was a bit of badinage about it. Prevent the pink elephants from crawling in, and all that sort of thing. Forgive me. Yes, I quite distinctly remember pushing the button and then trying the outside knob."

I let that lie for a moment. I wanted the jury to digest it. On the yellow pad I drew a horse that looked too much like a dog.

I said, "Some time after three-thirty you went over and rang the doorbell. Do you recall, Mrs. Forman, whether you tried the door at that time, or did you just ring the bell?"

"We tried the door. One naturally would, of course, under the circumstances. We would scarcely have called the police if it had been possible to investigate for ourselves. I mean, being close friends and neighbors. . . ."

"Thank you. I believe there are no more questions." The horse still looked too much like a dog. I added a mane, and now it looked like a dog with a mane. Under it I printed in block letters the word Horse.

63.

DR. ALBERT MAXWELL identified himself, gave his address, and admitted he was the Coroner. I conceded his qualifications. I realized that a horse would not have a tail that stuck up jauntily. I made a new tail that hung down and added some bush to it. I crossed out HORSE and printed MAN-O-WAR.

He testified that at or about four o'clock on the morning of April 27th he was called to 1918 Cedar Avenue, this city. At that time and place he examined a man, well-nourished, age perhaps forty-five to fifty, height six feet two inches, weight two hundred eleven pounds, apparently suffering from a fracture of the skull in the occipital region. Severe, with edema. Very evidently *in extremis*. Before the patient was moved, death ensued.

Yes, he made a *post mortem* examination. In his opinion death resulted from injury to the brain, as previously indicated. No, there was no other cause indicated. Apparently the subject had been in good health.

Bolden sat back.

I said, "If you wanted people like me and the members of this jury to understand it, how would you describe the injuries you found?"

"There was no attempt to be obscure. The record must be accurate. I merely used the exact terms of my profession."

I was trying to draw a table, but the legs wouldn't take on perspective. They appeared to be things of unequal length, hanging from a parallelogram that was a little sour. I said, "No reflections intended, Doctor. I just don't understand some of the words. There was something that sounded like Occidental. I don't get it."

"The word was 'occipital.' It means at the back of the

head, in the region where the big muscles of the neck join the skull. You can put your hand back there and feel it."

I put my hand up and wiggled my neck. Two of the jurors surreptitiously did the same. I said, "Thanks. How about that other word?"

He reflected a moment, looking at the ceiling. Then he said, "It means swelling, like when you sprain your thumb. That's the way flesh responds to violence."

"Does that happen when a person is killed instantly?"

"No, there's no edema after death."

"And Mr. Sothern was still living when you arrived at, perhaps, four o'clock Saturday morning or thereafter?"

"That's right."

"I see. Now what caused the injury you have described?"

He shrugged. "I wasn't a witness. I couldn't know that."

"Well, what *kind* of a thing?"

"A rather heavy object, I should say, or one wielded with extraordinary force. Round in shape, or even flattish. I am tempted to say something blunt, but the term 'blunt instrument' has been used so often in fiction that it is beginning to sound grotesque."

"A baseball bat or a brick or the leg of a heavy chair might have done it?"

"Conceivably."

"How about a fall?"

"Possible, but I would say doubtful. One doesn't usually fall with such great force as was indicated."

"How about if you were six-foot two inches and weighed over two hundred pounds, Doctor? Suppose you tripped and fell backwards and hit your head against something very hard. Would that produce such an injury?"

He shifted in his seat, restlessly. "I couldn't say it was impossible."

"Would you go so far as to say it was possible?"

"Theoretically, yes."

I got up and walked over to the corner of the jury box and leaned my elbow against it. I said, "Where did you find Mr. Sothern? I mean with reference to the fireplace in the room?"

"He was near the fireplace."

"And there's a tiled area there, isn't there?"

"Yes. There was a tiled area, as usual."

"As I understand your testimony, Doctor, the injury you have described could have been caused by tripping and falling backwards and striking your head against these tiles. Is that correct?"

He pursed his lips and looked at the ceiling a moment. Then he looked at Bolden and said slowly, "It is not my place to speculate on such matters. What I have said will speak for itself. You may draw your own conclusions and the members of the jury may draw theirs."

I put my hand to the back of my neck and said, "What was that word again?"

He said sharply. "Occipital!"

"Thank you. I expect the jury knows all about such things, but the defendant feels that he has learned something."

Bolden stood up and fiddled with a pencil. He said, "The Commonwealth wants to conform to the defendant's motion, but wonders if it is really necessary to require this witness to remain in court indefinitely. Physicians, the Court will understand, are faced with certain demands and responsibilities which are out of the ordinary."

I said, "If the Court please, the defendant is willing to excuse Dr. Maxwell, but no other witness."

Maxwell gave me a frigid nod.

64.

Zack and Beulah Mae Woods were the next witnesses and their testimony was so similar, even to the choice of words, as to indicate meticulous rehearsals.

They testified that they had served drinks and snacks at the party, and then before midnight, were excused and went to their rooms over the garage. Mrs. Sothern had told them they could take it easy until after the guests had gone, and then they should come back to the house, help with the last minute packing after Mr. and Mrs. Sothern had changed into travel clothes, handle the baggage, accompany them to the train, and bring the car home. They were told that they could then go on to bed, leaving the dirty glasses and dishes until Saturday.

They testified that when they left the kitchen they locked the back door behind them. They waited until about one-thirty, and when "Miss Marty" didn't ring for them they went over to the house anyway, let themselves in the kitchen door with Beulah Mae's key, and went to the second floor, using the back stairs.

Some time around two o'clock "Miss Marty" came staggering upstairs as if she were hurt, and right after that she fainted. Beulah Mae thought Miss Marty would have a miscarriage. Zack went down and talked to "Mr. Mitch" and received instructions to take Miss Marty to the hospital. He and Beulah Mae carried her down the front stairs, put her in the car, and took her to City Hospital. Later they called the house and could get no answer, so in the morning they called "Mr. Jess." Mr. Jess came down to the hospital after awhile, and then they went home and that's all they knew about it.

Zack testified first. When Bolden turned him over to me

– 219

I said, "The back door was locked after you left the first time, before midnight?"

"Yessuh. Nighttime I can't hahdly go out a door without I lock it behin' me. It was locked all the time only except when Beulah Mae and me come back in and go upstairs, an' even then we lock it behin' us."

"Now when Miss Marty came upstairs, Zack. Did you say you went down after that and talked with Mr. Mitch?"

"Yessuh. I want to know what to do."

"Was Mr. Mitch all right at that time?"

"Yessuh. We talk just like you and me talkin' here. He tell me what to do and I done it."

"And what time was that?"

" 'Bout two, Mr. Jess. Mebbe little after two. Beulah Mae an' me, we was afraid they was goin' to miss the train. Two or three times, Beulah Mae unpack Miss Marty's travelin' clock and look."

"Was I there?"

"No, suh. Nobody there. Mr. Mitch downstairs all by hisself."

"When you went to the hospital did you lock the door behind you?"

"Yes, suh. Sho did."

65.

JOE HERDT was slicked up as if he were on his way to a funeral. When his name was called he came through the gate in the railing, self-consciously, bringing with him a faint odor of bay rum. The back of his neck was freshly shaven almost up to the level of his ears, and his hair was combed over the top of his head where slick scalp was beginning to glisten.

He did not seem happy and would not look at me. He sat uncertainly on the edge of the witness chair, turned slightly sideways, so that only a part of one large buttock prevented him from making like an avalanche.

Joe said he lived in the 2100 block of Cynthiana Street and had been a bus driver for City Transit Company for eleven years. He used to work the day shift but his hours were now from eight in the evening until four in the morning. The company was a little short on drivers, and he could nearly always put in overtime if he wanted to. Friday he had come on duty at five-thirty, he could use the extra money. His little girl was sick.

The people at the garage knew he might get a call to come home, because he told them special. He was worried about his little girl. When he came in from a run about one-forty, a message was waiting for him and relief had already been arranged. Joe walked home, taking a route that brought him to the intersection of Cedar and Virginia around two o'clock Saturday morning—maybe two-five, maybe two-ten. At that time and place he saw the defendant walking toward him on Cedar.

Joe said he knew where 1918 Cedar Avenue was located, and if a person had left that address and started for the Albemarle Apartments, the direction such a person would take was the same as the direction in which he had seen me walking. His eyes were riveted on Bolden, and then on the freshly shined toe of the knobby shoe stuck out in front of him. He wouldn't look at me. I saw his wife sitting in the fourth row of spectators, staring at him formidably, her lips set in a grim line.

Under Bolden's questioning, Joe said that at that time he had not known me by name. However, he had known me by sight for some time, because when he was on the day shift I had ridden home on his bus almost every evening.

Bolden adroitly came back to his meeting with me at Cedar and Virginia and brought out that there was an arc light at the intersection, that he saw me clearly at a distance of not over forty feet, and that his identification was firm. Joe said he nodded to me and I nodded in recognition.

The assistant Commonwealth's Attorney consulted his notes and whispered with Bolden. Richmond went over and huddled with them. Bolden had been about to turn the witness over to me, but he nodded and resumed his questioning.

He said, "Mr. Herdt, you have stated that prior to Friday evening—last Friday evening, that is—you knew this defendant only by sight. Has anything occurred since that time to improve your acquaintance?"

Joe stared at his shoe and didn't answer.

Bolden left his table and went over and stood close to Joe, with one foot on the little platform where the witness chair sits. He said, "Just tell the jury what has happened since last Friday night to bring about a better relationship—a closer relationship—between you and Mr. London."

Joe continued to stare at his shoe.

I said, "Go ahead and tell him, Joe."

Joe Herdt brought his eyes up slowly and settled on a point northwest of the head of juror number twelve. He licked his lips and then said, very low, "Mr. London gave my little girl two blood transfusions."

Bolden bent closer and said, "I'm sorry. I'm afraid you didn't speak loud enough for the jury to hear. Will you repeat, please?"

Joe gave him a smoldering look and the answer was almost a snarl. "I said Mr. London came to the hospital and gave my little Joanna two blood transfusions. Is that loud enough to hear?"

"Thank you, yes. You may interrogate the witness, Mr. London."

I said, "Don't worry about it, Joe. How is she now?"

He looked at me, finally, with sweat popping out visibly on his forehead. His neck was a deep red. The lines of his face were set heavily and there was misery in his eyes. He said, "Saturday I am afraid she will die. Today she wants to climb trees in the yard. It is beyond belief."

"That's wonderful. I know you and your wife are very happy. You must give her my love."

I was sitting at my table. On the yellow pad, my pencil had done two pieces of mountain coming together in a valley. Over the valley there was something that could have been either the sun or a full moon. The foreground was supposed to be water with the sun (or moon) shining on it. There was a suggestion of perspective, which surprised me.

I put down the pencil and said, "If the Court please, the defendant does not wish to cross-examine at this time, but would like to have the privilege of recalling the witness later."

"No objection," said Bolden smugly.

Thornton said, "Granted. The witness will remain in Court, subject to recall. This seems to be a good time to recess for lunch. Court will reconvene at one-thirty."

66.

THE OFFICIAL stenographer put the cap on his ink bottle, the clerk gathered up the papers that a clerk always seems to have, the Judge disappeared, Bolden put his file in order and turned it over to his assistant. The spectators crowded into the aisles, pushing against each other, stepping on toes and heels, lighting cigarets, grousing irritably as hungry people usually do.

I let it all happen, not participating. If the water and

the suds wanted to rush out of the tub and leave me sitting there, it was strictly all right as far as I was concerned. While something had been going on I had not been conscious of fear, but now the muscles of my thighs and back and neck were almost in a state of cramp. My hands began to tremble.

I realized that trying to appear casual had drained most of my reserves of nervous energy. I was not sleepy, but my body wanted to yawn and I could do nothing to prevent it. The result was so satisfactory that I stood and stretched until my internal listening system heard a variety of cracking sounds. Then the blood seemed to flow freely again and messages of relaxation seemed to bustle along the nerve channels. My face felt as if it had been in a mud pack until I put up both hands and rubbed it vigorously.

When I came out of this psychic orgy there was no one left in the courtroom except Fant, George Stern, a deputy sheriff, and me. They were awkward, looking at me but not at each other. I wondered what impression had been produced by my re-activating routine but I didn't really care.

I looked at Fant and said, "I don't feel hungry, but I know I ought to eat something. How about Stovener's Grill? I want you and George to be my guests."

Fant looked at the deputy sheriff and didn't say anything.

I looked at him, too. I said, "What cooks?"

The deputy sheriff shifted his weight and was embarrassed. He said, "I'm sorry, Mr. London, but you know how it is. It's just a job, but I got to do it to get my pay."

I didn't get the connection. I felt like a lawyer, not like the defendant. I said, "That's okay. What is it you're paid to do?"

He looked at me steadily and stuck out his lower lip. Fant said, "The bail bond promises you'll be produced when the trial starts, Jess. It doesn't cover you during the trial. Maybe we could have done something about it, but the Judge isn't here and I didn't think about it."

I put on a grin that I didn't feel. I said, "Of course. My mistake. It's the first time I've been the prisoner at the bar, and I'm not used to the routine. See you later." I looked at the deputy sheriff and said, "Where are your bars? I'll get behind them without any fuss."

George Stern said, "It's simply a matter of being in technical custody. I don't see why we couldn't all go down to Stovener's Grill if the officer would come along."

I looked at the deputy sheriff. He was a small, shriveled-up type who couldn't have prevented me from breaking open a hard-boiled egg. I figured he was around sixty-two years seven months of age, entitled to his job solely by reason of voting the straight ticket during the entire span of my life. He looked as if the idea of going with me to Stovener's Grill was a mental crisis of the first degree. I had an idea he'd either have a heart attack or call a cop.

I said, "I meant I want you to be my guests at lunch the first day after the trial's over." I turned to the deputy sheriff and took his arm. I said, "Come on, Javert, let's wander through the sewers of Paris and look for the Bastille."

He said, "Huh?"

I said, "Don't worry about it. We sometimes use double-talk. Let's put me in the clink so you can take the bus home and eat with your grandchildren. By the way, how many grandchildren do you have?"

The turn of events had made him lighthearted. The crisis had passed. He said, "Two—a boy and a girl. But another one's due in August. My daughter's pregnant again."

I said, "That's fine." We were already on the way toward the door. I looked over his head at Fant and Stern and raised my eyebrows and grinned. Fant laughed and picked up his hat.

67.

Down the hall a door was ajar. The frosted-glass panel said "Commonwealth Attorney" in black letters. As we went by I heard voices and out of the corner of my eye caught a glimpse of Judge Abercrombie gesticulating across a desk at Matt Bolden and Lieutenant Richmond, both of whom showed expressions of exasperation.

I learned that my deputy sheriff was James Maloney, that in the eighth precinct of the sixth ward he was known as "Mr. Jim," and that at home he was called "Jamie." The grandchildren called him "Grandpa Jamie" to distinguish him from Grandpa Fred who had once been a famous tackle at Vanderbilt, had been a real estate agent, had fallen through some rotting cellar steps, and now used a crutch because for some obscure reason the bone wouldn't knit properly.

By this time we were walking up the steps to the entrance of the County jail. I hoped I looked like a social worker or a Baptist minister or a member of a committee appointed by the Governor, but I felt as if my suit had broad horizontal stripes. As we went in the door there was an odor of disinfectant, combined with what disinfectant is supposed to take the place of.

I guess there is a caste system in the Halls of Justice, pretty much as there is in India or in a hill of ants. Instead of being locked up in one of the better cells, I was ushered into the jailer's office. The jailer himself had political sense enough to be absent so that he did not have to choose between effusiveness, matter-of-factness, condescension, or superiority. After all, as far as he knew I might be Jack the Ripper or the next County Judge. It couldn't hurt anything to treat me diplomatically as long as he was away and could call it all a mistake if he had to.

I was not obliged to eat jail fare, either—a break which I later realized to be of economic origin. "Jamie" told me I could order anything I liked by phone, and then pointedly produced a soiled menu from a joint across the street. I wasn't hungry, but ordered a roast beef sandwich and a glass of milk. I wondered if the jail had a deal on such orders and cynically assumed that it did. This assumption gave me a feeling of sophistication.

Around one o'clock Judge Abercrombie came to see me in the jailer's office. He was wearing a celluloid collar and an old-fashioned string tie and his extreme age showed itself in the scrawny flaps under his chin. I stood up, instinctively, until he got himself into a chair that was, inevitably, a little too high for him. I tried to keep my eyes away from his button shoes which hung two or three inches short of the floor.

He said, "I won't waste time apologizing, Jess. You'll have to forgive an old man. You know, age makes people shortsighted."

I didn't say anything.

He said, "I've been sitting in the back of the room, listening to the trial. You've handled yourself passably enough, so far, but the idea of defending yourself is very foolish. You ought to have counsel. Against this kind of charge, one slip or mistake in judgment is too many."

I said, "I appreciate your coming, Judge. Your conclusion that I was either negligent or actually disloyal was pretty hard to take. It hit me where I live. I'm glad you've changed your mind."

He made a gesture as if to dismiss the whole thing. He said, "As a member of our organization you're entitled to our backing, Jess. I'm not the man I used to be but I think some of the old cunning is still here." He tapped his head. "Stoakes says you're stubborn about not taking any help, and things have gone pretty far already—probably too far to start over. But there isn't any reason why you shouldn't let me appear as

– 227

co-counsel and sit at the table with you. I think I have considerable standing in this community and even that would be a help." He gave me a wrinkled, grotesque sort of smile that showed his set of store teeth. "How do you know? I might even come up with a valuable thought, now and then."

I said, "Thanks, but it might give the impression that I'm running for cover. I started this alone, and that's the way it must be finished."

He accepted finality when he saw it. He squirmed until his feet touched the floor, eased himself out of the chair, and came over to put a bony hand on my shoulder. I didn't notice until then that he was chewing tobacco. He said, "Good luck."

I said, "Thanks."

68.

WHEN COURT reconvened the first witness was Charley Pitts. As in the case of Joe Herdt, he wouldn't look at me. All during his session in the witness chair he sat painfully erect, with his elbows drawn back on the arms of the chair as far as they could go.

After getting his name, address and occupation into the record, Bolden wasted no time. He said, "Did you see the defendant come into the Albemarle Apartments on Friday evening or Saturday morning?"

The witness nodded, yes.

"Just tell the jury what time that was."

Pitts ran his tongue over his lips. He said, "I reckon it was a little after two."

"That would be Saturday morning, April 27th?"

"That's right."

"How long have you known the defendant?"

"Several months, ever since he's been living there. I'd have to look at the records to give you the exact date."

"Have you seen him every day?"

"Except when it's my day off, I guess so."

"No difficulty about recognizing him—distinguishing him from someone else?"

"No, sir. I reckon not."

Bolden turned to me. "You may ask the witness."

I said, "How do you happen to say it was around two o'clock that I came in?"

Pitts sank his head down a little, between his shoulders. He said defensively, "All I know is to say what I know. That's what time it was, to the best of my knowledge and belief. I'm not telling no lies."

"Did anything else happen? Anything that's associated in your memory with my coming in?"

"There was some singing. I remember that. It was outside somewhere. They were singing when you came in."

"Remember the song, by any chance?"

He thought it over briefly, then shook his head. "Can't say as I remember."

"One person singing, or more than one?"

"More than one. A bunch, it sounded like."

"Men's voices, or women's voices, or both?"

"Both, I'd say, best I can remember. I wasn't paying any particular attention."

"Harmonizing? Sort of singing you'd do after a party?"

"You might call it that. Sounded sort of like a bunch of drunks. I wouldn't want to say for sure."

I said, "That's all, for now. I guess it's understood I can recall this witness later for further questioning."

Bolden nodded.

Judge Thornton said, "The witness will remain in the courtroom until the conclusion of the trial or until dismissed by agreement of counsel."

69.

THE NEXT FOUR witnesses were the occupants of the yellow Hudson sedan. They appeared, successively, and gave their names as Philip Thomas, Frank Hicks, and Alice and June Gravura. Except for minor details, their testimony was the same.

The four of them had been "going together" for some considerable time. Their ages ranged from seventeen in the case of Alice Gravura to twenty-two in the case of Frank Hicks. The girls were still in high school, so they stayed out late only on weekends. On Friday evening, April 26th, the boys came by and picked up the girls at their home along about eight-thirty. They were allowed the use of the Gravura car.

After going to a movie they drove out into the county and parked for awhile behind a church and just sat and talked. Frank had a bottle of whiskey and they had some drinks. They got back to the Gravura home about one-thirty or one-forty-five and stayed in the car, singing a lot of songs. The Gravura home was four doors away from the Albemarle Apartments, and on the same side of the street.

A little after two o'clock, or sometime in that neighborhood, a man came along the street walking toward the Albemarle Apartments. It was dark and they did not see his face well enough to recognize him, but he was about the same size as the defendant. Maybe they were a little tight by that time

—anyway they jokingly invited him to join them and he got into the car and had a few drinks and sang with them. He didn't stay very long and it was certainly no later than two-thirty when he left the group and walked up and entered the Albemarle Apartments. It might have been as early as two-fifteen, they weren't keeping track of the time.

The thing they noticed was that this man walked off with a hat sitting cockeyed on his head. When he approached the Albemarle where they could see him under the street light, they could see the hat was green. The man wasn't what they would call "pie-eyed drunk" but he had had plenty of drinks and didn't walk very steadily.

My cross-examination was brief. Philip Thomas will give you the gist of it. When Bolden had finished with him I said, "You mean this man was a total stranger who just happened to be walking along the street around two o'clock in the morning? You asked him to join you in the car with these two young girls and gave him some drinks without knowing anything about him?"

He squirmed. "Yes, sir. I guess it sounds silly, but that's what we did. It seemed to be a good idea at the time."

"You were pretty well oiled yourselves, I suppose?"

Sheepishly, "We'd had some drinks."

"Quite a few?"

"Some."

"Do the four of you sing together quite a lot?"

"Yes, sir. We like to sing. I'd say we have a few songs most every time we go out."

"What were some of the songs you sang Saturday morning? Remember any of them?"

"Oh, the usual stuff. Things we know the words of, and that sing together good."

"What, for example?"

"I dunno as I could say for sure. One thing and then another. Probably *Down By the Old Mill Stream* and *Gene-*

vieve and *Sweet Sue* and *I Been Working On the Railroad* . . . stuff like that."

"How about *Girl of My Dreams?*"

"We probably sung that too, I can't say rightly. Stuff like that."

"Now how about this hat again?"

"Well, just like I said. This fellow walked off, and then when he got in the light down by the apartment house, we could see it was green. I thought it was my hat and started to get out and chase him, and then he went in and I thought what the hell . . . I mean . . ."

"What made you think it was your hat?"

"Well, mine was green, too, and it was gone. You don't see many green hats."

"What are your initials?"

"P. W. T."

I went over and asked Richmond for the hat we had found in the Hudson sedan. He looked sour but he produced it. I brought it over and handed it to the witness. I said, "Here's a green hat marked 'Commonwealth Exhibit 7' with the initials P. W. T. in the band. See if that's your hat you were talking about."

He took it and examined it and tried it on. "Yes, sir, that's my hat."

I excused him with the same permission to recall for further questioning if I should see fit to do so.

70.

AFTER JUNE GRAVURA we had a ten-minute recess and I went into the clerk's office and had three cigarets as fast as I could smoke them. It was after four o'clock and I was tired. A dullness in the back of my head suggested that a headache was coming on. When I heard the gavel pounding for order I doused the last cigaret and went in and took my place. The witness was Mr. Block. Bolden got down to business fast.

Mr. Block testified that he lived in the Albemarle Apartments, was forty-eight years of age, and was state representative for a nationally known concern. His duties required him to travel all over the state and he was familiar with the hotel accommodations available at various places. Saturday morning, April 27th, he had an early appointment in a small town. Instead of driving down Friday and spending the night, he decided he would rather go to bed early, leave an early call, and drive down from the city Saturday morning.

He slept well until about twelve-thirty when he unaccountably awakened. He then remembered that he had failed to leave a call at the desk so he picked up the phone and left a call for four o'clock. After that he was unable to go back to sleep. About one-thirty he decided it was useless to try to go back to sleep and that he might as well get out on the road, using the time at the other end of the trip to have a leisurely breakfast and read the newspaper.

He then got up, shaved, bathed, and dressed. His bag was already packed and he went down in the elevator some time after two o'clock. When he left the Albemarle Apartments he saw the defendant. The defendant was walking north on the east side of the street, appeared to have had quite a few drinks, and wore a green hat which looked odd on him. Mr.

Block did not know the defendant very well, but had seen him many times in the elevator or in the lobby and had no difficulty in recognizing him. There was a street light near the Albemarle, and in addition to that the apartment house had a marquee which was lighted all night. There was plenty of light. The witness did not speak to the defendant, but nodded to him in recognition and received a nod in return.

Mr. Block was neither friendly nor hostile, simply matter-of-fact. He seemed solid and secure and I knew that his testimony was damaging. At the same time, I couldn't think of a damn thing I could do about him. The headache was growing in the back of my head. It was beginning to throb. Up to this time I had taken things in my stride, conserving my ammunition and managing to keep up my spirits.

Now I began to feel desperate. Here there was no question of the light, or drunkenness, or what the witness may have had on his mind. This guy was poison.

My mouth was dry. I said, "Where do you keep your car, Mr. Block?"

"In the Prince garage. It's the nearest all-night garage. I frequently have to go out in the night."

"That's north of the Albemarle, isn't it?"

"That's right."

"So when you came out Saturday morning, you naturally turned north, didn't you?"

"Yes, I turned north. I was going to the garage."

"And this man you have identified as being me. You say he was coming from the south?"

"From the south, yes. That's what I said."

"Then if you came out and turned north to go to the garage, you couldn't have had more than a glimpse of this man, could you? I mean, just before you turned?"

He said, "I didn't stop and stare, if that's what you mean. However, there was plenty of time to recognize a person, and

I recognized this one. If I were at all uncertain, I would say so."

"When you came out of the entrance and turned north, how far away was this person?"

"Under the marquee. A few more steps and we would have been at the entrance simultaneously."

"Haven't there been other occasions, recently, when you have encountered me under the same circumstances?"

"Not to my knowledge. In any event, I'm positive about this occasion on Saturday morning, if that's what you mean."

"Have you ever seen me wearing a green hat?"

"On Saturday morning around two o'clock. I don't recall any other time."

"Thank you. I guess that's all for the present."

"Am I at liberty to go?"

Judge Thornton said, "The witnesses will be required to remain in the courtroom, subject to recall, until expressly excused by agreement of counsel."

Block seemed to know I was responsible. He gave me a furious glance and I met it with what I suppose was a mixture of surliness and defiance. He hesitated a moment, apparently debating whether to make an issue of it, then stomped across to the gate in the railing, went through, and sat grimly in the chair he had vacated in the first row.

I did not look at him, but knew that he was mentally sending me to the electric chair and getting a nasty sort of enjoyment out of it.

71.

JUDGE THORNTON looked at the clock significantly, but Bolden knew his case was going well and chose not to notice. He quickly sent Richmond to the witness chair. The throb in the back of my head suddenly became almost unbearable. The corners of my eyes squinted in pain but I couldn't make them relax. Everything began to seem remote and unreal.

Richmond said he was Alpheus T. Richmond, Lieutenant of Detectives. He gave his home address, stated how long he had been on the force. Headquarters got him out of bed shortly after three-thirty on the morning of April 27th. A squad car picked him up and he went to 1918 Cedar Avenue. He arrived at the same time as the Coroner and was present when the Coroner made his examination of the person later identified as Mr. Mitchell Sothern.

Bolden skipped immediately to my visit on Saturday morning and I heard my confession repeated back to me as if it had been recorded. By that time each heartbeat felt like a minor explosion in my eyeballs and I was following the words only with great difficulty.

Before I was prepared for it, Bolden dumped the witness in my lap. I sat there, nearly blind and nearly deaf, teetering on the edge of nausea. I wanted more than anything to ask for a recess, but some sort of visceral intuition told me I could not afford any appearance of weakness at this time.

Bolden looked pointedly at me. So did Judge Thornton. Richmond looked at me, along with every other eye in the room. The air had a sort of legal gasoline vapor in it. If someone had struck a match, hell would have broken loose.

I forced upon myself a calmness that did not exist. I carefully, slowly, drew a five-pointed star and took some time off to equalize the points as best I could. The silence sounded like a striking clock.

I put aside the pencil, firmly, and looked at Richmond. I said, "Lieutenant, just tell the jury whether you believed that confession."

Bolden said, "Object."

Thornton said, "Sustained. We are not concerned with what the witness thought."

I said, "Very well, let's put it this way. After this confession, did you arrest me, Lieutenant?"

After a moment he said, "No, I did not."

"Did you take me down to headquarters for questioning?"

"No."

"I believe you said all this took place in a police car on the way to City Hospital. Is that correct?"

"You ought to know."

Thornton looked at me, expecting a complaint. I ignored the opportunity and went on. I said, "Will you repeat your statement as to who else was present when all this took place?"

"You and I and Corporal Lautzenheiser. No one else was in the car."

"I assume he will be available for questioning?"

"Of course. He's been subpoenaed. You know that."

"Thank you, Lieutenant, that's fine. Now when we arrived at the hospital after I had confessed to this crime, did you leave me in the custody of Corporal Lautzenheiser?"

"No I didn't, Mr. London, you know that. When I went into the hospital you went right along with me."

"All the way?"

"As far as the elevators."

"And then what? Why don't you go ahead and tell the jury what you did, Lieutenant? Isn't it a fact that you refused to let me go up in the elevator with you, despite the fact that I had just confessed in detail to the very crime you were investigating?"

He didn't like it, but he was stuck with it. He squirmed a little and then disciplined himself and stopped. He said, "I went up alone. I wanted to interview Mrs. Sothern and I didn't want you butting in."

"So you left the confessed murderer unguarded in the lobby of the hospital? You knew Lautzenheiser was out in the car, didn't you?"

He could have answered that he had no knowledge of what Lautzenheiser had done, but he was too smart. That kind of answer would only get him involved. He said boldly, "Yes, as far as I knew, the Corporal was out in the car. I left you alone in the lobby, yes. I wasn't afraid you'd get away."

I picked up the pencil and then put it down again. I got up and stood in front of the jury box, folded my arms and turned my back on the jury and leaned my rump against the railing that cut them off from the courtroom. I said, "According to my confession, how did I get through this front door that Mrs. Forman says was locked?"

"You said you had Mr. Sothern's keys. You said he had given them to you so you could go out and get some liquor. We verified that. You went."

I ignored the opportunity to object. I said, "Did you find the keys? I don't believe you saw fit to mention that point in your direct testimony."

"Yes, we found the keys. They were in Mr. Sothern's pocket."

"Reverting to my confession again, Lieutenant. To test your recollection. What reason, if any, did I give for this alleged return to the Sothern home some two hours after the party was over?"

"You *said* you went back to get your hat."

"Well, what about that, Lieutenant? Let's don't spar around and waste the jury's time. Isn't it a fact that you found my hat upstairs on a bed where I left it early in the evening?

238 –

Isn't it a fact that you have my hat over there, marked for identification and all that?"

"I don't know when you left it, or why you didn't pick it up when you went back. It's over there, yes. I found it on a bed in the guest room. It's marked for identification like the rest of the evidence. What does that prove?"

I was entitled to heckle him about an answer like that, but there was a sense of momentum I couldn't afford to lose.

I said, "This—this so-called weapon. This cigaret lighter, I believe you've got it marked Exhibit 3. Did I understand you to say you found it out in the hall—not in the room where Mr. Sothern was found?"

"You said you put it out there after you used it. You know that."

"It was in plain sight?"

"Right on the table where you said you put it."

"You examined it for fingerprints?"

"Yes, and found your prints on it. Sergeant Lohrman examined it first, and then I verified his findings. He's here and will testify when his turn comes."

"How about blood? Find any blood? How about hair? Did you find any hair on this—this so-called weapon?"

"No, we didn't find any. There wouldn't have been any. We didn't expect to find hair or blood."

"You mean Mr. Sothern was bald? He didn't have any hair where he was hit?"

"No, I don't mean that. Take a look at that cigaret lighter. It's embedded in a highly polished ball of steel. How would a man's hair stick to a thing like that? It was a bruising, crushing blow. Not a cut. There wasn't any gushing of blood."

"Wouldn't a shiny surface like that show an impression of having struck a hairy surface, just as it would show fingerprints?"

"Perhaps. Not necessarily."

I changed my position a little and folded my arms again. I said, "Perhaps my memory is faulty, or perhaps you were intentionally vague on one point, Lieutenant. Did you or did you not, at the time of this confession, question me as to wether Mr. Sothern was dead or alive when I'm supposed to have left the house?"

Even as practiced a witness as Richmond could not avoid a little movement that indicated his dissatisfaction with the question. It was only a slight movement—a turning in the chair and the uncrossing of his legs. He said, "I questioned you about it, yes."

"Well, don't stall. Why don't you tell the jury all about it."

"I was just getting to that, but other things came first. According to my recollection, you said Mr. Sothern was dead when you left the house. Of course, that couldn't be true. You heard the Coroner testify that death occurred while he was present. That was around four o'clock."

"Did I give any reason—any basis for saying he was dead before that?"

"Yes, you did. You *said* you felt for his pulse and didn't find it, and therefore assumed he was dead. Obviously you must have been wrong. The fact that there was swelling proves that, as you heard the Coroner testify."

"Why would I have added a fancy touch like that, Lieutenant, unless it was the truth? Or unless I was making the whole thing up?"

He said, smugly, "I wouldn't know, Mr. London. You ought to be able to answer that question yourself, and I don't know who else could. It was your confession, not mine."

I said quickly, "You thought it was fiction at the time, when you suspected someone else. Now it suits your purpose to pretend you believe it. Isn't that true?"

Bolden created a diversion by shaking his head and blowing out his breath as evidence of his exasperation. Judge Thornton was annoyed at both of us, but shut his lips in a tight line and said nothing.

Richmond said, "Certainly not." It was scarcely heard.

I said, "If the Court please, I'm tired and hungry and I'm sure the jury must be, too. The defendant asks adjournment until tomorrow morning."

Matt Bolden said, "Your Honor, two more witnesses will complete the case for the Commonwealth. I suggest a night session. Perhaps the case can be completed tomorrow and then the jury could be released."

Judge Thornton said, "There will be a ten minute recess. Counsel will join me in chambers."

People stirred and stretched and sighed and whispered. Bolden and his assistant walked briskly and I followed more slowly, feeling dead and trying not to drag my feet. It makes a lot of difference whose life is at stake.

When the door was shut behind us, Fant spoke first. I hadn't realized he was there. He said, "Judge, I guess it's none of my business according to the record, but I've been watching Jess and I'd like to call the Court's attention to the fact that he's all in. He's out on his feet."

Thornton said, "It's all right, Stoakes. I didn't think it should be discussed before the jury. Matt, under ordinary circumstances I'd be inclined to hurry things along but as things stand I'm inclined to adjourn until in the morning. Have you any real objections?"

I said stubbornly, weakly, "Anyway, Your Honor, the two witnesses won't complete the case for the Commonwealth. I haven't waived my right to cross-examine. I've only deferred it, with the consent of Mr. Bolden. Cross-examination is a part of the case for the Commonwealth."

Bolden said, "Oh, all right. It's consented to. Let's let the record show that the defendant gets everything he wants."

The Judge said, mildly, "I think we can all use a night of sleep. The sarcasm and irritation are beginning to show ragged edges. The Court will not permit this trial to get out of hand."

I said, "Yes, sir." There was a loud humming in my ears and my vision was beginning to be indistinct.

Fant said, "May I be heard as a friend of the Court?"

Thornton smiled out of the side of his mouth. He said, "I think so, Stoakes. You've always been heard, haven't you?"

It was Fant's turn to smile. He looked at Bolden who shrugged and lit a cigaret. After the hours in the courtroom, the fragrance of the cigaret was maddening, but it would never have occurred to me to ask a favor of the Judge, under the circumstances.

Fant said, "I understand the Court has entered an order, as provided in the Code, for the actual custody of the defendant during the course of the trial. That's within the sound discretion of the Court. If I may be permitted to speak unofficially on behalf of the defendant, I ask that the Court depart from the general practice in capital cases and admit Jess to renewed bail until the case is submitted to the jury. I'll be personally responsible to the Court and in addition I have made arrangements to give a new bond with good surety, just in case. Jess ought to have a good rest and he's unlikely to get it in jail."

"Have you anything to say, Mr. Bolden?"

Bolden said, "Judge, I don't think the Commonwealth ought to agree to that, but personally I think it's all right. Why don't we show a formal objection and then go ahead and do it?"

"Very well. The clerk will make the proper entries."

The muscles around my eyes were tired from squinting. The light hurt me, and the pounding, pounding, pounding, went on in my skull. I watched in a red daze while the bond was fixed up. I focused on the page, put my finger opposite the signature line as a guide, and signed my name jerkily.

I said, "I don't suppose Miss Wiggens was in court."

Fant looked away. He said, "She was there, but she left just before adjournment."

All the way out to Fant's house I was in a nightmare. If

he had spoken to me I think I would have sobbed like a fool.
By the time we reached the stairs the sands were running out.
I clung to the banisters with one hand, and Fant supported me
on the other side with an arm around my shoulders.

I remember things hazily . . . hot soup . . . Fant's getting my clothes off . . . a doctor . . . a couple of tablets
. . . a shot in the arm . . .

And all the time the impossible, intolerable, throbbing and
pounding and pounding in my head . . .

Then a smooth, soft blackness . . . no headache . . . no
dreams . . .

When my eyes came wide open, I was awake. It was
morning and I felt fine. I was hungry. I lit a cigaret and lay
on my back and thought about the trial. The panic did not
return. I reminded myself of all the things that had not yet
been done. I took a shower and shaved and dressed and went
down and was cheerful and ate a solid breakfast.

72.

COURT RECONVENED at nine-thirty and Corporal Lautzenheizer
promptly took the witness stand. Once more I heard my confession repeated. The performance did not take fifteen minutes,
and then it was up to me, again.

I said, "Did I understand correctly? You've been on the
police force for eight years?"

"That's right. Since nineteen thirty-two. August four-
teenth, nineteen thirty-two."

"And how long have you worked with Lieutenant Richmond?"

"Three years. July, nineteen thirty-seven."

"During that time have you worked with Richmond and other detectives much or little?"

"Much. More than that. All the time. When I'm on duty, that is."

"How about confessions? Is this the only one you've ever heard?"

"Oh, no, I've heard plenty of confessions. I'd say most of the cases are routine, Mr. London. It looks like someone did whatever we're investigating and we pick 'em up and they see it's no use monkeying around and they just go ahead and tell us about the whole thing."

I had not bothered to get up from my chair. I played with a pencil for a long moment and then put it down and looked at the jury. Still looking at the jury, I said, "I don't want you to answer this question hurriedly, Corporal. Just take your time and think back carefully. I want you to tell the jury, if you will, how many times in your experience the police force of this city has failed to place under arrest, immediately, a person who has confessed to a crime. If you can't be exact, an approximation will do."

Time went by and he didn't answer.

I said, "I'll ask the official reporter to read the question back to the witness."

He said, "I couldn't say."

"As much as five times?"

"No, I guess not."

"As much as three times?"

"I don't know as I could say."

"Now just tell the jury if you *ever* knew it to happen."

"Yes, I've known it to happen."

"You've testified it happened in this case. Give the name of the defendant in any other case."

"I don't know as I could."

I said, "I'm sure I don't have to remind a member of the

police force that he is under oath. Let's be specific. Whether you remember the details or not, just tell the jury if you've ever known of a case, other than this one, in which a person has confessed to a crime without being taken into custody."

After a moment, "No, I can't say as I can recall one."

"Let's be really frank, Corporal. Isn't it a fact that you told Lieutenant Richmond in my presence that you didn't believe this confession you've just testified—"

"Object," said Bolden. "It's hardly necessary to state the grounds for the objection, but for the record—"

Thornton broke in and said, "Sustained. We're not concerned with what the witness believed or didn't believe."

I said, "No more questions, Your Honor."

73.

SERGEANT F. LOHRMAN gave his name and address, said he had been on the police force for fifteen years, and was assigned to the laboratory. He gave an extensive account of his qualifications as a fingerprint expert. He then stated that he had examined the object marked Commonwealth Exhibit 3, and had identified thereon fingerprints of the defendant corresponding with the prints appearing on a card marked Commonwealth Exhibit 8. No, the prints on Exhibit 8 were not taken by him personally. I interrupted, examined the exhibit, and stipulated that the prints were mine.

My turn.

I said, "Did you find any other prints on this object?"

"Yes, I found prints of the deceased. There were also some other prints which were smudged and unidentifiable.

They were, in any event, overlaid by your prints and those of Mr. Sothern, the deceased."

"As I undestand your testimony, Sergeant, you aren't attempting to establish the *time* when any of those prints were made, are you?"

"No. Your prints and those of Mr. Sothern were clear, indicating that they were recent, as distinguished from latent prints which are remote in point of time."

"When did you make your examination?"

"I classified the prints on Saturday. On Monday, I was furnished Exhibit 8 and made the identification."

"Are you able to say whether my fingerprints were made at two o'clock Saturday morning, or at, say eleven or twelve o'clock Friday night?"

"No, I wouldn't attempt that."

"Now, one more thing, Sergeant. This—this *thing*—I'm referring to Exhibit 3—has a highly polished surface, hasn't it?"

"That's right, it has."

"You went over the whole surface with the utmost care?"

"Yes, sir. That's my job."

"Did you find anything that would indicate this object had come into contact with a hairy object—a human head, for example?"

"No, I didn't. I found no such evidence."

"Let me ask you this. If a highly polished surface such as this—a surface perfect enough to take perfect fingerprints —came into contact with some part of a man's head where hair is growing, wouldn't you find evidence of that fact on this object?"

"Possibly so."

I said, "No more questions at this time. I'd like permission to recall the witness later."

74.

Matt Bolden looked up at the bench and said, "I ask the indulgence of the Court for a moment."

Judge Thornton merely nodded. Bolden pushed his spectacles up his nose and gave his attention to the yellow pad in front of him, observing the check marks he had made against his pre-trial notes. The people in the courtroom relaxed a little and there was a faint stir of whispering. Bolden's young assistant looked over his shoulder and gave an indefinable impression of realizing his importance.

The job took several minutes. Bolden would finish a page, wait for his assistant to nod agreement, push his spectacles up his nose in the automatic gesture, and pass on to the next one. Feet moved restlessly on the floor. People blew their noses.

Judge Thornton fixed his eyes in fascination upon a shiny cockroach which sent experimental feelers over the edge of the bench and then heaved himself up and stood full in the presence of the Court. For a moment the cockroach and the Judge studied each other with equal gravity. Thornton appeared to forget the trial and the room full of people. His hand slowly closed on the gavel and I could see his knuckles turn white as he gripped it. I held my breath. Then, unhurried, the cockroach brought himself clumsily around, let his feelers inquire of the edge of the bench again, retreated with quiet dignity, flattened himself, and disappeared into a very thin crack. I strained my eyes and thought I could see his feelers sticking out, but I couldn't be sure.

The whiteness left Thornton's knuckles, his fingers relaxed, and his eyes surveyed the room almost furtively. Trying to be inconspicuous, he produced a handkerchief, wiped the palms of his hands, and then wiped his lips. His eyes caught mine and there was a scarcely perceptible flicker of sheepishness before he put the handkerchief away. I realized that I had been tense. I realized, too, that I had been pulling for the cockroach.

Bolden seemed satisfied until he got to the last page of his notes, where his eyes lingered and surrounded themselves with a frown. He pushed his spectacles up his nose three or four times in nervous agitation, then leaned back and took them off and polished them, blowing his breath carefully on each lens and afterward holding them up to the light for inspection. Then he hooked them over his ears, blew his nose emphatically, and put the polishing cloth back in his pocket. He beckoned, and Richmond came over for a whispered consultation. Bolden kept pointing to his notes in exasperation. At length Richmond nodded and returned to his seat.

Bolden said, "The Commonwealth will call Judge Milton S. Abercrombie."

Judge Abercrombie, being a respected member of the bar, was not sitting with the crowd. He had been sitting inside the railing, although I had not noticed him. Now he advanced to the witness stand, erect, ancient, small and pot-bellied. The scrawny threads of his neck were enclosed in a new celluloid collar. The shiny surfaces of his black alpaca suit suggested the dignity of extreme age, not the pressure of poverty.

Somehow while he was on his way to the witness stand an upholstered footstool had appeared without anyone noticing it. The thing was simply there, and it enabled old Judge Abercrombie to get into the chair without the embarrassment which his short legs would ordinarily have occasioned. When he was seated and stuck out his neck to look, a brass spittoon was situated at the right spot. The crowd appeared not to notice when he spat, gently, and then wiped the white stubble of beard on his chin with the back of a thin, bony hand. After that he sat back and worked his lips until his plates were settled comfortably into place.

Matt Bolden went over and stood close, not with an air of aggression, but with an air of solicitude. He bent his head and said, almost with reverence, "Judge, for the purposes of the record will you give your name, address and occupation?"

Abercrombie did so. The people in the courtroom were impressed.

Bolden said, "We don't want to keep you any longer than is necessary, Judge. Please tell the jury, if you will, what happened last Friday afternoon that might cast any light on the relationship between the deceased, Mr. Mitchell Sothern, and the accused, Jesse London."

Judge Abercrombie appeared to want to spit, but did not do so. He considered the question, with his thin fingers tip to tip in the shape of an umbrella. He did not speak until he had made sure his plates were under control. Then he said, slowly, "On last Friday afternoon, and by that I mean, to be precise, April twenty-six, nineteen hundred and forty, at or about the hour of three-thirty, possibly a few minutes before or after, Mr. Sothern, in my presence and hearing, instructed the defendant in this case to take a certain check to the office of the County Court Clerk of this County, to deliver the same, and to procure the signature of the said Clerk to a certain specified receipt therefor. Mr. Sothern emphasized the importance of this apparently simple transaction, and the significance thereof was apparently grasped by Mr. London. I believe that answers your question, doesn't it, Mr. Bolden?"

Bolden said, "Thank you, Judge. Now one more question, if you please. Just tell the jury whether or not that simple but very important act was performed by the defendant, as instructed?"

Abercrombie considered, verified the location of the spittoon, and spat with good intentions but characteristic inaccuracy. He said, "No, it was not."

"And now, one additional point. Assuming the tragic death of Mr. Sothern had not ensued, Judge Abercrombie, upon whom would the blame have fallen for the failure to present that check and get that receipt?"

Abercrombie paused, then said, "If Mr. Sothern had lived, the blame would have rested upon him. He would have been obliged to answer to the client for the fault of any member or associate of our firm."

Bolden said, "Thank you, Judge. That is all. You may ask the witness."

I doodled myself a sort of a duck, but it might have been a chicken. My mind was on Judge Abercrombie, but I was conscious of a feeling of irritation because I didn't really know the difference between a duck and a chicken, for drawing purposes. I made the bill broader, and then it looked like a chicken with a broad bill. It looked like hell.

I put the pencil down. I looked at Judge Abercrombie. He looked at me and wiggled his plates. Even in this process he contrived to look friendly.

I said, "Please tell the jury about firing me Saturday morning, Judge."

The old Judge shifted unhappily in the witness chair but the direct approach amused him, and I could see he was giving me a passing grade. He said, "When I saw in the morning paper that the property had not been redeemed, I—ah-well, fired you, yes."

"You gave me hell, didn't you?"

He grinned, "Yes, that's a fair way of putting it. I gave you hell."

"For carelessness and failure to carry out simple instructions?"

"Yes."

"Since that time, have you learned anything which has changed your opinion?"

He looked for the spittoon, missed, got out a clean handkerchief, wiped his white stubble, wiggled his plates, and put the handkerchief away.

He said, "You explained that Mr. Sothern came to your office, revoked his instructions, and undertook to deliver the check himself. I didn't believe you. Now I have reason to understand and believe what you told me."

Bolden was debating an objection, but gave up. He knew what was coming and didn't want to emphasize it.

I said, "What kind of a reason?"

Abercrombie took his time. He said, "I would rather not say this, but in justice I must. Mr. Sothern had acquired a substantial block of stock of Tremont Realty Company, but had not caused the stock to be transferred into his name on the books of the company."

"How do you know?"

"I have the stock certificates here. They were found in his baggage."

I said, "Wait a minute, Judge. I'm afraid the jury doesn't know anything about this Tremont Realty Company. Would you explain to the jury the practical meaning of the facts you've just stated?"

He said, "Of course. I'm sure the jury will have no trouble following this point. The delivering of the check was for the purpose of preventing the Tremont Realty Company from perfecting title to certain property which a purchaser had agreed to buy for a very nice price. Mr. Sothern had secretly bought up a substantial interest in the Tremont Realty Company. It's easy to see that the failure to deliver the check increased the value of his stock."

"By a substantial amount?"

"Very substantial."

"Then my so-called *carelessness* wouldn't have made Mr. Sothern angry, would it, Judge? It wouldn't have caused a quarrel between us, would it? Did I understand you to say you now realize I was telling the truth when I told you about Mr. Sothern coming to my office and undertaking to deliver the check himself . . . ?"

"Object," said Bolden. "The question called for a conclusion of the witness, based upon a fact which in itself is not in evidence . . ."

"Sustained," said Judge Thornton.

I said, "I'll withdraw the question. However, I'd like to ask another question which clearly calls for a statement of fact rather than a conclusion. Judge Abercrombie, I'll ask that you tell the jury whether I've been reinstated as an associate of your law firm."

The old Judge looked again for the spittoon, again missed. He said, "I jumped to an unwarranted conclusion, based upon insufficient evidence, and fired you. To state that you have been reinstated would be assuming that you are willing to resume the association, which may, in turn, be an unwarranted assumption."

I said, "Look. In plain English, do I have a job if I want it?"

He said, "To be short about it, yes."

There was a commotion in the courtroom and you could tell the crowd was amused and pleased.

75.

AFTER A CONSULTATION with Richmond, Bolden pushed back his chair and came over to me. He said in a whisper, "Another witness is under subpoena by the Commonwealth but her evidence is inconclusive and we see no point in putting her on the stand. Will you want to call her, or may she be released?"

I did not look at the jury but said, loud enough for them to hear, "You mean your witness, the nurse at the hospital?"

Bolden winced in annoyance. He wanted to shush me, but knew he couldn't. He nodded his head, yes.

I said, even a little louder, "Of course you don't have to call any witnesses you now think would help me, whether you've subpoenaed them or not. But I certainly don't want any witnesses released. I may want to call them to testify for the defense. I can't tell yet."

A flush of anger and frustration came up out of Bolden's collar and approached his ears. The artery in his neck pulsed against his collar. He turned abruptly and went back to his own table. He said grimly, "That's the case for the Commonwealth, if the Court please."

I was standing, too. I said, "May it please the Court, that's not the case for the Commonwealth. The defendant did not waive cross-examination, or further cross-examination, but deferred it with the consent of the Commonwealth. I will now, with the permission of the Court, exercise my right to recall the Commonwealth's witnesses and require them to explain many obvious loose ends which Mr. Bolden has overlooked or elected to ignore. I believe the case will come apart at the hinges, and out of the mouths of these very same witnesses."

Bolden stood his ground with resolution, not looking at me, but addressing himself frigidly to the Court. The tips of his ears were now pink and the tautness of his body, inclined slightly forward, showed fury in every line. His spectacles slid down his nose and he did not even bother to push them back.

He said, "The defendant deliberately twists everything I say, trying to squeeze out a morsel of sympathy and phychological comfort. I merely used the customary phrase to indicate that the Commonwealth has placed its evidence before the Court and the jury. As the defendant well knows, I agreed to his unusual request that the witnesses remain in the courtroom, thus giving him the opportunity to play one against another—"

I put in quickly, "Of course, if Mr. Bolden is afraid his witnesses can't afford to hear each other . . ."

The bang of the gavel cut me short. Now Thornton was angry. He said, "That will do! There will be no further baiting by counsel for either the Commonwealth or the defense. Argument of the case, within proper limits, will be made to the jury at the proper time. If there are any matters to be brought to the attention of the Court, there will be a recess and Counsel will be heard in chambers. Is that clear?"

Bolden sat down and stared at the table in front of him. I said meekly, "Yes, Your Honor."

"Very well. Mr. London, there is no question of your right to recall any or all of the Commonwealth's witnesses. You may proceed."

I said, looking at the deputy sheriff, "Philip Thomas."

76.

THE EXCITEMENT which I had not felt all morning was now enveloping me like a cold shower. I sat down, trembling as if I were having a chill. My lips suddenly felt numb and flabby and out of control, as they felt the first time I stood in front of the student body, in the sixth grade, to recite "The Wreck of the Hesperus." I rubbed my face with both hands while Philip Thomas came through the gate in the railing and sat in the witness chair. My hands were sweating. Now the ball was mine to carry, and I had better make some touchdowns.

I said, "I believe you have testified that on Saturday morning around two o'clock and for some little time thereafter, you were in a yellow Hudson sedan which was parked in front of the home of Mr. and Mrs. Garvin Gravura, a short distance from the Albemarle Apartments."

He was wary, on the defensive. He tried to speak, cleared his throat noisily, and finally said, "Yes, sir. That's right."

"Frank Hicks and the two Gravura girls were with you."

"That's right."

"Sometime after two o'clock someone about my size came along the sidewalk, slightly drunk, and you asked him to join you."

"That's right."

I looked at him steadily and counted slowly up to twenty-five. He looked at me a few seconds, then elaborately changed his position and failed to bring his eyes back to mine. The room became quiet.

I said, not raising my voice, "You have known all the time it was Don Stith who got into the car with you. Why did you want to leave the jury with the impression it could have been me?"

Agitation was spelled out all over his face. He wiped the palm of one hand on the knee of his trousers. He had to clear his throat again before he could answer. He said, "It couldn't have been Don. He was out of town."

"You mean, don't you, that he later *said* he was out of town that night?"

A long pause. "I—I guess so."

"Don Stith is married, isn't he?"

A pause. "Yes, sir."

"Did he use to run around with you and Frank and these girls, before he was married?"

"Well, we were together sometimes, yes."

"And you sometimes drove out together in this car and parked until the small hours of the morning?"

A long pause again. "Maybe we did and maybe we didn't. I just couldn't say for sure."

"Just parked? Is that all?"

Bolden said wearily, "Object, Your Honor. Where Mr. London expects to get with these insinuations, I'm sure I don't know. I fail to see any bearing on the guilt or innocence of the defendant in this case."

I said, "If the Court will bear with me a moment?"

Thornton said, "Within limits, Mr. London. Even cross-examination can be carried too far afield."

I shrugged for the benefit of the jury and waited before asking my next question. I said, "If Don Stith was out of town, as you say, then why did you tell Lieutenant Richmond that it was Don who got in the car and sang with you?"

The witness was very unhappy. He said, slowly, "I guess maybe I might have told Lieutenant Richmond I *thought* it was Don Stith. It was dark and he was the same build . . . but of course it couldn't have been Don if he was out of town, could it?"

"No, it couldn't have been Don, *if* he was out of town. Suppose you were married and had told your wife you were going out of town. What would you say if someone claimed—"

"Object," said Bolden, interrupting. "Really, this is too outrageous!"

"Sustained," said Judge Thornton severely. "If any inferences are to be drawn from the evidence, they may be argued to the jury at the proper time."

I raised my eyebrows and dropped my pencil noisily on the table. After a moment I looked up at the witness and said, "You *did* tell Richmond it was Don Stith who got in the car with you, didn't you?"

"Like I said, maybe I might have told him that, not knowing . . ."

"Just answer the question, Philip. You certainly know whether you did or did not tell Lieutenant Richmond it was Don Stith. Just skip all the palaver someone may have given you later. All I want is a fact. Now, what did you tell Lieutenant Richmond when he first questioned you?"

Unwillingly, and with a measure of defiance, "All right, I

told him it was Don Stith. Now I know I was mistaken, that's all."

I looked significantly at the jury: What I saw was alert interest. In some of the faces I saw encouragement.

I turned back to the witness and said, "Which one of the girls left her panties in the car that night, along with your green hat?"

Bolden started to come up out of his seat, but I beat him to the draw. I said in disgust, "Never mind. It doesn't make any difference. If Mr. Bolden doesn't like the question, I'll withdraw it. I'll also dispense with further examination of the other witnesses who were in the car. It's obvious—oh, never mind."

Judge Thornton had a debate with his temper. He said, "There will be a fifteen minute recess. The jury may retire to the jury room."

77.

I WANTED TO stand and stretch. I wanted to go to the can. I didn't do either. I sat with all the appearance of unconcern that I could muster and turned to a fresh sheet and drew my awkward conception of an outline map of the United States. I put in the southern edges of the Great Lakes with a fair degree of satisfaction but found I had no idea of the shape of the Canadian edges. I put in a round black dot for Chicago and a wavy line for the Mississippi River.

There was an empty chair at the table beside me and Fant came over and slid into it. He said, "You're about to wear out your welcome with Judge Thornton. I hope you know what you're doing."

I looked at him coolly. I said, "What can he do to me? Anything worse than the electric chair? Name three things worse than that."

He said evasively, "I guess you've considered . . ." He didn't finish.

I said, "No matter how the case sounds, I have not seriously considered asking the jury to make allowances because I was tight. Am I reading your mind?"

He didn't answer.

I said, "Maybe you can see now why I'm representing myself. I was home in bed, but apparently I'm the only person who believes it. I don't want somebody with weak knees trying to figure how I can weasel out cheapest. I'm going to stay here and needle these birds until I find out what's going on."

"And if you don't?"

"There isn't any don't. I will. Stick around and listen."

"Well, at least keep your questions within reason. You aren't going to help yourself being nasty. Before long you'll have Thornton down your throat."

I said, "There are only twelve people in this room I'm concerned with, and Judge Thornton isn't one of them. These witnesses are screwed up somewhere and they're trying to back me into a chair that's all wired up—and not for sound, either. I'm going to do whatever it takes to keep twelve hands off the switch. When I start making *them* mad, come and whisper in my ear."

Wiggie was near the back of the room, craning to look at me between two heads. When I caught her eye she turned evasively and sat back out of sight.

78.

I CALLED Richmond back to the stand. I said, "Tell the jury whether or not, the first time you questioned Philip Thomas, he told you it was Don Stith who got into that Hudson sedan about two or two-thirty Saturday morning."

"He did. Later he said he wasn't sure. Then he thought he was wrong."

"Did Frank Hicks and Alice Gravura and June Gravura say the same thing and later change their minds?"

"Yes, when they learned Don Stith was out of town. Then I guess they knew they must have been mistaken."

"How did they *learn*, to use your word for it, that Stith was out of town that night?"

"You'll have to ask them. You can ask Stith himself, if you like. We've arranged to have him available if you want to question him."

"That's thoughtful of you, Lieutenant. Now let's see if you remember our meeting in front of the Albemarle Apartments last Saturday afternoon. Do you happen to remember that?"

"Yes, I remember meeting you, Mr. London."

"Did we subsequently walk south along the street together?"

"Yes, we did. You offered me a drink. I agreed. Whiskey is legal and there's no reason why I shouldn't have a drink when I'm not on duty."

I said, "You do me an injustice. I'm not needling you or trying to embarrass you. I'm on trial on a charge of murder and I'm entitled to bring out the facts. Please tell the jury whether in walking south we passed a yellow Hudson sedan parked at the curb, facing north, with the two doors on the side next to the sidewalk hanging open."

"Yes, such a car was there."

"Tell the jury what, if anything, you oberved in that car at that time and place."

"It's not strictly accurate to say that I *observed* anything. The word is misleading. We were passing the car and you made quite a point of stopping me and calling my attention to certain things in the car. I then looked in and saw them, as you evidently intended I should."

"All right, I'm sure the jury is duly impressed. Now if you've completed your speech, let's tell the jury what you saw in the car. To refresh your recollection, I'll ask you if you didn't see a green hat and a pair of female panties."

"At your insistence, I saw them, yes."

"The hat is the one which has been introduced as Exhibit 7, isn't it?"

"Yes, sir."

"With the initials P.W.T. in the band?"

"That's right?"

"Did you hear Philip Thomas identify that hat as being his?"

"I heard his testimony, yes."

I paused a moment, looked at the jury, and then said, "These pink panties haven't been preserved as an exhibit?"

"No, there didn't seem to be any connection. The green hat was preserved in anticipation of the fact that you would try to make something out of it, and for no other reason. Your *discovery* of the hat in the car was very pointed."

I said, "I'm confident that the jury believes, as you would have them believe, Lieutenant, that I procured from somewhere a pair of pink panties and a green hat inscribed with the initials of Philip Thomas, and placed these objects in the car, knowing I would meet you on Saturday afternoon in front of—"

"Objection, Your Honor, for the reason which is now becoming monotonous."

"Sustained. The Court is trying to be patient in view of the severity of the crime charged. The question will be stricken. Counsel is once again admonished not to insinuate his argument during the questioning of the witnesses."

I said, "That concludes my interrogation of this witness."

Bolden said, "I have no questions."

I said, "I wish to recall the witness Joe Herdt."

79.

JOE CAME from among the spectators and sat in the witness chair. He carried his hat in his hand. After he had crossed his legs he turned his hat around and around. His appearance was not hostile or defiant, but sad. He looked straight at me with distressed, injured eyes, like an Irish Setter who feels himself in disgrace but doesn't understand exactly why.

I said, slowly, "Joe, when you were testifying yesterday some distant memory kept trying to tell me something, but I couldn't put it on the table and look at it. I think last night it came to me, but I'm not sure. Tell me, was your trip home around two o'clock Saturday morning the only time you went home during that night?"

He looked relieved. He said, "No, I went home two times, Mr. London. Two times I got a call about Joanna, and two times I went home."

I said, "Now I begin to understand. Was the other trip earlier or later than two o'clock?"

"Before. When I went home the first time, the doctor was

there already and the fever came down. With children it is always sick one minute, well the next. I had to go back to work for money to pay the doctor bill. Then things went wrong again. I got another call and I went home. This time it was very bad and we went to the hospital with Joanna."

"Do you remember the time of your first trip home that night? I mean, approximately?"

He was thoughtful. "I am paid by the hour, the work records will show. I'm pretty good at remembering when I work. I count up in my mind how much money every time I finish my shift . . . I think the first call was handed to me when I came in from a run about ten-forty, ten-forty-five."

"Go home the same way?"

"Same way, yes. Always I go home the same way."

"I understand. Now think about it and tell the jury what time you came to the intersection of Cedar and Virginia on that first trip. Never mind being exact. Just come as near as you can."

"Maybe ten minutes, maybe fifteen. I walk it many times."

"I see. That would mean you reached that intersection somewhere around eleven o'clock, wouldn't it?"

"Near about. A little sooner, a little later."

I stood up and leaned forward with my hands on the table. I said, "Do you know of a liquor store on Virginia Avenue, two blocks from that intersection?"

"I know such a store, Mr. London. I have bought wine there sometimes."

I walked around the table and folded my arms. "Suppose I left the house at nineteen eighteen Cedar Avenue some time around eleven o'clock Friday night and walked to this liquor store, Joe. Would I pass by the intersection of Cedar and Virginia? Tell the jury that."

"Yes, of course. You walk up to the corner and turn and go to the liquor store."

Now I went over close to the witness chair and put one

foot up on the little platform where it sits. I had the rapt attention of the jury, and even Judge Thornton leaned over the bench to make sure he didn't miss anything.

I said, "Let me try my nagging little memory on you, Joe. This is very important and I don't want you to answer until you've thought it all over very carefully. Have you torn a hole in your trousers recently? At or near the right knee?"

Somewhere among the spectators there was a sound. Joe's wife was standing, and her handbag had fallen to the floor. She pointed excitedly and shouted, "The right knee, of course! Look, Joe, the right knee!"

There was a momentary uproar. The deputy sheriff banged his gavel and Judge Thornton banged his, too. When things subsided, Thornton said, "I trust I shall not be obliged to clear the courtroom. Who is this person?"

Joe Herdt had meanwhile uncrossed his legs and stared at his trousers. He now turned in the witness chair and looked up at the bench. He said, "Please, Your Honor, it's all right. It's only my wife, she won't cause no trouble. It's the right knee, like she says. See, the mend is here, I show it to you." He turned toward his wife and said sharply, "Maybe it will be all right if you sit down and don't yell any more in the Court."

Thornton said, "What's this about your trousers?"

Joe got up out of the witness chair, stood on one foot in front of the bench, raised a knee, and tried to show him. He said, "The mend where my trousers are torn, as Mr. London says."

"I see. That's your wife, is it?"

Joe said, "Mr. Judge, Your Honor, my wife is only a woman. She doesn't understand how you should behave in Court. She is a good woman, only she gets excited. We must forgive such things, she won't yell any more. It will be all right."

Thornton could not help smiling. He said, "Mrs. Herdt,

we're trying to conduct a trial here, and the Court cannot tolerate any disturbances from the spectators. I will permit you to remain, but only if you keep quiet. Do you understand?"

Mrs. Herdt struggled with a word, and sat down heavily. She was pale with apprehension.

"Counsel may continue."

I said, "Apparently you're wearing the very trousers I referred to. I wonder if you'd go over and let the jury see the mended place you've shown to Judge Thornton."

He did so. The jury bent forward and craned their necks for a good look. Joe came back and sat down.

I said, "Now, Joe, let's don't lose track of what we were talking about. There's been a lot of commotion, but I'm afraid there's nothing specific for the record. Maybe we'd better go back and get your answer to the question. Tell us whether or not you've recently torn a hole in your trousers."

Joe became sober. The mend in his trousers had seemed to be a happy circumstance, but it was obvious he didn't know why. He looked at me and blinked and said, "I answer yes, Mr. London. The mend is here, the stenographer should see for himself and put it in his book. I have showed Mr. Honor, the Judge, and over there the jury, too."

I said, "All right, Joe. Now think carefully and tell us when it happened."

He put two fingers against his lips and looked up at the ceiling. He said, with a wrinkle between his eyes, "I got out of the bus and caught the knee, here, on a little something that sticks out. It happened when I am starting home, so it does not make any great importance. When I reached home, my wife made the mend here at the knee, like I showed you, the stenographer should put it all down in the book."

I said, patiently, "That's very clear. But when did this happen, Joe? See if you can remember."

He put his face down into his hands for a moment and

then looked up with a radiant smile. "I was hurrying to get home because Joanna was sick. It happened Friday night with the fever. Ask my wife. She sewed it up good while the doctor was at my house. Then I went back to work."

I looked at the jury and then back at Joe. I said, "How was that again? Did you say you went back to work after your wife mended the torn place?"

"It is true, Mr. London. After, I went back to work. I worked some more, drove the bus, then there came another call, I went home again. Now the fever was very high, we went with Joanna to the hospital."

I said, "Now, as I understand your testimony, you went home twice, first around eleven o'clock Friday night, and then somewhere around two o'clock Saturday morning. The first time, you had a hole in your trousers at the place you have shown us. Is that correct?"

"The hole, yes. Everyone can see."

"And your wife mended the hole before you went back to work the same night?"

He spread his hands and raised his shoulders. "Else my wife don't let me go to work, Mr. London."

"Then when you passed the corner of Cedar and Virginia the *second* time, Joe, around two o'clock, no hole was showing?"

"At two o'clock it had been mended. No one could see a hole at two o'clock. I have to think hard now, or I don't see it myself."

I went back and sat down at the table and drew a fish on the yellow pad. I said, without looking up, "Have you talked with anyone about this?"

He looked puzzled. "I don't understand."

"I mean, about this hole and your wife mending it and everything. Who have you discussed it with?"

"I haven't talk about it to anybody. I am forgetting all about it until you ask the question."

"You're sure you didn't tell me about it, even by accident?"

"No, I didn't tell you or anybody. I forgot all about it, Mr. London."

I let that sink in a moment. Under the fish I printed GLORIA.

I looked at Joe. "I believe you testified you saw me just one time at Cedar and Virginia that night?"

He nodded yes, and then said, "One time."

I put my elbows on the table and leaned forward. "If that was at or about two o'clock, Joe, instead of at eleven o'clock, tell the jury whether I could have seen a hole in the right knee of your trousers."

He sat up straight and his eyes widened. He stood up and then looked at the bench. He said, "Please, Your Honor, I do not tell a lie, but I have made a very great mistake. It was the first trip home I saw Mr. London, not the second. I am very sorry to make all the trouble, but it is true."

Bolden said in exasperation, "If the Court please, I object most strenuously to all this insinuation and suggestion which is both unfair and misleading. There has been no showing that the defendant *did* see anything like a hole in anybody's trousers, or anything else, at eleven or at two, or at any other time. Because something *did happen* at a particular time, the witness has mesmerized himself into thinking, without any evidence whatsoever, that the defendant *saw* it at that time—"

Interrupting, I said, "Then it appears the prosecution *admits* the hole was there at eleven and not at two."

Bolden gritted his teeth and said, "No, that's not the point at all. I don't admit anything of the sort . . ."

"Then why don't you put Mrs. Herdt on the stand right now and ask her? She's in the courtroom."

"Why don't you put her on?"

I looked pointedly at the jury and raised my eyebrows. I said, "When it's my turn to introduce evidence, Mr. Bolden, I'll certainly call Mrs. Herdt. I ask that a forthwith-summons be issued immediately and that it be served on Mrs. Herdt while she is present. I'm not afraid of the truth, whether you are or not."

Bolden said, "This whole business is most surprising. I would like to be heard in chambers."

Thornton said, "There will be a short recess."

80.

ONCE MORE the procession formed, shuffled in, and closed the door behind it. Bolden sat in front of Thornton's desk and pushed his spectacles almost continuously. He said, "Goddammit, I beg the Court's pardon, what am I going to do with a witness like this, Judge? He gave his evidence to Richmond and again to me, under oath. Then he signs a notarized statement in writing, and subsequently testifies under oath before the coroner. In this very Court he testifies that he saw Jess at this intersection at two o'clock, and now he claims he was wrong all the time. There's a stink of perjury that smells to high heaven and I ought to have a chance to get to the bottom of it. I hate to do this, but I feel I must ask a recess until tomorrow morning to investigate. This witness ought to be made to realize what perjury means. I ought to have a chance to verify the facts."

Thornton turned to me.

I said, "I don't see what all the excitement's about, Judge. Mr. Bolden's at liberty to argue to his heart's content, as matters stand, that there's been no evidence I *did* see a hole in Joe's trousers at eleven o'clock, or at all. Of course, there *will* be such evidence, as soon as I take the stand in my own behalf.

Otherwise I wouldn't have known to ask the questions which have demonstrated Joe's mistake. Meanwhile there's plenty of time for Mr. Bolden, using Richmond and the limitless resources of the police force, to question Mrs. Herdt, the doctor who may have seen her mending this hole, or anyone else. I'm now in the process of cross-examining the prosecution's pet witnesses and I certainly object to a long recess which will permit Mr. Bolden to give his witnesses a pep talk. I'm about to bust this case wide open right out of the mouths of Mr. Bolden's witnesses, just as I thought I would. If Bolden is making a formal motion for a long recess, I want the record to show my vigorous objection and furthermore I want to dictate a statement of my position so that the record will be clear on the point."

Richmond whispered hoarsely with Bolden and his assistant.

Thornton took a deep drag from a cigaret and said, "Frankly, and this is off the record of course, I detect no smell of perjury. It seems entirely possible the witness may have been confused. In any event, the jury will hear, in due course, whatever Mr. London has to say in his own testimony. Mrs. Herdt can be put in the witness chair, if her testimony should appear important . . ."

I said, "You may be sure it's important, Judge, to determine this time element about mending Joe Herdt's trousers. I saw Joe at eleven o'clock and he had a hole—"

"Now I object to that," said Bolden. "Let him be sworn if he wants to testify. This anomalous dual capacity of defendant and lawyer doesn't entitle him to try to influence either the witnesses or the court or the jury until he stands up to make his argument like anyone else."

Thornton said coldly, "The Commonwealth's attorney need not be afraid that the Court is subject to any improper influence."

Bolden said irritably, "Oh, hell, I didn't mean anything like that. I apologize, if an apology is in order. Upon reconsideration, I'll call Mrs. Herdt as a witness right now. That is," sarcastically, "if Mr. London will waive his right to insist that the Commonwealth has already closed its case."

I said, "I'll waive nearly anything to get at the truth. Let's go."

81.

MRS. JOSEPH HERDT came forward and was sworn by the clerk. She said her first name was Wanda and that she was the wife of the witness Joe Herdt who had just testified. Her lips were firmly joined in a thin line and she clutched her purse in both hands. She sat stiffly erect and defied Matt Bolden with her eyes and every muscle of her body.

Bolden said, "You heard your husband testify?"

"Of course."

"What do you know about all this business of holes in pants, if you know anything?"

"I patched the hole. I know everything."

"You want the defendant to be acquitted, don't you? Isn't it a fact that you feel deeply indebted to Mr. London because you think he saved the life of your child?"

I stood up for psychological reasons, and then made a face for the jury to see, and sat down.

Mrs. Herdt glared at Bolden and said rigidly, "I do not pay debts by telling lies, for anyone. You ask a question, I will answer it before God."

That was a stumper. Bolden seemed to debate the desirability of batting the idea around, and then gave up. He said, "Okay, tell us about this hole in Joe's pants."

She said, "Joe came home Friday night—that's last Friday night—while the doctor is there. My baby gets better, by and by she goes to sleep. The doctor says he will come back if there is reason, everything looks good. It is better my husband goes back to work, we should pay the doctor bill. He cannot go to work with a torn place very plain to see in his trousers. The other pair I am sending to the cleaners. I mend the place good, then he goes back to work. Later, he comes home again, we go to the hospital. Joanna is very sick baby."

"Are you sure it wasn't Thursday night, or Wednesday night?"

"It was Friday night. Joanna is not sick Wednesday or Thursday."

Bolden was obviously frustrated. He said, "You aren't going to testify whether the defendant *saw* this hole or not, are you?"

She said, "How could I know?"

Bolden signified I could take over. I said, "Just tell the jury whether the hole was mended before your husband went back to work."

"Yes, it was."

"And when did he go back to work?"

"Maybe eleven-thirty, twelve o'clock."

"There was no hole showing when he came home at two o'clock?"

"No, the second time there was no hole."

I said, "That's all. Call Charles Pitts."

82.

PITTS CAME FORWARD with apprehension and sat in the witness chair gingerly, guarding against tricks. He gave me the ghastly beginning of a smile and then looked nervously at Richmond and wet his lips.

I said, "Relax, Charley. There's nothing to be alarmed about."

He managed a smile and said, "No, sir."

I said, "Take it easy. Last night while I was thinking of a question to try on Joe Herdt, I happened to think of one to try on you. No harm trying, is there?"

This time his smile was less troubled. He leaned back a little in the chair and crossed his legs. He said, "No sir. No harm trying, I guess."

I said, "It's an easy question, anyway. Please tell the jury how many times I came in during the night all this talk is about."

He didn't have any trouble with that one. He said promptly, "Once."

"Not twice?"

"No. Just once."

"I see. Just one time." I got up and walked around the table and stood in front of him, looking down at my feet. I said, "And that was at or after two o'clock? Is that what you testified?"

"Yes sir. You understand I'm not aiming to take sides, Mr. London. I'm swearing the truth because I'm supposed to, that's all."

"And that was at or about the time when Mr. Block passed through the lobby of the Albemarle and went out the front door?"

"Yes sir."

"Do you see the picture clearly in your mind, Charley? Do you see Mr. Block going out, and me coming in, and where you were standing or sitting, and everything?"

He gave that a moment of reflection and even closed his eyes for a second, as if trying himself out. Then he said, "I believe I do."

"Look at that picture in your mind, and tell the jury whether I was wearing a green hat, Charley."

He stirred in his seat and frowned and looked down and put his lower lip between his teeth. He looked briefly in Richmond's direction and then at the window. He wouldn't look at me. He was not relaxed any more. At length he said, still looking away, "That was four, five days ago. I don't know as I could rightly say."

I crossed over swiftly to Bolden's table, picked up the green hat, and returned. I put it on my head and faced the witness. I said, "If you saw me like this, wouldn't you remember it?"

Somebody laughed. I looked up with a frown and then turned back to Pitts. I said, "I'm sorry if it's funny. I'm perfectly serious. Mr. Bolden and Block want the jury to believe I came in wearing this hat and I want to hear what this witness has to say on the subject."

Bolden stood up patiently, wearily. He said, "Now if the Court please, I'm trying not to lose my temper, but obviously an objection is in order. It's Mr. London's own idea that he's supposed to have been wearing this particular green hat, which the evidence shows belongs to someone else and was found in a car half a block away. The Commonwealth doesn't feel called upon to sit by and hear these distorted versions of the evidence cleverly insinuated for the benefit of the jury."

I said quickly, "If that's the position of the Commonwealth, I apologize, withdraw the remark, and myself move that it be stricken from the record. I naturally supposed, since this hat was marked as an exhibit . . ."

Bolden sat down and shook his head bitterly.

Judge Thornton said, "The jury will disregard at this time all that tends to be argumentative and concentrate upon the facts established by the testimony of the witnesses. The arguments will come later, when all the evidence has been heard. Mr. London, the Court realizes that you lack trial experience comparable to that of Mr. Bolden, but the Court cannot condone what appear to be wanton improprieties."

I said, "Yes sir. I'm sorry, Your Honor."

"You may proceed."

I turned back to Charley Pitts, rubbed the back of my neck, and let the silence congeal until it settled all the way to the floor. Then I looked up suddenly and said, "After I came in, did I call on the telephone and ask to be waked up Saturday morning?"

Charley thought that over. He said doubtfully, "Best I can remember, you did. I wouldn't want to say for sure. There are lots of calls like that."

"Try hard. See if you can remember."

After a pause he said, "Like I told you, Mr. London. I couldn't say for sure about any particular person on any particular night."

"Well, aren't there some records that would show for sure? I mean, how do you remember to call people if you don't write it all down?"

Charley said, "We write 'em down, of course. There's a book at the desk to keep 'em straight. People raise hell—that is, people get plenty mad if you don't call 'em. Like catching a train or something."

I said, "How about this book you're talking about? Does it show what time a call is placed?"

"You mean, what time a call comes in? No, it don't show

that, Mr. London. It shows what time the call is *for*, get it? I mean, what time I'm supposed to give people a ring, see?"

I said, "Come to think of it, I believe I've seen that book, Charley. Let's see, don't you write all the calls down on one page as they come in, and then copy them on the opposite page in the order you're supposed to wake people up?"

"That's right. About one o'clock I copy 'em over and put 'em in order, and then I watch the clock and ring people when I'm supposed to."

I said, "Then if I put in a call Friday night or Saturday morning, the book would show it right now, wouldn't it?"

"Yes, sir, but it wouldn't show what time, only the time I was supposed to call *you*."

"I see." I walked away, looking thoughtfully at the floor. I walked all the way to the jury box, and then turned and pinched my lip. I said, "What I mean, thinking about that book, Charley—no, wait a minute . . ."

One of the jurors finally came up with the idea. He cleared his throat timidly and said, "Your Honor, is it all right for a juror to ask the witness a question?"

Thornton said, "Certainly."

Everybody in the courtroom looked at the juror and his face turned a little pink. Now he was uncertain. He said, "Of course I don't know anything about this book they're talking about, Your Honor, but just listening, it looks to me if this witness writes down the people who put in calls, the order of the calls ought to show something. I mean, if there were any calls *after* the defendant put in *his*, and people happened to remember the time . . ."

I said, "That's a very good point, if the Court please. As a matter of fact, I believe Mr. Block has already testified that he called the desk around twelve-thirty. Now, if what I claim is true, and I came in and went to bed before that time, my call ought to be recorded ahead of his. I'm willing to stand on that record, Your Honor. I ask that the call book of the Albemarle Apartments be procured under order of the court and that my examination of this witness be recessed until that record is available."

The juror was now even more self-conscious than before. He tried to act as if he hadn't demonstrated he was smarter than the court, the lawyers and the witness. He leaned back in a happy sweat, not knowing whether to look at the floor, the ceiling, or his hands.

Judge Thornton said, "I'm not sure I understand the nature of the evidence in question, or just how it would bear upon any fact in issue. However, it is an opportune time to adjourn for lunch anyway, and if this book or record is readily available, I see no reason why it should not be produced." He turned to Pitts. "Is this book, or whatever it is, something you can produce voluntarily, or do you wish the court to issue an order requiring it to be produced?"

Pitts said quickly, "Oh, no, you don't have to put out any order about it, Your Honor. It's just a plain old book we keep to put the calls in."

"Very well. Court will be adjourned until two o'clock. Meanwhile, you will get this book which has been referred to. Come back at two, with the book. Do you understand?"

"Yes, Your Honor."

I said, with thick irony, "Perhaps precautions should be taken to prevent the defendant from forging the pages which are material to this case. If it pleases Mr. Bolden, I'll consent that Lieutenant Richmond take charge of the book until two o'clock."

Bolden said, "All right. And if the defendant should care to nominate a representative to prevent forgery by the Commonwealth . . ."

I said, "No, I'll trust the Commonwealth. However, if the Court please, and without knowing what this evidence will show, I'd like to make a request. If this book should show that I put in a call during the night in question, and if it should show that other calls were put in after mine, I'd like to have any and all persons who put in such later calls made available for examination, if they're within the jurisdiction of the Court."

Bolden said, "That's agreed to, Your Honor, but with the qualification that they not only be within the jurisdiction of this Court but can actually be located and produced within a reasonable time."

I accepted the qualification, and it was so ordered.

I saw Wiggie, going through the door with the crowd, leaving me without a word or a look.

83.

I WAS AS HUNGRY as a bitch wolf. I wanted to rush out and pick up the nearest hamburger and mash it into my mouth. I wanted to hold a piece of steak in my teeth and lunge forward and swallow it whole, like a starving leopard.

I sat very still and looked at my yellow pad. People got up and slid their feet against the floor, as people do when there are too many of them. I picked up my pencil, drew a bad circle and put a cross inside it.

Stoakes Fant sat on one side of me and George Stern slipped into the chair on the other side. I didn't say anything. I started printing, "A B C D E F G" and then impatiently scribbled all over the printing and threw the pencil on the table. People pushed each other and went out into the hall. I put both hands against my temples and wondered if the throbbing headache was returning.

Fant said, "The jury's beginning to take notice. You have the initiative, if you can just hold it."

I said, bleakly, "Thanks."

"There's no use getting short with me."

"I'm sorry."

"There's no use being sorry, either. I'm not trying to give you the harpoon, Jess. I'm your friend, remember?"

I said, "Yes, I remember. That's why I'm sorry. I guess I've got a chip on my shoulder, that's all. I have a feeling even my friends don't believe—oh well, what difference does it make?"

George Stern said, "Frankly, dammit, this thing's beginning to get next to me, Jess. There's something real about it. Up to this morning the thing has seemed sort of airy and theoretical, like x plus y equals z."

I said, "Yes, and I'm z for zero."

Fant said, "I hope you know what you're doing on this business about the book. If you get past that, there's only one thing that really worries me."

I said, "The book can't be anything but true, so I'm not afraid of whatever it shows. I came in around midnight and called down and asked Pitts to give me a ring in the morning. He gave me a ring, so he must have written it down. If this guy Block put in a call around twelve-thirty, as he says, it's got to be written down after my call. Maybe there were some others. Anyway, what can I lose?"

"Okay, let's assume that. Now what about the fingerprints?"

I said, "What about 'em?"

"Well, what about 'em? Suppose you tell me."

I said, "Hell, so my fingerprints were on this dingus, or whatever you call it. This cigaret lighter. So what? Your fingerprints might be on it, but what does that prove? My fingerprints are on this table, but that doesn't mean I hit somebody over the head with it. Or maybe I'm nuts."

Fant said, "Maybe you are. You're nuts if you forget two people have testified you confessed to hitting Mitch with this—

dingus, as you call it. I'm not forming an opinion about what happened. I'm only thinking about what the jury will *believe* happened. You'd better be thinking about the same thing."

I put my head down in my hands and let the business ride for a moment. I said, "My fingerprints are bound to be on the thing because I held it in my hand. I used it to light somebody's cigaret. Wait a minute . . ."

I picked up the pencil and held it in my teeth, crosswise, like a dog holding a bone. I looked up sidewise at Stern. I said, "What about it, George? Put your mind on this. The way I see it, you're on the stairs, almost at the bottom, looking across the living room at me. You holler something at me. Wait a minute . . . somebody wants a light . . . somebody coming across from the kitchen door . . ."

George opened his eyes wide. He said excitedly, "Wiggie!"

I leaned back and laughed. I said, "Of course. Wiggie. Pretty tight, wasn't she? Now I remember. She's walking along, sort of feeling her way. Bumping against the furniture. She's got a cigaret in her hand and she's looking around for a light. You're on the stairs and you see her and you holler across at me. Then I see she needs a light and I pick up this fancy cigaret lighter from the table . . . now I get the whole thing."

Stern frowned and said, "I can go that far with you, but that's all. I guess that's far enough, at that."

"How do you mean?"

"Like you said. I can tell what I saw, but I can't tell what I didn't see. I called, I remember that. Then you turned. You were standing between Wiggie and me. She got a light, but I didn't see *how* she got it. I can testify that far, for whatever it's worth."

"Was the cigaret lighter on the table by the divan? Can you remember that much?"

He closed his eyes. "If I'm honest, no. I can't remember."

I said hastily, "I'm not asking you to lie for me. Joe Herdt would have lied if I'd asked him to, and I believe Charley Pitts would have, too. I wouldn't let 'em. The truth is doing all right up to now, and it's going to hold out all the way. The truth is the truth, and when everybody has told it, you and the jury and everybody else will know the whole thing's a mistake. Even Matt Bolden'll know it. . . ."

"Look," said Fant, putting his hand on my knee. "You don't have to convince us. We're on your side. Let's go out and get something to eat."

84.

CHARLEY PITTS had his book with him when he came back in to resume the witness stand. Judge Thornton nodded to indicate I could go ahead.

I said, "Just for the record, you are Charles Pitts, who was testifying when we adjourned for lunch?"

He nodded, yes. Then when the reporter looked up he added, "That's right."

"And do you have that book with you?"

"Yes, sir, it's right here."

"Is that the book that shows what calls were put in on the night of last Friday and Saturday at the Albemarle Apartments?"

"That's right. They're all wrote down here, like I said this morning."

I went over and held out my hand for the book. I leafed through the pages. I said, "Mr. Pitts, I show you two pages, facing each other, marked 'April twenty-six' and ask you if these pages represent the record made by you, on that date, of requests for calls during the early morning of Saturday, April twenty-seven, nineteen forty?"

He craned his neck as if he had never seen the book before. He said, "Yes, sir, I wrote 'em down myself. That's what they are."

"Are these entries in your own handwriting?"

He craned his neck again. "That's right."

"Now, with reference to the left-hand page, Charley. Tell the jury what caused you to make those entries in the particular order shown."

"Well, I told you before. I put 'em down as they come in, Mr. London. One after the other, just when people call, that's how I put 'em down."

"And what's the reason for the entries on the right-hand page being in a different order?"

"Like I said before, that's all. People are mostly in and gone to bed by one-thirty, maybe two o'clock. Then I look over the list on the left side and copy 'em over on the right, in the order I'm supposed to call 'em. After that I'm reading a magazine, see? I simply keep looking at the clock, and when it's time to call, I give 'em a call."

"I see my name down here, and my apartment number. You wrote that, did you?"

"That's right."

"And after my name I see here it says 'Wright—four-oh-eight.' Does that men that someone named Wright in Room four-oh-eight called after I did?"

"Yes, sir."

"Now how about this entry that says 'Small—six thirty-seven'? Does that mean that someone named Small in Room six thirty-seven called after I did?"

"I just wrote 'em down in order, Mr. London."

"I see here the last entry is 'Block—six ten.' That isn't the same Mr. Block who has testified in this trial, is it?"

He took the book back and looked at it carefully. He

said, "There ain't but one Mr. Block, and he's in six ten. That's right."

"And that's in your handwriting?"

"Yes sir. I wrote it down, like I told you."

I walked over and handed the book to juror number one, then walked back and stood in front of Charley Pitts. I said, "If Mr. Block called the desk around twelve-thirty, as he testified, what does that indicate with reference to the time of my call?"

Charley had already examined the record during the noon recess. He was sitting rigidly, with his elbows drawn up tightly against his body. He said, "Your call came in before Mr. Block's call. It shows right there on the record."

I said, "I'd like to recall Mr. Block."

Bolden got to his feet. He said, "I have another question or two for the witness."

I went over and sat down.

Bolden said, "This call the defendant made. Do you know where it came from?"

Pitts now looked defensively at Bolden. He said, "I couldn't swear which *room*."

"You answer the outside phone, too, don't you?"

"Yes, sir."

"And they're both at the same desk, side by side?"

"That's right. Side by side. Two phones, one for outside calls coming in. That's right."

"And the inside calls and the outside calls are all through the same switchboard, aren't they?"

"Same switchboard, yes, sir."

"Now, suppose someone called from *outside* the Albemarle Apartments, Mr. Pitts. Called, I mean, and asked to be waked up at a certain hour and gave his name and room number. Wouldn't you mark that down, the same as a call from *inside?*"

Pitts hesitated. Then he said, "I guess I would."

Bolden came around the table and stood closer. He said,

"One more thing. You also operate the elevator at night, don't you?"

"Yes, sir, operate the elevator, too."

"And when you take someone up in the elevator, who's on duty down in the lobby?"

"Nobody, Mr. Bolden. I'm on duty alone, and when I go up I come down as quick as I can because there ain't nobody down at the desk."

"Then while you're going up or coming down it would be possible, wouldn't it, for someone to come in the front door and walk up the stairs, or walk down the stairs and go out?"

Pitts turned that over carefully in his mind. He said, "Well, if you put it that way, I guess I'd have to say it's *possible*, yes sir."

Bolden went back and sat down.

I said, "Tell the jury whether my call on this particular night came to the desk from inside or outside the apartment house, if you know."

Pitts said promptly, "I don't know as I ever had a call like that from outside. To be waked up in the morning, I mean."

"Then are we to understand the call came from inside?"

"Yes, sir, to the best of my knowledge, I'd say it did."

"Now," I said, "I'd like to have Mr. Block on the stand again."

85.

Mr. Block had heard the evidence and he was bristling with aggressiveness. He sat well forward in the witness chair, as if he might spring out into space at any moment. He admitted, with poor grace, that he was the same Mr. Block who had testified earlier in the trial.

I said, "As I recall, you testified that you woke up around twelve-thirty last Saturday morning and called the desk at that time, asking to be waked up at four o'clock. Is that correct?"

He said, "I could have been mistaken about the hour. It would be natural if I was. After all, I had gone to bed and had been asleep. When I woke up I was groggy, you might say. I believe I said around twelve-thirty, but it could have been later, and probably was."

"What time did you say you came down and left the apartment house?"

"Some time after two. I'd guess two-fifteen to two-thirty. Around that time."

"And before that you got up and shaved, and bathed and dressed?"

Uneasily, "Yes, sir."

"And you put in your call to the desk before you did all that, didn't you?"

A pause, "I guess so."

I said, "That's all. If the Court please, I've requested that any persons whose names appear after mine on this record book be summoned as witnesses. May I ask Mr. Bolden and Lieutenant Richmond whether these people represented by the names Wright and Small are present?"

Bolden said, "We've done everything we could, Your Honor. Mr. Wright seems to be out of town. Miss Small is here, I believe."

A tall, shriveled old lady who appeared to be in her eighties stood in the second row of spectators and held up her hand as if asking teacher for permission to go to the washroom.

I said, "Ah, of course, Miss Small. Will you come forward please?" I went over and opened the gate for her.

When she had settled herself officially and had taken the oath, I said, "I know you're busy, Miss Small. I'll be as brief as possible. Please tell the jury, if you remember, what time you called Charley Pitts on the night of last Friday, or Saturday morning. Do you have any recollection on the subject?"

Miss Small turned and addressed herself directly to the judge. She said, "As a matter of fact, I have a very distinct recollection, Your Honor. I came in from a special meeting of the executive committee of the Women's Auxiliary of our church. It was our annual meeting to report on the campaign to raise funds for the Daily Vacation Bible School, you know, and I'm afraid it was a good deal later than my usual hour of retirement. I clearly remember it was nearly twenty-two minutes after twelve o'clock when I called *dear* Mr. Pitts. At the moment I was afraid I was being *most* inconsiderate, but afterwards I recalled he's on duty all night and realized the absurdity of my qualms, as you might call them."

I said, "Thank you, Miss Small. I have no more questions."

Bolden stood up, opened his mouth as if to say something, hesitated, and then sat down with a grimace. He said, "No questions."

86.

EVERYTHING about a trial takes longer than you anticipate. Witnesses are slow in coming forward. There are pauses and delays and whispered conferences. Lawyers have to think between questions and look up things in files and memoranda. It seemed to me we had been at work only a short time since the recess for lunch, but when I looked at the clock it was after two-thirty.

I said, "If the Court please, I'm going to be the next witness. It hasn't been long since the recess for lunch, but I'd like to ask time enough to have a drink of water, smoke a cigaret and stretch. I'm sure the jury would welcome a short recess, too."

Thornton promptly said, "Granted. Recess for ten minutes. The jury will not discuss the case, either among themselves or with anyone else." He banged on the bench with his gavel, frightening the cockroach, who scuttled over the edge and into his crack. Thornton disappeared into his chambers, the jury rose to file into the jury room, and the inevitable murmur and scuffle grew in volume until it filled the room oppressively.

Fant came over and said, "Want to have a smoke in the library?"

I said, "If my bond's still good I'd like to get the hell out of here for a couple of minutes—out where people are."

Fant said, "Go ahead. The bond's good until the case goes to the jury."

I went out into the hall looking eagerly for Wiggie. There was no sign of her. I went down the cement steps to the first floor, and out the big front entrance beneath the portico with its great stone pillars. People were coming and going. A few gave me curious stares. I lit a cigaret. It didn't taste good. After a couple of drags I flipped it down the steps and turned abruptly and went in.

At the landing a broad window was open and fresh spring air was coming in. I stopped and spread my elbows wide on the sill, ignoring the fact that it was grimy, as window sills of all public buildings will always be. I rested my chin in my hands and looked vacantly at the courthouse lawn, which was beginning to break out in that fresh, pale green of life that spring produces. My stomach was nervous. I felt physically exhausted.

Behind me there were feet on the steps, going up. One man said, "Personally, I'm sorry for the boy. They're trying to frame him, or certainly *something* is screwy. That fellow Bolden is a slicker if I ever saw one."

Another said, "Maybe so, maybe not. Wait till we hear what he's got to say for himself when he sits up there and gets his workout. He'd better talk fast about that confession is the way I see it."

"Anyway, he's done pretty good. I'll say that for him."

The other voice said shortly, "So far."

I let them disappear into the crowd at the door of the courtroom and then went on up to the second floor. I walked around the crowd, past the door of Judge Thornton's office, and to the door marked "Library." When I went in, Bolden was relaxed in a tilted chair with his feet on a table and a cigar in his mouth. Richmond was sitting with his elbows on the table, and Bolden's assistant was about to fling a crumpled cigaret package at the brass spittoon. I said, "Sorry, I didn't mean to intrude."

Bolden said, "Come in the house, there's plenty of room. I guess you know Richmond. Have you met my assistant? Shake hands with Harry Meeks. Cigar?"

I held up my cigaret to show I didn't want a cigar, nodded to Richmond, and shook Harry's hand. I said, "A trial always makes me tired between the shoulder blades and in the small of my back. I feel as if I'm about to get the cramps. Does it hit you that way?"

Bolden took his cigar out of his mouth. He said, "It gets me here in the thighs, and in the back of my neck. Nervous strain, I guess. I don't know how lawyers live beyond the age of thirty-two."

I said, "I could use a little exercise of some sort. How about it, Lieutenant? Let's do a little of that Indian stuff where you try to pull each other off balance."

Richmond flexed his shoulders and rubbed his neck. He said, "I'm a little stiff, myself. Okay, let's have a go at it."

We put our right feet together, clasped our right hands, and braced in preparation. Richmond said, "How about it, Harry? Count to three for us."

Harry counted. When he said, "Three," Richmond got the jump on me and lunged forward and to his left, almost taking me off my feet. At the last possible instant I held him, taut and straining. I put everything I had into it, crouching and pulling my hand back toward my leg. There was a cracking sensation in my neck and my eyes bulged from the effort. Slowly I began to get the best of him. I regained my balance firmly, held steady a moment, and then applied the pressure. His face was drawn and a vein in his forehead became prominent. I could count his heart beats in it. When he could get his elbow against his side, he stopped my attack and held me. I could feel the business all the way down to my heels. Suddenly I went into reverse and pulled sharply, expecting to surprise him. He sensed the move just in time, relaxed and came with me all the way, then threw his weight into it and jerked down and to the left again. I staggered, lost my balance, and took three quick steps to keep from falling.

I grinned and said, "Too good for me. Thanks. That's what I needed. Funny how you can get up a sweat in a few seconds, isn't it?"

Richmond said, "I thought you had me. I'm getting too old for that sort of thing."

The deputy sheriff put his head in the door and said, "The Judge is ready."

"Okay," said Bolden, getting up and stretching. "Back to the salt mines."

87.

WHEN THE CROWD had simmered down there was a quick, expectant silence and Judge Thornton looked at me inquiringly. I left my table and stood in front of the witness chair. I said, "I guess I'd better be sworn."

I raised my right hand and took the oath. I sat in the chair, feeling unaccountably awkward. From this position, somehow the whole layout—the Court and the jury and crowd and the lawyers' tables—looked queer. My hands seemed large and clumsy and I didn't know what to do with them. Finally I sat back with my elbows on the arms of the chair and my hands clasped across my stomach. I remembered that this position gave the impression of being on the defensive, but I couldn't think of a better one. I remembered that I had seen witnesses relaxed and at ease, but I couldn't figure how they did it.

My throat was dry and constricted. I pulled at my collar, because it was too tight.

I said, "I'm the defendant in this case. My name is Jesse London. I'm a lawyer, or at least [trying to grin at the jury] I have a license to practice law and have paid my dues to the bar association. Until Saturday morning I was associated with the law firm of Abercrombie, Sothern and Fant, which is now only Abercrombie and Fant. From what I heard in this room awhile ago, it sounds as if I'm associated with that firm again, but I guess that depends on what happens in this case."

Now that the words had got out of my mouth, I felt a lot better. I sat forward, leaned over on my left elbow, and put my right hand in my coat pocket.

I said, "I live at the Albemarle Apartments, room three thirty-two. Maybe I'd better begin at the beginning. It's true, as Judge Abercrombie told you, that on Friday afternoon, my brother-in-law, Mr. Mitchell Sothern, called me in and gave me an important, though simple, job to do. I could have done it immediately, in the next ten minutes, but Mr. Sothern specifically told me to do it between four-thirty and five o'clock. I didn't know exactly why, but that was none of my business. While I was sitting at my desk, waiting for four-thirty to come around—I guess I ought to add that I was alone—Mr. Sothern came in and told me he had changed his mind. The thing was so important he'd decided to do it himself. So he took this paper and check that Judge Abercrombie told you about, put them in his pocket, and left my office. That ended my responsibility, and I put the matter out of my mind."

Holding a cigaret in my hand would have been helpful, even though I couldn't have smoked it. I said, "When it was time to go home, I went home. I took a shower and dressed, had something to eat, and went out to the Sothern home at nineteen eighteen Cedar, arriving there a little after eight. I don't have a car, so I walked. It's not too far—comfortable walking distance."

I shifted in the chair. "The party was going strong when I arrived. The front doorbell didn't seem to work so I waited for somebody to let me in. A Miss Wiggens was near the door and opened it. We talked a little—not much. Then my sister—that's Mrs. Sothern—saw me and introduced me to a lot of people. I had a drink and talked to people and had another drink—like at any other party. I didn't know very many of the guests—I was the kid brother-in-law who ought to be asked, that's all. I had a pretty good time, considering nearly everyone was older and I didn't know very many of them."

I hesitated and said, "Judge, is it all right for me to go on and just talk like this? I don't know—maybe Mr. Bolden would rather have someone ask questions, so he can object to them. I guess Mr. Fant or somebody could ask questions and let me answer them, if somebody would prefer it that way."

Bolden stood up and said, "No objection, Your Honor.

The Commonwealth will have a chance to ask questions on cross-examination."

Thornton said, "Continue."

I said, "Well, I'm only talking along, telling the things that happened. I hope the jury will stop me and ask questions, if they want to. Let's see—well, it was like other parties. I don't know what to tell you about it. I'd say it was some time before eleven o'clock that Mitch—that's Mr. Sothern—said more people had showed up than they had expected, and the liquor was running short. He said there was a liquor store a few blocks away and told me how to get there. Gave me some money, too. Of course, I said I'd be glad to go. Well, Mitch offered me the keys to his car, but I looked out the kitchen door and saw his car was blocked in the driveway so I said I'd go ahead and walk, and that's what I did. I didn't take the keys —what would have been the use? I walked down to Cedar and Virginia and then turned left on Virginia to go to the liquor store. At the corner I saw Mr. Joe Herdt and I nodded to him and he nodded to me. I saw he had a torn place in his trousers, down at the knee, and I'm glad I remembered it when I was worrying last night, or else he probably never would have known about his mistake."

I thought Bolden would put in his oar at that point, complaining about my assuming things, but he didn't.

I said, "I came back with the whiskey and—well, the party went on. People talked and had fun or were bored or sang songs. Pretty soon a few people started to go home. It was before midnight. I guess they started leaving that early because they knew Mitch and Marty were going away and the party had to stop some time or other. I was standing near the divan in the living room and Mr. George Stern—he's sitting right over there—called to me from the stairway out in the hall—something about someone needing a light for a cigaret. Marty was not far away, and when I didn't seem to know what the shouting was all about, she called too. Then I saw Miss Wiggens. She was coming from the direction of the kitchen with a cigaret in her hand, and she was looking for matches or someone to light her cigaret. Well, this unusual cigaret lighter that's over there on the table—or, as Mr. Bolden says, one exactly like it—was right there on a table. I simply picked it up as anyone else would have done, and lit her cigaret."

I looked at the jury innocently. I said, "Listening to all these witnesses, everything seems awfully important now—at least, important to me. But last Friday night things didn't seem so terribly important. Other people were going home so I went home, too. I did what you would have done—said thank you and good night and good luck. Then I went out with the other people who were going out, and started home. When I came to the party I was walking, so I started home the same way."

A cigaret would have tasted good. It would have been a relief to have had someone ask me questions, so I could answer them and stop and wait for another question. This way, it was all up to me. I changed my position, leaned on the other elbow, and put my left hand in my coat pocket.

I said, "Down near the corner of Cedar and Virginia some people were joking around, about who should get in the front seat and who should get in the back seat. When I passed them, they called on me to act as umpire or something—you know, just kidding around. So the way I acted as umpire was to get in the back seat and sit down. Sounds silly now, I guess, but I thought it was clever at the time, and so did they. Anyway, there wasn't any more argument, and they all piled in. My recollection is that Miss Wiggens turned up on my knee, all crowded together as we were. There had been some singing before we left the party, so someone started singing and we sang all the way.

"Everyone else was attached—couples. That left me, all by myself, so they naturally dropped me off first, near my door. It was pretty much trouble letting me out, because I was at the bottom of the pile. We were in the middle of "Girl of My Dreams" and I went on singing after I got out—even while I was walking away. Best I remember I was nearly at the door of the apartment house before the end of the song."

There was a water cooler inside the railing, and one of these gadgets that holds paper cups like they have on Pullman cars. I said, "Excuse me, Judge. Could I get a drink of water?"

No one said I couldn't, so I went over, pulled out a cup, trickled water into it, and swallowed.

I took my seat again and said, "I didn't look at my watch, because I had noticed the time before I left the party. But you can figure it for yourself—it's only a few blocks. I must have walked into the Albemarle right around twelve o'clock, or pretty close to that hour. I saw Charley Pitts and spoke to him —you know, a nod or a wave or something. I don't remember whether we actually said anything or not. Anyway, he saw me, too, and either spoke or waved or nodded. I'm only two flights up, and it's always been understood that when he's in the lobby on duty alone he won't run me up when it's late. I walked through the lobby and up the steps to my room. I guess I've done it fifty times before the same way, coming in from a late movie or a poker game or something. When I reached my room I remembered Saturday morning was something special—I had to go see a Mrs. Worthington rather early, to take her statement about an accident case. So I called down to the desk and asked Charley to call me in the morning, and he said he would. I knew where Mrs. Worthington lived because I had talked to her on the telephone earlier in the day and had got it all arranged."

I looked straight at the jury. I said, "Well, that's all of it. After I called down to Charley Pitts I simply went to bed and went to sleep. Saturday morning Zack called me from the hospital and told me Marty was there and she had been injured. I dressed as quickly as I could. When I opened the door, the morning paper was there, and I couldn't help seeing the headlines about Mitch being dead. I don't know about other people, but naturally my first thought was about my own sister. I was scared to death, for her. I went straight to the hospital and when they wouldn't let me see her I guess I got kind of panicky. I read the newspaper story again, about how the police were looking for her, and then on the spur of the moment I went down to the house and asked for whoever was in charge. It turned out to be this Lieutenant Richmond, and I did what he's called confessing to the crime."

I took a new position, being careful not to look away from the jury. I said, "Of course, it was a silly performance, and both Lietuenant Richmond and the Corporal who was with him recognized it as such. Richmond punched enough holes in my story to convince me I was being ridiculous. I'll give you some examples. He asked me how I got into the house when I went back to murder my brother-in-law, and I did the best I could. I said I had his keys with me. Of course I didn't have them, because I walked down to the liquor store and there was no occasion for me to have them. That's when I saw Joe Herdt and noticed the hole in his trousers. Not only that, Richmond told me right then and there that he had found Mitch's—Mr. Sothern's—keys in his own pocket, which will just go to show you. Why would I make up a story about having his keys, anyway, if I wasn't excited and foolish? He was my brother-in-law. If I wanted to go into his house, I'd simply knock on the door and say so.

"Well, that's not all. Richmond asked me why I went back to the party. I didn't go back at all, of course, so I had to do some fast thinking. I said I went back for my hat. That got a laugh out of them, too. Because naturally if I'd gone back for my hat I'd have taken my hat home with me. What happened was that I walked out of the party without even thinking about my hat, and I even forgot I hadn't worn it home. I made up something about a memorandum inside the hatband, and that much was true, but I didn't need the memo because I had talked to this Mrs. Worthington that very afternoon and I had fixed the address in my mind."

I leaned forward, talking straight at the jury. "Lieutenant Richmond was having plenty of fun with me by that time. Even the Corporal in the front seat was grinning. Richmond baited me by asking whether Mr. Sothern was dead when I left the house—you know, according to this confession of mine. I fell right into the trap, trying to make a good story out of it, and said he was dead all right. I even embroidered it, as any other amateur would. I embellished it with details—said I had particularly felt for his pulse and knew positively that he was dead. Richmond knew that couldn't have been true because he had just talked to the doctor and the doctor had told him Mr. Sothern didn't die until around four-thirty, as you've heard here in this trial.

"Next thing, Richmond kept on teasing me. He and the Corporal were exchanging glances in the rear-vision mirror and having a lot of fun. Every time he asked me a sort of sarcastic question, naturally I tried to invent an answer that would convince him. He asked me what weapon I had used to commit this crime with. Well, I had read the newspaper story and knew somebody had hit my brother-in-law in the back of the head. When I had gone to the door of the house I had looked in and seen this big, heavy cigaret lighter. I knew my phony story wouldn't stand up very long, but I wanted to make it stick for a few hours if I could—anything to take the pressure off my sister. On the spur of the moment I adopted this cigaret lighter—that thing right over there—as the thing I was supposed to have used. I didn't fool Lieutenant Richmond for a minute. He has a mind like a movie camera. Right away he knew I could have seen the thing through the door while I was asking for him. He even asked me about that, and all I could think of, right quick, was to say I had used it to hit Mr. Sothern and then had walked out and put it on the hall table. Of course, I had to say that, because that was where they found the thing, and that was where I saw it. I had to say something."

I was doing strictly all right with the jury. I said, "My fingerprints had to be on the cigaret lighter, because I used it to light a cigaret for Miss Wiggens, as I told you. I went to bed a little after twelve, and never left my room after that. All this stuff about singing "Girl of My Dreams" in this Hudson sedan with four perfect strangers a couple of hours after I was asleep is Greek to me. I never owned or even wore a green hat in my life. I didn't meet Mr. Block under the marquee at two-thirty Saturday morning, with or without a green hat because I had been in bed two hours or more, as Charley Pitts' written record shows you. I didn't see Joe Herdt any time around two o'clock or after that, because the only time we saw each other was about eleven o'clock when he had a hole in his pants and I saw it. I never had a quarrel with Mitchell Sothern in my life. He was the one who fixed me a connection with this law firm and I thought he hung the moon. I even ran errands for him, like going to buy his whiskey."

I turned and looked up at Judge Thronton. I said, "I'm kind of scatterbrained, I guess. I don't want to stop testifying until I've covered all the points. Will it be all right if I get my notes, Judge?"

Thornton arched his eyebrows at Bolden, and Bolden nodded, making notes industriously for himself. I walked over and picked up my yellow pad with GLORIA on it. I leafed back to the pages that had on them MAN-O-WAR and the table with the peculiar legs. There wasn't a thing on those pages except my doodles and I knew it, but I had to have time to think back and I didn't want to do it in the witness chair. I sat down and studied the pages blankly and turned them over, one at a time, making check marks on them to indicate that everything was going according to plan. Finally I stood up, made a last check mark, and went back to the witness stand.

I said, "As long as I'm talking, I guess I'd better try to cover everything. Just listening to the testimony of the witnesses, all I can do is guess about the motive I'm supposed to have had for this crime I'm charged with. The way I figure it, Mr. Bolden wants you to believe I failed to perform a simple but tremendously important job for Mr. Sothern, and because he found out about it I got into an argument with him and killed him. At least that may have been the theory Judge Abercrombie fired me on. But then you heard Judge Abercrombie testify awhile ago, so I don't see where that gets us. From what he told you, as much as I hated to hear it myself, the truth is obvious. Mr. Sothern came and took the papers back from me —and from all we know now, it looks as if *he* didn't do the thing *I* was supposed to have done—and he made a profit out of it. I'm not one to judge on the meager facts we have before us, and I hope it's all wrong. At the same time I'm very much alive and I want to live. I'm going to hope this all turns out to have another explanation, but I'm not going to cover up for anyone and put myself in the electric chair. You've heard the evidence and it's up to you to decide whether you've heard anything that proves, or even gives a pretty good indication, that I killed my brother-in-law."

I sat back and looked at the ceiling. I said, "Maybe I ought to cover one more thing. I don't own a green hat. I've never owned a green hat. I never in my life saw any of these people who have talked about being in this Hudson sedan you've heard so much about. I didn't leave that car, with or without a green hat, around two o'clock Saturday morning or at any other time in my life. I didn't run into Mr. Block or anyone else or Charley Pitts in front of, or in, the Albemarle Apartments anywhere near two o'clock Saturday morning, or at any other time after the neighborhood of twelve o'clock that night. I went in, left a call with Pitts as his record shows you, and went to bed."

I bowed my head in thought. I looked at the jury and said, "I want to tell you about that green hat. Lieutenant Richmond questioned me about it, even though these people in the car told him it was Don Stith who got in and sang with them. I didn't know a thing about the whole business, and I told Richmond so. Then, later, I ran into Lieutenant Richmond in front of the Albemarle. I guess it was Sunday, or it may have been Saturday—I've been through so much these last few days I just couldn't say for sure. Anyway, he questioned me and then we walked down the street together. We happened to pass this yellow Hudson sedan everybody talks about, and the doors were hanging open. Richmond himself will tell you about it if you call him back and ask him—or maybe he did, I can't even remember that very distinctly. Anyway, we were walking along and I happened to look into this car and I saw that very green hat you see over there on the table—that, and a pair of pink panties that no one seems to want to talk about. I insisted that the Lieutenant stop right then and there and try the hat on me, and of course he could see it didn't fit. But of course he wasn't satisfied, even then. I don't believe he would have marked the hat and brought it to court with him, if he hadn't been afraid that I'd—"

Bolden was on his feet. He said, "Really, Your Honor. Just how far can I be expected to allow this to go? There'll be plenty of time allowed for argument of the case. Just now we're supposed to be hearing the sworn testimony of a witness."

Before Thornton could comment, I said, "I'm sorry, Judge. That's all I have to say. Why don't we let Mr. Bolden argue his cross-examination right now?"

Thornton looked nonplused for a moment and then said, "I suppose the objection ought to be sustained, Mr. Bolden, but there's little point in directing that something be stricken from the record after the jury has heard it. Do you wish to cross-examine?"

Bolden said shortly, "Of course." He turned abruptly to me and said, "I suppose you know, Mr. London, that when you took the witness stand on your own behalf you waived any right you may have had to refuse to give evidence that might tend to incriminate you?"

I opened my eyes wide and said mildly, "That's always been my understanding of the law, Mr. Bolden. I've never been worried about giving evidence that might tend to incriminate me, because all I know is the truth and the truth will prove I was in bed during all the time you're talking about, as you've seen. After all, Charley Pitts showed you his record and it proves—"

"Object," said Bolden. "I ask that the Court instruct the witness, as in the case of any other witness, to simply answer the questions and not argue with the Commonwealth's attorney."

Thornton said, "Just answer the questions. Don't argue with the Commonwealth's attorney."

I said, "What is your next question, Mr. Bolden? I'm under oath and I'm going to give you a truthful answer to anything you want to ask."

Bolden looked as if he were counting slowly to ten. He went back and looked at his notes. Quiet descended on the courtroom, and it developed into a resounding silence.

Bolden pushed his spectacles up his nose and said, more quietly now, "So you now claim your confession was purely fictional, do you?"

I said, "Any resemblance to persons, living or dead, or to events, past or present, was purely coincidental. Richmond proved that to me so quickly that I never undertook to repeat my so-called confession. I was afraid you'd put me under oath before a Notary Public and then charge me with perjury."

Bolden looked helplessly at the Court and then at the jury. He opened his mouth and then shut it wearily. He said, "You didn't go back to get this memorandum that I found in your hatband? Is that what you want the jury to believe?"

I said, "I want the jury to believe the truth, Mr. Bolden. The truth is, I didn't go back at all—for any reason. Anyway, it would have been silly for me to go all the way back in the middle of the night to get something and then not get it, wouldn't it?"

Bolden said shortly, "Don't argue with me. Just answer the questions."

I said, "All right. Ask me sensible questions and I will."

Richmond crossed over to whisper again. Bolden listened, then gave me a bold stare. He said, "If you didn't go back for the memorandum in your hatband, then tell the jury why you insisted that Lieutenant Richmond give you the address that was written on it. If you already knew that address, why did you have to get it from Richmond the next morning?"

I said, "I didn't have to get it, Mr. Bolden. I was trying to make a good confession while I was at it and I simply threw that in on the spur of the moment to make the thing sound plausible. Naturally I knew the address of the lady I was to call on in the morning. I had talked to her on the telephone only a few hours before."

"You're pretty good at throwing things in to make a story plausible, aren't you?"

"Not good enough to fool an old hand like Lieutenant Richmond. You ought to have heard the way he took my so-called confession apart. If you think I'm smart, you could get a liberal education from him."

Bolden blinked at me, sat back, and pushed his spectacles up his nose again. He said, "I don't suppose it's any use asking, since your story's so carefully made up to account for everything. But since you're under oath, you might as well go ahead and tell the jury, again, how your fingerprints happen to be on that cigaret lighter."

I turned to the jury and made my eyes wide and innocent. I said, "As I told you before, I used the lighter to light a cigaret for Miss Wiggens. If she were here she'd tell you the same thing. I'd call her as a witness and let you hear it for yourself, but it seems she left town Sunday night. That's what I was told. I tried to get in touch with her. I thought I saw her over here in the courtroom, but during a recess I tried to find her, and couldn't."

Bolden sighed, audibly, for the benefit of the jury and the crowd. He said, as if his patience had been exhausted, "Okay, okay, okay, the Commonwealth doesn't desire to ask any more questions."

I said, 'That's the case for the defense, if the Court please."

"In that event," said Bolden promptly, "the Common-wealth will call Mr. Don Stith in rebuttal."

88.

Don Stith was so nervous he could hardly sit in the witness chair. His hands were trembling and he kept putting them up to his lips, so that his trembling was obvious to everyone in the courtroom. If I had written his script for him I couldn't have done better. A mist of perspiration glistened in the roots of his hair.

Bolden said, "Your name is Donald Stith?"

He licked his lips and said, "Yes, sir. That's right."

"Tell the jury whether you're acquainted with Philip Thomas, the Gravura girls, and this fellow Frank Hicks who have testified in this trial?"

A pause. Then, "Yes, sir. I know them."

"Did you hear them testify?"

"Yes, sir."

"Now please tell the jury where you were on the night of April twenty-sixth and twenty-seventh. That is to say, last Friday night and Saturday morning."

"I was out of town. I wasn't here. I left town in the afternoon of last Friday and went to Marvin, that's fifty miles away, and registered at the hotel. That's where I was until Saturday evening—working my territory. I come home Saturday night, and then's when I first heard about all this business about Mr. Sothern bein' killed Friday night. I didn't even read the newspapers and I didn't know a thing about it. I was clear out of town the whole time."

Bolden said, "You may ask the witness."

I got up and walked around and stood in front of him, with my lower lip stuck out. I said, with my eyebrows raised, "Now don't tell me you're married."

He said, "Yes, I am."

I said, "Really? That's interesting. How long?"

Bolden said, "Objection, Your Honor. It's most difficult to see how this kind of thing can have any connection—"

I said, "If the Court will bear with me . . . ?"

Thornton said, "Continue, for the time being. But come to the point."

I said, "Yes, sir." I turned again to the witness and said, "All right, let's answer the question."

The witness said, uneasily, "Three months."

"I see. Three months. All right, now let's tell the jury how well you knew these Gravura girls before you were married. Pretty well, didn't you?"

Stith said defiantly, "Pretty well, yes. I guess you'd call it that."

"Did you drive out and park in the country with them?"

Slowly, "Maybe once or twice."

"Just park?"

"I don't know what you mean."

I said, "I'm sure you don't. Now what about this pair of pink panties Lieutenant Richmond found in the Gravura car the next day. I don't suppose you know anything about them either, do you?"

He said stoutly, "No, I don't. I tell you, I was over in Marvin, and that's fifty miles away."

I said, "So I understand. So that's what you told your wife, is it?"

He half rose and clenched his fists. He said, "Listen, you. I ought to bust you one right in the snoot . . ."

I turned and walked toward the jury, folding my arms and looking as bored as I could. I said, "Okay, come and bust me one right on the snoot, if that's going to get you anywhere. . . ."

Thornton pounded angrily with his gavel. He said, "*That will do!* Have you any more questions, Mr. London?"

I said, "No more questions, Your Honor."

Don Stith's face was dark red and for a moment I was afraid he would pop his collar button clear across the room. I wondered uneasily about my snoot. Then Bolden went over to the witness and carefully accompanied him beyond the gate in the railing. I looked around for Richmond, but couldn't find him.

Bolden came back and stood behind his table, shuffling papers. There was an air about him that disturbed me. It disturbed other people, too. All at once I became aware that the whole courtroom was expecting something to happen. So was I, without knowing why.

A small delay became a very loud silence. The standard courtroom clock, with the jeweler's name on the glass door where the pendulum swings, suddenly went "tock, tock, tock."

Thornton said with a trace of irritation, "Very well, gentlemen. Let's get on with the trial. Have you any more witnesses?"

At that moment the hall door opened and Richmond came in. He stood aside and held the door open.

Wiggie came in.

The two of them came through the railing and sat down. Wiggie did not look at me.

Bolden said, "If the Court please, I realize it's unusual to suggest a new witness after both the Commonwealth and the Defense have closed their cases in chief. This is, of course, the time for strictly rebuttal evidence. However, there is a person in the courtroom who has been mentioned several times during the trial. I'm unable to say what she will say if allowed to take the witness stand. It might turn out to be rebuttal evidence, and it might not. Her name is Miss Inez Wiggens, and she's sitting over there with Lieutenant Richmond. I'd like to suggest to the defendant and to the Court that we waive the technical rules and let her testify so the jury can hear the whole story, or as much of it as we can piece together here."

I was frightened. More so than at any time since the trial had begun. I had no idea what Wiggie might say, but I knew she was angry with me. I also had reason to believe her memory of the party last Friday night was not too clear.

On the other hand, thinking of the effect on the jury, dare I object to letting her testify? What would the jury think if I either refused to let her take the stand, or objected to every question that was not strictly in the nature of rebuttal?

What would the jury think if I even hesitated?

There was no time to debate the matter. I couldn't take the chance. I stood up and said, "The defendant is perfectly willing to waive anything. By all means let Miss Wiggens testify. I'm willing for anyone to testify until the case actually goes to the jury."

Judge Thornton said, "Let it be noted of record that both sides consent to the introduction of new evidence, whether it be in the nature of rebuttal or not. I take it Miss Wiggens will be a witness for the Commonwealth, Mr. Bolden?"

Bolden did not appear too happy at the idea, because if he put her on the stand as his witness he would not be able to impeach her in case things went wrong, and the greater leeway of cross-examination would be mine. However, he had no choice. He said, stiffly, "Of course."

89.

WIGGIE LEFT Richmond, stepped sideways past people's knees, came through the gate, was sworn, and sat in the witness chair. She looked at Bolden gravely, her eyes a little wide. Her knees were demurely together, not crossed, and her black skirt was discreet. No cheesecake. I liked that. She looked very young and sweet. She looked honest.

I wasn't sure I liked the idea of too much honesty. I would have felt a little better if I had been confident she was ready to be, maybe, a little dishonest if she had to be—in my favor. I wanted very much to know what she was going to say when the vital questions came around. I would have given plenty to know how she felt about me, considering things that had happened—whether there was tenderness, or resentment.

My lips were dry and I moistened them slowly with my tongue. Then they seemed too wet and I took out my handkerchief and dried them.

Bolden said, "Please give your name, and where you live, and what you do."

"Inez Wiggens. I'm an assistant to the buyer at Harley and Farnsworth's department store. I have an apartment at six twenty-two Magnolia Drive but I think I'd say my home is in St. Louis. That's where my parents live."

An obscure something moved sleepily in my brain, but I didn't recognize it and it went back to sleep again.

Bolden said, "Will you tell the jury whether you were one of the guests in the home of Mr. and Mrs. Mitchell Sothern last Friday evening?"

"Yes, I was."

"While you were there did you see the defendant Jesse London? Or do you know him?"

Bolden's eyes turned on me and Wiggie's followed them. She looked at me steadily, without any change of expression. She looked back at Bolden and said, "Yes, I have met Mr. London. He was at the party Friday evening. I saw him there."

"About what time did you leave, Miss Wiggens?"

She gave that a moment of thought. She said, "I was enjoying myself. The people were a lot of fun, and someone was playing the piano, and there was some singing. Drinks were passed around and I had a few, along with everyone else. I could have stayed later than I did, but we knew Mr. and Mrs. Sothern were leaving and naturally they would have packing to do. Even so, I had no idea how fast the time was passing until my escort reminded me. I think that was a little before twelve o'clock. By the time I'd been to the powder room for my things and found the host and hostess to thank them, it must have been about twelve. I don't think I could be more exact than that."

Bolden pursed his lips cautiously. He said, "What, if anything, do you know about the time when Mr. London left the party?"

She said promptly, "I didn't see him leave, if that's what you mean. However, there was a group of us getting into the car down near the corner when he came by. He was walking. We were already more than a carload, but you know how people are. We were having fun and it wasn't very late. Someone suggested that Mr. London get in with us, and that's the way it worked out. As a matter of fact, I believe I sat on his knee."

"Oh," said Bolden, with a significant look at the jury. "And then what?"

"After that? Well, let's see. Nearly everyone in the car was in favor of going somewhere for something to eat—everyone, that is, except Mr. London. I believe he asked if we'd mind dropping him near his apartment, and that's what we did. He said he had an appointment in the morning, and besides—the rest of us were couples. We supposed he felt—well, perhaps a little out of place without a date. And then I guess we were a little—well, uproarious."

"How do you mean—uproarious?"

"Singing. You might say it was like a continuation of the party. Someone got off on a barbershop quartet piece almost as soon as we were in the car, and we went on like that—first one song and then another—until we found a place to eat."

Bolden did not like the way her testimony was going. He was visibly uneasy. He did not want to ask her any more questions, yet he could not be too obvious about excusing her. Braced and wary, he said, "When did the singing start, if you remember? Would you say before or after Mr. London got out of the car? I don't suppose you have any very clear recollection on that point and if that's a fact, don't hesitate to say so."

Wiggie smiled. "Oh, we started singing before he got out of the car, Mr. Bolden. After all, he was harmonizing practically in my ear, you know."

"How about right at the time he left the car? You weren't singing then, were you?"

She said, "Oh, yes! We were in the middle of a song when he got out. We kept on singing, and so did he. We could hear him until just before he went into the apartment house—that's when the song ended."

Bolden looked at the jury and said, "No one could very well expect you to remember the song. However, in view of previous testimony on the subject I suppose I must ask you the question. Do you remember it, by any chance?"

Wiggie frowned and looked up at the ceiling. She said, doubtfully, "He was in the car only a very short time. I know one of the things we sang was "Girl of My Dreams." According to my recollection, that's the piece we were doing when he got out of the car."

Bolden clamped his jaws together tightly. He put his knuckles on the table and leaned on them heavily. He glared at Wiggie and said, "Are you remembering, or guessing, Miss Wiggens? Let me remind you that you're under oath. Are you prepared to say to this jury, under oath, that around twelve-fifteen Friday night—or more accurately, Saturday morning —of last week, the defendant was in a car with you and a group of young persons, that you were singing "Girl of My Dreams," and that at that precise time, and no other, the defendant got out of the car and walked into the Albemarle Apartments?"

She said, "I'm trying to tell the truth, Mr. Bolden, according to my best recollection. I don't think I could be mistaken on any material part of it."

Bolden turned to me, almost with a snarl. He said, "No more questions. You may ask *your* witness."

I looked at Bolden in astonishment, then turned the same expression toward the jury, and finally faced the Court. I stood, looking as bewildered as I could.

I said, "Now if the Court please, patience has its limitations. I must remind the Court and the jury that this witness was called at the insistence of the Commonwealth under circumstances which might well have warranted an objection on my part . . ."

Judge Thornton looked bored and banged halfheartedly with his gavel to interrupt me. He said, "The circumstances are well known to the Court and the jury, Mr. London. The by-play between counsel is wasted on both sides, I'm sure. Have you any questions?"

I sat down and shuffled my notes and made a few random marks on my yellow pad. Then I got up again and stood with my back to the jury and folded my arms. I said, slowly, "When you were in the Sothern home, Miss Wiggens, tell the jury whether or not you saw a cigaret lighter of some peculiar or striking type?"

"Yes, I did. I was among the earlier guests to arrive and Mr. Sothern was showing a most unusual lighter to everyone. I believe he said a client has given it to him that day."

I went over and picked up Exhibit 3. I held it out and said, "Is that what you're talking about?"

She took it, examined it briefly, and handed it back. "That, or one exactly like it. I don't know any way I could tell if that's the very same one I saw."

I said, "This may be an unreasonable test of your memory, Miss Wiggens. If it is, don't hesitate to say so. However, if you do happen to remember, it may be important. Look at this cigaret lighter that's marked Commonwealth's Exhibit three, and tell the jury whether you recall if it was used in your presence, and if so, by whom and under what circumstances."

I turned and walked away and stood behind juror number seven, leaning against the fence that surrounded the jury. At the moment I would have given $2.98 for a drink of straight Bourbon whiskey. I looked steadily at Wiggie and she gave me an unblinking look in return.

She said, "It was used in my presence. You used it yourself. It was late in the evening. George Stern, who brought me to the party, was upstairs getting his hat. I was about to get my hat. I had a cigaret in my hand and couldn't find a light. Someone called to you, and this cigaret lighter that's marked as an exhibit—or another one like it—was there on the end table. You picked it up and gave me a light. Right after that, George came and said he was ready to leave. I went to the powder room, and then we left. I remember it distinctly."

I walked to my table, hoping I didn't look as unsteady as I felt. I sat down and picked up a pencil and drew three rapid triangles on the yellow pad. On the third one I broke the pencil point with an audible snap, but it didn't seem important.

I said, "I have no more questions."

90.

RICHMOND CROSSED over and whispered with Bolden. The Assistant Commonwealth's Attorney joined them and bent his head to catch what was going on. A low murmur and a movement of bodies pervaded the courtroom. Bolden looked up and pushed his spectacles. He said, "May I ask the indulgence of the Court for a moment?"

Thornton nodded without saying anything. The cockroach came out of his crack and walked horizontally across the front of the bench, hidden from the vision of the Court by the overhanging top. When he reached the corner he felt around it, seemed dissatisfied, and stopped. I was conscious of the vigorous whispered conference at Bolden's table, but I couldn't take my eyes off the cockroach. He seemed to be weighing the situation this way and that, counting up the odds, determining the course of events. I wanted him to go up over the top. I wanted to see what Judge Thornton would do.

Bolden whispered energetically, listened, and started making notes on his pad. The cockroach turned ponderously against the varnished surface of the bench, carefully making sure of his footholds before transferring his weight. Presently he was facing straight up, just under the lip of the bench. He put up his feelers, seemed to think better of the idea, and called them back.

Bolden cleared his throat. Richmond backed to his chair and sat down. The assistant crouched beside Bolden, apparently unwilling to disassociate himself with the center of gravity. The cockroach, electrified, became very still. The people in the room became apprehensive and settled down. The cockroach was precisely the color of the varnished wood, and equally as shiny. When I took my eyes from him and then looked back,

I was not sure whether he was there or whether he had fled to his protective crack. On my yellow pad I printed "Winnie the Pooh." Then I put two lines under the words. Not very parallel.

Bolden said, quietly, almost smugly, "On last Saturday morning, Miss Wiggens, you met the defendant in a drugstore, did you not, and conversed with him?"

Wiggie gave him the wide-open eyes. They were particularly lovely eyes, I thought, warm and capable of affection. She said, "The word *meet* is scarcely appropriate, Mr. Bolden. We bumped into each other in the crowd waiting to cross the street. He asked me to have a Coke with him, and I felt like having a Coke so I agreed. Is that significant?"

Bolden pursed his lips and consulted his notes. He said, "Tell the jury whether thereafter, on last Saturday evening, the defendant came to see you at your apartment?"

Wiggie did not hesitate, but might have turned a little pink under her chin. She said, "At my invitation, yes, he did. When we were in the drugstore that morning he had lost his job, his brother-in-law was dead, and his sister was in the hospital and appeared to be in trouble. I guess I'm the kind of person who takes in a wet puppy out of the rain. I—I guess I did the unpardonable thing, from a man's point of view. I guess you might say I was bold and forward. I asked Mr. London if he'd like to take me out to dinner."

Bolden wore an airy expression. He turned in his chair and hooked an arm over the back of it, looking wisely at the jury. He said, "And how long were you with the defendant that evening?"

Wiggie said evenly, "We went to dinner. Mr. Fant was there, too, at the same place. He came over and spoke to us about the—the arrangements—and things like that. About when the tax man would be at the bank to go through the safe deposit box and about the funeral. We were not out particularly late. I believe Mr. London took me home around eleven or thereabouts."

"He left you at the door, I presume?"

"No, as a matter of fact, he came in for a highball. I thought he needed something, or else he probably wouldn't get any sleep. He came in and joined me in a drink and then left."

Bolden looked at the jury again. Still looking at them, he said, "Now, the next morning. Sunday morning, Miss Wiggens. Tell the jury whether you went to the defendant's apartment in the Albemarle Apartments on Sunday, and if so at what hour. Tell the jury that, if you please."

She said, "On Saturday night we made a date to have breakfast together. I didn't think he ought be alone under the circumstances. I have a car and he hasn't, so I suggested that I join him, rather than for him to come by for me. I believe it was some time after ten-thirty Sunday morning when I went by. Am I supposed to have admitted something pretty awful?"

Bolden continued to look at the jury, with his back turned to her. He seemed rather happy about developments and appeared to feel that the jury would share his amusement. He said, "I'm not a censor, Miss Wiggens. I merely ask questions for the benefit of the jury, who are entitled to know the truth. Suppose you tell the jury when you and the defendant left his apartment to go out to—I believe you said breakfast, didn't you?"

Wiggie had ceased to be embarrassed and was beginning to be angry. There was no flush in her face, but there was a bright spot in each cheek and a deceptive gleam in her eyes. She said, "Your insinuations are bald and offensive, Mr. Bolden, but since the defendant doesn't object and the court doesn't interfere, I assume you are within your legal rights, although giving no evidence of good breeding. It is your desire to infer, of course, that there was something improper in the relation-

- *311*

ship between myself and the defendant. There was none. Now what is your next question?"

Bolden stared at her and she stared back. People waited, not moving. I took notice of the fact that the cockroach had made up his mind and was crawling up over the edge of the bench, with difficulty and in jeopardy, a foot slipping now and again in the most agonizing way.

Bolden said, "If the witness will quit her evasions, stop lecturing the Commonwealth's attorney, and simply answer the question already asked, perhaps it might not be necessary to ask further questions."

Judge Thornton looked expectantly at me. I didn't say anything. Wet puppy, indeed!

Thornton stirred and sat up. He said quietly, "The witness will confine herself to answering the questions, and the Commonwealth's attorney will confine himself to asking questions." He looked down at Wiggie and said, "You were asked what time you left the defendant's apartment. Answer the question, with any legitimate comments or explanations you care to add."

Wiggie said, "Shortly after I arrived at Mr. London's apartment, this bus driver—I believe his name is Herdt—came and asked Mr. London to go to the hospital to give a blood transfusion for Mr. Herdt's little daughter. The defendant agreed to do so, and went away with Joe Herdt. I don't know anyone human who wouldn't have done the same thing. I didn't want to intrude, so I said I'd wait where I was, and I did. Mr. London came back later, and we went to lunch, since it was then too late for the breakfast we had planned. Does that answer your question, Mr. Bolden?"

Bolden arched his eyebrows at the jury, pushed up his spectacles, and turned superciliously to his notes, which he studied with concern. After a long while he looked up and said, "Now about Friday evening at this party, Miss Wiggens. I believe you had, to use your own words, *quite a few* drinks. That's rather vague language, if you'll pardon my saying so. I'm sure the jury would like to know how many drinks you had. Suppose you tell them."

Wiggie said, "I didn't count the drinks, Mr. Bolden, if that's what you mean. I don't carry a score card around with me, you know."

Bolden said, "Ah, I see. No score card. Well, a rough estimate will do. Would you say ten drinks, or more than ten, or less than ten? That's a good round number, isn't it?"

"It's a round number, yes. But I didn't keep count, so anything I might say would be a guess. I just don't know."

"Then as far as you know it might have been fifteen? Or twenty?"

Wiggie realized the trap she had got herself into, and the spots in her cheeks were now very bright and ominous. She said, "The number of drinks is immaterial, as you well know, Mr. Bolden. The material thing is the condition you're in—what effect the drinks have on you. I enjoyed myself and didn't keep count and have no idea how many drinks I had that evening. To be very frank, I was what you might call *high* but I wasn't *drunk*. I knew what I was doing and I knew what other people were doing!"

Bolden looked pointedly at the jury and shrugged and spread his hands as if in helplessness. He said, "It satisfies me if it satisfies you and the jury, Miss Wiggens. These technical terms are over my head. High? Drunk? Well, I guess we'll have to leave it to the jury what you mean . . . Now, let's see. This incident involving the lighting of your cigaret by the defendant. I believe you said that was before you left the party —while you were—did you say you were *high* or *drunk* at the time? I'm sorry, I'm not sure I know the meaning of these terms."

Wiggie said, trying to be patient but with an edge on her voice, "I had had a number of drinks, but I knew what I was doing. What do you want to know?"

"You testified that the defendant lighted a cigaret for you.

– *313*

I'm sure I don't have to remind you that you're under oath. Do you *know* that he used this particular lighter that is marked Exhibit three, or are you, perhaps, rationalizing on that point —a sort of wishful thinking?"

Wiggie said, "I've said I don't know whether it was that particular cigaret lighter, Mr. Bolden. If there are others that look like it, I don't know how I could tell the difference. If Mr. London's fingerprints are on it, that ought to be corroboration. I simply stated my recollection, that's all."

Bolden got up and stood in front of her with his hands on his hips. He said, "Please examine your recollection, Miss Wiggens, such as it was in the condition you were in. At the risk of becoming boring, let me remind you that you have sworn to tell the truth. Now, please tell the jury whether it is your recollection simply that Mr. London lit your cigaret, or whether you really remember that he lit your cigaret *with this lighter or one exactly like it?*"

Wiggie did not answer immediately. She half closed her eyes and appeared to be thinking back very carefully. At length she opened her eyes, looked at Matt Bolden squarely, and said, "This is Wednesday and that was last Friday night, several days ago. As I said, I had had quite a few drinks, but I knew what was going on. Naturally I couldn't have known it was going to be important. With that explanation and the limitations necessarily implied, I must say, since I am under oath, that it is my distinct recollection that Mr. London lit my cigaret either with that very cigaret lighter, or with another one like it."

Bolden shut his lips tight, sneered at the jury, and went back to his seat. He let some silence take form, and then sat back and laced his fingers behind his head. He said, "Since you're so very truthful, being under oath, Miss Wiggens, suppose you tell the jury whether or not you're in love with the defendant, Jesse London. That's a very straight question and ought to bring out a very straight answer."

Wiggie did not answer immediately. I looked up in surprise and saw that the flush of embarrassment was replacing the red spots of anger. Her eyes went around the room, brushing mine in passing, but refusing to have a square look at me.

Bolden said, "Well?"

Wiggie looked down at her hands, then at Bolden. She said, "I knew Mr. London only very slightly before we met at the party on last Friday evening, Mr. Bolden. For your information, as it happens it has never been necessary for me to be forward about such matters. My father is Mr. Hosea Wiggens, who owns nearly all of the stock of Harley and Farnsworth and some eight or ten leading department stores in the Midwest and South. I encountered Mr. London on Friday evening at the party, saw him briefly on Saturday and Sunday, and have not seen him since. I believe that answers your question."

Bolden looked at Richmond and I saw Richmond shake his head almost imperceptibly. Bolden said, "On the contrary, I don't believe it does. I asked whether or not you are in love with Mr. London. Just say yes or no."

The silence was too long. I couldn't look at Wiggie. I couldn't think. I looked for the cockroach until my eyeballs hurt, but he wasn't where I had left him a few minutes ago. I raised my eyes to the top of the bench and saw him there, a few inches from the gavel, apparently looking at the Judge. The Judge was looking at Wiggie, waiting. I waited, too.

Bolden said, "I must remind you again that you're under oath."

Wiggie raised her head and looked at him full in the face. Then she looked at the jury. She said, "Yes, I'm in love with Jesse London. I hope you're satisfied. But I wouldn't lie for him if he were the Angel Gabriel."

Matt Bolden sat down very quietly. He said, "No more questions."

I stood up without knowing I was doing it. I opened my mouth and then closed it and sat down.

In a voice that sounded queer, even to me, I said, "No more questions."

Bolden looked at me and then at the Court. He said, "That seems to be the case, Your Honor. Unless Mr. London has something more?"

I said, "No, that's the case."

Juror number three sat forward in his chair and cleared his throat. He said, "Judge, I'd like to ask a question."

Judge Thornton said, "Very well."

The juror said, "As long as we're supposed to hear everything, I would like to hear from Mrs. Sothern. Is she too ill to appear?"

I looked at Bolden and Bolden looked at Richmond. I said, "If the Court please, the defendant is perfectly willing that Mrs. Sothern be heard, but the defendant is informed and believes that her physician will not permit her to leave the hospital at this time. However, Lieutenant Richmond has interviewed her a number of times. I suggest that we might be able to stipulate the nature of her testimony."

Judge Thornton looked at the Commonwealth's attorney and said, "What is your thought on the matter, Mr. Bolden?"

Bolden whispered with Lieutenant Richmond and then walked around and stood in front of the bench. He said, "Judge, the doctors won't let her be brought to the courtroom. We did not suggest the taking of her deposition as a substitute because of her condition, and also because her testimony was merely cumulative—that is, we ascertained nothing new. Nothing that has not been brought out through the testimony of other witnesses."

The juror said, "I'd like to know what time she went to the hospital, whether Mr. Sothern was alive and well at that time, and whether Mr. London had returned to the house after leaving the party."

Bolden and Richmond whispered some more. Neither of them liked this development.

I said, "I'm willing to let Richmond pass on to the jury what he ascertained on these points. Despite some of his testimony in this case, I have confidence in his integrity and am inclined to believe that I'll be willing to stipulate that if Mrs. Sothern were present she would testify to whatever he says."

Bolden was flustered but he couldn't very well refuse. By this time he was thoroughly exasperated and discouraged. He said, "I never heard of anything like this in a capital case, but if it's all right with the defendant and that fact is made to appear in the record, I see no reason why the Commonwealth should not agree."

Thornton pursed his lips meditatively and then said, "Well, all right. Lieutenant Richmond may represent to the jury what he believes Mrs. Sothern would testify to on those points. But let's limit it to answering questions of counsel or the jury. Right now, we have the juror's specific questions and Lieutenant Richmond will limit himself to them."

Richmond looked down at his toes and thought a moment, and then said, "Mrs. Southern told me, in the presence of another detective who can be produced if necessary, that she and her husband quarreled in their home about one forty-five or two o'clock on the morning of Saturday, April twenty-seventh, that she received an injury, and was taken to City Hospital by the servants who have testified in this case, a few minutes thereafter. She says her husband, Mr. Sothern, was alive and uninjured at that time and according to her story, the defendant, Mr. London, was not in the house at that time and had not returned to the house after leaving the party a couple of hours before. That's the story she told."

I said, "The defendant will stipulate Lieutenant Richmond's statement."

Bolden said, "I suppose the Commonwealth will have to agree."

Judge Thornton said, "Let the stipulation be made to appear in the record. Are there any more questions?"

Juror number three semed satisfied and the other jurors gave no indication of desiring to ask questions.

Thornton looked at me and at Bolden. He said, "Gentlemen, have you anything more?"

I shook my head no.

Bolden said, "That seems to be the case."

Thornton pounded with his gavel. He said, "Recess for fifteen minutes. Counsel will join the Court in chambers."

I looked all over the courtroom, but I couldn't find Wiggie.

91.

WHEN WE WERE all inside and the door was closed, Thornton took a cigar box out of a drawer, made a halfhearted gesture of offering them around, put the box back, lit one, and slid down comfortably on the point of his spine. He said, "It's time to talk about the instructions. Who wants to be heard first?"

I said, "Judge, I know there'll be an instruction that the jury is to find me not guilty if they don't believe I'm guilty. That's all I'm really interested in. I don't believe they can come to any other verdict on the evidence they've heard. If no one objects, I'd like permission to have Mr. Fant appear for me in the discussion of what the Court is going to instruct the jury. I'd like to have the library to myself for a few minutes and smoke a couple of cigarets and think through all the testimony so I can make up my mind what I'm going to say to the jury."

Thornton looked at Fant. Fant said, with dignity, "I'd want it noted formally, that I'm an attorney of record."

I said, "Of course. Let the record show whatever Mr. Fant thinks is appropriate. I'm content for him to dictate it, whether I'm present or not."

Fant drew me into the corner by the window. He said in a whisper, "We must be sure there's an instruction on reasonable doubt, of course. But then, that's automatic. Anything else?"

I shrugged and said, "Just make sure they've got a right to find me not guilty. You've heard the evidence. What else can they do?"

Fant made a face, almost involuntarily. He said, "Blue Larkspur was a cinch to win the Derby, but he ran second. And he wasn't running against capital punishment, either. They'll want to decide how much time will be allowed for arguments. How much shall I hold out for?"

I said, "Five minutes to a side."

He looked incredulous. "In a murder case? Are you crazy?"

I said, "On that point, I'll do my own talking."

I came back and stood in front of Thornton's desk. I said, "I'll leave the business of the instructions to Mr. Fant, if the Court please. But maybe before I leave the room we ought to discuss the length of the arguments. I'm willing to limit mine to five minutes, if Mr. Bolden will agree to the same limit on his argument."

Bolden sat up indignantly. He said, "Five minutes? In a capital case? I'll certainly agree to no such thing. The Commonwealth requests at least an hour for its summation. We'll agree, witl ut question, to a similar limit for the defendant."

Thornton took his cigar out of his mouth and looked at the accumulated ash. He tapped the cigar experimentally with his forefinger and seemed pleased that the ash did not fall. You could see he felt that his choice of brands had been vindicated.

He said slowly, "The charge is murder. The penalty is—serious. The court does not consider the Commonwealth's request for an hour to be out of reason. Of course the defendant will be allowed the same amount of time."

I looked at Fant and he raised his shoulders eloquently. I said, "All right. I agree to an hour a side. What I'm going to say won't take five minutes, but I can see how Mr. Bolden might have to talk half a day trying to make a case out of what he's got to go on . . ."

Bolden said wearily, "Frankly, I'm getting bored with the sales talk. It's bad enough in the presence of the jury, but we all know juries and perhaps it's understandable to get away with anything you can get away with. I suggest we ought to dispense with the crap when the door's closed and there's nobody here but just us girls. I hope you don't think you're going to convince me I ought to dismiss the case."

I said, "No, the kind of mentality that would bring a case to trial on this sort of evidence would naturally carry it through to its ridiculous conclusion. I don't suppose you've ever heard an innocent person react as an innocent person would react, but it might prove to be good for you, at that. There *are* innocent people, or did you know?"

Thornton said, "Gentlemen, this is neither amusing nor constructive. Mr. London, you have asked that Mr. Fant be recognized as your spokesman. Granted. You have asked the seclusion of the library until court reconvenes. That's granted, too. Now if you gentlemen please, the jury's waiting and I'd like to get down to business."

I hoped I was the personification of injured dignity as I gathered up my pencil and yellow pad and stalked into the library without comment. I closed the door. I threw my yellow pad on the nearest table, stuck the pencil behind my ear, and stood at the window with my hands in my hips pockets. We were on the second floor, overlooking the tar-paper roof of a one-floor annex. The expanse of roof was littered with stray objects and for a few moments I was lost in the fascinating business of identifying them—empty, crumpled cigaret packages of four or five different brands—cigaret butts in various stages of disintegration—empty paper match-covers, curled and weathered—paper cups, some upright, some on their sides, and some mashed out of shape—wrappers of such candy bars as "Baby Ruth" and "Mr. Goodbar" . . .

I was not in a very good frame of mind. I found it difficult to put the testimony of the witnesses in orderly rows so I could look at them sensibly. My mind kept jumping from one thing to another in the most haphazard fashion . . . I kept wondering why Wiggie avoided me during the trial . . .

I kept wondering if what Wiggie had said about being in love with me had been said because she thought it might help me with the jury . . . well, it might help me with the jury . . . people are incurably romantic . . .

. . . but then . . . all right, that was probably the explanation . . . the kind of person who'd take in a wet puppy out of the rain would be the kind you'd expect to perjure herself to help—well, a wet puppy in the rain . . .

Fant came in. He said, "Here's a copy of the instructions. I put in an exception, just in case, but only as a matter of form. Want to have a look?"

I said, "No, as long as the jury is authorized to find me not guilty if they feel that way. The rest doesn't make any difference. I couldn't be home in bed and half-guilty. It's got to be whole hog or none."

Fant said, "You have an hour, if you want it. Your turn's first, of course. Thornton's ready whenever you are, but nobody's rushing you."

I said, "Now's as good as any other time. Let's go."

92.

A COURTROOM can be without audible conversation when something is about to happen, but I doubt if it can be silent. It has to rustle. Somebody has to whisper, somebody has to move, somebody has to cough . . . that is, when something is *about* to happen.

It's different when something *starts* to happen, and everyone knows it. Then the whispering and moving and coughing stop. There is now an absence of sound. People crane their necks, afraid they won't see . . . won't hear . . .

They craned their necks at me. I stayed in the library until the last possible moment, pulling at a cigaret until it was almost too hot to hold. There was a trembling in my hands, an unbearable weakness in my knees. I was almost fainting for a moment. I was afraid. I wondered where the cockiness had come from—the cockiness that had carried me through the days of sparring and joking with Lieutenant Richmond, through the questioning of the witnesses, through my own moments on the witness stand, through the sarcastic exchanges with Bolden . . .

I had refused to let myself think about the meaning of being tried for murder. I had refused to entertain the idea of being extinguished in the electric chair. I had asserted my innocence, to everyone and to myself, and had used this assertion to exclude all other thoughts from my mind. But who was I kidding? Was it, after all, me?

I had killed a man. Would it have been better to have said so, and to have tried to explain why? Wouldn't it have been better to have told the whole story, the whole truth? Surely the jury would have understood . . . a sudden flash of anger in the face of something dispicable and violent . . . a thoughtless act in the heat of passion . . . perhaps, at the most, ten years in the penitentiary, or twenty . . . even a chance to go free . . .

But not death. . . .

And now, that was the possibility I had to face—a possibility I was wholly unwilling to face . . . a possibility I wasn't sure I was *able* to face.

Fant opened the door again, with a trace of impatience. He said, "The Court's ready. Everybody's ready."

I blew my nose, tucked the handkerchief into my hip pocket, and walked into the courtroom. That's when they craned their necks at me. That's when there was an absence of sound. I went over and sat at my table, and when the deputy sheriff had pounded for order, the Judge read the instructions to the jury.

"If you believe from the evidence . . ."

I think I listened to the instructions, but I'm sure I didn't hear them. Eyes were looking at me, and a calmness swelled in me to meet the challenge. I was no longer weak, or trembling, or afraid. I kept telling myself I was innocent and the evidence showed I was innocent and there was no reason why I should not face any man . . .

The instructions were over. Judge Thornton was looking at me. I stood, with dignity, and said, "May it please the Court . . ."

Judge Thornton nodded, "Mr. London."

I nodded formally to Matt Bolden, got a nod in return, and stood before the railing that enclosed the jury. Now the silence was intense. I took my time and looked at each juror in turn. Now I was not afraid.

I said, "Ladies and gentlemen, according to the law of the land you have been chosen to decide whether I did or did not kill my brother-in-law, Mitchell Sothern. You have been chosen at random from the community where I live. You have heard whatever evidence there is. I assume, and believe, that you came into this courtroom with open minds, and that you are about to make your decision on the basis of what you have seen and heard right here, without pressure and without fear of the consequences. Under our Constitution and laws, that is my priceless right. Under our Constitution and laws, that is your priceless duty and privilege.

"Perhaps you have wondered that I have shown no evidence of grief over the death of one so close to me. I can only ask that you try to place yourself for a moment in my position. My first knowledge of his death was accompanied by information that my own sister was thought to be involved. As between the two—the living and the dead, the blood kin and the relative by marriage—my first anxiety was for my sister. If the same circumstances occurred tomorrow, my response would be the same, and if it were otherwise I would be ashamed. I think you would feel the same way.

"I tried to see my sister at the hospital, and was not permitted to see her. I knew she was ill, and that she should not be subjected to grilling by the police. I don't know what you would have done. I don't know what I *should have* done. I don't know what I *would do* if the same circumstances should confront me tomorrow morning. But you've heard what I did, that morning, under those circumstances, and I don't know how I could have made a better decision. I went straight down to the core of the investigation—to Lieutenant Richmond himself—and I took the burden and the suspicion on my own shoulders. Correction—I *tried* to."

I looked at each juror, again. I let the silence take over again, for a brief moment. I said, "Tried to, is right. I made the best try I ever made in my life. I made up such a good story that it's about to cost me my life—if Lieutenant Richmond and Mr. Bolden have their way. But how good a try was it? Not good enough to convince Richmond and his assistant at the very time I was telling it! They saw the holes in that story *even while they were listening to it, and they haven't had the gall to deny that under oath in this courtroom!"*

I waited a moment. I said, "How did I get into this house which Mrs. Forman has told you was locked? By using keys I didn't have? Keys I didn't have any reason to have? Why would I kill Mitchell Sothern anyway? Do you think I would kill a man for something I didn't know about until the next morning? Would you? Would anyone?"

I needed to blow my nose so I paused and blew it, deliberately.

I said, "Who *says* I killed him? Nobody. Not one soul says so. Who says I *could* have killed him? Let's stop and look at that. Joe Herdt? Well, you heard Joe testify. What did he say? The most he ever said to anyone, at any time, was that he saw me at Cedar and Virginia around two o'clock Saturday morning. He didn't mean any harm. He thought he was telling the truth, God bless him. And then you heard him acknowledge his mistake. More than that, you heard the actual, physical, uncontrovertible evidence that proved his mistake, proved it beyond doubt to Joe himself, and to his wife, and to everyone.

"And then, of course, you heard the insinuation of Mr. Bolden that Joe and his wife and even his *pants* would lie, just because I did what anyone on earth would have done, guilty or innocent—gave a little blood out of my body for a sick little girl.

"Let's get back to who says I killed him. Charley Pitts? Why, Charley's all right, but even all right people can be mistaken. I didn't prove it to you, he did it himself. He wrote it down in a book in his own handwriting, and you saw the book for yourself. Charley told you I came in only once—singing "Girl of My Dreams," just as Miss Wiggens said. That's true. And when I got upstairs I remembered my appointment in the morning and called down and asked him to wake me up. When did I do that? Didn't Miss Small tell you? Didn't Mr. Block tell you?

"That reminds me of Mr. Block. Maybe he doesn't puzzle you, but he certainly puzzles me. Why he wants to get me in trouble, I don't know, but you must have seen the evidence of his animosity every minute he was sitting in that chair over there. Even in the face of the written evidence of Charley Pitts' own handwriting, he still wants to get me in trouble. What's behind it? What's this cock-and-bull story about a green hat? And at two o'clock or two-thirty in the morning, at that?"

I went over and got the green hat. I held it in my hands. I said, "This is the only green hat anybody has talked about in the whole case." I put it on my head. "Do you think I'd wear this hat, even if I were walking in my sleep?"

I walked over, slowly, and put the hat down. I came back and stood in front of the jury. I said, "Four young drunks who had been *just parking* have told you that someone about my size got into a yellow Hudson sedan with them on Saturday morning about two o'clock or thereabouts and sang songs. That's what they say now. What they said Saturday and Sunday was that it wasn't somebody my size, but this young fellow Don Stith. That's what they told Richmond. Now they've cooked up a story about Stith being out of town at the time, and you're supposed to conclude this person must have been me. How far out of town was Stith, anyway? Not over an hour, according to his own testimony. And what would you tell your wife, especially in view of this pair of pink panties which everyone admits but no one wants to talk about? Lieutenant Richmond admits there *was* a pair of pink panties with this green hat. The hat's here, all marked for identification in the hope that it'll convict me, but you don't see any panties, do you?"

I stopped and waited a long time. I said, "In mystery stories people are always dodging arrest because they figure a jury's going to find them guilty unless they *prove someone else is guilty.* That's putting the cart before the horse. I don't believe this jury or any other jury is going to find me guilty just because I can't prove someone else committed a crime. That's not my job. Under our system of justice, a man is innocent until he's proven guilty, not guilty until he proves himself innocent. And why shouldn't it be that way? What chance have I to prove I'm innocent? Do I have a lot of detectives working for me? Do I have an unlimited bank account? How would any of you, members of this jury, go about proving that *you* didn't kill Mitchell Sothern? See what I mean?"

I waited longer than ever. I lowered my voice. I said, "Judge Thornton says you are to find me not guilty unless you believe beyond a reasonable doubt that I committed this crime that has been charged against me. I don't ask that much of a break. As far as I'm concerned, you can find me guilty if you can make a reasonable *guess* that I *am guilty.* I mean, a guess that will enable you to leave this courtroom and look your grocer or your next door neighbor in the eye and not blush.

"My conscience is entirely clear. I have nothing to excuse, explain, or apologize for. I had some drinks at the party, but that doesn't make me guilty of murder. I came home singing "Girl of My Dreams," as maybe many of you have done. That doesn't make me guilty of murder, either. I went up to my room and went to bed. Joe Herdt didn't see me anywhere at two o'clock, and he now knows it, and so do you. Charley Pitts didn't see me at any such hour, and he now knows it, and so do you, as his own written record proves to you and to me and to everyone. Mr. Block didn't see me. Who he saw, or thinks he saw, or wants you to believe he saw, I don't know. As for Don Stith, give him the benefit of the doubt. Let's say he *was* a few miles away. Does that mean *I* was the person who sang songs with a bunch of drunks who thought it was Don Stith? Why pin this cockeyed green hat on *me?*"

I put my hands on the railing in front of the jury and looked down at them as long as I thought was reasonable. Then I looked up. I said, quietly and as simply as I could, "I can't think of another thing to say. I've said it all. You've heard the evidence, there's really no use in me telling you what it means. I'm an American and I'm happy with the system that leaves this kind of decision up to people like you. Now you can listen to Mr. Bolden, and when he's had his say, then it's simply up to you to decide my future—whether I'm a guy who ought to be allowed to practice law in this community, or whether I've got a big debt I ought to pay to honest, law-abiding citizens."

I gave them each a long look—as frank and guileless as I could make it. I said, "If you say I've got a debt to pay, I'll pay it. I don't believe you'll say that, because it isn't so."

I went back to my table and sat down. The people in the courtroom let out their collective breaths. I heard Matt Bolden clearing his throat.

93.

THE ROOM GRADUALLY became quiet again. The multitude of eyes were brought to bear on Matt Bolden. His sense of drama was good. He sat and looked at his notes until there was nothing in the courtroom but expectancy. Then he looked up, as if in mild surprise, surveyed the crowd, and slowly rose to his feet.

He said, "May it please the Court . . . ?"

"Mr. Bolden."

He glanced at me, but didn't bother to nod. I didn't nod,

either. He coughed into his handkerchief. He walked over and stood before the jury, surveying them. He let the silence tingle. Then he slowly removed his spectacles, held them up to the light, took out a little pink cloth, breathed on the lenses, polished them, held them to the light again, and slowly hooked them back over his ears. He folded the pink cloth carefully and put it into his spectacle case, snapped the case shut, and tapped it against the fingers of his left hand. Then he put the case in his pocket.

When he spoke, his voice was scarcely audible and everyone strained forward. He said, "I'm the Commonwealth's attorney. All that means is that I speak on behalf of the law-abiding citizens of this community—you who are in this room, the farmer, the merchant, the children in our schools, the laborer, the capitalist, the lawyer, the truck driver . . . I am your servant and your representative . . ."

He turned and pointed at me. "Jess London has been charged with murdering a respected member of this community. A Grand Jury chosen from among your number, heard the evidence against him and determined that he should be tried for his life in this courtroom and before this jury of his neighbors. You have heard the evidence. What does it show?

"It's true that no one *saw* Jess London murder Mitchell Sothern. Does that prove he didn't do it? Is a murderer to go scot free simply because no one *saw* him commit the crime?"

He stopped and turned to the jury. He waited for the silence. He said softly, "Wait a minute. Did I say no one saw the commission of this crime? I should have said only two people saw it." He held up two fingers. "Mitchell Sothern himself saw it, but he's dead and we can't hear the story from his dead lips." He took one of his fingers and bent it down. "Or *did* he see it? Did Mitchell Sothern see this blow, struck from behind by his own brother-in-law? We can only speculate."

He held up the other finger significantly and walked the

length of the jury box. "Who else? Only Jess London . . . Jess London . . . that's all. I suppose it's too much to expect *him* to tell us what happened, isn't it?"

He turned and looked seriously at me. His spectacles slid down his nose and he looked at me over them. Then he pushed them up his nose and turned and thundered, "BUT HE DID TELL US!"

His voice came down again and he leaned way over the railing of the jury box. He said, almost in a whisper, "Yes, sir, he told us all about it. In that first unguarded moment when his conscience had the upper hand, before fear and the instinct for self-preservation numbed and rotted his moral fibers, JESS LONDON HIMSELF TOLD US ABOUT THE MURDER OF MITCHELL SOTHERN!"

He went over and squirted himself a paper cup of water, swallowed it, and came back to the jury. He said, conversationally, "On last Saturday morning Jess London confessed to this heinous crime in the presence of two witnesses. He confessed to every detail of the crime. He told us why he came back to the house after the party was over, how he got in, and what weapon he used. The police examined that weapon, which wasn't in the murder room and might never have been suspected to be the murder weapon, and found on it the fingerprints of Jess London, precisely as he said.

"I'm sure I don't have to remind you that Jess London didn't deny that he made that confession. *Now* he simply says it isn't true. *He* says he was home in bed. Who *else* says so? Does Joe Herdt say so? *Does* he?"

Matt Bolden let that lie awhile. He stared at the jury. He stuck out his lower lip and stared some more. He raised his eyebrows. He said, mildly enough, "The *first* thing Joe Herdt said was that he saw Jess London a few yards from the scene of the crime about the time the murder must have been done. That doesn't sound as if Jess were home in bed, does it? Isn't it funny that Joe Herdt said the same thing the *second* time, in the statement he swore to before a Notary Public? Isn't *that* funny? And how about the *third* time, when he was under oath before the Grand Jury? Funny? Why, if I had Joe's sense of humor, I'd be in vaudeville."

He paused again, let his spectacles slide down his nose, and pushed them up again. He said, "The *fourth* time Joe Herdt opened his mouth—well, you heard him yourself. All of a sudden everything is different. It didn't happen that way. I was somewhere else, you were somewhere else, he was somewhere else, they were somewhere else. It wasn't this time, it was that time. I beg your pardon, I had a hole in my pants."

He stopped and looked at himself carefully. He said, "Maybe I've got a hole in *my* pants!"

That got a nervous sort of giggle out of the jury and out of the crowd. My mind began to wander . . . Matt Bolden could go on like this indefinitely. . . . I looked at the yellow pad and wondered how in hell I could have thought my drawing looked like a horse. . . . I looked idly at the crowd, seeing faces collectively . . . seeing nothing . . . observing that the eyes were pointing in the direction of Matt Bolden, flicking momentarily at me when I moved, but paying no attention . . .

The eyes were not all looking at Matt Bolden. Wiggie was sitting in the third row, looking squarely at me. I looked squarely back at her. Nothing was changed. It was the same courtroom, the same people, the same judge, the same jury, the same voice of the Commonwealth's attorney asking for my life . . .

But it was different.

I looked at Wiggie, and I do not know how much time went by. Bolden's voice rose and fell. There were pauses. Now and then I focused on a passage, without the context. . . .

". . . what else would you *expect* Charley Pitts to say? And all this monkey business about writing down calls in a book. You heard Pitts admit the call might have come in from *outside* the apartment house. And how does it happen Pitts didn't think of this so-called record until the suggestion *is made in this courtroom by Jess London?*

"And that brings us to Mr. Block. Why should Mr. Block come here and tell you a lie? Can you think of any reason? Jess London couldn't think of any reason, or you would have heard from him long ago . . .

"The green hat—a typical red herring if I ever saw one. Jess London conveniently *found* it, where it would do the most good, and when Lieutenant Richmond just *happened* to be with him . . .

"And that brings us down to the fingerprints on this cigaret lighter. The fingerprints of Jess London. The weapon wasn't even in the room, and the police would never have thought to look for his fingerprints on it—*except for his confession!* . . . Yes, gentlemen, he *told us where to look*, and we looked where he told us, and we found his fingerprints on the murder weapon. *Now* he says his fingerprints were there because he used the cigaret lighter for another purpose. For *what* other purpose? Isn't it funny that he used it, *so he says*, to light a cigaret for a young lady who admits she's in love with him? Isn't it funny that *no one else* corroborates that statement? No one else except a girl who'd perjure herself to save his life. . . .

Wiggie's eyes shifted to Bolden at that point, and she frowned. Then she looked straight at me. I did not take my eyes from hers. Somehow I sensed that half of the jury and half of the crowd were paying more attention to us than to Matt Bolden's speech, but it didn't seem important.

Then the silence seemed longer than usual. When I looked away, the Judge said, "Ladies and gentlemen of the jury, you have heard the evidence, the instructions of the Court, and the arguments of counsel. You will now retire to the jury room for your deliberations. When you have arrived at a verdict or if you wish to ask a question, you may knock on the door and the sheriff will unlock it for you. If you have not arrived at a verdict in, say, an hour, the sheriff will escort you in a body to a restaurant or hotel where you will eat together and then return and resume your deliberations."

The jury members stood, shuffled slowly out of their enclosure, and filtered into the jury room. The door was shut and locked before the crowd broke out in the inevitable chatter and babble. There was no formal adjournment of Court, but Judge Thornton turned and made an obviously informal remark to the stenographer. Then he left his seat behind the bench, came down, sat at ease in the witness chair, and lit a cigaret. People stood, stretched, lit cigarets, made remarks to each other, went out to the rest rooms. I could see Wiggie in the aisle, trying to push her way through to the gate in the enclosure.

There was a discreet cough at my shoulder. It was the timid deputy sheriff. He said, "You'll understand how it is, Mr. London. Bail runs out when the case goes to the jury. I'm supposed to take you into custody . . ."

I said, turning away to look for Wiggie, "Okay. Consider me in custody. I admit I'm in your power. Is that all? Or do you have to take me over to the jail?"

He said quickly, "Oh no. Not to the jail, Mr. London. As long as you're in custody, that's all."

Wiggie was coming through the gate. I said, "That's fine. Relax. Sit down and take a load off your feet." To Wiggie, I said, "I looked for you several times. I couldn't find you."

She said, "Thelma and I were powdering our noses in the ladies' room." Then she said, "I heard it all. I guess I owe you an apology."

Thurston Galloway had been talking with Matt Bolden. Now he broke away and came over to us. He said, "Anything to say for the press?"

I said, "Miss Wiggens, Mr. Galloway of the A & P or is it Kroger's? Mr. Galloway, Miss Wiggens. What did Bolden say for publication?"

Galloway looked down at his toes. He said, "For publication, he said he would predict conviction on an early ballot." He looked up and gave me a smile. "Off the record, he says he wouldn't bet a dime. Now what do you say?"

I said, looking at the clock, "How long have they been out? Well, call it five or ten minutes. They haven't finished taking turns in the washroom yet. Then give them credit for being rugged individualists who aren't on a jury but once and want to say their piece. Minimum of fifteen more minutes, maximum of forty-five minutes or an hour. I say acquital on the first ballot in forty-five minutes, so they can get out and go home or take a drink at the nearest bar. If it takes longer than that, maybe I'm in trouble."

"And you, Miss Wiggens?"

Wiggie linked her arm in mine. She said, "From what I heard, I don't know how it could take this long to make up their minds."

Galloway said, raising his eyebrows, "Maybe the two of you have something you ought to tell me. People aren't missing the human interest angle, you know. How about it, London?"

"Object," said Wiggie. "Don't answer that question. It's incompetent, irrelevant and immaterial."

I said, "The objection is sustained. The question is premature."

There was a sound, and then an electric silence in the room. Galloway frowned, looked at his wrist watch, and said, "Already?"

Bolden looked up anxiously from his chair. He said, half rising, "Maybe they want to ask a question."

Judge Thornton threw his cigaret into the nearest spittoon and resumed his place behind the bench. People sat down tentatively on the edges of the nearest seats. The word somehow permeated the whole building and people started bumping each other as they tried to push in from the hall.

The deputy sheriff had been eating a candy bar and he had chocolate around his mouth. He carefully put down the unfinished part on the window ledge over the radiator, wiped his lips on his sleeve, looked around sheepishly, and unlocked the door of the jury room. The jury came out in single file, heading for the space in front of the bench.

Galloway dug me in the ribs with his elbow and said in a whisper out of the corner of his mouth, "Hell, this is no question, bub. This is it."

Wiggie sat down suddenly. I looked at her and found that she was white, with her eyes wide and her mouth half open. My knees wanted me to sit down, too, but I was afraid to move. Bolden was still halfway between between sitting and standing, with his weight resting on his hands, which were spread wide on the table in front of him.

The jury members stepped on each others toes, apologized, nodded, smiled, moved this way and that, and finally arranged themselves to their satisfaction. Judge Thornton said into the silence, "Have you reached a verdict?"

The foreman said in a very loud voice, "We have."

"What is your verdict?"

The foreman looked at a piece of paper in his hand as if he didn't know what he was going to say. Then he looked up and said, "The jury finds the defendant not guilty. Is that all, Judge?"

You can't help but have a silence after a thing like that, and the silence must be followed, as it was, by bedlam. The deputy sheriff pounded on the table and hollered, "QUIET! QUIET!"

Judge Thornton said, "Do you wish the jury polled, Mr. Bolden?"

Bolden shrugged. He said, "No, Your Honor. When a jury brings in a verdict in fifteen minutes, they know what they're doing, I guess."

"Very well," said Judge Thornton. "The jury's discharged. The defendant's released from custody. Court's adjourned."

The deputy sheriff whammed his little hammer on the nearest piece of furniture and reached for his unfinished candy bar on the window ledge.

I looked at Wiggie. Her face was still white, ghastly. She said, wetting her lips, "You mean—that's all of it? It's over?"

My own speaking organs were paralyzed. I sat down very hard. Then I saw members of the jury coming my way and I had enough presence of mind to jump up and shake their hands.

Bolden came over and held out his hand. He said, "Congratulations. The case looked all right, and then it came apart. Did you know it all the time, or did you just get the breaks as you went along?"

I said, "All I know was I didn't do it. I hung on to that for dear life and kept pitching. I guess I'm just lucky I thought of the right things to ask. I knew it was all screwy, but I didn't know how it got that way."

Wiggie said, "I need a light."

She had a cigaret in her hand and was looking at me expectantly. I found my little black lighter in my pocket, thumbed up the top of it, flicked the wheel, and held the flame . . .

Galloway said into my ear, "*Now* what've you got to say to my dear readers?"

I started to answer, then realized that Wiggie had not bent to light her cigaret. I looked at her.

She was staring at the cigaret lighter in my hand. When I looked at her, she looked at me. Then she looked back at the lighter and back at me again. Was she still white, or had the color returned to her face and then left it again?

I held the flame steadily, with all the will power I could muster. I said, "Did you want a light, lady?"

She put her cigaret in her lips, then put up the other hand to guide the flame. Her hand was cold—icy. She had difficulty getting her cigaret to draw properly, but finally made it. She looked away and took several deep drags.

I said, "That does it." Then I said to Galloway, "Do you mind? I mean, just a shake or two."

He said, "Of course," and went over to ask a question of a juryman who was looking for his hat.

She turned and faced me. Now there were two bright spots, one in each cheek.

I said, "You said you love me, in front of God and everybody. I hope you weren't just taking in a wet puppy out of the rain. I hope you meant it, and mean it now . . ."

I waited, but she didn't say anything. She took a deep drag from her cigaret and then looked down and blew smoke out of her nose.

I said, "I love you with all my heart. I want you to marry me, I couldn't ask you until now. If you had said yes and we had been married, everyone would have wondered if I asked you to marry me only because a wife can't testify against her husband. I couldn't let them think that . . . I couldn't let you wonder about it, either. I had to let you sit up there in front of everybody and tell the truth, so you'd know I'm innocent and unafraid."

She still didn't say anything.

I said, "Now it's all over. I'm innocent and everyone knows it, and I'm a lawyer again, instead of a person accused of murder. I'm in love and I want to marry the girl I love. What do you think she's going to do about it?"

She looked into my eyes steadily, but only for the barest moment. In that flicker of a moment there was uncertainty . . . a visible doubt that recoiled upon itself, and disturbed itself, and blamed itself, and yet remained a doubt.

In an unconscious gesture of escape, she dropped her cigaret on the floor and stepped on it, turning her toe from side to side until the stub of the cigaret came apart and the light brown tobacco scattered on the floor. She turned away from me and wandered aimlessly to a window and stood looking out of it.

I walked over and stood behind her. Close behind her . . . not touching her, but very near . . . realizing the moment was fragile . . . untouchable . . .

I said, "Something has upset you. You needn't answer now, darling . . ."

She said, "No, I couldn't. Not . . . not now . . ."

She went out through the little gate in the railing and walked up the aisle toward the door. Thelma was there, but Wiggie appeared not to see her. Thelma looked queerly at me, and when I didn't follow, she turned and hurried after Wiggie, catching up at the heavy door and helping her open it.

I stood where I was, looking with despairing loneliness at the blank door that swung shut behind them.

Galloway was puzzled, and tried to be the nice guy he always was. He said, "Something happen? Sorry, everybody's been under a strain. If there's nothing to say just now . . ."

Without turning, I said, dully, "No. There's nothing to say . . . Just now . . ."

THE PERENNIAL LIBRARY MYSTERY SERIES

E. C. Bentley

TRENT'S LAST CASE
"One of the three best detective stories ever written." —Agatha Christie

TRENT'S OWN CASE
"I won't waste time saying that the plot is sound and the detection satisfying. Trent has not altered a scrap and reappears with all his old humor and charm." —Dorothy L. Sayers

Gavin Black

A DRAGON FOR CHRISTMAS
"Potent excitement!" —New York Herald Tribune

THE EYES AROUND ME
"I stayed up until all hours last night reading *The Eyes Around Me*, which is something I do not do very often, but I was so intrigued by the ingeniousness of Mr. Black's plotting and the witty way in which he spins his mystery. I can only say that I enjoyed the book enormously." —F. van Wyck Mason

YOU WANT TO DIE, JOHNNY?
"Gavin Black doesn't just develop a pressure plot in suspense, he adds uninfected wit, character, charm, and sharp knowledge of the Far East to make rereading as keen as the first race-through." —Book Week

Nicholas Blake

THE BEAST MUST DIE
"It remains one more proof that in the hands of a really first-class writer the detective novel can safely challenge comparison with any other variety of fiction." —The Manchester Guardian

THE CORPSE IN THE SNOWMAN
"If there is a distinction between the novel and the detective story (which we do not admit), then this book deserves a high place in both categories."
—The New York Times

THE DREADFUL HOLLOW
"Pace unhurried, characters excellent, reasoning solid."
—San Francisco Chronicle

END OF CHAPTER
" ...admirably solid...an adroit formal detective puzzle backed up by firm characterization and a knowing picture of London publishing."
—The New York Times

Francis Iles

BEFORE THE FACT

"Not many 'serious' novelists have produced character studies to compare with Iles's internally terrifying portrait of the murderer in *Before the Fact*, his masterpiece and a work truly deserving the appellation of unique and beyond price." —Howard Haycraft

MALICE AFORETHOUGHT

"It is a long time since I have read anything so good as *Malice Aforethought*, with its cynical humour, acute criminology, plausible detail and rapid movement. It makes you hug yourself with pleasure." —H. C. Harwood, *Saturday Review*

Lange Lewis

THE BIRTHDAY MURDER

"Almost perfect in its playlike purity and delightful prose." —Jacques Barzun and Wendell Hertig Taylor

Arthur Maling

LUCKY DEVIL

"The plot unravels at a fast clip, the writing is breezy and Maling's approach is as fresh as today's stockmarket quotes." —*Louisville Courier Journal*

RIPOFF

"A swiftly paced story of today's big business is larded with intrigue as a Ralph Nader-type investigates an insurance scandal and is soon on the run from a hired gun and his brother....Engrossing and credible." —*Booklist*

SCHROEDER'S GAME

"As the title indicates, this Schroeder is up to something, and the unravelling of his game is a diverting and sufficiently blood-soaked entertainment." —*The New Yorker*

Julian Symons

THE BELTING INHERITANCE

"A superb whodunit in the best tradition of the detective story." —August Derleth, *Madison Capital Times*

BLAND BEGINNING

"Mr. Symons displays a deft storytelling skill, a quiet and literate wit, a nice feeling for character, and detectival ingenuity of a high order." —Anthony Boucher, *The New York Times*

THE DANGER WITHIN
"Michael Gilbert has nicely combined some elements of the straight detective story with plenty of action, suspense, and adventure, to produce a superior thriller." —*Saturday Review*

DEATH HAS DEEP ROOTS
"Trial scenes superb; prowl along Loire vivid chase stuff; funny in right places; a fine performance throughout." —*Saturday Review*

FEAR TO TREAD
"Merits serious consideration as a work of art." —*The New York Times*

C. W. Grafton

BEYOND A REASONABLE DOUBT
"A very ingenious tale of murder ... a brilliant and gripping narrative."
—Jacques Barzun and Wendell Hertig Taylor

Cyril Hare

AN ENGLISH MURDER
"By a long shot, the best crime story I have read for a long time. Everything is traditional, but originality does not suffer. The setting is perfect. Full marks to Mr. Hare." —*Irish Press*

UNTIMELY DEATH
"The English detective story at its quiet best, meticulously underplayed, rich in perceivings of the droll human animal and ready at the last with a neat surprise which has been there all the while had we but wits to see it."
—*New York Herald Tribune Book Review*

WHEN THE WIND BLOWS
"The best, unquestionably, of all the Hare stories, and a masterpiece by any standards." —Jacques Barzun and Wendell Hertig Taylor,
A Catalogue of Crime

WITH A BARE BODKIN
"One of the best detective stories published for a long time."
—*The Spectator*

James Hilton

WAS IT MURDER?
"The story is well planned and well written." —*The New York Times*

HEAD OF A TRAVELER
"Another grade A detective story of the right old jigsaw persuasion."
—*New York Herald Tribune Book Review*

MINUTE FOR MURDER
"An outstanding mystery novel. Mr. Blake's writing is a delight in itself."
—*The New York Times*

THE MORNING AFTER DEATH
"One of Blake's best." —Rex Warner

A PENKNIFE IN MY HEART
"Style brilliant ... and suspenseful." —*San Francisco Chronicle*

A QUESTION OF PROOF
"The characters in this story are unusually well drawn, and the suspense is well sustained." —*The New York Times*

THE SAD VARIETY
"It is a stunner. I read it instead of eating, instead of sleeping."
—Dorothy Salisbury Davis

THE SMILER WITH THE KNIFE
"An extraordinarily well written and entertaining thriller."
—*Saturday Review of Literature*

THOU SHELL OF DEATH
"It has all the virtues of culture, intelligence and sensibility that the most exacting connoisseur could ask of detective fiction."
—*The Times* [London] *Literary Supplement*

THE WHISPER IN THE GLOOM
"One of the most entertaining suspense-pursuit novels in many seasons."
—*The New York Times*

THE WIDOW'S CRUISE
"A stirring suspense....The thrilling tale leaves nothing to be desired."
—*Springfield Republican*

THE WORM OF DEATH
"It [The Worm of Death] is one of Blake's very best—and his best is better than almost anyone's." —Louis Untermeyer

Edmund Crispin

BURIED FOR PLEASURE
"Absolute and unalloyed delight." —Anthony Boucher, *The New York Times*

Kenneth Fearing

THE BIG CLOCK
"It will be some time before chill-hungry clients meet again so rare a compound of irony, satire, and icy-fingered narrative. *The Big Clock* is ... a psychothriller you won't put down." —*Weekly Book Review*

Andrew Garve

A HERO FOR LEANDA
"One can trust Mr. Garve to put a fresh twist to any situation, and the ending is really a lovely surprise." —*The Manchester Guardian*

THE ASHES OF LODA
"Garve ... embellishes a fine fast adventure story with a more credible picture of the U.S.S.R. than is offered in most thrillers." —*The New York Times Book Review*

THE CUCKOO LINE AFFAIR
" ... an agreeable and ingenious piece of work." —*The New Yorker*

THE FAR SANDS
"An impeccably devious thriller....The quality is well up to Mr. Garve's high standard of entertainment." —*The New Yorker*

MURDER THROUGH THE LOOKING GLASS
" ...refreshingly out-of-the-way and enjoyable...highly recommended to all comers." —*Saturday Review*

NO TEARS FOR HILDA
"It starts fine and finishes finer. I got behind on breathing watching Max get not only his man but his woman, too." —*Rex Stout*

THE RIDDLE OF SAMSON
"The story is an excellent one, the people are quite likable, and the writing is superior." —*Springfield Republican*

Michael Gilbert

BLOOD AND JUDGMENT
"Gilbert readers need scarcely be told that the characters all come alive at first sight, and that his surpassing talent for narration enhances any plot.... Don't miss." —*San Francisco Chronicle*

THE BODY OF A GIRL
"Does what a good mystery should do: open up into all kinds of ramifications, with untold menace behind the action. At the end, there is a bang-up climax, and it is a pleasure to see how skilfully Gilbert wraps everything up." —*The New York Times Book Review*

THE COLOR OF MURDER
"A singularly unostentatious and memorably brilliant detective story."
—*New York Herald Tribune Book Review*

THE 31ST OF FEBRUARY
"Nobody has painted a more gruesome picture of the advertising business since Dorothy Sayers wrote 'Murder Must Advertise', and very few people have written a more entertaining or dramatic mystery story."
—*The New Yorker*